NOT
YOUR AVERAGE BEAR

&

Other Maine Stories

Jerry Stelmok

TILBURY HOUSE PUBLISHERS
Gardiner, Maine

Tɪʟʙᴜʀʏ Hᴏᴜsᴇ, Pᴜʙʟɪsʜᴇʀs
2 Mechanic Street
Gardiner, Maine 043345
800–582–1899 • www.tilburyhouse.com

First paperback edition: April 2007
10 9 8 7 6 5 4 3 2 1

Library of Congress Cataloging-in-Publication Data
Stelmok, Jerry.
Not your average bear & other Maine stories / Jerry Stelmok. -- 1st pbk. ed.
p. cm.
ISBN 978-0-88448-290-1 (pbk. : alk. paper)
1. Maine--Fiction. I. Title. II. Title: Not your average bear and other Maine
stories.
PS3619.T476465N68 2007
813'.6--DC22

2007000112

Cover and interior illustrations by Jerry Stelmok
Copyediting by Barbara Diamond and Genie Dailey
Printed and bound by Versa Press, East Peoria, Illinois

For David, Kristin, and Holly

Contents

Maxfield Ridge

Matt Nichols guided the white telephone van around the worst potholes, and skillfully sluiced his way out of the deep muddy ruts. It was mild for the third week in November and the seemingly constant rain since mid September had convinced even the most persistent skeptics that the two-and-a-half-year drought was finally over. The rear tires spun as Matt eased up the final slick grade, but he nursed the accelerator just enough to maintain minimal progress. Rounding the bend at the top, he caught sight of his destination—a modest microwave tower standing above the treetops and probing the low scudding clouds.

It had been several years since his last visit to the Maxfield installation, and the abandoned farmhouse on the left had fared worse than he would have thought in so short a period of time. It could now only be described as a dilapidated, falling-down structure beyond reasonable hope of restoration. The barn, as well as the connecting ell, suffered from a broken back with gables tilted back at a considerable angle, and the jagged weathered ends of rafters and purlins jutted up through dark holes in the gap-toothed, wood-shingled roof. The place had been empty for as long as he could remember—standing expectant and lonely—presenting a sad sight like so many other farmhouses in the area that deteriorated inexorably for lack of families to keep them up.

Matt stopped alongside the white, concrete-block cube that housed the communications equipment, pulling off to the side enough to allow a vehicle to pass. Not that it was likely to happen on this road, even during hunting season.

Matt, a tall man of about fifty, had a gaunt look about him, his chambray shirt and blaze-orange vest hanging loosely off his big frame. His belt was cinched up to the newest hole he'd punched into the leather, gathering the baggy jeans around his waist like a flour sack. His face was ashen, but reddened easily enough even with moderate exertion. The dark crescents sagging beneath his dull eyes bespoke nothing but overwhelming exhaustion.

He exhaled deeply, opened the door, and stepped out. Occasional flashes of brittle, late-fall sunlight swept the ridge as openings in the racing clouds revealed pale blue sky.

"Not a bad view," he thought to himself, zipping up his vest against the wind, which was beginning to bite. A shot rang out down toward the river over a mile away, and a minute later another.

"Must a got 'im," Matt said aloud. "Lucky bastard."

Deer hunting had been one of his favorite pastimes ever since he was a kid, but it had not materialized for him this year. "Christ," he thought. "All I've done is work, mostly to cover for those lazy-assed supervisors. They somehow manage to take a week or even two to go to their hunting camps, and most of them only for the cards and booze, unless the weather's perfect."

Matt, on the other hand, was a serious although not obsessive hunter. In camp he was out before daybreak, and seldom back before twilight. Only then would he knock back a few beers before sitting down to supper with his buddies.

But with all Marge's troubles the last couple of years, he was in no position to refuse extra work, even though his seniority technically left these decisions clearly in his own lap. The company health insurance covered all the tests and expenses during her hospitalization, but much of the extra help Marge needed at home, as well as the exotic items in the diet prescribed by her homeopath and some of the more unconventional therapies, came straight out of Matt's pocket.

Not that it mattered to him, not so long as his wife's health was improving, anyway. But he wished he wasn't so completely wrung out himself. And he did genuinely miss the chance to go out looking for deer a Saturday or two during the month.

Returning to the van for tools and supplies, he saw a red Ford pickup pull up alongside. Taking a closer look he recognized Ben Turcotte, a friend and former colleague, dressed in orange, his window rolled down.

"Jesus Christ, Matt, don't you know it's Saturday and only one week left to hunt? Don't tell me you got one hanging up already."

"Hell, no, Ben. I haven't even been out. How come you're still hunting?"

"No luck yet. Christ, look at you, Matt. You look like a scarecrow. Don't they have anyone else back at the farm they can send out to take care of shit like this? And on a Saturday?"

"You got out just in time, Ben. Mitchell's run out so many good men since he took over, it's just the desperate ones like me left to do everything. Of course, His Majesty does even less than when he was just a crew boss."

"That doesn't surprise me one bit. Say, how's Marge? Billie said she saw her outside Griffin's and Marge looked pretty rested. Told Billie the tests since the operation been negative. That's great news."

"Marge is doin' great; we're lucky for that. She's still way down on her energy level, though. The doc says that's not unusual, especially with the anemic condition she'd had even before she discovered the lump."

"Well, good to hear it from you. Soon as Marge is up to it, give us a call and we'll have you over for dinner. Feed you, then take all your money playing Twenty-One," Ben laughed. "Look, you still carry your rifle in the van?"

Matt nodded.

"Finish up here and join me over at the old Kinneson place. It's just a couple miles down this friggin' road. You remember that ten-pointer I got five or six years back in the orchard on the east side of the road? Well, there's some serious scraping going on there, and there's plenty of space for two to hunt."

"Thanks, Ben, but maybe another time. I've got one more stop after I finish here, off the Carson road. But I like your new truck."

"Not new. Eighty-two, but you wouldn't know it was four years old would you? Twenty-three thousand original miles. Driven by an old lady once a week to church and back."

"Go get your goddamn deer, and let an honest man get back to his work."

An hour later Matt had the job finished, the building locked up, and everything back in the van. It was mid afternoon. He paused before getting in and craned his neck to take in the top of the tower.

"Christ," he thought, "I'd better check the automatic switch at the receiver before I go. If I don't, it probably won't restart and I'll have to drive all the way back here and climb the damn tower, anyway. Hell, I'm too beat to do this today," he tried to convince himself, but all he could see was an image of himself driving back and struggling up the frost-coated rungs in the middle of the night.

Ten minutes later, with his safety harness and satchel containing a few tools and extra relays, he was halfway up the steel structure.

"Damn good thing this is only a fifty-footer. Otherwise they'd have to get someone younger," he thought.

A door slammed shut. Not a car door, but a wooden one like anyone's front door. It seemed to come from the rundown farmhouse, but surely no one was living there now. Still, the closest house beyond that was nearly a mile farther along and there was no way he could have heard a door close at that distance.

"Must've been the wind," he decided, and proceeded up the tower, working harder at it than he could ever remember.

Matt felt much better as he climbed back down, the job completed. A third of the way down he stopped to take in the rolling panorama that extended to the mountains marching to Katahdin. Each receding layer of ridges was a shade paler and less distinct than the one preceding it, like a serigraph. Even the view close at hand of the overgrown pastures, fields, and fence rows was extraordinary from this vantage point.

Across the road the former hayfield was becoming clogged with milkweed and burdocks, and along the stone wall clumps of alders, poplar, and ground junipers were crowding in. The wall descended gently to another wall growing up to birches and alders. The old pasture beyond was a half generation ahead in terms of young volunteer trees, including dozens of healthy little spruces, bushy and reaching up to seven or eight feet in height. A movement in the far right corner of the old pasture caught his eye. Unbelievably a whitetail buck was walking diagonally across the pasture with the surprising speed and determination of a buck on a mission. Even at a distance of over two hundred yards, Matt could see the body of the animal rippling in shades of gray and brown, the wide ivory antlers gleaming in the afternoon light.

"Holy Christ," Matt muttered, "wouldn't you know it?" Certain that he stood no chance of descending to the ground, reaching the truck, retrieving the rifle, loading it, and getting a good shot at the deer, he began doing exactly that.

His heart was pounding audibly in his chest as he disengaged the safety lanyard from the rung above and began climbing down without its bother or benefit. Reaching the bottom he wiggled out of the harness dropping it as he half ran to the van that now stood between him and where he supposed the buck ought to be. He reached behind the seat and drew out the iron-sighted .32 Winchester Special that had belonged to his father and wished he'd been less sentimental and instead brought his .308 with the scope. He scooped up a small handful of cartridges from the otherwise empty ashtray and grabbed a cap, that looked like Sherlock Holmes's, except for its blaze-orange color.

Hastily he fed three shells into the spring-loaded port while still behind the sheltering van. The solid metallic *kajunk* when he jacked a shell into the chamber was more than loud enough to send the deer fleeing into the next county.

Carefully Matt extended his head and neck around the back of the van, expecting nothing, but hoping for a broadside view of the buck standing in the weedy field across the road. The field was empty. But before making any sudden movement, the experienced hunter scanned the field thoroughly, as well as what he could see of the pasture beyond. But the deer was nowhere in sight. As he stepped clear of the truck, his peripheral vision alerted him to a flicker of white, on a little rise to the left, partially concealed by a thick stand of young poplar and birch.

"How could he have gotten way over there already?" he thought. But it was the buck all right. Through the brush Matt could see the shadowy silhouette of the deer through the thicket and the white spread of his rack when he lifted his head from feeding, apparently on dropped apples from the scraggly trees that had once constituted an orchard. The good news was that a column of bushy young field pines marched toward the orchard at an angle and would afford Matt cover that might just allow him to stalk close enough for a shot. The wind would be mostly in his favor, but errant little gusts were also about and might betray him by suddenly casting his scent to the vigilant quarry.

Matt knew full well how hopeless it was to try stalking a whitetail buck in this country, unless the deer's immediate attention was on a receptive doe. Nonetheless he found himself walking carefully behind the screen of pines in a half crouch, watching each footfall to prevent a snapped twig or other minor noise from sending the buck bounding off without waiting around to ask questions. Finally, the hunter found himself literally crawling on his belly through the tall pale grass, and brittle milkweed stalks the final twenty feet to a huge fallen elm trunk that afforded both cover and a solid rest for the muzzle of the rifle.

With steady, almost impossible, slowness Matt raised his brow above the smooth silvered trunk actually expecting to see the animal still crunching the frost-crinkled apples on the knoll just ahead. But again he was disappointed. The orchard was empty and Matt figured the deer had continued on into the tangle of brush that would provide cover for it all the way down to the cedar and fir woods below.

Just as he rose to his knees, he saw movement again to his left, and turning his head he was surprised and excited to see the brown hide and white antlers moving along toward the road behind a stand of naked sumac only thirty yards away.

Still on his knees, Matt rolled to his right and back as the deer cleared the woody-stemmed sumacs and continued up toward the dirt

Jerry Stelmok

road sheltered only by a thin screen of spent raspberry canes, his antlers gleaming above the tops. In about five seconds the buck would disappear behind a dense clump of cedars that would shield him from the hunter until he eventually entered the alder-rimmed woods across the road by the tower.

Matt swung the barrel in line with the unhurried target, placed the bead in its notch in the solid brown just below and behind the swaying rack, and pulled the trigger. Instantly the deer dropped from sight. Knowing better, Matt envisioned his arrival at the tagging station with an enormous buck—at least a ten-pointer—in a hastily cleared space in the back of the van. He imagined Ben's surprise, along with that of other hunters he knew who had hunted hard all season with poor results, when they saw this trophy hanging from the big oak alongside his garage.

A rustle in the raspberries—the buck's final reflexive kicks—assured Matt of his success as he approached the spot with the rifle ready, a fresh cartridge jacked into the chamber. The decaying remains of an old logging scoot shrouded by the prickly canes lay forlornly in the tall dead grass at his feet as he topped the little hillock. Beyond the scoot, lying perfectly still on his side, a stream of scarlet oozing from his mouth and running along his jaw, was a white-haired man in an olive-drab fatigue jacket.

Matt refused to believe it. He closed his eyes, then opened them again, but the gruesome scene had not changed. Where was his foolish buck and what was this thing doing here? Gradually the reality of what he had done crept into his consciousness, and the impact slammed into him like a cement truck.

"Jesus Christ. Holy shit," the rifle fell from his hands, the hammer still pulled back in firing position. He sank to his knees. He looked away, stood up and walked in a circle. He looked again, still half believing there would be a deer emptying its blood into the grass. But, of course, it was only the angular old man, his eyes wide open in perfect astonishment.

"Holy Christ! What will I say? Who'll believe me? Not Marge. She'll say, 'Not Matt, Matt has hunted most of his life.' Not Ben. He'll say, 'Not Matt. He's the one who makes a major issue over the slightest lapse in safety!' Everyone will say, 'Not Matt. He's taught the hunter safety course at the high school for a dozen years.'"

He started running for the road, which was farther than he remembered. The going was ridiculously difficult. Someone had plowed the field years before and never gotten around to harrowing it. Besides the hidden furrows there were thistles, vines, vetch, and raspberries, all grabbing his pants, trying to pull him down. He tripped over the rusted shaft of some derelict piece of machinery and went sprawling through the weeds, landing in mud on his hands and knees. He was perspiring heavily and breathing with great difficulty. His chest seemed to be seizing up. He got up, turned around, and lurched back toward the body.

"What if he's still alive? What if I've only wounded him?" he mumbled. "I have to check. What do I say to him?"

The scene was still the same. The shot man looked pitiful. The fatigue jacket was frayed and mended a dozen times. The visible breast pocket was two-thirds ripped off. His trousers were once good dress pants but were now torn and threadbare from hard use. He looked pathetic. And he did not appear to be breathing. It took all Matt's courage just to touch him, and then even more to grasp the left arm, which he imagined felt like a skeleton's would inside the sleeve. He moved the arm forward exposing the wound in the middle of the rib cage. It was a small hole, perfectly round through the jacket now sopping with blood, but the glimpse of imploded flesh and fractured bone and coagulating blood was enough to make him gag. He let go of the arm, stood up, whirled around, took a few steps, and vomited. Tears were running freely down both cheeks.

"Why me? Why me? How could this happen? Why? Can't we turn back the clock? Just a few minutes? This must be a dream. I know it is."

Suddenly he remembered the radio in the van. He should call someone—the state police, the wardens, the hospital, Marge. He sat down trying to quiet his heart and restore control of his breathing. Then he bolted back up and thrashed toward the tower and the van, the sour taste of vomit in his mouth, the sense of dread overwhelming.

As he stumbled onto the gravel road, he heard a car approaching from the right. He looked up. It was Ben in his new red pickup. The driver's side window was rolled down.

"I heard the shot! What did you get? Holy Christ! Look at you, Matt. What the hell happened? Did a bear get you?"

"I ...I shot a man...an old man, Ben. I k-killed him."

"What! Are you crazy? Get hold of yourself, buddy," Ben said as he climbed out of the truck. He put his hand on Matt's upper arm and said calmly, "Tell me what happened to you."

"I c-can't, Ben, we gotta call the sheriff or somebody, maybe the game warden. I don't know who we should call."

"Look, Matt, let's talk a second. I think you're way overtired is all. You need to get some rest. You need a real vacation. Just get in my truck. I'll drive you home, and they can send someone out for the van."

"I *can't,* Ben! I tell you, I *shot* someone! C-come with me." He was off into the underbrush at a fast walk, stumbling but not falling, not looking back, and no longer talking. Ben had no choice but to follow.

Ahead by fifteen yards, Matt topped the little rise. He looked around. Nothing! "This can't be," he thought to himself. "I know he's here somewhere." He looked around frantically, but couldn't find the victim, the scoot, nor his rifle. Ben had caught up and was looking at him with concern in his eyes.

"Listen, Matt, you've had a hell of a fall. Let's you and me...."

"NO!" Matt practically yelled at his friend. He saw there were several of these little hillocks around. All looked much the same to him now. "This is the wrong hill. It's over there."

Despite Ben's protests he was off running unsteadily down the little grade. Reaching the top of the next rise he was sure he had found the fateful spot, and somehow he felt relieved. He looked around, but there was nothing familiar, not a body or even an old scoot. Then he spotted a clump of cedars to his right and next to it a mound he knew was the right one. Ben had given up trying to reason with him and was following behind, walking, a worried look on his face.

"Here! This is it!" Matt called in triumph. "I've found it." He clambered up the steepest side and saw the old scoot before he reached the top. When Ben caught up, Matt, his hair wild, his eyes wilder yet, was stamping around, obviously agitated and raving. "Where did he go? Where did the son of a bitch go? He must have crawled off. We've got to find him so he doesn't die!"

Ben saw the scoot. It was something, but there was no body, and no blood that he could see. "Easy, Matt, let's not trample the place flat. Let's take a good look here."

A minute later he spotted the .32 Special lying in the grass and picked it up. The safety was off. Carefully holding back the hammer with his thumb, he squeezed the trigger, gently letting the hammer forward. Then he drew it back one click to the safety position. He could smell that the rifle had been recently fired. Matt came up to him, looking a bit calmer.

"See, I told you it was here. And there's the sled. The body was right here. Shot in the side of the ribs." He couldn't believe he'd said that. Not to anyone.

Ben was carefully looking around. He had good eyes and was an excellent tracker. "Hey, I've got something." He lowered himself to one knee, closely inspecting the ground before him. "Look, Matt," he said, "there's a small spot of blood on this leaf, and here too." Then he picked up a little swatch of coarse white deer hair.

"It's a coincidence," Matt insisted. "There's a man shot here and he's in serious condition. I saw him."

Ben was following the hoof prints in the tall, late-season grass, much of which was lying almost flat. "Here's another drop of blood," he said. Then, five feet farther he added, "Here's another one and another small clump of hair. Blood's dark. And this white hair? I think you shot low, Matt, and grazed his belly."

Matt wanted to believe him in the worst way, but he knew better. "I didn't wound any deer, Ben. I shot a man and I think I killed him."

Ben figured the only way to convince Matt was to find some conclusive evidence. What few signs there were indicated the deer was

Jerry Stelmok

running downhill in long bounds headed for the nearest woods. It was easy to miss the depressions in the weeds, but luckily just before the stone wall and the woods there was a slick ribbon of green grass and mud forty feet wide. There he found clusters of hoof prints—one set at the edge and three more across the mud to the stone wall. The deer had easily cleared the wall, but Ben found another clump of hair on the barbs of a sagging rusty fence the buck must have caught on his way over. There was no more blood after that.

But Matt would not give up looking for the body until darkness forced them to quit. His face glistened with perspiration, his orange quilted vest was unzipped, his blue jeans were muddy and covered with burdocks. They left the company van parked alongside the cinder-block shack, and Ben drove Matt home. The whole way, he tried reasoning with Matt, who insisted they must call the police.

"Listen, Matt, it's dark, there's nobody out there, you're overtired. You winged a deer, but he's long gone."

Matt would have none of it, sticking to his story and his determination to call the authorities.

"Listen, I'll drive you out first thing in the morning, if that's what you want," Ben offered, "and we can have another look around. But I think once you've had some sleep you'll remember what really happened."

Marge was not at home. Matt now remembered that she was staying at her parents' house down in Richmond until Thanksgiving, resting and visiting with her sister, who was home from Spokane, Washington. Their son, Jamie, was at the university and wouldn't be home for a few days yet.

Ben said, "I don't like leaving you alone in this condition, Matt. Why not grab a few things and stay at our place tonight?" But Matt flatly refused, and finally, after making some coffee for him, Ben got ready to go.

"Billie was expecting me for supper about an hour ago, I've got to go. If you change your mind, come on over and join us. And in the meantime, don't do anything foolish. Things will look a lot different tomorrow; you'll see. Just get some sleep."

But Matt couldn't sleep or get the horrible picture of the wounded man out of his mind. He sat at the kitchen table a long time trying to remember details of the deer walking through the sumac and raspberries. He tried to reconstruct what he'd seen when he squeezed the trigger.

"It was a deer, goddammit. It was long and horizontal. It wasn't a man." But then he'd remember the fallen man, each time as unpleasant as it had been on the little hill. It was real. There was too much detail. It had happened! He went round and round with these images, but could make no more sense of it. Several times he picked up the telephone to call the police or to call Marge and tell her what he'd done. Twice he had the number at her mother's punched in, all but the final digit, but had put down the receiver. He couldn't bring himself to tell her. With all the lights out, he sat in his easy chair going over the entire incident, from spotting the buck from the tower, to squeezing the trigger, to discovering the gunshot man. Then he pondered the body's disappearance and the deer hoof prints and the blood. Still, he couldn't make any sense out of it.

In the morning Ben brought over a couple of warm muffins and made a fresh pot of coffee, but Matt just wanted to get back out to Maxfield Ridge to find the body and get it all over with. He looked even worse than the evening before and Ben had to insist that he take a warm, weatherproof jacket because there was a cold steady drizzle.

Back on the ridge, things looked different mostly because the drizzle had turned into a steady icy rain. Matt went right for the site where he'd seen the body, but of course it wasn't there. He found the rotting scoot right off, but that was all. The rain had washed away even the few drops of blood Ben had discovered, along with the deer's prints. Matt worked his way over to the fallen elm where he had taken the shot. It was closer than he thought, about twenty-five yards to the raspberries that had screened the deer—or the man. He knelt down and reconstructed the shot. In his mind, the shape of the deer was clear—no mistaking it—certainly not for a man. He couldn't comprehend what had happened. He looked around and found the spent brass shell beaded with rain droplets, but still smelling of burnt powder. That part of the incident at least was real.

Ben, dressed in rain parka and pants, methodically searched the hilltop for signs of the body or the deer, making widening circles through the rough country around the spot where he'd found the blood. After an hour, he gave up and sat in his truck, the engine idling, watching his perplexed friend dash here and there, peer around, and scratch his head, seemingly impervious to the cold rain.

Finally Matt walked up to the truck. He was sweating despite the raw conditions. His weatherproof parka was open and clusters of burrs clung to his clothing. He appeared out of breath and totally distressed, the bags under his eyes heavier than the day before.

"I don't know what the hell's going on, Ben, but there's no sense you sticking around here. Go on back home and watch some football or something."

Ben tried talking Matt into following him, but Matt insisted he'd stay. "I'm not sure of anything at this point," he told Ben, "but I've got to keep looking a bit longer. There's gotta be some explanation. If I haven't found anything by noon I'll drive the van home, take a shower, and try to sleep." He then added distractedly, "Thanks for all your help, buddy. I know you think I'm crazy, but I know what I saw and there must be some explanation."

By eleven the rain had pretty much soaked through to his skin, and despite his exertion Matt was chilled to the bone, as well as exhausted. He'd searched as much as one man could, and there were no further clues. He stood up from a crosstie on the scoot where he'd been sitting and thinking, and headed resignedly toward the road. He hadn't gone a dozen steps when for no particular reason he glanced down and spotted something unfamiliar. He stooped to pick it up.

"Holy cow!" he exclaimed. "How could we have missed this?" In his hand was a small cruising axe with about a two-pound head. The varnish on the hickory handle was still in good shape and the side that had been facing down, protected from the rain, was spattered with what looked like dried blood.

"Holy shit!" he yelped, dropping it as though it was red hot. Then he picked it back up and examined it closely. It was no relic, he was sure of that. "That poor old fella must've been carrying this when I shot him. Wait till Ben sees this." He noticed that the blood was starting to wash away wherever he touched it with his wet hands, so he gripped it by the head between his thumb and forefinger, and rushed off toward the van.

—

Billie came to the door, a look of concern on her pretty face.

"Oh, Matt, you look a mess, and you're soaked through. Ben's so worried about you. Come on in. I'm having tea with Wanda and Beverly in the front room. Go right on down the stairs, Ben's doing something or other down in the basement." She squeezed his arm and gave him a little peck. "You're going to be all right, Matt," then she turned back toward her guests.

Ben turned around from the bench where he was planing a length of maple for a table leg. He was a careful and resourceful woodworker and had a well-equipped shop.

"Well, thank God you've given up, Matt. I was planning on driving back out to the Maxfield place in a little while to make sure you weren't frozen to death."

"Take a look at this, Ben." Matt's voice was a hoarse whisper, his throat was sore. "I found it right by that woods sled. I don't know how we could've missed it." He drew a black trash bag from under his coat, glancing nervously around as if he were trying to sell stolen goods on the street. "The old guy was carrying it when I shot him."

"Matt, you didn't shoot...."

Matt interrupted him, "Wait till you see this before you're so sure."

He drew the axe from the crumpled plastic bag. Only it wasn't the axe he'd found on the ground. That one was practically new, with a shiny head, a varnished helve and spattered blood on the varnish. This was an old, abused axe. The head was badly rusted and pitted, the handle had weathered to a grayish brown, and the finish was gone, leaving the grain standing out. It had been outside a long time.

"W-what the hell?" Matt stammered. He couldn't believe what he was seeing. He looked from the axe to Ben, then back again. "What the hell kind of trick is this? This was a new axe. At least almost new. Holy Jesus. The handle was varnished smooth as could be and there was blood on it, blood from the old man I shot. No kidding."

Ben wasn't looking at the axe. His eyes were on Matt and they registered deep concern. He said nothing as Matt excitedly told him how he'd found the axe where they had already looked a hundred times and how new it was, and about the spots of red blood where the rain hadn't struck it. Ben put his hand on Matt's trembling shoulder.

"Look, Matt, I've talked this over with Billie, and we're going to give Marge a call at her mother's. I know she'd want to be here. You've had a little breakdown—or something. She can go with you to the doctor and call Mitchell at work and...."

Matt cuffed the comforting hand aside and shook his head.

"You don't believe anything I'm telling you. Christ, I'm telling you the truth, Ben." He bolted up the stairs, pushing past the women who were taking their leave at the doorway. They shrank from the soaking wet, crazed man with an axe, and watched in horrified fascination as he hurried across the wet lawn and jumped into the telephone company van.

Monday morning, Matt had no choice but to call in sick. He had a burning fever, a sore throat, and he ached in every joint—not to mention his nervous exhaustion. He said nothing of the weekend's incident, but had the feeling that perhaps Ben had called up his old boss and at least told him how worn thin Matt was, and how badly in need of rest. He doubted his friend would have told the supervisor that he was delusional.

Marge arrived back home at noon, her sister with her. By then Matt really needed the care. His fever was raging, his breathing was labored, and his throat was raw. Whenever he'd drift off to a troubled sleep, he'd relive the shooting, especially the discovery of the crumpled, white-haired man with the bulging eyes. He'd awaken thrashing and soaked with perspiration, trembling like an aspen leaf in the breeze.

Later in the week, he somehow managed Thanksgiving. Marge

drove the three of them down to her folks', where Jamie joined them for dinner. For years, Matt and his son had had difficulty communicating, so along with Marge's father and the brothers-in-law, they pretty much absorbed themselves in football before and after the meal—Matt's preoccupation going largely unnoticed. Jamie came home for the rest of the holiday weekend but spent most of his time in his room and evenings visiting a few of his old high-school buddies.

Bert Mitchell, Matt's supervisor, had uncharacteristically extended Matt's sick leave through the first week of December without Matt having to beg or fight for it. The snow was still holding off and by Wednesday he was feeling considerably stronger. A bitter chill that had gripped the region since Thanksgiving broke and even the weak, low-angled December sunlight made the day seem almost balmy.

Matt drove slowly past the nearly collapsed dwelling that had once commanded the ridge named for the house's owner. Parking by the tower, he got out and looked over the receding fields, lovely on this bright day even in their muted tones of umber and sienna. The skeletal forms of the bare maples and birches added graphic accents against the brownish-green spruce that dominated the bordering woods, as did a patch of subtle red osier. But for the disturbing event embedded in his memory, Matt would have called it a beautiful view.

Instead of heading directly for the wood scoot, he walked back along the road a couple of hundred feet to the old farm site. Unlikely as it seemed, perhaps some explanation for the bizarre occurrence could be uncovered within the farmstead's sagging remains.

The driveways, lawns, and whatever else once constituted the yard were now overgrown with dead witch grass, burdocks, and milkweed. Paths beaten down by wild creatures crisscrossed the site. Two towering stubs were all that remained of what once must have been huge elm trees, the ground at their bases littered with decayed branches. A single maple, a dozen feet around, was still half alive, the barkless branches of the dead side beginning their descent to earth, as well. Beside the collapsing porch was a large patch of Japanese knotweed, the dead canes temporarily halted in their takeover of everything around by the arrival of the dormant season.

Warped gray clapboards hung precariously or had already been shed by the standing walls and were piling up around the granite foundation. Much of the glass in the windows was either missing or cracked in spider-web patterns. Matt walked slowly around the rambling wreck in the tall grass and weeds, being careful not to step on anything that might conceal an abandoned well. The side of the house farthest from the road appeared to be in the best shape. Matt stepped up to a window and peered inside. It was not as dark as he had expected once his eyes got accustomed to the gloom. The room had probably served as a bedroom or den. A fireplace framed in ornate wooden moldings painted white had long ago been bricked over. Slate-colored wallpaper with a floral pattern still covered two of the visible walls, although much of it was water-stained from leaks and was peeling off in large patches that revealed the original plaster walls. The other visible wall had been roughly sheathed in dark, weathered barn boards. The job had not been especially well done and through the numerous gaps and spaces the relatively light wall-paper beneath showed through. The ceiling plaster sagged in huge bulges, especially around the old brass-plated overhead light fixture fitted incongruously with a pair of compact florescent light bulbs. Where large patches of the plaster had fallen, light gray laths were visible. A floor of six-inch-wide spruce boards had been mostly covered with a cheap linoleum that showed wear, if not actual cracks, along every plank seam beneath it. On the wall opposite the window, above the fireplace was pinned a faded print of what looked like a jaguar or a black leopard engaged in mortal struggle with a large python.

Removing his hands which had been sheltering his eyes from the outside light as he peered inside, Matt was jolted by the reflection of a figure standing just behind him. In the imperfect glass of the old window the figure appeared tall, wrapped in some sort of brown clothing, and had a bushy head of intensely white hair.

"Don't let me stop you from snoopin', mister," said a croaky voice that sounded more female than male. "But it's curiosity gets lots a' folks in trouble."

Matt whirled to face the speaker, prepared for an encounter with unspeakable horror. Instead he found himself looking almost directly into the intense eyes of a willowy and ageless woman. In her arms she carried two paper bags full of dark, speckled apples. She was clad in a fake suede coat with a fake sheepskin-lined collar, much too large for her slender frame. The coat was not buttoned and under it she was wearing at least two sweaters, and beneath those was a faded denim dress that hung about mid calf. Below the frayed hem, Matt glimpsed seasoned blue sweat pants tucked into gray woolen socks. On her feet were black, high-cut canvas sneakers, the white rubber borders green with grass stains, and the canvas around the eyelets starting to let go. Matt exhaled a sigh of relief, happy to face anyone besides the white-haired man he still thought he had shot.

"Pardon me, ma'am. I didn't mean to be spying into your house or anything. It's just I was curious about who used to live in this place."

"It's not my place. Who in the world could live in this rundown heap, anyhow? What do you take me for, a tramp?"

"Oh, no, it's just that you startled me is all," Matt explained.

"Well, didn't mean to scare you, made enough noise walking up, I should think. Place belonged to the Maxfield family from when it was built in about 1870 till about 1950, I guess. Then it set empty for a spell of maybe ten years until a man named Rodrigues bought it. He taught at the college and was plannin' to fix it up for some gentleman farmin', but no one's lived here now for a dozen years or more, and you can see what's become of it."

The woman's name was Carrie Stiles, and she lived a mile down the road, back in the woods a bit, and had lived nearby for over thirty years. She seemed not only informative, but also happy to have someone to talk with.

"Got to get back home right now, Mister Nichols. You can follow me if you like, and maybe I can answer some of your questions." From out of the weeds she righted a fenderless direct-drive bicycle with balloon tires and about as much rust as green paint on the frame. The relic was fitted with a pair of baskets like panniers over the rear wheels, and another in front of the straight, rusty handlebars that were missing their rubber grips. Refusing Matt's offer to take the apples in his car, she set a bag in each of the side baskets and put a small white dog Matt had scarcely noticed in the forward one. Guiding the rig out to the road, she pushed off, swung her leg over the seat, and located the pedals with her sneakers. The little dog began barking with delight, and she was off. Matt would not have been surprised if the whole outfit had lifted off and flown away like Mary Poppins.

Following the wobbly cyclist down the road in his car felt as ridiculous as anything he'd ever done, but thankfully there was no one around to see the spectacle. A little over a mile past the tower the woman veered suddenly to the left, as though deliberately steering into the ditch, and disappeared. Reaching the spot, Matt stopped the car and by looking carefully could just make out a little dirt path leading up into the woods. Twenty feet up it, Carrie was standing beside the bike, the dog already out of the basket and sitting on her feet, yapping at him.

He followed the odd woman into a little clearing a hundred yards from the road. There were a number of variously shaped garden patches, all of them cleared of weeds and spaded over for the winter. Dominating the clearing were two boxes wrapped in green rolled roofing. One had a wooden door standing open and appeared to be an animal shelter. The other, equipped with a window as well as a door, had a stovepipe leaning out the side and out of the pipe floated faint puffs of wood smoke. A number of flop-eared Nubian goats came running to Carrie from all directions, including a couple from the "barn." Chickens scattered, dodging the goats who playfully tried to butt or kick them as they ran by. The dog ran past the goats to a near twin lying in front of the cabin door, barking like crazy. As Matt watched the two dogs greet each other, it was obvious that one had lost the use of its hind legs. However, it appeared to be doing fine pulling itself across the grass as its pal repeatedly jumped over its recumbent back, licking his handicapped buddy's face at every opportunity. Both barked incessantly.

"Built this place myself, I did," Carrie announced proudly over the noise, "after my house burned and I found myself without insurance. Did it all without borrowing a cent, too."

As they ducked through the door, a half dozen cats erupted from their perches on the table, chairs, and daybed that stood against the back wall under a second window. Only a regal yellow tabby with a white bib and a perfectly round hole in one ear kept his place on the sideboard with a view out the window to the chaotic yard.

Along the inside walls were stacks of books and copies of *National Geographic* magazine. Strung from the open rafters, a web of baling twine sagged under its burden of dried herbs and flowers. On a card table near the woodstove was a huge jigsaw puzzle about two-thirds completed. The image was of three kittens playing with a ball of yarn. Dozens more puzzles, in their colorful cardboard boxes, were stacked beneath the table. Although it was probably ninety degrees inside, even with the door open, Carrie stepped outside and grabbed a pair of wrist-sized billets of firewood from the tarp-covered pile by the door. She opened the front of a little woodstove, tossed them in, and placed a blackened kettle on the stove's surface. "We'll have some tea in a few minutes," she announced.

Carrie indicated Matt should sit on a stool—what was left of a wooden kitchen chair that was missing its back—while she eased into a rocking chair whose seat was well padded with old newspapers and various articles of clothing. She rocked the chair back and pulled out a pipe.

"Now, what is it you wanted to know about the Maxfield place?" She tapped a wad of tobacco down into the bowl of the pipe, clamped it between her gums, and lit it.

Before very long the conversation settled on the owners of the property after the Maxfield family had lost interest in the place. The man's name was Bernardo Rodrigues and, as she had mentioned, he was a professor at the college. He'd bought the farm from the bank for very little, and before moving in had hired work done on the roof and the failing underpinnings of the barn. He and his young wife had

Jerry Stelmok

planned on doing the rest themselves. Interestingly, "Dr. Rodrigues," as Carrie referred to him, was a scholar of the world's indigenous religions.

"Not your everyday Buddhism and Hinduism and such," Carrie assured him, "but the really weird fringe stuff." She knew a lot about him, and had actually worked for him and his wife, Eliza.

"Believe it or not, Mr. Nichols, but in a former life, before moving back to this godforsaken valley, I was nearly a college graduate. After that I was a personal secretary for a successful businessman in New York, a truly wonderful man, who treated me and everyone else right, I can tell you. Should never've left that situation."

"Well, why did you...?"

"Never mind that, that's none of your business, mister." She grinned a warm smile, the absence of her top teeth giving her smile the quality of a young child's or perhaps a gnome's. Her clear eyes sparkled with energy. She poured tea out of a pot with no lid into two large cups without handles.

"There's some goat's milk just outside the door coolin', I got sugar here somewheres, and that's wild bees' honey in that jar on the table next to that stack of magazines."

She'd started working for Dr. Rodrigues typing the manuscripts for a series of books he was writing. Before long she was cleaning the farmhouse once a week and preparing an occasional dinner for colleagues, students, and mysterious guests of all descriptions.

"That place was some popular let me tell you, mister. And there was some odd ducks among 'em. Not ordinary folks from around here, you know, but people from all over—South America, Indonesia, Africa, and especially the Caribbean. Lots of Rastafarians—you know, dreadlocks and 'Hey' mon, take it easy.'" She laughed at her own bad stereotype, and Matt taken by surprise, had to laugh with her. The yellow cat had jumped down from its perch and onto his lap, looking straight up into his face. Matt scratched him behind the ear with the hole.

Carrie relit her pipe, took a few puffs, and continued. "It was all cool enough, this being the sixties and all, but it was getting a little out of hand, if you ask me. Some of these jokers didn't know when to leave, you know. They'd stay for weeks, months in some cases, and they'd call their friends and they'd show up, too. Few of them ever saw fit to lend much of a hand with the chores or cooking or anything.

"It was his wife, Eliza, started the trouble, if you ask me," Carrie continued. "She was a lot younger than Dr. Rodrigues, come from Haiti or the Dominican Republic, claimed to be some kind of priestess, and there seemed to be plenty who believed her. I think she was just a plain witch. They'd 'a burned her at the stake in the old days—if they'd dared to.

"Anyways, she was beautiful, dark skin and jet black hair, and eyes even blacker still. And she knew how to dress to drive a man crazy. And she did just that all the time. I was embarrassed for the professor just bein' around the way she flirted with all these men always around—and with the women, too! She loved keeping things stirred up and all the attention it give her."

A dirty white duck waddled in the open door. He was male Muscovy with an ugly wattle around the bill and eyes, his body horizontal to the floor, not upright like an honest duck's. Spotting Matt, the duck commenced hissing like a snake, his head darting back and forth, his tongue extended.

"Oh, stop your hissing, and eat your damn corn," Carrie admonished, "and shut up while I'm talking to the gentleman." Carrie scattered some cracked corn on the floor and the Muscovy stopped threatening. He took a sloppy drink from a bowl of water and began vacuuming up cracked corn, his tail feathers wagging back and forth horizontally.

"Still, it was tolerable for a few years, mostly because they'd go back to the Caribbean or Central America every December. Then the doctor'd come back alone to teach after about a month and Eliza'd stay down there until May or even June."

According to Carrie, things began getting a little weirder each year, with the doctor becoming more obsessed with his research. This wasn't necessarily a bad thing, but things around the farm began to deteriorate for lack of attention.

"When he first bought the place he was working around it all the time. He hired a young carpenter to help him put up those ugly boards all over the inside walls. 'Course *all* the hippies was doin' that. But they fixed up the barn and the chicken coop and got some nice hens, a few goats and pigs. Started a big garden, too. But after awhile he seemed to lose interest. The book I'd been typing for him got put aside and he got obsessed with some much stranger stuff.

"The real trouble started when Dr. Rodrigues hired a young man to help around the farm so he could spend more time at his work. The boy was from Springfield, Massachusetts, but had an Indian name— you know, the subcontinent. Rashir or something like that. A gorgeous young man. Tall, polite, soft-spoken, but as lazy as a minister on Monday mornin'. Doctor'd ask him to do something, and he'd just smile that beautiful sleepy smile of his and sit there. Finally, the doctor'd just turn around and leave. Rashir would look back at Eliza, grin some more, and the work never'd get done.

"And it was no surprise to anyone that the two of them got together. You know how opposites attract, her with all the fire and energy and ambition, him with that maddening dreamy-eyed laziness. They got together all right; I caught 'em right in the act! Went out to the barn to throw some vegetable scraps to the hogs, and on my way through the haybarn, I hear these voices—only it's not voices, it's moaning. This is about five o'clock in the afternoon—in August or early September. There they are, a blanket spread on the hay, in plain sight! An' she's on her back, just looking at me with the scary smile she had—just daring me to say something or tell the poor doctor. Rashir just goin' at it with that foolish smile on his face. I didn't know what to do. I dropped the vegetables and run out of the barn. I couldn't bring myself to tell Dr. Rodrigues—although he must've known well enough. It led to me endin' work there for good."

"So you quit?"

"It wasn't just that, although that was plenty enough. Another thing, they was taking me for granted—expected me to be there at the snap of Eliza's fingers, mop up the place and cook for a bunch of wild bohemians—but then I might have to wait a month to get paid. But mostly it was the wild goin's on at night. Couldn't call 'em parties, really. Rituals is more like it. I could abide the heavy drinkin' and the drugs even, and what's nudity? Hell, I seen it all before. But it was the drummin' and the bonfires and the screamin'. The final nail in the coffin, so's to speak, was the sacrifices—killin' innocent chickens and goats, you know, just for the blood. Makin' a real thing about it. Well, I told 'em just what I thought about that, let me tell you, and I walked out and I never come back!"

Matt was fascinated by the stories of life on the farm under Professor Rodrigues, his mysterious young wife, and a sinister cast of characters which Carrie painted in brilliant detail. He sat through two more cups of strong tea, and as many unnecessary fillings of the woodstove. But the real impact didn't surface until near the end of the tale. According to Carrie, Eliza eventually moved in with Rashir, but the three of them continued to live together in the farmhouse in a precarious equilibrium. It seemed Dr. Rodrigues could not bear to see Eliza leave and preferred even this unnatural arrangement.

"Seems Eliza had no funds of her own and it's for sure her lover didn't and wasn't about to go to work to earn any, either. Things got so strained around the place, even the freeloaders stopped coming."

"But, how did it end?" asked Matt. "Something had to snap."

"Well, that's for sure. Late that fall, Dr. Rodrigues turned up missing. It was around Thanksgiving. That'd be just about a dozen years ago. Seems longer than that somehow. Eliza and Rashir were away at a conference in Boston, so they claimed, and when they came home during a big northeaster snowstorm, there was no sign of the doctor. Nothing was missing—they'd taken his car to Boston, but his pickup was still in the yard. A stew or something, burned to a crisp, sat on the kitchen woodstove which, of course, had gone out. He'd just up and disappeared."

"Was anyone notified?" Matt asked, getting more intrigued by the minute.

"Oh, sure, they made a show of having the sheriff out and everything, but there wasn't much to go on. They made a halfhearted search of the property, but twenty inches of new snow and all made it pretty useless. Besides, the doctor had a history of disappearing—taking off for Haiti or Mexico or somewhere with no warnin'. Folks at the college told 'em that."

"And it was never solved?"

"Oh it was solved all right. By Christmas Eliza and Rashir had packed up and left the place. Headed for parts unknown. George Harvey down the road rescued the livestock that'd been left behind. In the spring, April I guess it was, a deputy checking out the place—just routine—spotted a bunch of crows makin' a racket in the pasture just across the road."

The hair on Matt's neck stood up straight and his skin began to crawl.

"Went to have a look, and sure enough, there was Doctor Rodrigues—or what the birds and coyotes had left of him. He'd been shot with a deer rifle. It was in November he went missin', so the deputy had to assume it was a huntin' accident. You okay, Mister Nichols? Mister Nichols!"

Matt's head was spinning and his stomach was on a roller coaster. "Oh, ah, sure, I'm all right."

"You don't look it. Anyway, the doctor was probably out doin' some early prunin' on his apple trees. He'd never a' thought to put on some orange, wasn't practical that way. But I don't think it was any huntin' accident."

"Y-you think...."

"You bet. It was Eliza shot 'im. She was cold-blooded enough. That Rashir guy was useless. Anyway, she come back up from South America somewhere and pretended to be grieving, but she didn't fool no one. They had to settle the estate, and 'course it was that witch got all the assets. But real estate was way down, and no one ever bought the place, run down as it was."

Matt Nichols was trying to put a frame around this incredible piece of information and square it with his bizarre experience. He took his leave, but was back the next morning and had Carrie go over the story in greater detail. He'd brought a box of donuts from the bakery and Carrie inhaled them one after another.

"Well, I've got a picture of Dr. Rodrigues right here some-where—it's on the back of one of his books. One of his early ones that I helped with—not the wild foolishness he started with later." From under the bed, piled high in blankets and afghans—covered with a solid mat of cat hair—she pulled out a hardcover book and blew off the dust before handing it to Matt. *Gods in Their Satchels* was the title. There was a silhouette of a big South Seas outrigger canoe and under that the subtitle, *The Migration and Transformation of Religion in the Pacific Archipelago*. It looked like an important book.

Matt turned it over and gave a visible start. Looking up from the jacket was a younger version of the man he had shot! "Bernardo C. Rodrigues," he read. "Born in Panama City, 1929. Educated in Rio de Janeiro and at Columbia University."

"You look like you've seen a ghost, Mr. Nichols." Carrie's know-ing grin and twinkling eyes possibly betrayed knowledge she had not chosen to share.

"Is this an old photograph of Doctor Rodrigues?" he finally asked.

"Is now, but it was taken when the book was published in 1970, I think."

Matt checked the copyright date and nodded.

"So his hair was just starting to turn gray?"

"A little, but in fact he still didn't have much gray at the end of it."

"Interesting," Matt thought to himself. "How can a body age after it's dead?" Then he said aloud to Carrie, "And you think it was his wife who killed him?"

"I think she might a' done more than that."

"What do you mean?"

"There's some things you can do to a body and a soul that's even worse than killin' it, if you know what I mean."

"No, Carrie, I don't. What *do* you mean?"

But she clamped her gums shut and clearly wasn't ready to discuss it further.

Matt tried another tack. "Tell me honestly, Carrie, have you noticed any strange occurrences around here having to do with

Dr. Rodrigues?"

The old lady's lips remained closed, but the thin line of her mouth seemed almost to be smiling as did her twinkling eyes, but it was apparent to Matt that this conversation had come to its conclusion.

———

Matt Nichols leaned up against a straight ash trunk, the old .32 Special in the crook of his left arm. He was watching a recent cutting below for the movement of a deer. His mind was focused only partly on the hunt, however, and he was indifferent as to whether or not he would get a shot. His thoughts kept drifting back over the events of the past ten years that had somehow landed him here. He was positive he would not be hunting here or anyplace else had it not been for the pressure from his son, Jamie. Not only had Jamie recently taken up an interest in hunting, but also—for the first time in fifteen years—he seemed to take an interest in his father, as well.

A year after her surgery, Marge's cancer had returned and spread rapidly. Her condition had declined steadily, and without another respite of hope, she had died within a few nightmarish months. Matt had thrown himself totally into caring for Marge, and with help from hospice had managed to keep her mostly at home where she at last gave up her desperate struggle. Matt had been left exhausted, empty, and in total despair. But despite Matt's extraordinary efforts, Jamie seemed to blame him for his mother's death, and would have nothing to do with him. Worse yet, the son seemed to throw over his own fortunes and plans to take up a life of pointless wandering.

He dropped out of the university during his junior year, driving out west with a couple of buddies. After knocking around a year or so, he enrolled in a college in Colorado but quit before the semester ended to work construction jobs there, and in Oklahoma. Next he was in Idaho and finally California. For over four years Matt didn't see his son. Then Jamie turned up briefly to announce that he was getting married and went back out west for another two years.

Now Jamie had been back in Maine for three years with his wife and son, living less than an hour's drive from his father. He had a good job as a propane technician, and the young couple had purchased their own home outside Skowhegan. Matt was surprised and pleased when his son invited him down to ask some advice on needed house repairs. There Matt met Jamie's friend, Butch, and the two somehow started talking about hunting. Matt was clearly surprised when he learned that Jamie was also taking it up. The previous season the three of them had gone out a few times and this year they'd hunted together every Saturday.

Matt had been surprised this morning when Butch, who was driving, turned onto what had to be the west end of the old Maxfield Ridge Road. Now paved over, it was scarcely recognizable. Two grandiose new homes stood in what had been the old orchard of the Kinneson farm where years before Ben had enjoyed hunting. Butch drove on about a mile, to the point where the road started to climb, and turned right onto a gravel tote road. This road went up toward the summit of the second-highest spine of the long ridge. Without saying anything to his companions, Matt figured he was at most a couple of miles from the old farmstead and the microwave tower site. He knew the obsolete tower had been taken down some years before.

After Marge's death, Matt never regained interest in his work. Everything in the industry was changing over to fiber optics and cellular phones, and Matt simply didn't have the interest or the ambition at his age to learn the new technology. When Ben offered him a job at his father-in-law's electrical supply warehouse, Matt accepted the offer and took an early retirement package from the phone company. He enjoyed the low-keyed pace of the work behind the counter and had no regrets.

Once Butch and Jamie had Matt positioned on high ground with good visibility, they disappeared into the thick woods below to hunt carefully and perhaps scare something his way. There were a couple of inches of new snow but the temperature was climbing and since the ground had not yet frozen, the snow would not last long. Scanning the hilltop, Matt spotted a more promising-looking stand about fifty yards away and decided to make for it. He'd taken just two steps when a crashing of brush alerted him to a pair of deer—a doe and a fork-horn buck—forty yards away. He had failed to see them coming, probably because he had been for the most part daydreaming. They offered no opportunity for a decent shot, so Matt simply shook his head and watched the two whitetails bounce off toward the east. As was his habit, he stalked carefully over to where he'd first heard the commotion. Sure enough, the deer had walked up the ridge from the softwoods essentially in plain sight, and had he been paying attention, he would surely have seen them coming.

The snow was ideal for tracking, and since the deer couldn't have gotten Matt's scent, it was possible he could catch up to them. Following along their tracks it became evident that they were not running full out. Within two hundred yards they had slowed to a walk and were moving through relatively open hardwoods. Matt was being led away from the planned hunt, but he was not about to abandon this possible opportunity. He struck out for the ridge top and was thankful to find there a dense band of young hemlocks to screen him from the open woods below.

He made good time working along the spine of the ridge, before long reaching a stone wall that ran up the hillside from below, separating the hardwood lot from a stand of mixed softwoods. He worked carefully down along the wall expecting at any moment to spot the deer feeding on beech mast as they moved toward him. A quarter mile from the top he was surprised by the sharp blowing of a startled deer in the softwoods behind him. He whirled to see a pair of white flags bounding off through the pine trees that were overtaking an old pasture. Apparently the deer had moved faster than he had anticipated and beaten him to this spot. His strategy had been good, but his timing a little slow. Matt grinned and shook his head. "Well, good for them," he thought. "It's probably a hell of a drag down to the road from here, anyway."

The temperature had by now climbed well above freezing and he suddenly discovered he was quite warm from the exertion. He unzipped his orange vest, unbuttoned his wool hunting coat beneath it, and glanced around. Most of the snow had already melted. Below, he heard a vehicle moving along the road and thought that perhaps it was closer than he had figured. If so, it would be his quickest and easiest way back to the car.

He continued downhill aiming for a patch of snow that lingered on the surface of a small ledge or a fallen tree. He was surprised when it turned out to be the slanting roof of a small structure at the edge of a weed-choked clearing. There was something familiar about it, and a closer inspection confirmed his suspicion that it was the asphalt-covered hovel that had served Carrie Stiles as a barn for her creatures. The door had long since fallen off, and Matt couldn't resist peering inside. When his eyes adjusted to the gloom, he could make out a moldy heap of blankets in the far corner. Coarse white and brown hairs matted the blankets. The hay on the floor appeared flattened smooth, as if it had been recently crushed. Outside the doorway and around the hovel were numerous droppings, obviously deer. In a patch of shade nearby, a remnant of shrinking snow clearly revealed fresh hoof prints. It wasn't making any sense, but he was struck by the ridiculous idea that deer had been using the abandoned shack for shelter. Then he came to his senses.

"Of course, it's the goats!" he said out loud. Obviously, the poor old woman had abandoned the property for whatever reason, and apparently the goats had been left behind to fend for themselves.

His curiosity rising, Matt couldn't help checking out the site thoroughly—even though each small discovery added to an uneasy feeling about the place. The entire field, including the gardens, was growing up into weeds, alders, and saplings. It took him several minutes to locate the cabin site, largely because the cabin itself had burned and collapsed. The forlorn aspect of the warped woodstove leaning against a pile of charred boards and timbers filled him with a combination of sadness and apprehension. He shivered as prickles migrated up his spine, arms, and neck. He hoped in his heart that the fire had occurred after Carrie had left. His only other discoveries were a garden hoe and a rusted roll of page-wire fencing. By the time he had finished nosing around, he was feeling not only unsettled, but parched, as well. He remembered a spring of ice-cold water out back that Carrie had shown him during one of his visits. It was some of the best water he had ever tasted, and he badly needed a long drink of it now before walking down to the road—Jamie and Butch were probably starting to worry about him.

The path to the spring was still discernible, but the back field was mostly grown over. What had been six-foot-high pines and spruces were now good-sized trees. Former grassy patches were taken over by clumps of alders and poplar saplings. The rock-lined spring itself was still protected from leaves and debris by a coarse metal screen, now badly rusted. Lifting this off, Matt knelt and scooped the clear, cold water directly into his mouth with his hand. It tasted as good as he remembered. After drinking his fill and feeling completely refreshed, he wiped the water from his chin with his red bandanna.

He had just placed the screen back into position when he heard a twig snap behind him. Carefully he reached for his rifle, then slowly straightened up and turned toward the sound. The deer continued moving noisily through the brush. Matt craned his neck and caught a glimpse of movement. Some pine boughs shook, there was another blur of motion, and then Professor Rodrigues lurched into the opening. There was no mistaking the shock of white hair, the intense expression on his face, the round eyes bulging from their sockets. His hair was longer and wilder than Matt remembered and the fatigue jacket was in tatters. The figure was stooped as he stood staring at Matt with a mixture of surprise and confusion. The hunter was equally startled, but relieved that he felt no actual fear of the apparition.

"Dr. Rodrigues," he said, too softly. Then, much louder, he called again. "Dr. Rodrigues."

The old man, who had dropped his gaze and seemed to be pondering his escape, shot his head back around toward Matt, registering astonishment at hearing his own name. With just a hint of uncertainty, he turned away slightly and stepped hurriedly toward the shelter of another island of bushy pines. The boughs moved and the man disappeared.

"Dr. Rodrigues, stop! Please! I won't hurt you. Look, I'm dropping my gun," and Matt set the Winchester down in a clump of ground junipers.

He called again, then hurried to the spot where the professor had been standing moments before. But the man—or ghost—had disappeared into the adjacent thicket.

"Wait, Professor Rodrigues!"

The old field was a maze of thick cover and small weedy clearings. With surprising agility, the old man—or whatever he was—kept just enough ahead of Matt to deny his pursuer another close look. Soon Matt found himself standing in one of many similar openings, breathing heavily, with no idea which way the old man had gone. By now there was no trace left of the snow that might have revealed a footprint, and it appeared Matt would have to abandon the weird chase.

Then suddenly he heard a commotion and saw the tops of some alders swaying in a thicket ahead. The cover looked all but impenetrable, but there appeared to be a trail around the patch to the left. Matt took off running. He rounded a pine tree at the end of the thicket and hurried forty feet or so past some thick alders and poplar. Emerging into yet another opening, Matt, sucking in his breath, was pulled up short by the sight before him.

Not fifty feet away stood a ten-point buck, looking back over his shoulder directly at him, his tense muscles rippling beneath the brown hide. Then, with no snort or hint of alarm, the deer turned, and in two great bounds disappeared into the thick firs.

Jerry Stelmok

Not Your Average Bear

—◆—

Awet wind, raw for so early in September, swept across the lake and lashed a small knot of men engaged in a discussion of obvious gravity. Pulled up onto the gravely beach was a thirty-foot logging bateau, a pair of birch canoes, and the wherry from the small tow steamer that stood just offshore. Inland, just beyond the beach, was an impressive stand of white pine and red spruce that marched in an uninterrupted phalanx over a series of drumlins before continuing up the gentle flanks of the mountain, where they disappeared behind curtains of low scudding clouds. The beach stretched across the end of a wide point. To one side, where the shore was steep, a small river boiled into a protected cove of Big Bear Lake; on the other side, an extensive marsh worked its way inland among the lower hills.

On maps pre-dating the Civil War, the mountain and the long lake at its foot were designated Kchee Awasoos, which was the cartographer's phonetic interpretation of the Indian name—*Kci Awesus.* After 1880 both features were labeled Big Bear on most maps because some bureaucrat found the Native American name difficult to get his tongue around.

The men on the beach had reached an impasse, a situation that clearly exasperated a large man in a slicker and a felt fedora. He scuffed impatiently at the gravel with the toes of his tall leather boots and scanned the forest behind the two Indians without making eye contact. He spat, then directed his unsettling glare at a shorter man to his right, also in a hat and slicker.

"C'mon, Carl. We're just wastin' time trying to talk sense into these trespassers. You know we got all the legal papers in that satchel of yours. That's why I brung ya here. I'm losing patience. Tell Mr. Solis and Mr. Sacobie here, them and all their women and friends has got to leave my woods immediately, so's we can start settin' up our operation."

The younger of the two Natives, a handsome man with straight cheekbones and obsidian eyes who might have stepped out of a Frederick Remington painting, regarded the infamous timber baron, Horace Tardiff, with neither impatience nor fear.

"This land is sacred to my people."

"That's the trouble with you Indians. Everything's sacred to you. Haven't you got Katahdin? Seems to me you have your ceremonies up there every year. No one tries to stop you, do they?" Tardiff countered.

"Ktaadn sacred, yes. Kci Awesus sacred, too."

"If I'm not mistaken, Solis, there's at least one church settin' on that reservation of yours. Now that's what I call sacred! This is just plain woods, and I bought it legal from your own council, even though you didn't even have a deed for it. Isn't that accurate, Carl?"

"Mr. Tardiff's right there, John." Carl Hastings, the sheriff, spoke up. "I've got the papers right in here, and also a court order from Judge Hardwick demanding you leave this land so Horace can begin getting ready for the winter's logging."

"Papers lie. Call wrong brook, Fish Brook. We never sell land west of real Fish Brook. Your map wrong."

"Jesus Christ, it's the same goddamn map we had when you signed the deal, for Chrissakes!" shouted a lummox of a young man, spittle spraying from his fat lips, one eye all over the place.

"Easy, Bim," Tardiff cautioned his son, placing a restraining hand on his trunk-like arm. "We're in our legal rights here and Sheriff Hastings will do his job. We've said all we're sayin' about it."

With that the timber baron turned on his heel, and pulling his gorilla of a son by his damp wool shirt, strode down to the boat.

Carl Hastings was left standing alone with his deputy facing the Indians. Obviously uncomfortable, he shook his head, looking mostly at their moccasins, and produced the court order.

"Sorry, John. Truly I am, but we got no choice in the matter. Mr. Tardiff's within his legal rights, and he ain't one to fool with. I'm afraid you and your companions will have to leave Big Bear Mountain and the lake by sunset tomorrow."

The Indians made no reply, but turned and walked silently into the forest. The sheriff and his deputy, Fred Collins, watched them disappear, then shrugged and joined two loggers who were holding the bateau against the waves in the shallows, ready to ferry them out to the steamer, where they'd join the Tardiffs for the thirteen-mile passage down the lake.

As the bateau approached the steamer, they could hear Tardiff below, lambasting Bim for having spoken out of turn. The harangue ceased as the law officers climbed aboard, and in a couple of minutes Tardiff and his sheepish-looking son emerged from the cabin, a bottle of whiskey in the father's hand. He produced a pocketknife, slit the seal, removed the cap, and passed the fresh bottle to the sheriff. Hastings took a healthy slug, and then at Tardiff's nod handed it to Deputy Collins, who knocked back a gulp and wiped his mouth with his sleeve. Reclaiming the bottle, Tardiff helped himself to a double swig but withheld the bottle from Bim, who stared at it hungrily.

"Well, that's that," Tardiff grinned. "By Thursday, any Indians stupid enough to stay behind will be run off by my crew carrying pick poles and peaveys."

The towboat was still within view of the beach while the engineer was tinkering with valves on the boiler of the new vessel.

"Take a look at that, will ya?" Deputy Collins gestured toward shore with his chin.

"Well, Holy Jesus!" Horace Tardiff exclaimed. The two Indians had emerged from the woods back onto the beach, another pair behind them. Soon a woman appeared with two young children. Presently, alone or in small groups, more Indians materialized, emerging as though they had been given up by the dark forest behind them. Some carried baskets, blankets, or rolled-up moose hides. A few had pots or bundles done up in deerskin. Two of the men carried shotguns. Within ten minutes there were about two dozen people on the beach, all largely silent except for quiet exchanges among themselves.

Some of the men stepped back into the woods and reappeared with five additional bark canoes, which they placed on the shore alongside the two already there. The previously stiff wind had diminished to a breeze. Quickly and without fuss, everyone including two dogs was aboard a canoe. The stern paddlers stood to guide the heavily burdened craft away from the shore, then knelt and bent to their work. The small ragtag fleet glided past the steamer, the Indians silent, looking straight ahead down the lake.

———

Foreman Ian Cassidy stamped his cold feet, rolled and lit a cigarette, and watched the skid trail for signs of the horses. He couldn't remember a more poorly planned logging operation, nor one fraught with as much bad luck. It was now January 1912, and what might have been a phenomenal harvest operation, given the quality of the timber, was limping along at a rude half-finished base camp. The planning had certainly been deficient, but the weather had also been a contributing factor.

From that day in early September when the Indians were run off, there had been heavy rain for most of the month, and for two weeks after that the ground was too soft for serious work. Crews were unable to harvest the good wild hay that was to be used to feed the horses over the winter. It grew tall and thick along the winding marsh, but by the time they were able to cut it, in mid-October, it had lost much of its value.

Then there was the freakish bad-luck accident that further hampered preparations and sapped the crew's morale. Louis Bissonette, the best axe man and builder in the outfit, was crushed along with Billy Hollander when a log they were hoisting onto a log wall—a task Louis had done practically without thinking a thousand times—got caught up, broke free, and pinned the men against a huge stump. Aside from the loss of two competent and good-natured workers, another consequence was that the crew, only half the size it should have been anyway, was sleeping in a drafty bunkhouse and eating meals in a homely little cook shack. The blacksmith and the rigger shared a dismal shed, and besides the horse hovel, the only other building was a small cabin serving both as the office and quarters for the woods boss, Norm Belanger, and Lenny Hekinen, the scaler.

The seven teams on site, instead of the usual fourteen, were fast eating through the insufficient hay supply as well as the oats brought in before the lake froze. Everyone was waiting to see if the Lombard log hauler Tardiff had promised to send, with its train of sledges carrying fodder for the horses and supplies to replenish the shrinking stores, would be able to negotiate the half frozen bogs and possibly weak lake ice in time to save the operation.

The logistics of the whole operation were ass-backwards in the first place. The logical thing would have been to start at the south end of the lake, adjacent to where they'd cut the year before, then over four or five seasons work their way up to the mountain at the north end with its prize timber. But doing it the way they were, they'd had to hurry all summer building a half-assed dam at the south end of the lake just to get up enough head to float logs down the measly outlet stream in the spring. And Tardiff had spent a fortune having the steam-driven towboat built on the beach at least three years sooner than he'd had to.

Oh, Cassidy knew the reason for this madness all right, but he still couldn't swallow it. It was all for Tardiff's idiot son, Bim, who'd gotten into his empty head that he had to have huge trees to cut after visiting his brother in the Pacific Northwest. Once Bim had seen the gigantic Douglas-fir, Sitka spruce, and red cedar on that Canadian island, it was all Tardiff could manage to get him to come back east.

Big Bear Mountain had the biggest timber in Maine—not half so big as the trees in the northwest, but plenty big enough to keep his youngest son in the family business even if he was an idiot. Bim had always been exceptionally strong and impulsive, but since being conked by a falling limb a couple of years back, that would have killed anyone else, he had become unpredictable, aggressive, and possibly even dangerous to have around.

And the whole idea of gypping the Indians out of their sacred holdings by using capital, political connections, and trickery made Cassidy sick. So ridiculous had Tardiff's scheme seemed at first, the tribe had not even thought to hire a good attorney.

But all Horace Tardiff's conniving did not prevent another tragedy from staining the operation, even though there were some around camp who were not exactly heartbroken by the event.

Just before Christmas Bim had gone on a crazed rampage, claiming he was sick and tired of knocking down small trees for building and swamping twitch roads. One morning he stormed into the cook shack and upset the rough table that had just been piled high with breakfast fare and hot coffee. When Gustav the cook protested, Bim flattened him with a right to the head. On his way out the door he announced that he for one was going to start dropping some real timber no matter what Belanger had to say.

He collared Emile Dupuis, and grabbing an eight-foot crosscut saw and their axes, the pair snowshoed out of camp and headed directly up the mountain to an impressive stand of white pine growing on a precariously steep slope. By noon they had dropped and limbed three enormous trees and were setting up to fell the biggest yet.

Emile had several concerns, but had to be careful about expressing them to his berserk partner. For one, there was no way to drop the behemoth without it shattering upon impact down the slope. His second concern arose when they removed the wedge of wood that produced the felling notch. Inspecting the resinous rings inside the notch, Emile pointed out numerous voids where the growth rings had separated along possible splits running up the tree inside the bark. This would indicate the structure of the trunk might have been compromised by wind, or simply by growing on such a steep slope.

Bim would have none of it. Dragging the saw to the uphill side, he thrust one end of it over to Dupuis and glared at him, eyes bulging and mouth actually foaming, until out of fear the experienced Canadian grasped the handle. The pair then began the practiced give-and-take strokes that fed the hungry teeth efficiently toward the notch. The eight-foot blade was barely as long as the pine was wide and the men had to work their way around the trunk to cut through. The giant tree was just beginning to nod in the intended direction when a contrary gust rocked it back uphill and pinned the saw. For a moment the tree seemed unable to decide whether to obey the call of gravity or the force of the wind, and swayed back and forth with great creaks and groans on its little hinge of solid wood.

Dupuis, knowing what could happen, released his grip, wheeled about, and floundered away from the dangerous tree. But Bim stood his ground, yelling obscenities at the Frenchman until the stricken tree decided on its own course of action. The internal splits became sufficiently aggravated by the swaying, and all the tension that had built up within the trunk over a hundred years was released as the tree twisted and fell. The concentric layers exploded and cast off great sections of bark as well as countless slivers and splinters with the force of a catapult. Those fibrous shards still attached to the tree as it fell shot outward with equal power, several of them hammering Bim with enough force to all but dislodge his head, while others sliced open his torso like broadswords.

Word was sent out and on Christmas day, Horace Tardiff, Sheriff Hastings, and a handful of cronies arrived at camp to collect Bim's remains. They had driven pungs over the relatively new ice, and anticipating their arrival, Belanger had kept the snow on the mile-and-a-half road between the lake and the camp well packed.

Tardiff insisted on visiting the site of Bim's demise, so Belanger led the little party on showshoes to the remote stand with the shattered tree trunk strewn across the slope. Tardiff paced up and down looking over the site chomping on a cigar.

"That foolish bastard," he muttered, and it was all he said about the horror that had claimed his son.

After supper back at the camp, while the full moon was high, the party left, figuring to clear the lake by mid-morning the next day. Bim's remains would make the journey out in a wooden coffin they'd brought in on the bed of one of the pungs. The temperature was beginning to drop, heralding the first really sub-zero freeze of the winter, and by morning the thermometer registered twenty-eight below.

―

Cassidy was not overly sorrowful about Bim Tardiff's death. But it didn't bode well for any operation, especially one hamstrung like this one, to have the owner's son killed on the job. Especially so early on.

He was starting to feel the cold, and wondered why the two woods-wise Percherons, Ham and Eggs, were not yet back with another log to add to the growing brow. This team was so well trained it needed no supervision in twitching logs from the staging area to the site of the brow above the frozen stream. At the yard end Willy DuJours would hitch a giant log to the doubletree with a choker chain, and the handsome pair would waste little time hauling the timber along the well-packed trail a quarter mile to the brow. Cassidy would uncouple the log and by means of a log ramp and jig pole, would use the horsepower to slide the log up to the top of the stack. He would then release the team and they would head back down the trail for another skid. The foreman would straighten out the new addition with his peavey if necessary, and in April the logs would be rolled into the swollen stream for a ride down to the lake.

Cassidy rolled another smoke and started down the trail with his peavey to see what was holding things up. The horses were usually smart enough to work free a fetched-up log by pulling side to side, and he couldn't think what else could be causing the delay.

Rounding the final bend above the wood yard, Cassidy suddenly stopped in his tracks and the bent cigarette dropped from his lips. Before him, old Ham and Eggs lay flat out like two giant broken toys. It was easy to see their necks were broken, and bright red blood was saturating the snow as it seeped from slash marks along their necks and withers. Cassidy walked around the gruesome sight unable to believe his eyes. His calls to DuJours went unanswered. There were prints the size of snowshoes in the new snow alongside the trail, but they were indistinct, the light snow having partially refilled them.

Jerry Stelmok

Those on the packed snow had been pretty much obliterated by the terrorized horses.

"DuJours! Where the hell are you?" Cassidy yelled again as he struck off across the wood yard, but there was no reply. At the far end he found a rough furrow of a trail slicing through the deep snow. It almost appeared as though DuJours had been trying to run, but again the soft snow had refilled most of the actual prints making it all speculation. Thirty yards into the trees he came upon another trail, this one suggesting great lunges of a much larger creature. This trail converged on DuJours's trail, and there, half buried in the snow, was the savaged body of Willy DuJours. Brushing away the pink snow with his moosehide mitt, Cassidy recoiled at the sight. Whatever it was had apparently taken the logger's head entirely into its jaws and delivered a crushing bite to his lower neck, shoulders, and thoracic cavity.

Cassidy straightened up, stunned, and stepped back, still staring in astonishment at DuJours's remains. He was jolted back to reality by a disturbance in the woods to his left. Disbelief turned to palpable fear as the brush in a willow thicket began to shake and a drawn-out guttural rumble emanated from the throat of whatever lurked behind the snowy screen. Cassidy could barely make out a dark amorphous shape behind the brush, but it was startlingly huge. His mouth went dry and his pounding heart seemed to leap to his throat. His stomach contracted as though in the grip of a giant hand.

There was a second long growl, louder than the first, and for a moment the willows shook wildly. Cassidy himself was shaking, frozen in his tracks. Then there was a crashing of brush, and good-sized branches snapped as the creature moved off into the deep woods. Cassidy retraced his steps on the run, sheer terror propelling him back to camp.

Norm Belanger, the experienced camp boss, didn't know what to make of the attack. During his many years in the woods he'd seen a few strange things, but the violent deaths of Willy DuJours and the team of horses went beyond anything in his experience by a country mile. It was the same with everyone else in the little party that had gone out to retrieve DuJours's body. Belanger knew of no creature in the forests of the northeast that would attack a man unprovoked, and the only instance he recalled of a horse being attacked was a mare slashed and bitten badly enough by a cougar that it had to be put down. That had been more than forty years earlier when he was a kid visiting his grandfather's logging camp over at Mattagamon. He hadn't even heard of another credible sighting of an eastern mountain lion since, and by the looks of it, Ham and Eggs had been dispatched almost instantly by something of tremendous strength, beyond the capabilities of a hundred-and-fifty-pound cougar. Even a good-sized black bear couldn't do what had been done to the team, and not only were bears hibernating in the winter but they were generally not in the habit of attacking horses.

Settling the crew down back at camp was the first order of business. Fear and anxiety were growing out of control as the men discussed over and over the details of the carnage, and speculated about just what sort of monster or demon had now targeted the cursed operation. In an effort to calm them, Belanger gathered everyone into the cook shack around the glowing pot-bellied stove and delivered a rather unconvincing talk. He told them that DuJours's death was an isolated incident and in the light of day he and Cassidy would track down the critter and make sure it would cause no more trouble.

But that night and the next day over a foot of snow fell and the trail was buried almost before they could get started. Late that morning two visitors came snowshoeing into camp, one pulling a toboggan behind him. Russ Kelly was a new timber cruiser for the company and he had brought in Stewart Fischer, a pain-in-the-ass bean counter from Tardiff's main office. Fischer had no business setting foot in the woods, but supposedly to gain a better understanding of the timber business, insisted on bothering at least one woods operation for a couple of weeks each winter. Fischer had brought along his handsome, mostly black shepherd, Turk, who snapped at anyone who came near him, and was about as unappealing as a dog could get.

It had taken them five days to reach the camp from Pittston Farm.

Jerry Stelmok

Each evening Kelly had set up a wall tent and a small tin stove that heated the shelter and cooked the day's one hot meal. Fischer would read while Kelly cleaned up the pot and tin dishes and split more kindling for the morning coffee. Turk, the shepherd, would find himself a comfortable spot between his master and the canvas wall and growled menacingly whenever Kelly stirred.

Kelly was stunned by the account of DuJours's and the horses' deaths. He'd never heard of anything remotely like it, and he volunteered to snowshoe to the site the following morning to look over the horse carcasses for any clues. But as it turned out he didn't have to wait that long.

A small crew had been working an easily accessed stand close to the river for the past three weeks. They had built a rough slab-wood hovel as shelter for two teams to save them the time and energy of plodding back and forth between the main camp and the worksite each day. So even though the choppers couldn't work because of the blizzard, and enjoyed a day of rest and personal chores at camp, teamster Zeke Slater was not excused from his duties and was still responsible for feeding the teams at the shelter. Early that morning he headed off into the storm pulling a boxed sled stuffed with hay and a pail of oats to tend his charges. He would draw their water from the spring fed brook that twisted past the structure.

Now, as Belanger, Kelly, Fischer, and a few of the crew were discussing the attacks over coffee in the cook shack, Slater came charging into camp, gasping for breath and clearly hysterical. The men got him into the kitchen and sat him down in front of the stove. His mackinaw, wool trousers, and face were encrusted with frozen snow. He apparently had lost his mittens and snowshoes, and must have run through the deep snow the whole way. Enough ice had accumulated on his ample mustache and beard to effectively freeze his mouth shut, but his wide bulging eyes spoke eloquently of his terror.

Gustav, the Slovakian cook, passed a steaming mug of tea back and forth before Slater's beard hoping to melt the restraining icicles as Slater tried desperately to speak. Belanger had a better idea and after soaking a towel in a pot of hot water on the stove surface, he wrapped the steaming cloth around Slater's head and whiskers. Before long the teamster shot to his feet and let go a howl of pain, for not only had this steam treatment melted the ice, but at far as he was concerned, it had also scalded his face.

In a couple of minutes Slater's breathing had returned to near normal and he began gaining control of his blubbering. Apparently the creature had struck again, this time attacking the four helpless horses tethered in their hovel. All were badly maimed, three were dead. The beast had collapsed the rickety shelter on top of his victims and when Zeke finally lifted his eyes from the carnage, the creature was standing across the brook from him challenging or taunting him with the same drawn-out rumbling growl earlier described by Cassidy. Even through the swirling snow the enormous bulk of the creature was apparent.

"What was it, Zeke?"

"What did it look like?"

"Can you describe it?"

"It, it was a bear. A huge black bear. Only it was tall as a moose. Bigger 'n a' ox."

"A bear, Zeke? Are you sure?"

"It was a bear all right. Standin' acrost the crick. A'growlin'. It was the biggest bear in the goddamn world, I'm tellin' ya."

"Ridiculous," declared Fischer. "Bears are hibernating this time of year and that's not black bear behavior, anyway. Now I've read accounts of grizzlies out west, where...."

"Stow it, Fischer," Kelly interrupted, still irritated by the past few days spent guiding this prig. "Now, Zeke, it didn't attack you?"

"No. No, I guess it didn't. I took off runnin'. Lost one snowshoe, then t' other. They was only trippin' me up, anyways. I never looked back. But ya know? He could've catched me, easy as pie. But, no, he didn't!"

Within a few minutes a group of men was assembling in the camp yard. Like most working logging camps, this one was not heavily armed. In his office, Belanger kept a twelve-gauge double and slugs that would pack a real wallop at close range. Kelly drew a .45-70 lever-action rifle from his outfit still lashed to the toboggan. The scaler, Hekinen, kept a .30-30 in case a tasty moose unwittingly wandered near camp during the winter, and Fischer had a .45-caliber revolver on his belt. The men tied on their snowshoes and struck off at a trot toward the hovel.

They could smell the thing even before they reached the scene. A dense musk hung in the air despite the wind and the larger wet flakes that were still pirouetting down. The sight that greeted them was gruesome in the extreme. After Slater had fled, the beast had returned, killing the surviving horse, ripping open the carcasses, tearing off limbs, even pulling out viscera. As more debris from the collapsed shed was removed the greater the extent of the mutilation became evident. For all the gore, it appeared as though nothing had been consumed or dragged off, which was mystifying in itself. There was, however, physical evidence pertaining to the true nature and size of the attacker. Several prints in packed snow revealed unmistakably the distinctive pads, with the five toes and claws associated with a bear. These, however, were more than twice as large as the largest prints either Kelly or Belanger had ever seen.

Fischer's shepherd, Turk, had enthusiastically led the charge along the trail, but since reaching the scene his manner had changed dramatically. The big dog slunk around sniffing at the mess, his ears flat against his head and tail down like a puppy that had just been kicked. Now as the storm again intensified and the men discussed whether or not to take up the creature's trail, Turk's ruff bristled and he retreated to stand behind his master. He peered intently at the thicket across the brook and emitted a low growl. Almost instantly firearms were shouldered and hammers were cocked as the men strained to see though the snow into the heavy brush ahead, ears alert for any revealing sound. They had not long to wait.

Something large was moving through the stunted gray birches that clogged a one-time beaver flowage off the brook, and it was snapping off the spindly, closely spaced trees as it proceeded. The pattern of the sounds, however, was not consistent, and no sooner had the men trained their guns on a particular spot than the sound would shift and appear to come from someplace different.

Turk started whimpering pitifully, and when the first growl rumbled from behind the screen of brush he yelped, wheeled, and galloped off in the direction of camp.

The sinister growls continued, always coming from a slightly different location, and the visibility continued to diminish. If the thing were to charge, no one would see it until it had cleared the brook.

Sweat was now beading on every brow, and Fischer was shaking like an aspen leaf, his eyes wide with terror. His .45 revolver wavered so wildly it would have been comical under different circumstances. A gust of wind dislodged a dead limb from an old pine and as it crashed into the thicket below, he began firing randomly into the driving snow. He got off three shots, all of them striking the woods yards from one another and at least fifteen feet above the ground, before Norm Belanger grabbed his wrist and twisted until the pistol dropped into the snow.

Russ Kelly, Belanger, and Hekinen all expected the careless shots to trigger a full-out charge, but to their relief it didn't happen. The creature continued to move, always out of sight, through the dense undergrowth, cracking wood and occasionally growling. Eventually the sounds receded into the deeper forest and after a time ceased altogether. By now every man was shaking considerably, as much from the weight of holding his gun at the ready as from apprehension. With heavy snow still falling and the gloom of late afternoon descending, there was no further thought of tracking the beast. The small group retreated cautiously, guns still cocked, expecting a cataclysmic ambush at any moment as they made their way back to camp.

———

There was a young man in camp named Jeff Partridge who had no business being part of any logging crew. He had grown up in privileged circumstances in the Boston area, and had attended the finest schools. What change of fortune or romantic disappointment had turned him away from a more conventional path was a matter of conjecture only, because he never spoke about his past. But something had propelled him toward the north woods, and the Tardiff office in Bangor, desperate to put together a crew to work Big Bear, had overlooked his shortcomings. He was among the last handful of loggers deposited on the beach at Big Bear Lake in the fall. It wasn't that Partridge was lazy or lacked motivation, it was just that he was soft, unintuitive, and unschooled in any of the dozen skills that distinguished a seasoned logger. Beyond being green, he was so incompetent with any logging implement as to constitute a hazard to himself and anyone nearby. After Partridge's second week, Belanger was ready to send him out of the woods on the towboat that had just made its final supply run before freeze-up.

But with personnel in such short supply in the teamster crew especially, Zeke Slater had told the boss he could use Partridge, if only to help him feed and care for the horses. His intuition proved accurate and Jeff's easy manner was effective around the horses. He was eager to take on any task Zeke suggested, and caught on quickly. At this point he could handle two teams hitched to a loaded scoot and was finally considered a contributing member of the hard-pressed woods crew.

Since the slaughter at the brook, the four remaining teams were kept at the larger stable at the main camp. To their credit, Zeke and Jeff moved their bedrolls onto the dwindling haystack at one end of the stable and courageously spent their nights with the spooked horses. Belanger lent Zeke his twelve-gauge, but doubted its effectiveness if the bear launched a nighttime attack.

There was no sign of the creature for several days after the hovel incident, but a week later the whole crew was jolted awake in the middle of the night by two gunshots followed by shouting and the squealing of terrified horses from the crude barn. Nearly everyone responded, most in their union suits despite the minus thirty-degree cold, bearing peaveys and double-bitted axes. Russ Kelly and Hekinen were first on the scene brandishing their rifles, but once again they were too late.

The bear had called again. Around midnight young Partridge had still been awake, shivering with the cold, although Zeke Slater was sleeping as soundly as—well, a hibernating bear. Although he heard nothing unusual, Partridge noticed the horses getting edgy. Soon they became extremely agitated, tugging at their tethers, stomping about and whinnying nervously, which apparently was still not enough commotion to rouse Zeke from his snoring slumber. Jeff had grabbed the shotgun and tried to sort out which sounds were coming from outside the hovel. A rank, musky smell permeated the air and he heard the first of several signature growls but could not get a bearing on their origin because of the noise made by the terrified horses. Still Slater did not wake up.

By this time Partridge was frozen with fear, his muscles as well as his bones seemingly turning to mush. He wet himself. Still, when a black shadow blocked out the moonlight that had been streaming through the open seams of the slab sheathing, he let fly with a load of double-aught buckshot from the first barrel and a heavy slug from the second.

The blasts were sufficient not only to wake Zeke up, but nearly caused him to jump out of his skin. One team pulled free its stanchion and dragged it through the canvas door into the yard. The others neighed and screamed as though caught in a fire.

But the beast had retreated. Partridge, who had apparently collapsed from fright, was carried to the cook shack and the breakaway horses were secured back in the hovel. It appeared the apprentice teamster had prevented another massacre. By moonlight and kerosene lantern, Russ Kelly located a number of the enormous prints. It was evident the bear had stalked around the rear of the shelter and was very likely about to bust his way inside. A good-sized hole from the shotgun slug was too high up the wall to have connected with anything but a giraffe. Partridge's first shot with the buckshot, however, had been well placed, but most of the pellets spent themselves cutting in two some harness that hung on the wall. But a few pellets had passed cleanly through the cracks between the slabs, and these had struck the creature. On the snow just outside were a few tufts of long black hair with bits of hide attached, along with several spots of crimson. The wounds would most likely be of minor consequence to so large and strong a creature, but it was the first hard evidence that their nemesis was at least flesh and blood, and it had apparently been driven off.

In the kitchen Jeff Partridge was revived with tea and a medicinal shot of the whiskey kept on hand strictly for such emergencies. He was clearly shaken and not altogether coherent. Belanger made a point of telling him that he had probably saved the lives of the horses and his own and Zeke Slater's as well. And he had wounded the giant bear. But even this unusual praise had little effect on the young man, and a pair of choppers had to help him to his bunk.

By first light the weather front had changed. Clouds had moved in and once again snow was falling heavily. Belanger and Kelly took up the trail, but it was fast being smothered. They stuck with it until it entered a tangled blown-down swamp, then had to give it up.

Work resumed for a couple of days, but the boss kept the crews within earshot of the camp. Everyone was still so edgy, little harvesting actually got done. Partridge still had not emerged from his shell and seemed not to hear or comprehend when spoken to. At breakfast the third morning after the incident a crewmember told Belanger that Jeff had gotten up sometime during the night, and his bunk was empty at wake-up. No one had seen him at the latrine or anywhere else around camp and a quick investigation proved this to be true. Missing were his knapsack, bedroll, and snowshoes. Kelly asked Belanger if he wanted him to try to catch the young man.

"No, I guess maybe not. He's made up his mind to get out of here. The lake's good travelin'. If he makes it down the lake today he should be all right."

The following morning was bright and cold. Smoke rose straight up from the stovepipes with no drift whatsoever. After breakfast Kelly engaged in a little conversation with Gustav, and by the time he stepped outside, the rough buildings with their snowy roofs and the patches of bright sunlight dancing amid the blue shadows beneath the pines struck him as almost normal. The crews had already entered the nearby woods and he could hear their friendly shouts and taunts interspersed with the rhythmic zips of a crosscut saw and the satisfying *tunks* of a well-directed axe.

He was heading toward the blacksmith's shack when a disturbance down the trail toward the lake caught his attention. For a few moments he didn't know what to make of it, but eventually he identified it as a team of dogs being driven up the trail toward camp. It was something Kelly had never before encountered in the Maine woods.

The apparition only became more mystifying as it drew nearer. For one thing, the dogs were much smaller than he would have imagined, and unlike the handsome, long-haired Eskimo dogs he'd seen in pictures, these were short, rather homely creatures with wide chests and short muzzles. All were one shade or another of brown or gray, and if their ears had been any more round, they would have looked like wolverines as much as anything.

The driver looked like a mountain man character from a romance novel, and jogging behind him was an Indian as tall and lean as the musher was short and squat. Russ Kelly could only stare at the outfit in amazement as it pulled up alongside the office.

"Arrett, Chien, Arrett!" called the driver and the sled glided to a smart stop. He stepped off the back of the runners and nodded a greeting to Kelly from across the yard. He removed his long-cuffed fur mitts and glanced around the camp with obvious disapproval. Although he wasn't much over five feet in height, he cut a colorful figure with his full chestnut beard and long hair beneath his beaver cap. His coat was cut from a scarlet five-point Hudson Bay blanket and bound around his considerable waist with an embroidered sash in royal blue. His short legs were done up in Eskimo-style mukluks with leather ties wound up around his calves.

The Indian, who had appeared to be very tall at first when compared with the driver, was actually of average height. He wore an anorak and pants of caribou skin tanned to retain the insulating hair. He wore the same type of moosehide mukluks as his companion.

As soon as the sled stopped, the well-disciplined dogs sat or reclined in their traces, looking about curiously but making not a sound. As the Indian undid the lead dog's harness, the office door swung open and Norm Belanger stepped out to greet this obviously familiar figure.

"Monsieur Belanger, comme 'ça, you ol' hore dog?" bellowed the visitor, laughing.

"You camp, eet look like shet."

With a wide grin, Belanger responded "Jean Batiste, you sonofabitch. I'd've bet anything either a Mountie or a jealous husband would have taken care of you by now."

"Mountee, he no probleme. Jean Batiste geev heem leetle scratch," and he made the universal gesture with his stubby thumb and fingertips that translates to passing currency, especially as a bribe. "Yealous husban'? Dat 'nudda story. Husban' can be trés dangereux. Haw, haw, haw."

Kelly had crossed over to the gathering.

"Jean Batiste, this is Russ Kelly, a new timber cruiser for the company. Russ used to survey for that Brown outfit, but he's lowered his standards and come over to Tardiff."

"He's certainly got that right," Kelly thought to himself.

The two men shook hands seriously, each possessing a grip like a steel trap, and neither would let up, their unblinking eyes locked. Finally Belanger was called upon to end the foolish stalemate without either man losing face.

"Okay, you two bulls, that's enough. What use is either of you with a broken hand?"

Batiste turned toward the Indian, who was unlashing a moosehide tarp that covered a sizeable load on the *komatik*.

"Thees ees me brudder, Michael—hees be St. Francis Injin from Kébeck and bes' tracker in de woods." Batiste placed his hand alongside his cheek and as though in an aside to Belanger said, "Bedder even den Jean Batiste. But he wan' more money if when he hear dat. Haw, haw, haw." And again he brushed his fingertips with his thumb.

Acknowledging nothing, the Indian pulled off the cover to reveal a pair of butchered moose neatly quartered and stowed. He grabbed a sack of less desirable cuts and began dispensing the gristly chunks to the harnessed dogs. Each waited obediently for his turn then fell ravenously on his portion.

"See dat, Belanger? We breeng you two fat mooses already. Jean Batiste tink crew mebbe like moose meat for der supper, no?"

"I'm not sure this crew remembers how to eat anything besides beans and biscuits," Belanger retorted with a wide grin. "Slater's been worried the way some of the crew's been eyeing his horses."

Russ Kelly had heard about this hunter from Québec, but had never met him. He operated along the inaccessible border woods, poaching Maine moose, and some winters provided logging outfits like this one with welcome but illegal game. Batiste liked working with Tardiff because he always paid, entertained no scruples against such transactions, and was well enough connected to have the appropriate authorities paid off. Besides, even the most dedicated game warden—charged with patrolling twelve hundred square miles on snowshoes—had little chance of catching up with Batiste's swift and tireless dog team plying the wind-packed lakes and river systems.

Other years, when fur prices were high, Batiste would head north, often as far as Hudson Bay, where he had spent several years as a factor at a trading post. It was during those years that he became familiar with the skills and accoutrements of the northern tribes, later adopting those that were useful to his work along the border country.

"Well, Belanger, Jean Batiste recall whiskee no allow in dees camp, non? So, by gar, we pour dees Canadienne me'dcin on da snow." He produced a bottle of fine amber Québec reserve and pretended to empty it on the ground.

"Haw, haw, haw!" Then he tucked it under his arm and entered the office with Kelly and Belanger to talk business.

⬤

A few minutes later Fischer returned from the nearby yarding area where he'd gone to get some figures from Hekinen. Spotting the sled dogs by the office, he instinctively reached for Turk's collar to restrain him. Turk's ugly habit of nipping at passersby had pretty much disappeared after several serious kicks to the snout and ribs by intolerant loggers. But now, Turk's back bristled, his ears lay back against his head, and he snarled menacingly through his curled lip. Once Fischer realized that all but one of the dogs were still hitched to the komatik, and saw how small the dogs actually were—Turk had a good forty pounds on the lead dog—his face relaxed into a smile, and he let go of the collar.

"Go get 'im, Turk," he urged, anticipating some cruel fun.

Étienne, Batiste's prized lead dog, had turned his attention toward the shepherd at the first growl. Now as Turk covered the distance between them in great bounds, he braced his sturdy legs and held his ground. When Turk slammed into him full tilt, it was almost like running into a tree. Étienne absorbed much of the impact, then rolled backwards sending Turk sailing over him to land with a jarring thud on his chest and chin. Before the shepherd could begin to gather his feet under him, Étienne was on top of him sinking his teeth into the side of the big dog's neck. With a powerful twist, Étienne had Turk helpless on his back, his feet scrabbling in the air and his bleeding neck still locked in a death grip.

Fischer's grin had turned to an open-mouthed gape in fewer than twenty seconds. He ran up to the dogs, assessed Turk's predicament, and kicked Étienne a good one in the ribs—with no apparent effect. The big dog was whimpering pitifully, and Fischer was by turns shocked, furious, and embarrassed. He reached under his coat, pulled out his revolver, leveled it between the sled dog's bulging shoulders. He was about to retract the hammer when the maple billy that Michael kept to control the rare dogfight came down on his wrist like a pile driver.

The pain was sharp enough to turn Fischer's world bright white, and then searing red. He not only dropped his pistol but dropped to his knees as well. As he rocked back and forth grimacing and clutching his wrist, Michael walked up to the dogs, said something in his own language in a normal tone, and Étienne released his lethal grip and backed off. Another short command and he trotted over to his position at the head of the team, which had watched the encounter with just barely enough discipline to keep themselves from joining their leader in tearing the attacker to ribbons.

Turk, on the other hand, lay still for half a minute, rolled his eyes around to be sure his adversary wasn't preparing to pounce, then leapt to his feet and ran off toward the hovel. The splash of bright red on the snow was as large as a dinner plate.

When Belanger, Kelly, and Batiste stepped out the door, Fischer was shaking his swollen wrist and glaring at Michael with intense hatred. The Indian met his eyes with total equanimity.

"Cool off there, Fischer, before you really get yourself hurt," Belanger warned.

"Are you serious?" spat Fischer. "Sitting Bull, here, tried to get Turk killed."

"We saw the whole thing from the window, Fischer, and the only one at fault here is you. You're lucky Michael didn't bring that baton down across your skull. I might have. Now, if you've any concern for that dumb-ass dog of yours, you better find him and get him sewn up before he bleeds to death," advised the woods boss.

Enraged, humiliated, and outnumbered, Fischer turned and stalked off in the direction Turk had fled. Numerous crimson spots the size of silver dollars marked his path.

"Haw, haw, haw, by Jeeze!" bellowed the hunter. "Mebee now Jean Batiste git look dem tracks you tol' heem 'bout?" Batiste was impatient to see the prints left by the so-called bear outside the stable. From what Belanger had told him—which was backed up by Kelly, who seemed reliable—the Frenchman couldn't tell for sure whether or not he was about to have a joke sprung on him. But his first look at the tracks left him speechless for almost five seconds.

"Holy, Jésus, Joseph, et Marie. Wha' kine o' creeter leeve track like dat? He look like bear track, sure, but so beeg! Even greezly bear not so beeg lak dat and Jean Batiste know dere no ice bear dis country. An' black bear? Heem sleep mos' da winter."

He shook his head and looked at Michael, who had squatted beside one of the prints, but the Indian's expression was inscrutable.

"Tell me 'gin 'bout de choppere and dee two horse," Batiste inquired, and Belanger repeated the story of Ham and Eggs and Willie DuJours.

Jerry Stelmok

Michael stood up and walked over to the cook shack, where, judging by the sounds, Fischer was having difficulty controlling and tending to Turk. At first the accountant refused Michael's assistance and the Indian stood back. But eventually Fischer's concern for Turk, whose wound was still bleeding, forced him to accept Michael's help. Michael got the dog to relax almost at once, then he took some crushed herbs from a pouch beneath his anorak, mixed them with hot water, and applied the mix to the small but deep wounds and held it in place. In a few minutes the bleeding had stopped and he applied a pitch-like salve to the wounds. Finally, without raising a single yelp from the grateful dog, he laced in a few neat stitches of fine babiche.

"Give him water, plenty rest," was all Michael said as he stood, turned, and went out the door.

Jean Batiste was now familiar with the particulars of the bear attacks and was rather eagerly anticipating the challenge these strange events presented. From deep within the komatik he pulled out an expensive fleece-lined leather gun case and removed a magnificent large-bore double-barreled rifle. It looked brand new and was stunning in every respect, from the almost microscopic checkering pattern on the walnut stock, to the fine engravings of African wildlife around the breech. Clearly this was a beautifully crafted piece built by old-world gunsmiths and intended for use on dangerous game such as lions, tigers, Cape buffalo, or even elephants.

"Holy shit, Batiste," Belanger said. "Where did you ever come by a piece like this?"

"Ees luvly, non? Tree-sev'nty-five Holland wid tree-hunret-grain bullet. Thees babe, she's take good care of trouble bear, don' you tink? Riche man geeve Jean Batiste as pre'sen', haw, haw, haw!"

"Someone gave you this rifle?" Kelly asked incredulously. "What did you do, save his life?"

"Haw, haw, haw. Dat good one! Non, Jean Batiste not save hees life. He geeve gun eef Batiste ee's promis' stay clear dis man's wife! Haw, haw, haw!"

"Wait a minute, Batiste. You mean someone actually gave you this rifle to stop fooling around with his wife, instead of using it on you?"

"Haw, haw. Dat good one too. Oui, ees true. She trés fine woman, too, and she's can't résiste Jean Batiste. But she not so fine as dis here gun."

"It looks like it's never been fired," the timber cruiser commented.

"Dat's true eenuf. Don' wan' spoil too much meat on dem moose. Use soon eenuf on beeg, bad bear, haw, haw, haw."

Then Batiste told Belanger that as they'd been traversing the north bay of the lake from the west, making for the camp, Michael's sharp eyes had spotted birds, mostly ravens but also an eagle, about three miles down along the east shore. Belanger and Kelly both felt it should be checked out and the trapper said Michael would run one of them down the shore with the team. Kelly was quick to volunteer and in a few minutes was sitting on a caribou skin in the komatik, which had been hastily relieved of its moose meat by Gustav and his helper. He held his octagon-barreled .45-70 across his knees and was much impressed with his first experience behind a good team driven by a competent musher.

In half an hour, with Michael running alongside much of the time, the team and sled were approaching the scene. Ravens perched in trees and on the ground were patiently waiting their turn at whatever the eagle was ripping at on the blood-stained snow. They all reluctantly flapped off as the sled approached. Most of the ravens landed in nearby trees to watch the proceedings with intelligent curiosity.

Russ Kelly had always felt he was as tough-minded and had as strong a stomach as the next guy. But the sight of what was left of Jeff Partridge after the bear had ripped him to pieces and the scavengers had begun their important work left him at first dizzy, then nauseous. He turned into the scrub brush along the shore and retched until his stomach was empty and his sides were sore.

Meanwhile, Michael had gathered up Partridge's slashed knapsack and a few other items like his sheath knife and bloodied hat and was preparing to wrap up his remains in a moosehide. Kelly helped him finish this gruesome chore and they placed the knobby bundle into the sled. Following behind the makeshift hearse on the trail back to camp, Kelly cast frequent glances over his shoulder, the heavy Winchester at the ready.

Jean Batiste and Michael set up their neat balloon-silk tent just beyond the office, insulating the packed-snow floor with an interwoven carpet of fragrant fir boughs and setting up a small tin stove with a pipe that ran out through a sewn-in thimble. The confident hunters added a palpable measure of security to the besieged outfit, and Zeke the teamster was perhaps the most thankful of all. Now he didn't feel he had to spend his nights in the freezing hovel with the horses, waiting for the bear to come roaring in to tear him—or his teams—to pieces. Jean Batiste stationed his capable dogs around the stable each night and after hearing what Étienne alone had done to the arrogant Turk, most of the crew figured nine of these dogs, left untethered, would be a match for even this formidable beast.

The first few nights were peaceful, the dogs remaining quiet throughout. By the second night the camp had relaxed and for the first time in a couple of weeks, the men were actually able to sleep soundly. But after four days of this respite, the peace was suddenly shattered around two A.M. by the growling and barking of the dogs followed by the stamping and neighing of spooked horses. Russ Kelly was the first to arrive at the barn, his rifle at his shoulder. But it was a dark night and the thing stayed out of sight in the shadows.

A minute later Batiste and Michael came running up, the Frenchman with his big game rifle, and Michael now carrying a ten-gauge. By the time Belanger joined the party the horses were settling down, and at a command from Batiste the barking ceased also. Still, the peculiar musky odor hung in the air, keeping the animals as well as the men uneasy. Clearly the bear had paid a call, but for some reason had not followed through with an attack.

The next night at about the same time pandemonium once again broke out at that end of camp. One moment the stillness of a frigid winter night embraced the slumbering logging camp and in the next moment it was replaced entirely by the snarling and yelping of dogs, the squealing of horses, and an unholy bawling somewhere between the braying of a donkey and the barking of a seal.

Jean Batiste was out from between his caribou skins and through the tent door in seconds, impatient to test the handsome .375 against this arrogant intruder. From the sounds, he feared his dogs were being tossed around quite violently, but there was no sign they were giving up. Belanger had beat him to the melee by a few seconds, and it was already becoming apparent that the skirmish was retreating into the woods beyond the hovel, with at least some of the dogs still pressing the attack.

Suddenly there was a bright flash and a concussion from Belanger's shotgun. Still there was yelping and whimpering from the sled dogs apparently determined to stay with the beast even as it moved at a surprising rate away from the camp.

Belanger was excited but unhurt and coherent, and the horses had been saved. But Jean Batiste's dog team had paid a heavy price. Four of the courageous defenders lay dead in the immediate vicinity of the hovel, slashed, bitten, and dashed to crumpled heaps in the bloody snow. A fifth, essentially eviscerated, lay gasping his final breaths a few yards farther along the path of the beast's retreat. At least two of the dogs were still worrying the bear, their yelps fading as the struggle moved deeper into the woods. Without hesitation Jean Batiste was on the trail. There was enough light from the quarter moon to distinguish it, and Kelly was right behind him.

Michael checked each of the bloodied dogs, but they were beyond help. Belanger soothed the agitated horses, surprised that none had been hurt during their desperate thrashing. Soon the distant yelping stopped—the dogs had either given up the chase or, more likely, been killed.

Ten minutes later Batiste and Kelly returned to camp, a badly mauled dog cradled in the Frenchman's arms. Étienne likewise appeared seriously injured but was limping along behind his master under his own power. Ozette, the team peacekeeper, padded in ahead of the others, bleeding from a large U-shaped swatch of hide that had been nearly stripped from his side.

Batiste laid the dog in his arms on the snow before Michael. The Indian looked him over, gently running his hand over the dog's shoulder and pelvic regions. He looked up at the hunter and shook his head. Batiste knelt, speaking softly to the stricken dog while stroking his head with his left hand. With his right he drew his long knife from its sheath and sank it squarely into the suffering dog's heart.

Michael carried Ozette to the tent for treatment and signaled Étienne to follow. There had been nine dogs on the team and one was still unaccounted for. Hekinen, the scaler, solved the mystery when he spotted a carcass on the hovel's low roof where the beast had flung the dog after crushing it.

"Monsieur Belanger. You heet 'im ver' gude. Dat bear, he be bad hurt, ver' much."

"How can you tell?" the boss retorted. "There's goddamn blood and hair everywhere."

"Ah, Jean Batiste can tell, sure. Beeg spots blood on de trail, an' track he say bear not peek up much de lef' paw. Haf' ower 'fore de sun rise up, we start on hees trail. We fine heem, by gar, den we feenish 'im wi' dis," and he brandished the polished Holland and Holland.

A few hours later, with the sinking moon still casting a pale light and the first blush of dawn defining the eastern horizon between the black trunks, the party set off on the bear's trail. This time no new snow obscured the prints. Michael led, followed by Batiste, with Kelly bringing up the rear. The Frenchman had been right about the blood. There was plenty of it, in plate-sized blotches along with tufts of straight black hair. And as the hunter had reported, the left front paw was scuffing the snow, making a comparatively shallow impression. How Batiste had determined this the previous night was beyond Kelly's comprehension.

As the men followed the trail over the foothills and up onto the flank of the mountain, the blood trail diminished substantially. The creature was clearly avoiding the thickest tangles and concentrations of blow-downs, another indication it wasn't operating at its normal strength. The trail led up along a good-sized stream that tumbled wildly down the slope in its own steep-sided gorge. The turbulence was enough to prevent the water from freezing beyond a little shelf ice along the edges of the pools between drops. But the spray had frozen, coating the ledges and boulders at stream level as well as partway up the walls. Batiste could not imagine the bear committing itself to this slick trap and his presumption was correct. Before long the trail, now showing very little blood, turned abruptly east and Russ Kelly had a pretty good idea where it would take them.

Halfway up the mountain's southern slope, below an ancient rockslide, a split dome reared its head a hundred feet above the surrounding gradient. The two sheer rock faces opposed each other across a thirty-yard corridor or slot running down it. This fed a little stream that had twisted down the gully and nurtured a stand of huge white cedars, not common in any surrounding stands. For decades the thriving cedars sent out thick twisted limbs that tangled with one another in their competition for sunlight. Then, about thirty years ago, a strong sheer wind accelerated up the notch, tearing the old trees out by their massive shallow roots and tumbling them back in a hopeless snarl. The wide crowns and root clusters held many of the trunks well above the rocks, and these formed a mat of interlaced cedar with the stream continuing to wind its way down the slope beneath the snarled trees. With the winter's snow accumulated on the exposed trunks and branches, the cave-like notch presented an easily defended sanctuary to anything that might take refuge inside its formidable maw.

This proved to be exactly where the beast had headed. The hunters found themselves peering cautiously into any number of dark portals, some at ground level, others as high as a dozen feet off the ground. The now bloodless tracks disappeared into one of these openings, and no one was in a hurry to follow them inside.

"Holy Jésus! Never see anyteeng lak dis nowhere before. How far eet go?"

"Follow me and I'll show you." Russ Kelly had been equally impressed with this unique formation when he'd first come across it surveying the standing timber. He led his companions to the eastern half dome, and the men had little trouble negotiating the slope along the edge of the face. From the apex they looked down on the tangled mat of cedars and realized that the bear or anything else in there was pretty safe from an attack from above. They continued along the edge that descended to the rockslide defining the northern end of the slot. Batiste and Michael combed the snow thoroughly for any signs that the bear might have exited at this end.

"F'rsure he no leave cover on dis en'." Batiste concluded. "Bear, he still inside dis win'fall. Make 'im fine place for to res', grow strong."

"Well I for one don't think I care to crawl in there after him," Kelly observed.

"Oh, non, 'course not do dat, bear keel you f'sure. Dat be foolish. But Jean Batiste have good plan."

He climbed back up along the edge of the dome and carefully surveyed the two-hundred-foot length of the cover from end to end.

"We go now back ta' da camp. Get hunter tings. Nex' day we come back wi' beeg su'prise for monsieur bear, non? Haw, haw."

"But how do we know he'll still be here tomorrow?"

"Oh, he be dere, sure. Heem sick bear, sleep two, tree day 'fore he's leeve cover."

Without a word Michael turned and began retracing their path, Batiste behind him. Russ Kelly looked back at the hopelessly tangled fortress, then hustled to catch up.

—

Back at the camp, Norm Belanger had arrived at a decision. The next day he would close down the ill-fated operation and take the men out of the woods. Things had gotten altogether too dangerous, and in any case it was not going to be a profitable venture for Tardiff this season. Meeting with all the men in the cook shack, it seemed nearly everyone approved the boss's decision, and there were relieved smiles on many of the rough, stress-lined faces.

Fischer, nearing the end of his planned stay anyway, was the sole dissenter. He had the brass to remind the loggers of their contracts with the company, and proposed that they give Jean Batiste a few days to hunt down the bear. Then with fresh supplies, and—hopefully—recruits arriving within a couple of weeks, they could still pull off a decent season and be in a position to have a great one the following year.

Fischer's reference to their contracts with Tardiff brought back the worried looks, and Belanger again took the floor.

"Listen, Fischer, if you want to stay and deal with this critter on Tardiff's behalf, feel free to stay. The contract these men signed guaranteed them decent food, adequate shelter, and reasonably safe working conditions. All you need to do is look around here and you can see that none of these provisions has been met."

"Try telling that to Mr. Tardiff," Fischer shot back. "Anyone doesn't finish out the season according to the contract is entitled to no part of the agreed-upon pay. Anyone leaves now, he won't get a cent from the company, let alone half his wages just because half the season's over."

Now, Belanger was right in Fischer's face. "I wasn't talking about half pay, buster. With what these men have gone through, they're entitled to the full amount of the agreement."

Fischer was getting uneasy with the woods boss's chin so close to his, but surprisingly did not back down. "Well, Mr. High and Mighty, we'll see just how big you are in front of Tardiff's lawyers in court in Bangor. Just how do you think you're going to get him to pay a crew that ran out on an operation at mid season?"

Belanger considered this point for about half a minute. "Well, Mr. Bean Counter, Tardiff owns thousands of acres of woods. Isn't that right?"

"Of course he does."

"Well, I don't suppose he'd want to lose any of that timber to forest fires, now would he?"

"That sounds like a threat to me, Belanger, and you'd better hope I don't pass it along to Mr. Tardiff."

"If that's what it takes to get him to pay off these boys, go ahead and tell him." Belanger answered, erasing any doubts about his seriousness. He turned again to address the anxious faces of the men who trusted him.

"So, boys, after supper tonight get your kits together and be ready to roll out of here at first light. If Batiste and the Indian get that critter, we'll have a real operation here next winter."

Muttering to one another the men gathered up their things. Fischer stood silently against the wall, but the sour expression on his face seemed to say, "We'll see about that."

—

Jean Batiste and Russ Kelly entered the cook shack just as the crew was sitting down to their last meal in the crude but familiar building. Michael had gone directly to the tent to tend to the two convalescent sled dogs. The rough plank tables were heaped with great platters of moose meat, mealy spuds, beans, and biscuits. The standard rule against conversation had been lifted, and the kerosene-lit room was awash in speculative chatter, mostly about the trip home. Most of the men were ready to get out from beneath the shadow of the killer beast, whether they got paid or not.

Silence fell across the room as Kelly and Batiste reported what they had discovered. Batiste concluded, "T'morrow be da las' day for dat bear. We breeng heem beeg su'prise. He not hide from Jean Batiste now. Dat f'sure."

"Well, Jean Batiste, old friend, I hope you're right," Belanger said. "But the men here have had enough. We've lost five men already this season, and we're just about out of grub. I'm taking them out tomorrow morning," Belanger explained, adding, "and if you're smart, you'll forget about the bear and come with us."

—

Daylight had not even begun burning its way through the thick overcast the next morning when the logging crew began preparing for departure. The depleted crew was now down to twenty-three including Belanger, and despite his tough talk the previous afternoon, Fischer was one of the first to lug his gear out into the yard. Turk, looking good as new, was a much better mannered dog than he had been before meeting the rough loggers and Étienne.

Two teams were hitched to a sledge carrying provisions for the five- or six-day trek out to Pittston Farm, as well as tarps for shelter at night and a wanigan for cooking outdoors. The load was topped off with the last of the hay and oats for the horses. A third team would pull a pung carrying a few tools and the frozen remains of the last two casualties, DuJours and Partridge, in rough pine coffins held together with horseshoe nails.

Zeke and Cassidy were astride the last team of Percherons, which were otherwise unencumbered so they could break trail in the deeper snow. The two riders hoped that the snow on top of the lake ice would be sufficiently wind-packed to make preparing a trail unnecessary.

Everyone had a blanket rolled and strapped across his shoulders and a knapsack or flour sack containing his meager personal belongings. Most had a pair of snowshoes. Norm Belanger carried his shotgun, Hekinen his .30-30, and Fischer ostensibly had his revolver. Everyone else was armed with a double-bitted axe, a pick pole, or a peavey. In the morning's half-light the troop resembled a frozen mob preparing to storm the Bastille.

Russ Kelly had decided to remain behind to help Batiste and Michael eliminate the deadly bear, and the three stood in the yard as the crew prepared to leave the beleaguered camp.

Jigger Olson, the blacksmith and an old friend of Jean Batiste, stepped out of the sorry smithy toting a pair of heavy contraptions and dragging a length of boom chain. He dropped them with a clatter at the feet of the hunter, who bent to examine the work and then released one of his booming, deep belly laughs.

From spring steel and metal scrap, Olson had built two enormous traps with thick jaws armed with steel teeth a couple of inches long. Each was shackled to a length of boom chain capable of resisting a force of fifty tons. These Baptiste could keep on hand in the event his first surprise plan failed to kill the huge bear.

"Holy Jésus. You make deez beeg trap, Jigger? Jean Batiste never see no such heavy trap. Deez trap hol' dat mean son'agun, no mistake. Haw, haw!"

The Frenchman then marched over to his tent and returned with a nearly new bolt-action rifle, which he presented to the blacksmith.

"Dis a new cartridge, an' a good one, too. Turty-ot-six dey call 'im. Ver' good for moose and caribou far'way distance. Shoot flatter den forty-fi' sev'ty. You take and keep eet. Gift from me, Jean Batiste."

Jigger was more than pleased with the rifle and everyone in the crew was relieved to have an increase in their rather meager firepower should the bear decide to stalk them.

"All right, boys," Belanger yelled. "There's daylight in the swamp, and time to get your sorry asses on the trail." And with that the unlikely looking band of refugees silently began their long, cold trek out of the deep woods.

As Fischer turned to join the troop, Batiste yelled after him, "You, make sure tell Monsieur Tardiff, Jean Batiste take care dat beeg bear f'r 'im."

"You kill that bear so we can have a real operation here next winter, there'll be a reward in it for you, Batiste."

"Jean Batiste no forget dat promise, Haw, haw, haw."

—◆—

The three hunters wasted no time setting out on their mission. Michael settled Étienne and Ozette in the tent. They obviously wanted to join the party, but would not disobey the Indian's command. Batiste picked up the traces of a toboggan, on which two metal kerosene cans and a wooden box of dynamite were lashed. With Kelly packing the trail the three men made for the gargantuan tangle of uprooted cedars where the wounded bear had disappeared. When Batiste was satisfied that the beast had not left the cover by either end of the wood-choked notch, he put his plan into action.

At the south end he poured the contents of a three-gallon kerosene can onto the bone-dry softwood trunks and limbs while Kelly and Michael split up a few armloads of the driest material for kindling. This was likewise drenched with the accelerant. Certain that the whole end would erupt in flames within seconds of being touched off, Batiste then produced a torch of tightly rolled birch bark. He handed it to Kelly and instructed him to light the torch in twenty minutes and set the whole end ablaze. Then he was to stand back off to the side with his rifle ready should the bear attempt an exit through the wall of flames. Then Batiste and Michael hurried over the half dome to the north end and similarly prepared it for a quick hot blaze.

Right on cue they saw thick black smoke rising from the other end. Batiste waited for the fire to grow and advance another fifteen minutes, his .375 ready in hopes the bear would panic and appear at the mouth of the shelter, giving him a chance to break in his new possession. When nothing appeared but a pair of hares, he gave Michael the signal to set fire to the north end, closing the trap with a second wall of leaping flames and black smoke.

The first fire was now advancing with astonishing speed despite the blanket of snow. The fuel was perfectly dry and had retained much of its original resin. Now the fire was large enough to produce its own accelerating wind as it advanced up the natural flue. Anything living in the once-secure sanctuary now faced imminent destruction in the conflagration. A solitary porcupine fifty feet back from the end climbed a doomed treetop with unhurried deliberation as though this were his ticket to survival. But there was still no sign of the giant bear.

In half an hour the initial fire had traveled halfway up the draw, burning hot enough to consume its fuel completely. Leaving Michael at the rockslide, Batiste hurried along the lip of the dome to execute the second half of his plan. At the top, he pulled three bound sticks of dynamite from a moosehide sack slung across his shoulder. Touching a match to the short fuse, he tossed the explosive into the ravine a few yards ahead of the flames. Then he crouched behind a boulder a few steps back.

The force of the explosion sent torn and shattered sections of trees and branches, some already ablaze, twenty and thirty feet into the air before they toppled back into the inferno. Moving along the edge ahead of the flames, Batiste was forced to avoid exposing himself directly to the intense heat from below for fear his hair or even his clothing might catch fire. From points well back from the edge, he tossed down a new charge every fifteen or twenty yards.

Batiste was certain the beast had to be in there, but it had yet to show itself despite the holocaust. He had longed for a glimpse of the creature with its hide afire, roaring in agony as it tried in vain to scramble up the steep face and offered itself as a target for his heavy slugs. Or at least he wanted to hear its bawling screams as, wounded and unable to move, the pulsing heat caught first its hair, than its hide and finally its evil flesh on fire until the whole abomination was consumed. He began to think that perhaps the thing had actually perished in there from Belanger's shot and the multiple rips and tears from the dogs, but he could not quite convince himself.

At the height of the conflagration, trees along the edges of the containing walls caught fire from the withering heat welling up from below. Snow along the cliff tops melted, and water ran down both faces, evaporating into steam before reaching the bottom. Batiste had never dreamed the fire would be so effective. At this rate everything in the draw would be reduced to ash instead of the jumble of charred roots and trunks that seemed more reasonable to expect.

As darkness fell, most of the smoke and flames had played out, and the whole corridor was buried by a shrinking mat of live coals and embers that cast a ruddy glow onto the walls clear to the top. The heat was so intense that if there was a way of adhering an egg to a vertical surface it would have fried in a fleeting few seconds.

By ten o'clock Jean Batiste was convinced they had done everything possible. If the bear had been anywhere within that snarled mess, which it should have been, it was by now reduced to ash. The three walked briskly down the trail to the empty camp, shocked by the twenty-below temperature after half baking in proximity to the inferno. Étienne and Ozette were wild with delight at Michael's return, and he stayed with them in the tent while Batiste and Kelly took up quarters in the office.

A light but steady snow was wafting in from the east the following morning and the conditions were such that it was likely to last a day or two. Jean Batiste cooked a couple of his famous trail breads on top of the little cast-iron stove in the office, brewed a pot of stiff black tea, and sliced up moose meat to fry. He was in a good mood and he kept his pipe lit while he cooked and regaled Kelly and Michael with tales from the far north. His initial two-year contract with the Revillon Frères, rivals to the Hudson Bay Company in the eastern subarctic, had stretched into a ten-year sojourn stationed at various posts along the coast of Hudson Bay and Baffin Island. The Frenchman was still very much enchanted by the Arctic and had endless stories of the Inuit and of hunting polar bears, walrus, arctic foxes, and caribou. Other stories tumbled forth of extreme weather, celebrations, epidemics, and more, some of them amusing or exciting, some tragic.

Batiste had an appreciative audience in his two exhausted companions, and the unsettled weather provided the perfect opportunity for the three friends to relax and rest. They all hoped the fire marked the end of the ordeal, but the evidence was far from conclusive. This unsettled weather provided the perfect opportunity for the three friends to relax and recharge.

"Wen dis snow, she's stop in day or two, perfec' condition for look an' see eef dere's new sign of bear on dis mountain. Jean Batiste bet no track we fine. Beeg fire between de rock take plenty care of dis bear. Den we leave dis trés mal place. Go trap up nord, eh Michael? Make beeg money on de white fox 'fore spreeng is come up dere."

Three days after the fire, the persistent snow finally stopped drifting down, the front swept out by an icy blast from the northwest. Only six or eight inches of new snow had accumulated, but it had been gray and raw the whole time. By contrast this morning was as crisp and dry as a winter day could be, the thermometer again registering twenty below under a bright blue sky.

The three hunters strapped on snowshoes, slung light packs over their shoulders, and checked their guns carefully, just in case. The two dogs wanted desperately to be included, but Michael confined them to the tent so they'd be ready to travel out the next day.

They found it a pleasure swinging along the familiar paths without the dread of the bear hanging over them, and they made good time. Within half an hour they were cutting over toward the little river. Michael was breaking trail when he came to an abrupt halt after topping a little rise. He stood perfectly straight looking down at something at his feet. When Batiste and Kelly came up alongside, the three men stood a full minute without speaking.

Crossing their intended path were great craters in the new snow, and there was no doubt they had been freshly laid down by the diabolical beast. The bear was still favoring its left forepaw and was missing two great claws. The heavy musk of the animal still hung in the air.

"Impossible! Impossible!" growled Batiste in a gravelly whisper. "Dat bear, he has no right for be alive. Holy Jésus, Marie, et Josef what it take to keel 'im, dat bear?"

Neither Kelly or Michael had a reply to the rhetorical question, but what they didn't say spoke volumes about what they were beginning to suspect. The prints were remarkably fresh and the men half expected to hear the creature moving off through the underbrush.

"He head for de rivere, sure, he's make beeg mistake. Now we 'ave 'im in da beeg trap." But his colleagues' expressions did not indicate they shared the Frenchman's optimism. Still, neither was about to lose face and do the sensible thing, which would have been to abandon Jean Batiste and his suicidal mission and put as much real estate as they could between themselves and Big Bear Mountain before dark.

Instead they soberly nodded their assent to Batiste's plan: They would split up, Batiste making the best time he could on a beeline to a big outcrop that crowded the edge of the little river gorge. There he would be in an excellent position to intercept the bear, which would need more time following the convoluted course of the stream. Meanwhile, Michael would parallel the gorge a quarter mile in from the edge, in case the bear broke off his likely path and headed east. His slug-loaded ten-gauge would be like a small cannon at close range. Kelly would continue following the prints, putting pressure on the bear from behind, his .45-70 cocked and ready. Each of the men understood that this tactic could very well develop into a shot at their nemesis, and no one was positive that the firepower he carried would be effective in stopping a direct charge from the mysterious beast.

Michael had been working his way carefully along the interface of a mature birch stand and a ribbon of young hemlocks that separated the birch from a strip of spruce and hemlock that extended along much of the stream. His sense of smell more than anything alerted him to his proximity to the deadly predator. He froze in his tracks at the first whiff of the pungent musk but was unable to detect any sound or movement in the green growth directly below him, although he was certain the bear was hidden within it. The wind was in the Indian's favor and he had been moving silently. Still, he felt sure the bear knew exactly where he was and was hunkered in the dense thicket contemplating its next move.

Due to the thick cover, Michael had strapped his snowshoes on his back, and his moosehide mukluks made no sound in the new snow. After waiting five minutes with no further sign of the bear, he climbed onto the recumbent trunk of a fallen birch whose thick branching crown held it well off the ground and afforded him an elevated view into the heavy growth below. As he worked his way toward the radiating limbs, one foot slipped on the new snow covering the already slick surface, and Michael found himself tumbling seven feet into the snow beneath the trunk. From there his momentum carried him over the lip of the natural bowl and he careened down the slope amid rising clouds of fresh snow, coming to rest at the bottom of the little depression next to the thicket.

Although not seriously hurt, Michael realized at once that he had lost his grip on his gun, which now lay in the snow a dozen feet above him near the top of the slope. Carefully he gathered his legs beneath him, keeping his eyes riveted on the edge of the dense growth a few yards away. He was about to stand when a gravelly rumble caught his full attention. Twenty-five feet away the saplings shook and an enormous black shape materialized from the cover.

From Michael's perspective where he sat on the snowy ground, the creature appeared to tower over him by a dozen feet, though it was probably a little over six feet at the shoulder. Still, this was half again as tall as a large polar bear he had seen taken by Inuit hunters in the Arctic. Resigned that he would very quickly be meeting his death, the Indian drank in all the details of the terrible beast before him. Just as impressive as his huge proportions were the grizzly-like characteristics, which included a prominent hump at the shoulders and a broad head with tiny ears. Below the large flaring nostrils at the end of the snout were wrinkled and very pliable lips that revealed gleaming teeth. The great paws were the size of a woman's snow-shoes.

Most remarkable was the intense black of the long hair that covered every part of the bear. Even the snout, which was generally covered with brown or tan fur on black bears, was completely black. And though nearly all black creatures have coats that ripple blue, violet, and bronze in certain light conditions, the blackness of the bear before him was complete. It was as black as a vein of coal at the bottom of a very deep mine on a moonless night. More than anything else it seemed to represent the absence of light. Sunlight did not illuminate the form, reflect off it, or pass through it. It was simply absorbed or consumed by the blackness.

The bear, barely a couple of bounds away, regarded the Indian with close-set eyes that glowed with the intensity of a white-hot flame. Michael realized that he was perfectly defenseless against this beast, and thought gratefully that it would all be over for him very quickly once the bear attacked.

The creature swung its great head to the left toward the river, then back again toward Michael. A rumbling growl rolled down upon the Indian and clutched him with a frigid grip. Then, incredibly, the bear turned toward the river, and with a gait that was at once shambling and liquid smooth, disappeared into the thicket.

Michael slowly gained his feet, wiping the beads of nearly frozen sweat from his forehead. He then brushed off the snow that covered his anorak and mukluks, all the while watching the opening in the hemlocks where the bear had disappeared. He gathered his snow-shoes, climbed to the top of the rise, and found the ten-gauge half buried in the snow. He brushed it off, opened the breech, and took out the two heavy slugs, placing them in his sack. Then determining the most direct route to the overhang where Batiste waited for the bear, he set off in that direction at a rapid pace.

Twenty minutes later, Batiste was surprised and a little annoyed to see Michael coming toward him on snowshoes in a less than careful manner. Not wanting to raise his voice, he waited until the Indian had nearly reached him before speaking.

"What for you hurry to Jean Batiste like dat? You scare de bear if 'im hear you. Mus' be ver' quiet."

Michael's response was preempted by the crack of a rifle, barely audible over the thunder of the nearby waterfall. It came from downstream, how far was difficult to guess, but it was definitely Kelly's .45-70. They listened for a second report, but none came, and the two hunters set off along the rim of the gorge beside the surging river. Little attention was paid to watching for the beast, and it occurred to Michael how easy it would be for the bear to rush out at them from any of a hundred concealed grottoes and send them sailing over the edge.

A half mile downstream they came upon a little ledge where some violent activity had disturbed and packed down a patch of snow in an area the size of a small room right at the lip of the gorge. Spots of blood were sprayed across the snow and there were prints belonging to Russ Kelly as well as to the bear. The familiar musk saturated the air.

Apparently the bear, whose trail Kelly had been following, had circled back around and surprised him from the thick cover. Michael suspected the bear had returned to intercept Kelly after leaving him at the site of their encounter.

Kelly must have heard his attacker in time to get off a shot, but to what effect it was difficult to gauge. There was plenty of blood on the snow but it may have come from Kelly, the bear, or from both of them. Since the timber cruiser's tracks ended right there and he was nowhere to be seen, the hunters surmised that the bear might have thrown him down into the river. The rifle lay partially buried in the snow. A second round had not been jacked into the chamber. The bear's prints continued on back into the forest and after a few yards displayed no further traces of blood. Back at the ledge Michael pointed downstream to the next pool below a rapid. "Down there."

The pair hurried down along the edge a couple of hundred feet and peered over the lip. Russ Kelly's body, minus its head, had come to rest on a shelf of ice alongside an eddy in the ice-rimmed pool. The gorge's steep walls coated with ice made retrieving the body impossible.

Uncharacteristically shaken, Jean Batiste exclaimed, "Holy damn, dat bear keel 'im one fine man dere. We go back camp, tink da way to keel heem, by Jésus."

———

Back at camp that night Michael told Batiste that he would be leaving the next morning, and he advised the Frenchman to do the same.

"That no ordinary bear. You cannot kill him. You stay, hunt him, he kill you," Michael explained.

But, hardheaded as always, Batiste resisted. "Jean Batiste keel 'im sure. Bear beeg and he smart, but he bleed all da' same. Belanger shoot 'im with slug, he bleed an he lame. Jus' not shoot 'im in right place." He patted the .375 Holland and Holland resting against a wooden chest.

"Jean Batiste shoot 'im with dis rifle, it keel 'im, sure by Jésus. Jean Batiste run from no bear."

Michael tried convincing his friend that this bear was quite different, perhaps even a spirit guardian of the mountain. But Batiste would have none of it.

"You best leave, friend. Mebbe bear let you go. Mebbe not. You stay here, he hunt you for sure. An' he kill you," Michael concluded. He then stood up from his chair and left to spend the night in the tent with the two dogs.

Jean Batiste picked up the gleaming rifle and stroked it like a cat. "Pretty gun," he thought to himself. But not so pretty as his dearest love, Clarisse. He considered B. N. Talbot, the husband who had tried to bribe him with the rifle, as the biggest fool in all Québec. Talbot's firm in Toronto had reassigned him to their Montreal office and he had courted Clarisse knowing nothing of her relationship with Batiste. After she and Talbot married, it was only a matter of time before she resumed seeing her earlier lover. So in his stiff and insipid English manner Talbot had confronted Batiste, and told him to leave his wife alone. He offered the Frenchman money to disappear, a gesture that naturally offended Batiste. A little checking around would have revealed to Talbot that Batiste was actually the wealthier man by far. Still, Jean Batiste had no qualms about taking the magnificent rifle, even though he had no intentions of abandoning his relationship with Clarisse.

"What a fool eez dat Monsieur Talbot," Batiste now said aloud. "As eef rifle make Jean Batiste forget mon chère Clarisse. Oh, non! Jean Batiste not abandon heez love. But first he use gun to keel dis bad bear."

Then he relit his pipe, tossed a couple wood chunks into the glowing stove, poured another mug of good Canadian whiskey, and contemplated just how he would go about accomplishing his mission.

———

Next morning Michael was at the office door, snowshoes under his arm and a knapsack and caribou skin over his shoulder. He stood the ten-gauge inside the doorway, apparently satisfied to walk out with only his .25-20 Winchester. With it he could shoot enough game or even a deer to get himself and the dogs to the St. Lawrence.

"You need this gun more than me," the Indian advised. "Put it somewhere you can get it fast."

"Tanks, brudder. Betta you put rope on Étienne an' Ozette, take dem out. Dey wan' stay wid Jean Batiste. Betta dey go."

Michael nodded. Both men knew Batiste was only saving face. Ever since the attack at the horse hovel, the dogs had stuck to the Indian like glue. Should Michael have, for some reason, shinnied up a greased pole, the dogs would have found a way to follow.

"You tell me, Michael," said the trapper, betraying his first sign of misgiving, "how bes' Jean Batiste hunt dis bear?"

The Indian stood for a moment before answering. "You no need hunt bear, Batiste. Bear know you here. He come hunt you by an' by. You be ready."

Batiste nodded soberly as though this was a great revelation. He handed his friend a small sack containing a couple of loaves of his trail bread, some dried caribou meat, tea, and tobacco, although he knew the Indian already had everything he would need.

"Make safe you journey, brudder. Jean Batiste keel dis bear, den he come git you. We travel nord, trap some white fox, oui?"

"Oui, Batiste, you come get me. Now you be ready. Bear come. He waste no time. Au revoir."

Batiste stood outside the cabin watching Michael swinging easily on his snowshoes down the trail to the lake, the exuberant dogs romping like puppies beside him.

"Au revoir, Michael," he called. "Au revoir, Étienne. Au revoir, Ozette."

As soon as Michael and the dogs were gone, Batiste hustled to put his next plan into action. He lugged one of Jigger Olson's heavy traps out behind the hovel. The horses were now gone, but the bear had approached the camp from this direction at least twice. He scooped out a depression in the snow and set the steel monstrosity down into it. Even with the lever Jigger had provided, it took all his strength to open and set the jaws. Batiste covered the trap with a few light fir boughs, then some powdery snow, and finally a little horse manure. He didn't bother baiting the trap since the bear never appeared interested in food. He ran the end of the attached boom chain around a ten-inch birch tree trunk, shackled it to itself, and covered it with snow.

He set the second trap out behind the office cabin where he would sleep and stand vigil. Smaller than the other crude buildings, it was more comfortable and easier to defend. It also had three small windows, just big enough for Batiste to monitor activity in at least three directions. It was built of stout logs and the doorway was too small to admit the enormous creature. The bear's only way inside would be through the snow-covered slab wood-and-shake roof. Should the bear try that, the roof would not support him for long, but maybe long enough for Batiste to empty both barrels of the big game rifle into him before he crashed through. If still alive he would be momentarily trapped, and the hunter would be out the door in a flash, tossing in behind him a stick of dynamite with a sizzling short fuse. If that blast didn't finish the bear, the second explosion from the dozen sticks inside the door surely would. Across the yard, Batiste would be crouching behind the blacksmith shack, safe from the explosions. Having blown the bear to bits, Batiste would retrieve the pack, bedroll, and shotgun stashed in the smithy and be ready for his walk out to collect his reward.

———

Before the early darkness descended on the camp, Batiste was snuggly ensconced in the little office building. He had plenty of bread and moose jerky, but was more inclined toward the last of the whiskey and his pipe. His loaded rifle was at hand and the bag of dynamite was in position near the door.

It wasn't until two or three in the morning that he was startled from a fitful nap by a sudden flaring up of the shrinking fire in the stove, followed by a low rumbling growl that seemed to come from behind the cabin. Batiste was instantly alert, the rifle in his hands, tensely waiting to hear the first screams from the beast as the steel teeth of Jigger's trap buried themselves in its foreleg.

When this failed to happen, Batiste, crouching in the darkened room, concentrated on the end window facing the cook shack, rifle ready should this square of blue winter night suddenly darken with the black form of the bear. But it was the window behind him that for an instant winked, as the creature ghosting past shut out the moonlight. Batiste wheeled, rifle at his shoulder but not quickly enough, catching only a glimpse of the shadow as the pale light was restored.

Perspiration now stood out in droplets on Batiste's neck and face. He turned toward the front window, which was the largest, and looked out on the yard bathed in silver with deep purple shadows. Surely this was where the elusive beast would next appear. However, held at the ready, the rifle grew heavy and there was no sign of the bear skulking across the yard. The Frenchman began shaking, the strength to support the gun melting away.

Another rumble from outside provided Batiste with a rush of adrenaline, but it was impossible to tell from which quarter the sound had come. Setting the rifle down on the table that served as a desk, the hunter reached for the nearly empty whiskey bottle and drained it in a single gulp. And in the next instant a dark form twenty feet out in the yard crossed the field of vision afforded by the window. By the time Batiste had again taken up the rifle, the chance for a shot had passed.

Several more times before dawn, Batiste heard the bear growl or caught a fleeting glimpse of a black shadow disappearing around a building or emerging from the edge of the woods, only to be swallowed up instantly by the darkness. A few times he was sure he heard the bear out behind the cabin and wondered why it hadn't stepped into his carefully set trap. Batiste began to realize that he had planned poorly, after all, confining himself to the vulnerable cabin. He was like a sitting duck without much of a chance for a good shot at the elusive target. Still, he was surprised that the bear had not tried to get at him, either through the roof or by tearing at the walls.

By the time the first light of dawn began to replace the receding light of the moon, there had been no sign of the bear for more than an hour. Jean Batiste was an exhausted bundle of nerves, consumed by his rage at having planned so poorly, and greatly irritated by the fact that he was now out of tobacco as well as whiskey. He was tempted to walk straight across the yard to the smithy where there would at least be more tobacco. But even in his distracted state, he thought better of it and forced himself to settle down. He then remembered back a few days when he'd smuggled a quarter-full bottle of the forbidden whiskey into the shop to share a snort with Jigger Olson. The blacksmith wasn't there but as Batiste prepared to leave, Jigger came walking across the yard with Belanger. Quickly Batiste had stuffed the bottle under the crude bench on which Olson fabricated all his amazing metalwork, and later forgot about it. Chances were good that it was still tucked away there, and the thirsty hunter could almost taste the smooth yet biting amber potion.

Although the bear had apparently left, Batiste exercised great caution, first cracking open the door, then swinging it open quickly, the rifle at his shoulder. He systematically scanned the entire yard before stepping outside. Then he took a few steps, turned, and scrutinized the cabin and the woods behind it, listening intently and using his nose, which detected only a faint trace of the bear's musk. Again the enormous size of the prints in the packed snow startled him. They were just so unbelievably large.

Satisfied that the creature had indeed left, Batiste proceeded warily across to the blacksmith shack. Inside the door stood the loaded shotgun and his emergency traveling supplies. But even before digging out his tobacco pouch to fill the empty pipe in his mouth, he squatted down and felt around a support of the cluttered bench and located the hidden whiskey bottle.

"Mon Dieu! Merci! Merci!" he whispered gratefully

Two healthy swigs from the bottle went a long way toward restoring a sense of calm in the hunter. Next he filled the bowl of his pipe, lit it, and stood in the doorway, his rifle held across his chest. Surveying the camp, his eyes were drawn to a big white pine that stood sheltering the end of the cook shack and bunkhouse.

"Dat's de answer, Jean Batiste," he assured himself. "Dat perfec' place wait for dat bear."

Since the logging camp was built in an expanded natural clearing, the few trees left standing for shelter were not tall clear timber like those in the woods. Instead they were mostly field pines with great sweeping branches starting almost at ground level. Climbing one would be incredibly easy and this one was missing a few boughs that would afford him a good view down onto the yard. Batiste strode over to it, his gun in the crook of his left arm and the whiskey bottle in his right hand. He walked around beneath the great branches, looking up, nodding approval. He imagined himself up twenty feet or so cradled in the limbs with a perfect view of the yard below. He would have not only the .375, but also a few sticks of dynamite he could hurl down onto the incapacitated beast after shooting it. He'd lay a fire in the office stove to trick the bear, and from his lofty vantage point he'd likely get a good shot no matter what direction the beast came from.

Greatly pleased with his new plan, Batiste took another belt of whiskey and was about to chase it with a few tokes on his pipe, when he caught a smell other than the fine Turkish tobacco. Lowering the pipe he drew a deep breath, and the scent registered—the musk of the bear! But now it was again faint. He turned from the tree to go back to the office and sixty feet away, regarding him from the middle of the yard, stood the bear. Somehow it was even larger than he had imagined. The pipe and bottle both dropped onto the snowy ground and the rifle leapt naturally to his shoulder.

"Now we see how strong Monsieur Bear really be," he thought as he tucked the beautifully balanced firearm against his cheek and clicked off the safety. The bear had not moved. It stood in all its terrible glory essentially broadside to Batiste, its head turned toward the hunter. Batiste put the bead exactly where the enormous head met the short neck, and squeezed the right-hand trigger.

Instead of a deafening blast and a satisfying jolt to the shoulder, there was only a crisp metallic click.

"What da' heck eez dis?" the stunned hunter muttered under his breath as his finger found the left-hand trigger, which responded with a similar result.

Batiste couldn't believe it. He lowered the rifle and stared at it, then up at the bear, which was now facing him and starting to walk purposely toward him. He ran back a few yards and whirled about. The bear had stopped. Opening the gun's breech, he replaced the two dud cartridges with two more from his pouch. They all looked and felt good. Again he shouldered the rifle and again got two empty clicks.

"Sachariste!" Batiste jerked open the breech and removed the two shells. Instinctively he ran a finger over the tips of the firing pins. There was nothing there. Only smooth metal. Of course!

"Haw, haw, haw," he bellowed out loud. "That son'abitch Talbot. He get Jean Batiste in the end, after all. Son'abitch!"

The jealous husband had filed down the firing pins, rendering the gun impotent. He could never have dreamed how dire the situation would be when Batiste discovered his little trick. How he would celebrate if he knew!

And how stupid could Batiste be? A professional hunter like him, never even trying out the rifle? It was unbelievable!

The low rumbling growl wrenched Batiste back to the present. The bear was again advancing, but not hurriedly. The hunter's survival instincts kicked in. The bear was positioned between him and both the smithy, with the loaded ten-gauge inside the door, and the office with all the dynamite. He had only one slim chance now. Slowly he backed up a few more yards, the bear keeping pace, but not charging. Against its blank black face the small eyes burned like bluish-white fire.

At the appropriate spot, Batiste dodged quickly around the back of the cook shack and ran through the deeper snow, tripping once on some runners buried in the snow. Back on his feet he glanced over his shoulder. The bear was not following, but instead was keeping roughly parallel to him on the other side of the building. Batiste dashed across the gap between the cook shack and the office cabin. If he could round the far corner ahead of the bear, he might just be able to dive inside the door and reach the dynamite. His chest burned as he pounded through the deep snow.

Suddenly his entire world turned a brilliant white, then red with blazing pain. He had stepped into his own trap! The excruciating pain was beyond anything he had ever experienced. The trap's wide jaws had closed on his right calf just below the knee, the steel teeth meeting somewhere in the shattered bone. Blood was already saturating the snow, and he blacked out for a moment. Coming to, he regarded his smashed leg in the jaws of a trap he had himself set. The lower part of his leg was twisted at a ridiculous angle. It was *all* so ridiculous. How had he not inspected the gift rifle? And how in hell had he bumbled into his own goddamn trap?

Searing pain surged to his head, threatening to burst it, and again he blacked out. Jean Batiste's colorful life did not pass before him—

only one brief defining event:

A clean-shaven young man stood in the cavern-like train station in Québec City, a large duffle at his feet and a canvas knapsack over his shoulder. He was getting ready to board the train that would take him along the North Shore to the mouth of the Saguenay, where he would board a northbound schooner belonging to the Revillon Frères trading company.

On his arm was a beautiful raven-haired maiden—Clarisse, the woman with whom Jean Batiste planned to build a life. She was the daughter of a successful but aging Habitant, with no sons to take over the sun-drenched farm that occupied a blessed patch of fields and woodlots overlooking the St. Lawrence. It was clear enough the pair loved one another, and she made no effort to stanch the big tears that rolled down her cheeks from the long-lashed hazel eyes.

The only sensible thing for the young man to do would be to forget this nonsense about the north, marry this lovely woman, and raise a large family on the well-established, immaculate farm. But with remorse undiluted by the twenty years that had since passed, Batiste watched his younger self kiss Clarisse and promise her he'd return with a pouch of money after his two years with the trading company and make that his contribution to the farmstead. Then he gathered his duffle, and just as the train broke its inertia, swung himself into the slowly moving doorway of the passenger car.

Another jolt of pain rocked Jean Batiste and he was jerked back into the nightmare that had become the present. The merciless throbbing was more intense and his vision was beginning to blur. Still, lying with his head to one side he saw clearly enough the corner of the cabin against the snow, the tops of the pine trees, and the blue sky above. And he watched with calm detachment the great black bear round the corner and with a ponderous and deliberate shamble close the distance between them.

―

The small frame house at the end of the road on the island reservation stood against the bright, brittlely cold February night. Inside, the cast-iron parlor stove glowed copper as it worked to heat the two modest rooms and open loft. At the round table in the kitchen, beneath the hissing gas lamp, John Solis sat reading the day's newspaper. Across from him, his wife Mary was beading a pair of her exquisite deerskin moccasins. Between them their son Patrick was cutting in the details of the carapace on a wooden turtle with the small sharp blade of his pocketknife.

Solis looked up from his reading and regarded Mary's patient and meticulous proceedings. Her moccasins were among those most prized by the summer folk around Bar Harbor when the family traveled to the coast in August to sell their wares and gather the coast's natural bounty which seemed to be diminishing each year. John wondered if he'd be making the trip this year, now that he'd taken a job at the canoe factory. If he didn't go, he'd certainly miss the annual event, which came just after the blueberry raking. The pay at the canoe factory was adequate and certainly more reliable than the money he'd been making trapping, making baskets, and doing a little guiding in the fall. But already he suspected that with this passing of the seasonal work he'd be giving up something that was integral to his very being. Perhaps there would be a lull in production at the plant at the end of the season, before they had to gear up again for the spring orders. Maybe he could take the voluntary layoff as others had done.

"Well, Patrick, there's school tomorrow," Mary said, smiling at her serious-minded son. "Maybe you should finish that carving tomorrow night. Time to bring in the wood and go to bed."

Patrick's carvings were also becoming popular with the tourists. The previous summer, between selling them and pounding out ash splints for several basket makers, he'd earned enough to almost buy a .22 rifle. Mary had put in the last dollar and taken him to Montgomery Ward to pick out the single-shot bolt-action along with a box of .22 shorts.

Patrick had gotten good with the gun and regularly brought home squirrels, hares, muskrat, and a few grouse he'd shot out of trees before they flew. This year he'd already split enough brown ash for island basket makers, that the money earned, along with what he hoped to get for his carvings in the summer, should be enough to buy a used twenty-gauge shotgun. He'd had his eye on a single-shot Harrington Richardson at the sporting goods store in town.

Patrick put the nearly finished turtle and his knife on the windowsill, then brushed the shavings off the oiled tablecloth and put them in the kindling box. At the door, he put on his jacket and mittens and went out to get an armload of firewood from the shed for the next morning's fire.

He'd been gone only a couple of minutes when he rushed back in, slammed the door, shoved the firewood into the wood box, and turned excitedly to his parents.

"He's back, Papa," he announced. "I saw him."

John Solis turned to his son. "The Great Bear?" he asked.

"Yes, Kci Awesus! He's brighter than ever. Come see him, Papa!"

It had been around the first of January when Patrick had run into the house without his armload of wood and announced to his parents—but especially to his father—that the Great Bear constellation had disappeared from the sky.

John Solis knew this was impossible, but knew also that his son would not lie. He might joke around a little but he could always be depended upon to tell the truth. So John had stepped outside with Patrick to see what he was getting at. By then thin clouds had covered most of the northern quadrant of the sky, and naturally the constellation was not visible.

"It's just a cloud, Patrick. Great Bear hasn't gone anywhere."

"But he *was* gone, Papa! Little Bear was in his place, and the Hunter was in his." He pointed to Orion stalking just above the treetops in the southeast. "See, he's still there. But where could Great Bear have gone?"

"Maybe he's gone hunting?"

"No, Papa. It's only stars, you know. Sister Margaret's taught us a lot about stars."

"Maybe the stars burned out?"

"No, I don't think so. Why whould just *those* stars burn out all at once?"

The cloud had drifted and now the Big Bear shone brightly in his upended position.

"There's the Great Bear. He's standing on his head." Solis spoke softly.

"Please don't tease me, Papa. I don't see him."

And John Solis was convinced that for some reason Patrick could not.

"What did Grandpa call him?" the boy had asked.

"Kci Awesus," Solis answered, reflecting how rarely they used the old tongue now that the grandparents were gone.

Patrick tried the pronunciation carefully: "Kchee Awasoos, like the mountain?"

"Like the mountain. Where we can no longer hunt."

Each night for almost six weeks now, Patrick had searched the northern sky for Kci Awesus when he got the firewood. The weather pattern had been unsettled for weeks and there were many nights when clouds and light snow obscured the constellation along with everything else. On two occasions the northern lights had glowed bright enough to wash out most of the stars behind their shimmering curtains. But even on clear evenings the Great Bear seemed to be invisible to Patrick, although John Solis found the constellation easily and saw nothing unusual about it.

Now Patrick said Kci Awesus was back, so Solis pulled on his plaid wool jacket and joined his son outside. Sure enough, the constellation was in its usual position, and Patrick seemed unusually excited about seeing it.

"Kci Awesus. Isn't he beautiful? Sister Margaret says his real name is the Big Dipper and that's what she wants us to use. And she said I was talking nonsense when I told her he had disappeared."

"Not everyone understands these things," Solis commented. "At school you call him Big Dipper. At home and in the forest you call him Kci Awesus."

"I'm going inside to bed, Papa. It's getting cold."

Solis stood outside a few more minutes. The stars of the constellation did seem exceptionally large and bright this night. Brighter than diamonds. More like the brilliance of a white-hot flame. He wondered what all this could have meant.

He went inside and hung his coat on its peg. Mary was putting away the sweet, smoky-smelling deerhide, and Patrick had gone up to bed in the loft.

"He has the sight," Mary Solis stated matter-of-factly.

"Yes, very strong," her husband replied.

"Just like his grandfather." Mary took the hot kettle from the stovetop and poured boiling water into the little decorated teapot.

THE SAMARITAN

Gagging from the cloud of dust and feathers, and reeling from the stench, Leo Miller staggered to the freight elevator, three chickens hanging upside down from each hand. A co-worker, Manny Acosta opened the hatch of a wooden crate and, using his left hand to keep the prisoners inside from escaping, used his other to relieve Miller of half his catch and deftly guide them into the already tightly packed cube of white feathers, scaly feet, and staring eyes.

The other three, roused from their stupor, suddenly came to life in a flapping, squawking frenzy, producing a noxious dust cloud largely directed up at Miller. He started sneezing uncontrollably, inadvertently letting go of the captives, who half flew and half ran back into the darkened depths of their low-ceilinged shelter.

Leo blew his nose into a filthy bandanna, tears streaking the black dust that covered his face, and apologized for being such a klutz.

"No problemo," Manny grinned, his wide smile revealing dazzling white teeth that matched the whites of his ping-pong-ball-sized eyes. His pal, Raoul, materialized from the gloomy depths bearing eight hens, all swinging as docilely as if their throats had already been cut. Raoul grinned, too, as the last escapee dodged past him, and kicked playfully at it as it scooted by. The difference between Raoul's smile and Manny's was mainly that Raoul's was practically toothless, save a handful of dark uneven stalactites. But it was just as warm and Leo could never get over how cheerful the two Guatemalans remained no matter how grim the task at hand.

As soon as his hens were caged and the full crate deposited on top of the others in the elevator, Raoul pushed back his sleeve revealing what looked to Leo like a pretty nice watch.

"Douze a'til," he grinned. "Time take break."

The three headed over to a hatchlike door and swung it open, out over the feather-filled yard three stories down. A half dozen rats that were scavenging the ground for spilled grain scattered in as many directions. Otherwise the early summer evening with its stars, purple shadows, and scores of winking fireflies could not have contrasted more starkly with the stuffy, dark, metal space in which they had been enclosed for the past three hours. The men were less than halfway through capturing a flock of several thousand pullets that had finished their initial egg-laying period and were now being sent to a processing plant to be rendered into the less fancy packs of bargain chicken.

Manny produced a crushed pack of Lucky Strikes, extracted one for himself, and offered the bent and leaking leftovers to his co-workers. Raoul had his lighter out and everybody lit up almost at once. The three sat on sacks of laying mash, looking out at the night and taking in the cool sweet air along with their smoke. The two Guatemalans spoke softly to one another, ending each exchange with a smile and a chuckle. Leo didn't understand Spanish, and if he hadn't been so exhausted, might have wondered if they were making jokes at his expense.

The break, although welcome physically, also gave Leo a chance to take stock of his current situation, and that wasn't quite so pleasant. Here he was nearly forty, less than a year out of prison, his ex-wife and, more importantly, his two kids were living a hundred and fifty miles away, and he had few opportunities to see them and few resources to take advantage of those he *did* have.

And he had this shit job, working like a dog at this immense poultry concentration camp for poor pay, no chance for advancement, no way out, and ruining his health to boot. And he had no one to blame for it but his own goddamn self. Hell, he wouldn't even have *this* job if it wasn't for that sonofabitch lay minister or whatever he was who'd "embraced" him into his mother's adopted church, and given him this "chance at an honest start, despite his fallen past." Christ! This job gathering eggs from the filthy conveyor ten hours at a turn, mucking out barns that were two feet thick in stinking layered chicken shit, and worst of all, culling out and dispatching sick pullets, all for just over minimum wage, apparently with no overtime since this qualified as an agricultural job, wasn't exactly his idea of a generous opportunity.

"Boss come. Quick. We look busy." Sure enough a pair of headlights was bouncing down the drive. Shortly Leo could see they belonged to a big white car that was no doubt "Big Jim" Brenner's Lincoln Town Car. Manny and Raoul had already melted into the tin barn's depths, but Leo, standing back from the opening, concealed in the shadows, could not pull himself away as easily.

The big Lincoln, wheel covers flashing, pulled past the mercury security light, the queer glow turning the white paint a shade of mint green, and rolled to a stop in the dappled shadows under a maple tree.

Since all but a few lights on the floor had been turned off to aid in the chicken capture, Leo was sure he couldn't be seen from below. On the other hand, from his vantage point he could readily see down into the car's front seat. There was Big Jim all right, the sleeves of his white shirt rolled up and a thin black tie loose around his trunklike neck. A pretty dark-haired woman was snuggled up against him and Big Jim's right hand was tucked up between her legs, which were exposed by her pushed-up skirt. Without removing his hand, the boss bent his flattop-coifed head down toward his passenger and the two shared a prolonged and passionate kiss, her dark arms wound under his suspenders and around his neck. Then, smiling broadly, he turned from her, withdrew his paw from her crotch, and stepped heavily from the vehicle. The woman smoothed down her skirt and slid over to the passenger side, reaching for a pack of cigarettes on the dash.

Leo turned from the hatchway and stepped back into the nitrogen-enriched stench, as Big Jim, heavy thighs rubbing together, bobbed his way into the barn's entrance. Leo found everyone at the elevator, which now was nearly full with about thirty crates. Manny and Raoul stood watching Big Jim use his calculator, operating it with

THE SAMARITAN

91

one hand, the other on his hip next to his beeper. The boss didn't acknowledge Leo, so he just stood behind the Guatemalans.

Finally Big Jim said something in Spanish, and Raoul responded, causing the boss to shake his head. Raising his voice, Big Jim made another point. Manny and Raoul looked at one another blankly. Then Manny tried communicating something that seemed to further exasperate his employer.

"No!" Big Jim bellowed, and finally noticing Leo, "Oh, Miller, there you are. Where the hell have you been? Never mind. Anyway, we need to get more birds in each crate, otherwise there won't be enough, and it will cost us another trip."

Leo looked over at the crates. Already the contents of each looked like they'd gone through a trash compactor.

"There's already two dozen in each crate, Mr. Brenner. I don't see any way we could...."

But Big Jim interrupted him. "Oh, don't give me that. Them hens'll puff out and take up all the space no matter how many's in the crate. There's plenty of room. I need to have thirty hens in each crate. Understood?"

No one said anything. They looked back and forth at each other and at the stuffed crates.

"Watch!" And with that Big Jim opened the door to one of the crates, pulled out a chicken by its feet, and ordered Manny to open the crate next to it. With his huge hand he stuffed the hen into the mass of feathers and flesh, releasing a chorus of squawks and cackles. He repeated this five more times, actually stuffing the last two in with his foot. The three bystanders winced and averted their eyes as the shiny, black-leather piston compressed the birds into the crate amid squawking, gurgling, and crunching noises.

"Don't be so damn squeamish. What are ya, a bunch of pansies? These birds aren't on their way to a vacation for cripessake."

Before leaving, Big Jim pulled Leo aside and asked him how his co-workers were doing, but before Leo could tell him Manny and Raoul worked hard, and knew the work far better than he himself did, the boss went on with his own concerns.

Jerry Stelmok

"Listen, Miller, we have to stick together when it comes to these Latinos. They're not like us, you know. They haven't been raised like Americans, see? You always gotta keep an eye on 'em. That's one reason why I put you here, see? Someone's gotta keep an eye on 'em. Otherwise they'd never finish the job. Know what I mean?"

Leo saw little chance to tell Big Jim that he was the one holding up the job if anyone was. Big Jim was not in a listening mood. He told Leo he was also carefully watching him.

"Just like Reverend Burnes, I believe in giving someone like yourself a second chance. I heard you're a pretty good mechanic, Miller. You keep up the good work and we'll be thinking about transferring you over to the garage. Takes twenty-seven vehicles to keep Brenner Poultry moving. You think about it. And oh, yeah, see you in church Sunday. Make sure you clean that black dirt off your face first." And he laughed woodenly.

When the boss left the building the three men gathered around a window in the darkened space. Below them in the Lincoln, Big Jim's companion had slid back over next to him, giving him a welcoming kiss. As they drove away Leo turned to Manny and Raoul and asked, "That's not his wife, is it?"

Both shook their heads and grinned.

"Wife fat, big as boss," and Manny indicated her girth, pretending to put his arms around a huge invisible tree. Then, chuckling, "That Maria, works in office." Then Leo remembered the pretty dark-eyed señorita with perfect teeth and perfect English who had helped him fill out an application when the Reverend Justin Burnes drove him over to Brenner Poultry Farms after he had settled in with his mother.

The three shared another little laugh, then Leo turned grimly to the stuffed crates.

"What about these? Was he serious?"

Raoul flashed his familiar grin and threw up his hands as though in despair.

"Latinos stupid," he mocked. "No understand boss," and he rapped on his head with his knuckles as though it was empty. "We forget already. Put in twenty-four hens. That plenty."

—◆—

Leo was making good time gliding along Route 11 as it threaded the
rolling ridges between the expansive potato fields of Masardis. The
fields stretched like corduroy to the mixed woods that marched uninterrupted to distant mauve hills. Listening critically to the rattles in
his mother's sedan and glancing at the clock, he allowed himself to
enjoy some of the highlights of the two great days he had just spent
with Kate and Stevie, his two kids. It was the longest period of time
he'd been able to be with them in over four years, and surprisingly, it
had seemed pretty natural.

Kate had not forgotten "Grammy Miller," as they called his mom,
and naturally she was thrilled. That was probably part of the reason
she let Leo use her car to drive them all the way to Ashland when
Berry, Leo's ex, consented to let the children spend an additional
night. Since Berry and her new husband would be attending church
in Houlton on Sunday, they would be unable to meet in Lincoln for
the planned exchange. No one was more surprised than Leo when his
mother said she would go to the morning service at church with the
Heberts from the next trailer over so that Leo would be free to make
the drive. The only condition was that they start early so that Leo
could get back in time to attend the late afternoon service at the barn-
like church between Holden and Orland. Church attendance was
pretty much mandatory in Reverend Burnes's organization, and Leo
had been quite surprised at how strictly his mother had conformed to
the rather invasive conditions that had to be met to remain a member
in good standing. It was not her usual pattern, and formal religion
had barely been a part of Leo's growing up. Perhaps it had to do with
the loss of Leo's stepdad, Henry, who'd struggled at length with a
wasting disease that had consumed most of Henry's, as well as his
mother's, modest nest eggs, including a neat little house just inland
from Searsport. Leo had had his own troubles to deal with while that
was going on, and had not been as helpful as he might have been.

After prison, with no money and few prospects, Leo had felt fortunate that his mother offered to let him stay with her in the small but tidy trailer, even under the conditions that he promise not to drink, and also to join her church. He had little choice but to submit to the humiliating process of contrition and finally acceptance into Reverend Burnes's Church of the Blinding Light, which was well named as far as Leo was concerned. He still gritted his teeth when he recalled the "Service to the Lord" he was required to complete before being brought up before the congregation for formal forgiveness and enrollment. Mostly it consisted of showing up at Burnes's pretentious mansion where he stood around waiting until the Pastor's arrogant twenty-something son, Isaiah, put him to work cutting grass, sweeping walks, and washing and polishing one of Burnes's luxury cars or his enormous powerboat.

"Christ," Leo thought to himself getting angrier by the second. "What could I have been thinking?"

But his futile fretting was interrupted when an indecisive moose stepped out onto the road in front of him near Knowles Corner, demanding all his attention and considerable driving skills to avoid a collision. Leo breathed a sigh of relief, his hands shaking a bit on the wheel, and at Sherman, at the interstate, he pulled into a service station that actually offered service, and, by the looks, probably even did repairs on site. He checked his own oil and had the kid add a quart.

In the open bay of the garage stood a gleaming Harley Davidson the young man had obviously pampered. His bored girlfriend leaned against the doorway taking tiny sucking puffs on a cigarette. Boy, did that bring back memories. The bike was a newer version of the model he himself had rebuilt in high school. In those days he went by the handle "Slick." Among his friends it was an allusion to the racing tires he kept on his neat little street rod. To others, snobbish or perhaps a little jealous, it probably referred to his well-maintained "duck's ass" hairstyle. Either way he had a reputation of being tough enough so few guys actually gave him any trouble. And if he didn't exactly date cheerleaders and prom queens, he ran around with plenty of more interesting chicks who liked fast machines and were fast in other ways as well.

"That'll be twenty-three dollars, sir," the buzz-cut attendant interrupted.

Leo paid and got back in the car. He couldn't get used to the price of gasoline these days.

"One-thirty," he thought to himself. "Better step on it a little."

The late-afternoon service recently introduced by the pastor relieved some of the overcrowding as more and more converts were drawn to the church for reasons Leo could never understand. But he had to admit that Justin Burnes was an animated and charismatic, even entertaining, preacher. He was a small man in stature but had a commanding presence that emanated enormous energy. Burnes adorned his slight form with unique and flashy attire that included a pleated, pointy-collared tuxedo shirt and bow tie under a tailored white coat with heavily padded shoulders. The coat was snug at the waist and flared at the hem, and a gleaming gold Crusaders' cross flashed on one lapel. His white trousers were pegged sailor-style over expensive, high-heeled cowboy boots of supple exotic leathers. Three or four sparkling rings on each hand caught and reflected any source of light, imparting the illusion that Burnes's very hands were charged with visible energy.

But the subjects of his sermons were predictable, and the same topics came up week after week. In just the ten months or so since Leo began attending, he'd heard more than enough about the unspeakable blasphemies of abortion, homosexuality, and sexual intercourse outside marriage. Burnes had repeatedly railed against the teaching of evolution and human sexuality to innocent children in public schools at the expense of compulsory prayer. He espoused the glories of family values in the male-dominated household, as well as the right and might of aggressive U.S. foreign policy. To hear him go on one would think the Lord Jesus himself held permanent seats in the president's cabinet, the Supreme Court, and the Joint Chiefs of Staff, and that the Constitution was handed down to the founding fathers on tablets of stone.

Leo had also gotten his fill of advice on a woman's proper role in the home, where her duties included caring for the children, doing all

Jerry Stelmok

household chores, and offering unquestioning obedience and service to her husband. Burnes punctuated these sermons with recommendations of acceptable books and videos for the family, all available at the church's high-priced Bible bookstore. Just the previous week, the preacher had exposed the "conspiracy" among prominent scientists who supported the theory of evolution, railed about the effects of so-called global warming, or supported legislation to allow stem-cell research. Leo wasn't exactly looking forward to today's message.

Pulling off the interstate in Bangor, Leo had to slow down for the fairly heavy traffic on Route 1A. Along the Brewer strip he passed one car dealership after another, bringing to mind another period of his mismanaged life. In his junior year of high school, Leo was working afternoons and Saturdays at a hot rod shop, what today would be called a performance center. But it served a rougher crowd back then, and Leo had no difficulty fitting in. After graduation it seemed natural to come aboard full time as Flip Skilling's business continued to grow. The pay was nothing great, but adequate for Leo's needs, and he could buy parts and accessories for his Camaro and his bike at discount prices. And nights and weekends he could work on them in the shop. He began drinking a lot more than he was used to, and more and more he found himself accepting the proffered joints at the frequent wild parties that tended to run out of control. After his folks kicked him out he had little trouble finding compliant chicks to shack up with. He went through quite a string of these, a few of them smart, surprisingly sensible women who encouraged Leo to get his destructive habits under control.

But naturally Leo wasn't listening. He kept to his precarious lifestyle, somehow avoiding serious accidents while driving drunk or stoned, until inevitably he was busted for possession and possibly trafficking in nonscheduled substances. Upon his lawyer's advice, Leo pled guilty to the first charge, not guilty to the second, and ended up serving six months in the county jail, followed by a year's probation.

By the time he was released the hot rod shop had gone out of business. Leo got part-time work at a second-rate body shop, while squatting in a little hunting camp down by the river. Then one day Bud

O'Brien, owner of the Chevrolet dealership, walked into the body shop and told Leo that if he stayed clean he could come to work in his service department.

O'Brien's brother Charlie, a raging alcoholic and the family's black sheep, lived at the end of the Millers' street. Leo was one of the few neighbors, and certainly the only teenager, who regularly stopped and gave poor Charlie a lift when he spotted him stumping along the highway from Bucksport with a bag of groceries and wine clutched to his breast by fingers numb with the cold. A couple of times Leo had even driven Charlie to the hospital when he began experiencing the heart problems that soon killed him, and Bud O'Brien had never forgotten these kindnesses to his brother.

Recognizing a sincere offer of help during a spell of bleak prospects, Leo accepted the offer and within a couple of months was living in a small apartment over Barrons' Insurance Agency. Wearing his pressed blue Dickeys uniform, Leo worked all day on a wide range of vehicles in an orderly, well-equipped, and up-to-date service center.

Leo's talent was obvious and he had never been afraid of work. O'Brien's service manager recommended him for a number of service schools, most of them a few weeks long, where he learned the intricacies of transmissions, air conditioning systems, and the new computer diagnostic equipment.

Leo still wore his hair in his signature DA, but he was clean and looked and felt healthy. He put some of his energy into restoring a fifties pickup, jazzing it up with magnesium wheels and chrome pipes and running boards. But he kept his promise to stay clear of drugs, and, surprisingly, seldom missed his earlier wild times. He sold the pickup and drove around in a black Jetta and spent most evenings alone in his apartment watching television. And for a time this seemed to work. He couldn't say he didn't miss girls, but he didn't miss his old crowd, and outside of it, interesting single women seemed few and far between.

This all changed practically overnight once he met Berry Whittemore, a new teller at the bank, originally from up in the County, neat as a pin with a soft wave in her shoulder-length chestnut hair. But it was her exquisite mouth that most attracted Leo. It might have been too wide on just any girl, but it was balanced perfectly by Berry's prominent cheekbones, garnished with just a dash of freckles. Beryl was her real name, and in some ways she seemed as old-fashioned as the name implied. She had recently graduated from business school in Bangor and was staying in a little apartment behind her cousin's house on the water. He and his wife owned the marina down from the town dock, and after struggling for three or four years, things were beginning to take off for them.

Leo came to Berry's aid one rainy day after work when she couldn't start her wreck of a car. He removed the distributor cap, dried it out and replaced it, and away it went. She thanked him and when she told him she probably couldn't afford to bring it into the shop for a new one just then, he made a date for the following Saturday afternoon to replace the distributor, along with new points, in the empty lot out behind his place. When he'd finished the work she bought him an ice cream and they sat under a tree while she told him about her close family up north, and how she felt a little lonely so far from home.

Dating a nice quiet girl was a new experience for Leo and he found it refreshing. They went to movies at the Grand in Ellsworth, and window-shopped in Bar Harbor. A wild day might include riding the go-carts around the track in Trenton. She was a great kisser but that was as far as it ever went. She wouldn't think of inviting him to her two rooms alone, nor would she let him talk her into coming up the stairs to his place. They did, however, have dinner frequently at her cousin's, and enjoyed many evenings watching TV and playing cards there.

Within a year they were married. He'd been promoted to assistant service manager and not quite believing it all, Leo found himself a responsible provider and soon-to-be father. Those early years with Berry, Leo often thought, represented the best and brightest period of his life.

At Holden Leo turned left toward East Orland, and as he passed a classic New England church with white clapboards and a steeple, he was struck by how normal and relaxed the congregants appeared as they chatted in front of the steps, nodding and smiling. He also couldn't help noticing that most seemed to be at or near retirement age.

It wasn't like that at the Church of the Blinding Light. There, a palpable tension filled the air, and by design it increased as the sermon progressed, until the congregation was lashed into a frenzy by the combination of Reverend Burnes's showmanship and the intensity of the message. The feelings of urgency and pressure that permeated the tabernacle were more those of a sales meeting than a worship service—or at least that's how it seemed to Leo.

By the time Burnes's pulsating diatribe, complemented by his athletic gyrations, reached its climax, sweat would be pouring from his furrowed brow and running freely down his blotchy reddened face. He would then stop his prancing, mop his brow with an oversized silk handkerchief, and throw his hands into the air—it was time for the *coup de théatre.*

"And now brothers and sisters, it's time you did your part," he would start in a lowered raspy voice that would build again rapidly. "The Lord Jesus has spoken to you. And He has shown you the terrible things that go on every day when His benevolent grace is withheld. And these unspeakable blasphemies go on not only in darkest Africa, not just in godless Russia or China, not just in soulless Arabia. Oh, no, brothers and sisters, these terrible affronts to Our Lord go on each day right here in the U.S. of A., right here in the great State of Maine, ladies and gentlemen, and would you believe it, right in your own cities and towns.

"So, brothers and sisters, you know what time it is. I want you to take out your shades. If you've forgotten your eye protection, or don't have any, don't worry. Just reach right into that little cubbyhole right there on the back of the seat in front of you and take out what you need. And remember, sisters, make sure your little ones have theirs on first, 'cause we're gonna let in the Light of the Lord right now. That's right, your generous contributions are going to energize the Light of the Lord. And with your help His Light is going to beam into every town, every house—yes, brothers and sisters—into every nook and cranny where the darkness still reigns. And because of your generosity, His Word, the Word of your Lord Jesus Christ is going to spread. And the Light of it will drive Satan and all of his minions back into the darkness so deep, they can never climb out and work their evil on innocent people again. EVER."

And as he spoke a panel in the ceiling above the podium would slide open. Slowly and regally a polished glass sphere, half again the size of a disco globe, would descend on a slowly rotating shaft until it hung, still turning, a couple of feet below the ceiling. The regular lighting would be extinguished and a hush would sweep over the anxious congregation, followed by a communal gasp as a dim light shone in the heart of the globe, flickering weakly as though about to die.

"Brothers and sisters, the Light of Lord Jesus is weak this morning. It needs your help to grow. Now you know what to do. Those at the left of each row, pick up that energizer from its holster, there, and punch in your code number. Then search your blessed soul and punch in the amount of the gift you want to give today, so that this ministry, your chosen church, can shine the Light of the Lord, and do His Work."

And as the parishioners adjusted their glasses and punched in the numbers, the light would begin to slowly grow in intensity.

"Good, good, thank-you. Thank you! Now pass the energizer along to the person on your right, there. Yes, just like that and look!"

And the globe would grow brighter at a fairly steady rate, but occasionally, when one of the remotes was in the hands of one of the wealthier or showier supporters, there would be a leap in the intensity, and Burnes would acknowledge that generosity.

"Praise be to you Brother Stambaugh, the Lord thanks you."

Leo doubted that the brightness or the light was actually connected to the transponders; he bet Jim Brenner or another deacon out back was controlling the light. There was no doubt, however, that the transmitted offerings were received and recorded by the church business office. Each member was assigned a registered code, and after the service, if you didn't keep an account at the rectory from which your pledge would be automatically deducted, as was encouraged, you were expected to settle up. Those who failed would be called at home Monday evening and if the pledge was not received before the next week's service, your name would appear on the pastor's "Register of Shame," which was prominently posted weekly in the vestibule. Anyone appearing on the register more than twice in any quarter would be asked to stand at their seat and be chastised during Burnes's painful "Warning to the Disgraced."

As the globe would shine brighter and brighter, the choir would strike up with a rocking gospel number and the preacher would dash from one end of the dais to the other, shouting encouragement and cheering on the generous contributors. Near the end the dozens of halogen bulbs in the sphere would produce an incredibly intense light, and Burnes would be running up and down the two aisles holding out transponders, encouraging members to add just a little more to help cast the Lord's Light and Word just a little deeper into the darkness. The choir would be joined by the congregants swaying and singing and clapping their hands above their heads, until finally Burnes would collapse into an armchair alongside the podium, wiping his brow, one hand spread on his chest. The globe would dim and for a moment the singing would stop. Then, as the globe ascended back into the ceiling, a pair of American flags would descend and Burnes would regain his feet and lead his flock in a rousing rendition of "God Bless America."

—

As Leo drove along the twisting woods-lined road his thoughts went back to his brief married life with Berry, and he wondered for the millionth time why he couldn't make it work. Looking at it from the outside, it was a case of a wild young man finally getting his act together with the help of the right girl, but maybe Leo had been just a little *too* wild.

All of a sudden he had a wife, a family, a decent job, and he and Berry had even bought a starter home. Once Kathleen was born, Berry had quit her job at the bank and fell naturally into the roles of full-time homemaker and mother. Two years later, with Stephen's arrival, they decided to buy a two-bedroom house off the Bangor Road. Leo loved the kids and was an attentive dad, but was strictly limited by Berry as to which were acceptable activities for the children, and which were not. Although the kids loved it, roughhousing was out, as were any activities that resulted in their getting even the slightest bit dirty. Pets were out because she thought the children might develop allergies, and rides on his motorcycle were definitely out.

Things began feeling just a little tiresome to Leo and he was feeling penned in. After the kids were born Berry had pretty much lost interest in sex. It wasn't the end of the world, but was surely the cause of some of his frustration. Berry's cousin sold the marina and moved back to Presque Isle, and they found themselves without any friends their age. Berry didn't like going out. Finding reliable babysitters was difficult, and she'd just as soon stay home and watch TV every night, weekends as well as weekdays.

Berry kept a beautiful house. Her meals were tasty, and she stayed within her self-imposed, reasonable budget. She wasn't crazy about shopping like many women, and in fact seemed not to have any close girlfriends to do such things with.

On warm summer nights, Leo would cruise around town or out in the country on his motorcycle. She had no objections to his joining a local bikers' club—the respectable one. Berry didn't drink and she disliked it when Leo had a beer. He had to buy a bottle or two each night after work because she wouldn't let him keep it in the refrigerator.

One thing led to another, no one really planning anything, but he started staying out more. Inevitably he ran into his old buddies and that was not good. He wasn't without responsibilities these days. Leo tried to keep his drinking down to a reasonable level and refused their pot, but it wasn't easy. His old habits had only been dormant, not dead. When he'd come home late with stale beer and cigarette smoke on his clothes, Berry wouldn't confront him or chew him out. She just pretended she was asleep, which made him feel doubly guilty.

Things might have gone along like this for some time if Leo hadn't run into the old gang outside town by the river celebrating Dizzy Dudzik's thirtieth birthday. The Bud was flowing freely, the music was loud enough to drown out the occasional passing train, and the humid air was saturated with the aroma of good marijuana. Leo hadn't yet had dinner and the alcohol hit him early on and hard. He had no recollection of accepting the first joint, but later he figured he'd smoked more than one or two. Eventually the cops broke up the party and several belligerent revelers were arrested. Not Leo, however. He'd passed out a good hour before the bust, and looked so sick his friends were concerned about leaving him lying on the gravel. Several of them shoved him into a van and drove him home.

When Berry, in nightgown and robe, answered the door at eleven, there was Leo out cold, being propped up by two disheveled biker chicks, one of whose ample breasts were all but hanging out of her unbuttoned leather vest. Berry stood there staring, unable to speak as the girls and a huge man standing behind them—with a beard like Santa's and a long white ponytail swinging from beneath his Nazi helmet—tried incoherently to apologize on Leo's behalf. Six-year-old Kate came to the door dragging her teddy bear, and upon seeing her father, apparently dead, and these scary strangers, started screaming uncontrollably, waking up Stevie who began crying from his room.

The next morning, before Leo even had a chance to come to, Berry had packed up a surprising amount of stuff, put it all, along with the kids, in the minivan, and headed north for Ashland.

No amount of reasoning, apologies, or promises had any effect on Berry, whether delivered by Leo over the phone or in person after a four-hour drive, standing on her parents' front steps, since he wasn't invited inside. He was ashamed. He was filled with remorse, he was sorry. But it was too late. Berry had made up her mind and it was over. No second chances, no real discussion.

Leo felt lost. He stumbled around in a stupor for a month, automatically performing his job, more or less, but otherwise directionless and awash in self-pity. He found solace in the excesses of his old ways, and before long he could no longer be counted upon to show up on time for work. When he did, he was apt to be unwashed, and a few times he was stoned. He made a number of costly mistakes on customers' cars before Bud O'Brien had to let him go. He felt, somewhat justifiably, that he had just ruined his own life.

That was how Leo ended up working at Tiny Beech's Pre-Owned Auto Rama. Tiny, who had a mysterious past, weighed at least three hundred pounds. He purchased cars in lots at out-of-state auctions, largely lemons and flood-damaged time bombs, which he foisted off onto desperate customers for more than they were worth at exorbitant interest rates. Any major work required to make them temporarily operable was done at Tiny's large facility out behind his legitimate Jeep dealership. All Leo got to do was stop up leaky radiators, add gallons of motor oil, and clean the rigs up. He was supposed to be selling the things the rest of the time, which included lashing colorful balloons to antennas and stringing up those annoying flapping pennants. It didn't take Tiny very long to realize that Leo wasn't really cut out for sales.

One afternoon an old threadbare couple looking at a used-up Buick found Leo killing time in the garage. They had just test-driven the car and asked him if the thumping they had felt in the front end was just tires out of balance as Chris, the other salesman, had assured them it was. Leo looked past the stooped gentleman through the window behind him, where Chris, standing outside by the wreck, was giving Leo the "okay" sign.

"No, sir," Leo said, "I'm afraid it's not just the tires. It's the ball joints and tie rods that are shot, and I wouldn't feel safe driving that vehicle as far as Ellsworth."

"Oh, my," the woman replied.

Surprisingly, Tiny didn't fire him on the spot. Instead he told Leo he could use him for out-of-state deliveries, and that the money would be quite a bit better, especially since Leo wasn't exactly earning many commissions.

So about three or four times a month, Leo would be given five hundred dollars in cash and a reasonably late-model sedan, and would be instructed to drive it to a certain coffee shop or hamburger joint outside Boston. There he would meet the customer, who had been well described, and turn over the keys. He'd have lunch or a coffee, then take a taxi directly to the bus station for the trip home, or perhaps to a sleazy motel north of the city where he'd spend the night with a bottle of booze and some professional company, and catch the bus the following day.

Leo never asked what was in the trunks of these cars although he had his suspicions—especially since he discovered that they couldn't be unlocked with the car's regular set of keys. It wasn't exactly uplifting work, but Leo still wasn't over the divorce and separation from his kids, and he really didn't give a damn.

Late one afternoon Tiny came by Leo's cabin off an old section of Route 1 that had been by-passed years before. His rental was the last semi-standing cottage in a row of about a dozen at a defunct motor court. Shriveled black locust leaves and tough, emaciated seedpods had recently fallen and covered everything up to about the second rickety step. It stood nearest the neglected bungalow where the owner still lived, which still bore the "office" sign over the door. Each cabin beyond Leo's was in progressively worse shape, with junk piled on the little sagging porches and knotweed growing out of control.

Leo's furnishings consisted of an old iron bed, a Formica kitchen table with a television on it, and two chrome and vinyl kitchen chairs. His clothes and belongings spilled out of a doorless closet onto the floor. An ancient, curiously rounded refrigerator hummed along, apparently still functional. Empty beer bottles surrounded it like a tiny amber forest.

Tiny had come to get Leo to help him pick up another car to be driven to Massachusetts. Leo had no idea where these cars came from, although normally they were not from the car lot. He was surprised when Tiny headed down the coast toward Deer Isle, taking one gravel road after another before finally turning off onto a narrow dirt track that took them down to the shore. There, at the edge of a gravel clearing, tucked up under the trees, was a gunmetal gray Oldsmobile.

"Good," Tiny grunted, "It's here." Seemingly relieved, he handed Leo a set of keys.

"Want this at the lot?" Leo asked as he moved to get out of Tiny's car.

"No, take it back with you tonight and drive it down to Boston tomorrow." He handed Leo the customary envelope. "Call me at home at nine tomorrow morning and I'll give you directions to the customer."

He rolled up the window, his doughy face still turned toward Leo, then peered ahead and drove back up the path. Leo looked around. It was a nice evening. Behind the thin clouds, the moon gave off considerable light and gentle waves lapped against the boulders at the water's edge. A gull mewed. Leo could see well enough to tell this was a good-sized cove with dark spruces ringing the shore like ramparts. He thought he heard the rumble of a boat engine, but there were no lights out on the water. All this pretty much dispelled any doubts Leo held regarding the true nature of Tiny's vehicle exchanges. He was going to have to think about changing jobs. He wasn't getting paid enough to take these kinds of risks, especially for an asshole like Tiny.

Just before he got into the car, the moon momentarily slipped its shroud of clouds and the cove sparkled like a sheet of dancing silver light. Far out near the mouth, Leo spotted the silhouette of a dragger of some sort rocking easily on the swells, all lights extinguished. He got in, started up the car, and drove back to his cabin.

The following afternoon in Saugus, Massachusetts, he pulled into the parking lot of a Thai restaurant doing business in what must have once been a gas station. Stiff from driving, he climbed out of the Oldsmobile and stretched, and two federal agents were out of their unmarked car and on him like ducks on a June bug, one flashing his badge, the other holding his drawn handgun down along his thigh. Another unmarked car wheeled in, skidded to a stop, and two more plainclothesmen jumped out, followed in another minute by a police car with its strobes flashing and siren wailing.

An agent pulled the registration from the glove box, glanced at it, and tossed it onto the seat.

"This isn't my car," Leo offered from his spread-eagled stance, hands on the roof.

"'Course it isn't, pal. It's stolen." And this was no doubt being confirmed by the officer rummaging under the hood. Then he handed Leo the keys.

"What say we have a look at what's in the trunk, Slick?" Leo couldn't believe the coincidence. No one had called him by that name in twenty years.

"These keys won't work," he said.

"Try 'em."

To Leo's surprise the trunk key fit fine, and the big lid opened to reveal three plastic buckets of vermiculite and a half dozen fully automatic assault weapons. Once the seals were broken on the plastic buckets they proved to be about two-thirds full of cocaine in sealed plastic bags under a few inches of the insulation material.

"Fucking Tiny," Leo said to himself. Still, he realized this was far too expensive a trap just to nab *him*.

By cooperating with DEA agents and the district attorney's office, Leo got his fifteen-year sentence reduced to five, and got to serve his time at the Maine State Prison instead of a federal penitentiary. Yet his testimony did not lead directly to Tiny's arrest—at least, not right away. But about a year later both Tiny Beech and his nephew Chris were nailed good, and Leo found himself being transferred to the minimum-security facility near Dover. There he worked on the logging equipment used in the prison's woodlots, and after two years there as a model inmate, he was released on probation

—

Leo never tired of running that chain of events through his head. He glanced at the clock, relieved he would make the service on time. It was just a couple of miles to the church.

Then up ahead he spotted a car pulled over on the gravel shoulder. "Car trouble," he said to himself. "Too bad. I've got to show up at

Jerry Stelmok

church. Mom trusted me."

But instinctively he slowed down. He crawled by, noticing an old man struggling to open the hood of the dilapidated compact. Steam was escaping from around the seal and from underneath. Against his better judgment Leo stopped. A horn blared as a SUV roared up from behind and swerved around him. A church-bound family in showy clothes, pasty faces to the glass, scowled at him. He moved over onto the gravel as a second car speeding toward Reverend Burnes's church veered and honked angrily.

A thin man, shaggy white hair ringing his bald crown, stood mopping his brow with a dirty rag, an embarrassed grin on his face. From behind the windshield his wife forced a wide smile, waved at Leo, and shrugged her shoulders. Leo thought she looked like Edith Bunker. The panting black dog next to her appeared to be blind.

"Ayeh, yeh, yeh yeh," the man began, almost as a wheeze. "Guess she overhet a bit. But can't get the dang hood open fer the life o'me." His bib overalls were worn almost to the texture of silk and had been patched a dozen times. The sleeves of a frayed grayish shirt were rolled up over his bony elbows.

"Scared it might be the radiator hose. Replaced it last week, I did. But mebbe the clamp's worked loose. Ayeh, yeh, yeh, yeh. Sorry t' be botherin' ya, mista. Been here a half hour now and you're th' only one stopped."

Leo reached for the latch but the scalding steam made him quickly yank his hand back. He pulled a neatly folded clean handkerchief from his back pocket, and looked apprehensively at the oily hood and grille. Personal appearance was of primary importance to the Reverend Burnes, and he made sure his congregation took it seriously. "Slovenly dress is an affront to the Lord," he liked to say. "It shows a flagrant lack of respect for the Savior, who died on the cross to save our souls."

Men were expected to wear a jacket, preferably a suit, a white shirt, and a proper, not flashy tie or a bolo tie. Footwear was to be black dress shoes, polished as though ready for a military inspection. Women wore dresses, loosely fitting and mid-calf in length. Nylons were acceptable, but no high heels. For boys under ten or so it was slacks with a white shirt and tie, no jeans. But most were made to wear a sport coat, anyway. Some wore ridiculous little business suits. A surprising number of parishioners were well off, and for them it was a chance to strut around showing off their fine worsted wool suits with vests during cold weather and linen and silk blends in the summer. Some of the women appeared to have striking new outfits nearly every week of the year.

But for many families the dress code represented a real challenge if not an actual hardship. There were men who had but one polyester suit the year 'round, and threadbare but clean shirts washed hundreds of times by the wife, who made do with a couple of dresses that were also laundered almost to death.

Leo thought about this as he rolled up his sleeves now that he had the radiator cap off and most of the steam had dispersed. As it was, he was going to have to attend the service in his shirtsleeves and tie because the kids had gotten chocolate on his light blue blazer.

Leo quickly discovered that the radiator hose had slipped off the flange because the clamp had been poorly installed.

The old man kept repeating "Ayeh, yeh, yeh, yeh" as he watched the proceedings over Leo's shoulder. When Leo finally got the hose reseated, he wondered how he was going to squeeze the clamp open without pliers. He straightened up and the man was pawing through a shapeless cardboard box filled with oil- and grease-covered tools and miscellaneous parts. While Leo waited for the man to find a pair of pliers, he saw his boss, Big Jim Brenner, rocket past in his white Town Car without so much as a glance in their direction.

To complete the operation under the hood, Leo was forced to lean forward as far as he could into the oil-blackened oven, his shirt and pants rubbing against a fender that was a study in black smudges, both old and new. When he'd finished, sweat was pouring off his brow and neck and saturating his shirt. He kept brushing at the limp forelock that hung down into his eyes, and in so doing applied a black smear across his forehead and cheek. He couldn't have looked much worse if he'd just climbed out of a chimney.

Jerry Stelmok

"Ayeh, yeh, yeh, yeh," the old gent observed. "Thought that might be th' trouble with 'er when I see th' steam."

His sweet wife was somewhat more helpful. With no small difficulty she climbed out of the vehicle, looked at Leo, and shook her white dandelion head. "Oh, my, just look at your nice clothes, deah." With a clean towel that had been covering some strawberries in the back seat, she was able to rub off a fair amount of the worst grime, but the remaining stains and smudges were still pretty obvious.

Naturally, there was no coolant left in the flat plastic jug the old man fished out of the trunk, but there was a stream flowing through a culvert up the road and Leo grabbed the container and hurried toward it. Approaching the stream, he spotted a painted turtle that had crawled a few feet out onto the road surface, then froze in confusion. The driver of a pickup noticed it just in time to swerve and miss it. Glancing back, Leo rushed to rescue the turtle before being overtaken by a line of six or eight vehicles that would surely do it in. When he realized he wasn't going to be able to snatch it up in time, he decided to crowd the road just a bit himself, figuring the drivers would get the idea and swing around the creature since there was no traffic from the other direction. This strategy seemed to work as one vehicle after another veered left to avoid Leo as much as the confused turtle, which most of them probably never noticed. Several drivers laid on their horns and gave Leo dirty looks as they passed without slowing. One even flashed the one-finger salute. Just as the final car in the procession started its jog to the left, the turtle got back its nerve and with a determined burst of speed, scuttled to the crown of the road—just in time to be grazed hard by a front tire and sent scaling through the air to land lifeless in the ditch near the culvert.

Feeling sad and utterly defeated, Leo descended the grassy bank to the brook. As he struggled to remove the childproof cap on the jug, he lost his footing and slid from the wobbly hummocks of grass on which he'd been balancing into the soft black muck that reached well above his ankles.

THE SAMARITAN

By the time Leo filled the couple's radiator, jumped the dead battery with the man's greasy cables, and rinsed most of the muck off his shoes and pant cuffs, he was running forty minutes late for church. In gratitude, the wife had handed him a quart of beautiful berries, and the husband had given him a handmade cedar birdhouse from the car trunk which was filled with them.

The parking lot at the huge unadorned church was divided unofficially into two sections. The paved upper lot next to the newest part of the edifice was pretty much filled with the vehicles of the wealthier congregants, starting with Reverend Burnes's and Big Jim's twin Town Cars, and ran heavily to dark-hued SUVs and polished luxury cars. The gravel-surfaced lower lot alongside the much smaller original church had mostly sedans, pickups, and a disproportionate number of minivans, mostly blue, of increasing age and deteriorating condition the farther you got from the macadam. Leo guided his mother's beat-up K-Car well down toward the end of the lot.

As usual he was struck by how most of the bumper stickers voiced support for two disparate messages. Oddly, it seemed to Leo, both themes were sometimes promoted on the same vehicle: love for and by Christ, and solid support for the NRA. A case in point was an aging Jeep Cherokee. On the back passenger-side bumper was a lavender sticker decorated with daisies and the message, "Put the love of Jesus in your life." The sticker on the driver's side was blood red and displayed the graphic image of the business end of a double-barreled shotgun. It read, "Sure, come take my guns. I need the target practice." Strong support for this second message was evident by the number of gun racks, most in use, in the rear windows of pickups. "The only message missing," thought Leo, "might be 'Jesus died on the cross for your right to bear arms.'"

Leo's bladder was bursting. He stepped out into the empty lot and as inconspicuously as possible took a leak alongside the car. As he reluctantly started toward the church he saw the pastor's son, Isaiah, crush a cigarette, then turn and enter the side door of the older structure that accommodated Sunday school, youth groups, and other activities. "Christ!" he thought. "He must have seen me."

Leo's plan was to sneak into the vestibule at the back; usually the doors to the tabernacle were left open. If there were any empty seats in the rear, as there might be during the evening service, he'd quietly take one. If not, he'd stand in back and leave promptly at dismissal, drop his offering at the office, and disappear before many members got a good look at his sorry appearance.

His first problem was that the sanctuary doors were not open. He could hear the final refrain of "God Bless America" indicating the blinding globe had just been retracted. Normally Burnes would then reinforce the theme of the earlier sermon with a five- or ten-minute summation, followed by a few announcements of coming events and a reminder to members to honor their pledges. Then, after a brief final blessing, the congregation would be dismissed.

Ordinarily, once Leo saw the closed inner doors, he would have turned and left, because opening them always attracted attention, especially late in the service when everyone was getting a little antsy. However, one of the deacons was seated in the vestibule beside the door reading a pamphlet. He glanced up at Leo, then back at the bulletin, then quickly back at Leo with an expression of stunned disbelief. Leo swallowed, pulled himself up to full height, and chin held high, walked past the deacon and pulled on one of the huge oak doors. Reverend Burnes was reinforcing his views about the folly of immigration, illegal or otherwise, emphasizing that most of the new-comers—in addition to being deadbeats—were not even Christians. Considering his point of view that even Roman Catholics did not fall into that category, this was probably an accurate statistic.

The sustained creak of the door was louder than Leo expected, and it was compounded by the widening arc of light that washed into the darkened auditorium. Burnes stopped in mid-sentence and looked up, and about half the heads in the congregation turned to see the source of the disturbance. The door creaked shut and Leo stood stock-still. His only ally now was the dim lighting. He didn't dare breathe. He waited for a merciful axe to cleave him in two, or a bolt of lightning to strike, but neither event came to pass and, remarkably, Reverend Burnes resumed his address and gradually the curious faces swiveled back toward the podium.

After a of couple minutes Leo spotted an empty seat at the end of a nearby row. He stole quietly toward it, but when he put his hand on the back he noticed in it a young child slumped over sleeping, his head on his mother's lap. She turned and looked at Leo with a mixture of disgust and horror, and Leo backed away. Unfortunately, as he retreated, he backed into one of the large urns of lilies which flanked the exit. It tottered noisily on its stand and clunked audibly against the oak paneling. Leo made a grab for it but succeeded only in knocking it over with a loud crash that was immediately followed by the rush of water spilling onto the hardwood floor, and the subsequent rumble of the vessel rolling back and forth in a little arc.

There was a communal gasp and rustle as every head in the tabernacle turned again toward the back, and some of the faithful actually jumped to their feet. The pastor's impassioned rhetoric came to a halt, and quietly over the murmuring he called for the lights to be turned on.

More gasps ensued as the congregation got a clear look at the offender. Leo crouched next to the unbroken urn, which he'd righted and was now refilling with lilies. He stood slowly, revealing his filthy shirt, pants. and hair, and his smudged face.

After a minute of silence, the Reverend Burnes spoke quietly. "Brothers and sisters please take a close look at the gentleman at the back of the tabernacle," he said, not that all six hundred souls were not already staring agape at the spectacle.

"Here we see the thanks we get, and the respect our Lord gets, for opening our hearts and our church to a fallen sinner. Here stands a wretch who has spread the evils of narcotics not only among the youth of our community, but to other communities in our the state and elsewhere." And his volume built. "And who, upon completing a far too lenient sentence in a so-called house of corrections, came crawling back to his mother, our beloved sister, Barbara Miller...."

"God, what is she doing here?" Leo wondered, spotting her drooping head halfway down the center aisle.

He stood numbly in a trance, as though he was not actually present, but was instead watching from outside like any interested observer. Burnes yammered on and on about the church's capacity for forgiveness and Big Jim Brenner's generosity in providing honest work for this ingrate who had so violated the church's trust.

"And how are we repaid for this generous reaching out? You can see for yourselves, brothers and sisters. He stumbles into the sanctuary of our divine worship. Into the Lord's own house. Waiting until the offerings that energize the Blinding Light have already been generously fulfilled by his fellow members. Making a spectacle of himself in his blatant disrespect for Our Lord. Dressed in filthy rags, insulting our faith.

"Brother Miller, and I'm using the title 'Brother' only out of the purest spirit of Christian grace, not because it is a title you deserve. Please come up here. Come on up here, beside me, so the whole congregation can get a look at your sorry appearance. And then tell these honest, hardworking people just what you have in mind, desecrating this shrine of Our Lord, showing up looking like a tramp, a hobo, a n'er-do-well."

Leo's eyes were riveted on his mother, who looked so frail and heartbroken sobbing into her handkerchief. He took a step toward the aisle, but then something inside him rebelled and his spine stiffened. He would not succumb to Burnes's demands; he would not be disgraced, and then used by the preacher as a lesson in "ingratitude" to be rewarded with condescending conditional forgiveness. He wheeled about, made for the doors the deacon had just opened, and walked through the atrium out onto the wide granite steps and into the fresh air.

"Leo Miller, you come back in here!" He could just hear Burnes calling over the jabbering of the congregation.

The sweetness of the late summer afternoon enveloped him, and he stood for a moment in a daze of mixed emotions—confusion, shame, humiliation, anger—and finally an altogether different feeling swept over him—a sense of pride and freedom.

He inhaled deeply, descended the steps, and strode off through the paved parking lot, down toward his mother's car. The children had been released from their catechism and in small groups were enjoying the unstructured time. A sister and brother about the ages of Kate and Stevie were scooched down poking at the gasoline rainbows in a puddle. Leo smiled. "Thank God for the children," he thought to himself.

Then he noticed a knot of kids over by his car. They dispersed and ran tittering as he approached, and as he drew closer, he saw what they'd been up to—with chalk from the classroom they had scrawled over and over on every surface of the vehicle the word "SINNER." Most of the kids had run to the side door that led to the meeting rooms, and standing beside it, with arms crossed and a smug grin on his face, stood Burnes's surly son, Isaiah.

Stunned, Leo turned again toward the car. Nearby, atop a rock retaining wall, stood a half dozen of the older children, their eyes squinted almost shut, unsettling grins stretching their cheeks. They leaned out toward Leo like a six-headed cobra and chanted in chorus:

"Something rotten, I do smell. Sinner, sinner, burn in Hell."

Maggie

John Brighton was the most hateful, meanspirited man in all of Franklin County, and to top it off he was dishonest and lazy. All of these sad traits were greatly enhanced whenever he drank too much, and that was as often as he possibly could. As is often the case with such scoundrels, his wife Mary was as kind as he was cruel, as thoughtful as he was thoughtless, and as honest as he was crooked.

They lived on a run-down place off Harrington Ridge that had been in Mary's family since the Civil War and that Mary had inherited upon her mother's death. Her brother had been killed when his marine battalion was decimated taking a tiny Pacific atoll from the determined and well-entrenched Japanese defenders. A nearly lifelong boyfriend whom Mary had hoped to marry after the war had also failed to return home from his hitch—not because he was killed in action, but because he fell in love with a girl he'd met while on leave in San Francisco and had decided to start his life over out west.

The McCorison place, as it had been called since Mary's great-grandfather purchased it after the Civil War, sat just below a windswept hilltop on a gentle southern slope. Aside from the usual abundance of rocks and boulders common to all tracts in the region, it was a fertile and productive piece of ground with sweeping views to the south between the intervening foothills that lay halfway to the coast. Hard work on the part of Major McCorison, who came home after Vicksburg with a poorly fitted wooden leg, and help from a former slave who had accompanied him north, had added twenty-seven acres of arable fields to the fifteen originally purchased. There was also a vigorous mixed woodlot of about seventy acres, and later on Mary's grandfather, Henry, nurtured about five acres of the hardwood lot nearest the barn into a productive sugar bush.

Henry Jr., his brother, and three sisters came late into the first Henry's life after he had married for the second time, and the children were expected to do their share of the chores. Another thirty acres of fields were wrested from the stubborn forest and the existing barn was built before the younger son left for France during the Great War and got himself machine-gunned at Verdun. The daughters married and moved on one by one, leaving Henry Jr. the sole proprietor and sole heir of the farm. He did his best to continue the McCorison tradition of productive croplands, well-kept buildings, and sound and contented livestock, but without a son to help with all the work, the unmistakable signs of a place too big for the owner to manage began to show. Unpruned orchards, weathered clapboards on the south side of the house, sagging fences, and leaning outbuildings bespoke neglect despite a growing interest in the farm by Mary, who worked tirelessly in an effort to help her father keep up.

Mary ran the place single-handedly in the five years between her parents' deaths, slipping back just slightly each year in terms of milk and vegetable production and equipment maintenance. Her mother's condition during her final year of life demanded a huge share of Mary's attention, and with a lazy hired man doing most of the farming, the sheen of prosperity quickly faded from the operation.

At twenty-six and single, Mary couldn't be expected to keep the place up by herself, no matter how much she was willing to work. She took on a series of hired hands—all of whom were lazy, incompetent, or merely interested in marrying into the established farm their own circumstances had denied them. Mary was quick to fall deeply in love with one such opportunist, without knowledge of the business debts he'd run up out in Illinois, which eventually followed him all the way to Harrington Ridge. To prevent her lover from extradition and imprisonment, Mary sold twenty-two acres of pastureland to the Richardsons, who owned the next farm over. But six weeks later the man picked up and left anyway, and by then Mary was almost glad to see him go.

Another hired-hand-turned-lover hit the ground running, and in a few months made some major strides toward getting the farm back into shape and ready to roll. To replace the dairy herd sold down since Henry's death, Mary sold the Richardsons another twenty-six acres, half of which was woodlot, and then this partner was off to a cattle auction in western Massachusetts. There he unexpectedly ran into the brothers of the wife he'd neglected to tell Mary about. All she ever heard from him was a brief phone call from Springfield expressing his regret and begging her forgiveness—she never did get her cattle money back.

That's probably why John Brighton didn't look so bad to Mary when he slid into town from the coast where he'd been a pipe fitter at a shipyard. At thirty-two Mary, while still pretty, had clearly lost the blush of youth, and lines on her forehead and around her eyes and mouth told the story of a life of hard work, disappointment, anxiety, and despair. Brighton was handsome in a rugged way, with deep lines creasing his leathery skin and a disarming smile that hid a few missing teeth. He generally wore a clean white shirt and a dark wool vest, like the one Mary's grandfather had worn. He spoke with seeming authority on a variety of subjects and was an endless source of stories and jokes, many of them ribald, which got him lots of free drinks in any bar. And he had a charming way with women that could bring a flush to the cheeks of a chosen target and even send her heart racing.

One day he drove out to the farm to meet Mary. He'd heard of her circumstances from time to time during his stay in town, and aimed to propose leasing some land and who knows what else. He'd operated a truck farm years back before the shipyard work, and had a plan for raising vegetables and hay that might profit them both.

"Don't know," Mary replied, looking at her shoes. "To tell the truth, Mr. Brighton, I haven't had much luck farming this place under *any* plan, and it seems it always ends up costing me money I don't have."

Brighton waited until she glanced up, then caught her blue eyes with his steely ones, locking onto them and using all his charm to press his case.

"Listen, Miss McCorison, all you have here now is a Jersey milk cow, a bunch of laying hens, a small garden—albeit a lovely one—and a big old place ready to fall down on top of you. And the way I hear it around town, you've also got a neighbor trying to rent more land for nothing and eventually steal it."

"Hold it right there, Mr. Brighton," Mary said as she straightened, a different aspect transforming her whole bearing. "Will Richardson and his father are good farmers and good neighbors, and they never stole a thing from nobody, and anybody tells you different don't know what they're talking about. Furthermore," she continued, cutting Brighton off from an attempted response, "without their generous advice and help I wouldn't be living here today. And that's not to mention Claire's kindnesses. The Richardsons are the best kind a' folk in this county or anywheres else."

Mary's defensiveness took Brighton completely by surprise; he'd clearly taken the wrong approach. He apologized, back-pedaled, apologized again, and with his gray fedora in his hand, bid Mary good day and left.

It would have been better had it ended right there, but Brighton had sniffed an opportunity and could be as persistent as he could be charming or ruthless. He drove out to the farm again a few days later with a lovely long-necked vase as a peace offering and never brought up the subject of renting land. Next time he brought some flowers to put in the vase. These were flowers from an actual florist and not those picked alongside the ditch, or from someone's unattended garden, as all the other bouquets in Mary's life had been. He engaged Mary in pleasant conversation and from a zinc-lined wooden chest in the back of his car, pulled out a pair of ice-cold ginger beers, droplets of condensation stippling the bottles with their rich amber contents.

By late September, the opportunity for any farming was swept away by the first hard frost that coated every blade and stem, lifting them to the light in sparkling glory before shriveling them into a wasteland of drooping and twisted brown weeds. Brighton drove out to Mary's place that afternoon and presented her with a simple pewter tray and an annotated edition of Elizabeth Barrett Browning's poems, having learned over the summer what an avid reader Mary was. The book had been purchased for almost nothing—the "Discarded" stamp from the town library clear evidence. Still it was a touching, personal gift in Mary's view, after so many empty disappointments.

She was thrilled and embarrassed all at once and could not look Brighton in the eye. When he announced he was heading back down to Portsmouth to earn some money, the news hit her like a sledge-hammer. All the disappointments she had ever known from men welled up inside her, and she feared that once again she'd been criti-cally mistaken.

"Come spring," he told her, "I'll have a little stash and I'll be back, Mary. You can count on it. And I'm gonna show you how we can be partners, and use this place to make life easier for both of us."

She stood numbly watching the gray Plymouth with the rusted rocker panels wind down her rutted driveway. Then he was off, trail-ing a plume of dust around the first bend and out of sight. Mary was far more devastated than she thought she would allow herself to be. She tried everything in her power to suppress the glimmer of hope that he would ever return.

About that time, Mary started seeing a strange dog in the field beyond the garden where she dug carrots and parsnips. Other times it would be along the stone wall at the foot of the orchard, where she'd use a hooked pole to shake down the dark red Baldwins and nearly black Oxfords to be bagged up and sold to Hutchins's cider mill. Usu-ally this chocolate-colored dog was hunting mice like a fox. Mary watched as the dog moved along the wall, her head down her and ears forward. Suddenly she'd stop, cock her head one way, then the other, then in an arching leap she would pounce, usually trapping the field mouse between her paws. The dog would dispatch the rodent with a quick bite, toss it in the air, catch it in her mouth, crunch it once or twice, and swallow. When not hunting, the dog would lie in the sun a respectful distance off, her head up, watching Mary attentively. Since she appeared in good condition and didn't skulk around like most stray dogs Mary had seen, she figured the dog must belong to one of the several farms along the road.

One late October afternoon Mary was setting lids on a batch of halved Bartlett pears when she heard a commotion from the vicinity of the henhouse. Most of the fencing had long ago collapsed, and Mary preferred the hens having the run of the place, anyway. Well before twilight the flock would always gravitate back to the dusty yard in front of the coop, where Mary would coax them inside and close them in for the night.

Now a cacophony of squawks, murderous shrieks, and flapping wings was turning the usually peaceful hen yard into a maelstrom, and the chocolate bitch was right in the midst of it. Mary grabbed a hoe leaning alongside the back door and lit out with only one thought in her head—to save her precious hens. Before she covered half the distance to the henhouse, a desperate fox she hadn't at first seen erupted from the cloud of billowing dust and feathers and shot over the sagging chicken wire in one corner of the pen, his eyes white with fear and saliva streaming from the corners of his mouth. Right behind him, spitting a wad of fox fur from her mouth, was the mysterious dog, an expression of fearsome determination in her golden eyes. Twice before they reached the edge of the woods, the dog latched onto the tail of the dodging fox causing the creature to tumble, but each time the dog's own momentum sent her rolling right over her quarry and the fox was first on its feet and off in a slightly different direction. In half a minute they both disappeared into the gloom of the ground hemlocks and pine.

"Land sakes alive!" said Mary, shaking her head. "Here I was worrying about the stray bothering my biddies and all the time she's been watching out for that old fox."

The dog didn't show up again until the next morning, when Mary found her lying expectantly next to the empty tin bowl she'd set out for her the night before filled with rich milk and cream from old Bessie the Jersey.

As the hard edge of November took over October's spot on top of the ridge, and skim ice formed most nights along quiet bends in the stream, an occasional pickup truck stuffed with hunters in plaid wool jackets prowled slowly along the road, the occupants scanning the fields for an easy shot at a deer. Once in a while, around twilight, this lazy strategy proved successful and Mary would hear one or two shots from down toward Simeon's place, and a half hour or so later the truck would come swinging back by the foot of the drive with the feet or antlers of a deer sticking over the sides of the bed, just visible in the gloom. In their exuberance, if the hunters saw Mary's porch light, they'd honk the truck's horn to announce their success. Mary had lived among these men all her life and so had come to accept this violent rite of autumn, but she could never approve of it.

The chocolate dog stayed around and Mary left milk out for her, along with meat scraps from the kitchen, which weren't plentiful since Mary seldom ate meat these days. Sometimes she'd cook an egg for the dog, and she'd begun to call her Maggie after a school chum she'd had in the fourth and fifth grades, before the girl had moved with her family to Pennsylvania. Mary had at first been a little concerned that the dog would bother her old yellow tomcat Vincent—so named because he was missing most of an ear when he first turned up at the farm—but the two appeared to tolerate one another with mutual respect and indifference.

Maggie was a tall, lean dog of perhaps fifty pounds with a short sleek coat that looked like the color of milk chocolate at first glance. But in the dramatic light of a late autumn afternoon, her coat rippled in shades between honey gold and glossy black. She had matching white stockings on all four feet, a diamond-shaped white patch on her chest, a white tip on her tail, and a thin white blaze running between her wide-set eyes, from her knobby crown halfway down her long, thin muzzle. Mary thought she recognized an intelligent, rather thoughtful expression in her countenance, which seemed to be borne out in her behavior. Maggie seemed always to be watching things, not in a casual way, but with intense curiosity, as though actually studying them. Despite the milk and scraps she tentatively accepted, she seemed most content when she was hunting mice along the edges of the fields and around the farm's collapsing sheds and outbuildings.

Maggie would wag her tail slowly whenever Mary petted her, and although she would venture into the house for a few minutes if invited, she preferred spending nights outside. With November's heavy frosts and early snows, she moved into a corner of the barn next to Bessie's box stall, and slept curled up on an old quilt Mary had spread out on a nest of sweet-smelling hay.

———

The cold April rain pelted the tin roof of the sugar shed, and outside the last defiant patches of rotten snow were shrinking into oblivion. Mary tossed a few broken branches into the firebox beneath the evaporating pans to keep their sweet contents rolling in an easy boil. Clouds of steam rose from the bubbling surface and escaped through gaps in the shed's porous walls or condensed into heavy droplets on the inside of the tin roof. Vincent slept curled up next to one end of the huge stove and Maggie next to the other.

"That's just about the last of the fuel," Mary remarked, wiping her brow with an old dish towel. "Good thing the sap's about stopped running or I'd feel obliged to scrounge up some more."

Will Richardson's wife, Claire, leaned against a narrow bench that held a motley collection of capped whiskey bottles, each now filled with rich amber syrup. "Looks like you've done really well for the late start this year," she offered. Then, smiling, she added, "I'd be more afraid you would run out of whisky bottles."

Mary flushed even though she knew Claire was just teasing her. "You know darn well it's not me drinks all the whiskey. It's a lucky thing Winnie Taylor works at the hotel and saves me all these empties from the bar." Then she giggled, "Wish just once she'd bring one over had a little of the original contents left in it!"

"Not likely, knowing Winnie," Claire laughed. "No doubt she sucks them empty with a straw if there's any trace left a' tall."

Claire Richardson, was Mary's one true friend. Without pitying Mary's circumstances she helped out whenever she could, bringing by an "extra" apple pie, some cuttings or bulbs for Mary's growing perennial garden, or a flat or two of pansies. Knowing that Mary loved reading as much as she did, Claire loaned her the latest books from her book club as soon as she finished them, and the two would discuss each thoroughly over tea in Mary's kitchen or in Claire's parlor whenever they got the chance. Claire's life was very comfortable at the Richardsons' prosperous farm. The only thing that kept it from approaching perfection was the couple's inability to have children. It was a glaring rent in the otherwise rich fabric of their marriage, and it was one with which Mary, never having had the chance to bear children herself, could well empathize.

"That's a nice dog you have there, Mary. She seems real smart. Will likes it when she comes over to our place and catches mice around the silo. What's her name, again?"

"Oh, I call her Maggie, I guess. Not *my* dog really, but she's made this her home since last fall and nobody's come looking for her."

"She comes over some days and visits our old dog, Bull. He's getting arthritis quite bad and doesn't get around much these days. They seem to like sitting together. By the way, Mary, Will tells me that John Brighton's back in town."

Mary, who'd been taking clean bottles out of a box, nearly dropped one as she turned quickly to Claire. "You don't say?" She didn't seem to know where to look.

"Yes, it's true enough." Claire continued. "Will saw him going into the Rusty Nail yesterday with Lenny Chandler. Two of a kind, I'd say."

"You don't say?" Mary repeated distractedly. "Wonder how long John...um..he's been back."

"Just pulled, in according to Will. Something wrong, Mary?" Claire asked.

"No...no, of course not," Mary answered too quickly. "Just tryin' to think how many of these bottles I'm going to need."

"Well, looks like the rain's let up. I'd better run down the path 'fore it starts back up." Then she added, giggling, "Hope I don't slip and fall on my backside! Bye, Mary."

After a pause, "'Bye, Claire," and too late, "Thanks for stopping by and for the books."

It was a long, nearly sleepless night for Mary McCorison. After twisting and turning hopelessly in bed for hours, she ended up in the rocking chair before the kitchen woodstove, finally catching a few brief catnaps. She was still in the chair in her worn chenille bathrobe and flannel nightgown, cobwebs still clouding her thinking, when a knock on the door startled her out of a bleak daydream she'd allowed herself to shrink into.

"Just a minute," she called out to the dark-paneled door. "Who's there, anyways?" Mary wasn't used to morning callers, not since Father LaCroix, who'd come by for an occasional chat and coffee, had left this hardscrabble rural parish for a more important one near Boston.

The door swung open, flooding the room with the brightness of a fresh spring morning. Standing there, backlit by the sunshine, bigger than life and more real than Mary dared believe, was John Brighton. He wore the familiar white shirt and vest and, once Mary's eyes grew accustomed to the daylight, she noticed he was clean-shaven except for a neatly trimmed mustache. In his big left hand was the battered gray fedora, in his right a big bouquet of pastel tulips, and on his ruddy face was a grin from ear to ear.

"You still got that vase I give you last summer, Mary? Hope it's big enough for these babies," he boomed, tipping his head toward the tulips, and stepping forward as if to gather Mary into an embrace.

But Mary shrank back and he stopped. She made a visible effort to gather herself, her pupils shrinking against the flood of light. Then, looking at the worn linoleum, she finally managed to speak.

"John, what a surprise! I mean...it's a surprise to see you here. I haven't heard anything at all...from you. Sit down, please. I'll get dressed." She paused at the door that led up the stairs and looked back at Brighton, the hat and flowers now hanging down on either side. "Them are real lovely tulips, John," she said shyly. Then she fled up the stairs to get dressed and quiet her wildly pounding heart.

Back downstairs, seated across the table from her visitor, drinking tea, and watching John Brighton eat stove-top toast with butter and last summer's blackberry jam, Mary began to regain her composure, and her mood brightened noticeably as he talked.

"Reason you haven't heard from me, Mary, is I've been working my tail off—pardon the expression—down at the shipyard," Brighton explained. "Overtime, holidays, weekends, anything I could get, and just like I said I would, got a little stash we can use to start some serious farmin' and make some real money for both of us."

Mary opened her mouth to respond, but before she could get a word out, he cut her off, adding "Oh I know—same as you—you don't exactly get rich farmin', and I know about hard work, too. But you've got yourself a farm and land here with some real potential. All you need is a little capital and a partner to help get the work done and start the place bringing in a little income.

"Mary McCorison, I'm thinking we gotta team up here and get this farm of yours back up into the condition your father—bless his soul—left it in."

It was a convincing argument in many ways, and Mary was in no position to dismiss any proposal that might end up saving the farm. This was surely the first time anyone had offered to invest capital along with promised work. And she had to admit that, even as jaded as she was about romantic entanglements and for good reasons, she did not find this rough yet handsome and ebullient man unattractive.

Brighton ended up staying on for a midday dinner of parsnips and most of a roasted chicken Mary had reluctantly culled from the flock when she was expecting Fanny Longel to join her for their annual Easter dinner. But Fanny had failed to make the trip out from town because of her health, and most of the chicken had gone uneaten.

"There's nothing in the whole world better'n roasted chicken, 'less, of course, that's leftover roasted chicken, and that's the truth," Brighton declared, and the way he was attacking the carcass and wolfing down the pickings made it obvious he spoke sincerely. Mary had planned on some nice scraps the next couple of days for Maggie and Vincent, but it was clear there'd be nothing left but bones.

"Skin's the best part," he added, sucking down the greasy membrane like a starving wolf.

Brighton said he had $300 with him—hardly a fortune—but he

had left another $750 with a friend back in Portsmouth who had let him in on a real estate deal. According to the contract, Brighton would collect an even thousand in May, when the deal closed.

"Not bad, huh? Thirty-three percent interest on my money in just over two months, and just in time for plantin' season. But there's a pile a work to do before we'll be doin' any plantin'—that is, if you want to give this a try."

All afternoon they talked about the possibilities and drank enough tea to drown a cow. Mary was at first uneasy when Brighton asked to use the bathroom. She was unaccustomed to sharing her private facilities with a man, but Brighton made himself so obviously at home her shyness and embarrassment seemed to melt away.

His plan was to first get the old Case tractor on the place into shape, confidently claiming he was good with machines. When the fields immediately around the house dried out enough, he'd plow up five or six acres for sweet corn and tomatoes. "We'll have to use a commercial grower to start the tomato seedlings this year, but if this works half as good as I'm thinking, we can build our own greenhouse in the fall."

"You really think so, John?"

"Yessiree, Mary. You got sweet land here, and you're high enough up on the ridge, the late spring frosts won't touch us like them down in the valley. Same with the first freeze in the fall. Plantin' early and pickin' late, that's the key to makin' money with tomatoes, yessiree."

The second part of his plan didn't sit as well with Mary. Brighton suggested overhauling the mowing machine and cutting the thick clover hay growing in the fields to the east. For now they could hire someone to bale the hay and then sell it. There were always farmers willing to buy really good hay.

"There's a problem with that plan, John," Mary finally forced herself to speak up. "Will Richardson and his father have been buildin' up those fields for seven or eight years now, and they take the hay and pay me for half. It's how I've been payin' the taxes and lights, mostly."

Brighton's mouth was set in a grim line of disapproval as he asked, "And just how long is this contract in effect, Mary?"

"Friends and neighbors 'round here don't need written contracts when they make an agreement, John. Them fields were goin' all to thistles and milkweed when the Richardsons started cuttin'. They couldn't even use the hay for heifers the first couple years. There'd been nothin' I could do about it. Now it's about the best hay in the county."

"Harrumph," Brighton puffed, clearly still irritated, but in no position to be anything but diplomatic. "Well, that's that, I guess. We're gonna have enough work without hayin' for a while, anyways. There's work to do on the barn roof and underpinnings for sure. And in the fall I got firewood to cut for us—er, you—here and maybe a few cords to sell for winter money."

Mary still found it hard to believe anyone would be making plans to stick with her that far in advance. For supper she cooked up a pan of fresh eggs and baked a batch of biscuits. Brighton made little effort to contain his appetite or his enthusiasm for fresh country food.

That evening when Mary walked out onto the porch with her visitor to see him off, Venus and the first bright stars of the lengthening evenings had already burned through the cerulean membrane stretched above them. In the fields out back a male woodcock was performing his spectacular aerial antics in a last-ditch effort to attract a mate with all the *breeping,* spiraling, and singing he could muster.

As Brighton descended the rickety wooden steps, Maggie, who was sitting off to the side in the shadows, emitted a low, guttural growl. Startled, the man missed the last step, stumbled, and nearly fell.

"Jesus! Where'd that come from?" He whirled to face the dog, who had not moved, though her upper lip remained curled as she issued another low growl.

"Maggie!" Mary yelled, ending the growl instantly. "What's got into you anyway? You never growl at anybody. This here's John, and we're going to be partners runnin' the farm." She smiled nervously at John while she petted the dog.

"Since when did you get a dog?" He didn't take his eyes off Maggie, but slowly the hand that was raised to strike came down.

"Oh, Maggie's been here since last fall, John. She's real good at catching mice."

"I'd be worried for my hens, if it were me. Well, good night, Mary. I'll be out in the morning to look over that tractor. Course I'll keep my room in town, just like I said." He lowered another suspicious glare at Maggie, then walked to his car and got in.

Mary watched the taillights bounce down the twisting drive. Brighton gunned the engine to blast through the muddy ruts at the foot of the hill just before the intersection with the road. Without slowing, the Plymouth wheeled onto the hard gravel, spun its tires, and shot off down the road.

In a confused mixture of elation, weariness, relief, and uncertainty, Mary went back inside to face the mess left by three hurriedly prepared meals, too much talk, and Brighton's signature untidiness at the table. He'd made no mention of lending a hand cleaning up, and Mary had to clear and wash, as well as cook and serve. Now the top of the stove, the sink, and the sideboard were piled high with just about every pot, pan, dish, and cup Mary owned. Vincent crouched above the dishpan licking up the last bits of chicken on Mary's dinner plate. The exhausted woman added kindling to the nearly cold firebox and poured water into the big pot on the black-lidded surface to heat for washing.

The next morning Mary went out at 6:30 to feed the hens and collect eggs and was surprised when Brighton rolled in to begin work on the tractor. Maggie barked and growled furiously as he got out of the car, and Mary had to jerk her back by the scruff of the neck and order her to be quiet.

"She's not used to having company this early, John. I'm sure she'll be gettin' used to seein' you."

"That bitch needs to learn her place, I can see that." He opened the unlocked trunk, which sprung open at a crazy angle, and took out a greasy metal tray of tools. To Mary's surprise and mild disappointment he declined breakfast.

"Already ate, thanks just the same, Mary. I'd best get started on that relic you call a tractor, if we're gonna plant anything this spring."

At noon he downed three apple butter sandwiches, a quart of Bessie's rich milk, and coffee, leaving black oily smudges on everything he touched. "Nothin' better'n good, rich Jersey milk," he opined, and then followed with a hearty belch.

"Goodness!" Mary jumped, then collected herself. "About the last of it for a bit, I'm afraid. Bessie'll be drying up and should produce another beautiful calf this summer."

"That's the trouble with havin' just one cow, Mary. In dry times there just isn't any fresh milk." He seemed to be blaming Mary for this circumstance. He got up, belched again, and headed into town to get parts.

Three days later he had everything rebuilt, cleaned, and installed, and was ready to start the antique. Despite a lot of fancy handwork and a fair amount of cussing, all he got from the recalcitrant old machine were a few oily coughs. On Friday the tractor actually started, although once put into gear it covered only fifteen feet before hesitating and dying.

Brighton continued work Saturday morning and in a moment of triumph maneuvered the old Case around the driveway several times, but the staccato roar of the engine and the black smoke billowing from the exhaust did not fill Mary with confidence regarding the tractor's reliability. John, on the other hand, was pleased as could be with the progress, and obviously with himself, as well, judging by the way he beamed at the machine and at Mary.

"Well, Mary, there you go! We're in business for sure. This old thing's got lots of life left in it. Just need to let it run for a bit to clear itself out."

Brighton jerked the knobless shift lever out of gear, grinding the gears in the process, and jumped off the snorting, rocking beast. He shoved a flat rock under the left rear tire, dusted off his hands on the filthy bib of his overalls, and approached Mary.

"This calls for a celebration, Mary. When's the last time you had dinner at the hotel, huh? Probably can't remember. Well, tonight we're dinin' in style, partner—steak in the Stagecoach dinin' room, and it's on John Brighton."

To punctuate the proclamation, the old Case coughed, spit out a wad of clotted black motor oil, wheezed, and fell silent.

Mary wore her one decent dress, organdy with a full skirt printed with a flower pattern on a plum background. It had been years since she'd eaten in the hotel's restaurant and she was at once relieved and proud when Brighton came down from his room scrubbed clean, hair greased and combed back, wearing a clean white shirt and pressed tweed trousers held up by leather suspenders. He ordered a double whiskey for himself and a glass of white wine for Mary—against her protests. He teased the youngish waitress a little too familiarly for Mary's comfort and ordered steak, mashed potatoes with gravy, and peas for them both.

"Man's gotta eat somethin' besides just pancakes, apple butter, and parsnips if he's gonna keep workin' everyday," he proclaimed in obvious reference to the meals Mary had served—which he had consumed at the time with relish if not actual gluttony. The comment stung Mary like a yellow jacket, at once minimizing and deprecating her tremendous efforts in the hot kitchen to provide this ungrateful bottomless pit with wholesome, tasty, and nourishing meals with what little resources she had available.

Brighton had another whiskey with his meal and when Lenny Chandler happened by, invited him to join them and ordered two more. Mary had never cared much for Lenny, who supposedly worked at his father's spool mill. Everyone knew he was kept around the establishment just enough so folks wouldn't say he drew his salary without even stepping into his office. His serious-minded father had little use for him and would probably have paid him just about anything if Lenny would just pack up and head out for parts unknown. Chandler was the worst kind of slacker for a man like Brighton to get involved with. He had time on his hands, money in his pocket, and a sense of entitlement to do anything he felt like doing because of the importance of the mill to the local economy. And although Lenny was quite dense when it came to understanding even rudimentary principles of worthwhile endeavors, he was diabolically clever, even gifted, when it came to dreaming up any kind of trouble.

Brighton was making a mess of eating his apple pie, and was paying much closer attention to the whiskey bottle he'd had brought over than he was to his dessert or to Mary.

Embarrassed and desperate, Mary fled to the ladies' room. A few minutes later Claire Richardson stepped in. Claiming an upset stomach, Mary asked if she and Will might drive her home.

Back in the dining room Brighton was too drunk and too engaged in talking nonsense with Lenny to really care. He tried standing, but fell clumsily back into his chair, mumbling.

"Be glad t' drive you home, honey, soon's I have jes' one more little drink with Lenny here. Right, Lenny? His daddy owns 'bout half this town, don'cha know." All the while he smiled idiotically with a big wad of apple pie stuck to the corner of his mustache.

"You and Lenny enjoy yourselves. I got a little upset in my stomach and Claire here's going right by the house, anyway. Thank you for the dinner, John. It was real delicious." She turned, wishing she was invisible, and joined the Richardsons at the door.

Brighton drove out Sunday afternoon, sober, clean, his hair combed. "Guess Lenny and I got a little carried away last night at the restaurant," was as close as he could come to an apology. Mary fed him a ham dinner, which he downed voraciously, and Monday morning he was back at work. Later in the week he returned from town with most of a new plow projecting from the cavernous trunk of the Plymouth, the lid bouncing wildly as he rumbled up the drive, the inside of the wheel wells rubbing on the tires. He announced he'd ordered enough sweet corn seed for six or seven acres, plus three thousand Red Valiant tomato seedlings from the grower.

"Goodness, John, sounds like a lot of money to me, especially with the plow. I didn't know you had that much."

"Well, Mary, I don't. But I'll have plenty in a few weeks when I drive down to Portsmouth. Meantime your credit's good enough at the Seed and Feed for now."

Mary's eyes widened appreciably at this news and her jaw actually dropped open, but she was cut off from expressing her distress.

"You see, Mary, we're partners and if this is gonna work we both need to take some small risks. I went and bought this plow for your tractor with my money, don't forget. Without the plow we can't plant crops. And without the corn seed and tomato seedlings we don't have any crop."

"I guess that's true enough, John, but I wish we'd discussed the details a little before you went ahead and used the farm's credit, which is thin enough as it is."

"Your father's name still counts for somethin' 'round here, Mary, and I'm certain he'd be glad to see you'll be farmin' the land again."

May was working its emerald magic on the hilly farm country. The new grass was sprouting a brilliant yellow-green, warblers and thrushes of all varieties were celebrating the season in song amid the new poplar and birch leaves, and red buds were bursting in the maples. Mary was busy reclaiming more of the old kitchen garden for the anticipated increased demands. Vincent took delight and repose in every nook that received the strengthening sun's warming light. Maggie sought the sunshine just as eagerly only selecting her napping spots more carefully, and whenever Brighton came near she would silently disappear.

Adapting the secondhand plow to the old tractor was more challenging than Brighton had expected, and figuring in the frequent trips to town for this and that, it ate up more than a week. When it was finally operable he couldn't wait to get out on the fields. The first day he turned over three acres of neglected field behind the barn. It was certainly not a perfect job. The brush should have been cleared first, and as the blade scraped through the tangle, rocks broke the plow tip three times. But even that didn't dampen his enthusiasm.

Over the next three days, between frequent stops for repairs, Brighton managed to turn over five more acres before hopelessly burying the rig in the wet ground along the lower stone wall with its ever-widening belt of scrub. Mary feared he had snapped when he came rushing into the house red-faced, breathing hard, and covered with mud. The last thing she expected from this fierce yet irresistible man was a proposal of marriage.

Claire Richardson found Mary in Bessie's box stall brushing the contented Jersey with an old currycomb. Vincent crouched over a small pan of yellow cream singing while he licked up the treat, his tongue moving too fast to actually see. It was the last bit of milk Bessie would be producing until she calved in June her September visit to Will Richardson's bull obviously fruitful. Maggie got up and wagged her tail while Claire scratched her ears.

"Maggie here's a real wonder," Claire began. "Will was havin' a devil of a time with two heifers that kept breakin' down the fence and gettin' into the next field that's got plenty of fresh grass, but isn't nearly dried out. Maggie watched Will and Andy—he's the new hired boy—tryin' to get them back into their pasture and figured it out. Will says she'd catch up to a heifer and bite her ankle just hard enough to show 'er she meant business. Then she'd herd her right back to where it broke out. Did that a couple times and those heifers been stayin' put ever since."

Claire looked shocked when Mary announced her engagement. As a true friend she had to confess that she really didn't trust John Brighton. But since Mary knew him better and was willing to take the step, Claire said she would be happy to stand up for her at the simple ceremony, even though it was unusual—Claire being married and all.

"I can't say I don't wish it was someone else, Mary, but I guess you know your own heart and circumstances. I'd be happy to help you get ready, and I'll be there by your side when you exchange your vows. 'Course I will, Mary."

Mary knew her circumstances, all right, and it was not great expectations but rather a desperate glimmer of hope that was propelling her forward.

While the lower fields continued to dry out, Brighton had driven down to the coast to collect his share of the so-called real estate investment. When he returned, supposedly with a thousand dollars in cash in his pocket, there'd be a simple ceremony at Harlan Ricker's, the justice of the peace. Attending besides the couple would be Will and Claire Richardson; Lenny Chandler, as the best man; Mary's sister,

Ginny, from outside Boston; and Ginny's daughter, Annette. After the ceremony everyone would have dinner at the hotel. Brighton would gather up his things, and he and his bride would drive out to the farm for a one-day honeymoon before resuming work on Monday.

Mary wondered if Brighton would really come back from Portsmouth at all, and if he did, would actually have the money he'd talked about. A part of her almost wished he wouldn't return, because more and more Mary McCorison was getting the feeling she was in over her head.

Thursday night the heavens opened and a cold heavy rain began drenching the countryside and everything in it. By noon Friday Brighton was three days late and the wedding was scheduled for the next day. Lenny had gone with him to Portsmouth, and it was easy to imagine the two on a bender if the money was really there, or even the two of them on a purposeless trip across country, living high and wild until the money was gone.

Mary was beside herself in restless anxiety and true disappointment, and nothing Claire, Ginny, or Annette could say would console her. Once again she had allowed herself to believe in what for her was a miracle—that a man would want her and be willing to share with her the happy and hard times of life—and once again that trust was proving to be misplaced, and the vision an illusion.

Annette was as distraught as Mary herself. A lovely twenty-year-old with golden curls yet a dark complexion, and eyes like black diamonds, she had a smile that could melt an iceberg. She was strongly attached to her aunt, although they'd never really spent much time together. She worried about Mary living alone on the dilapidated farm and wrote to her frequently. The wedding was nearly as important to Annette as it was to Mary.

The rain let up about mid-afternoon on Friday, and to escape the gloom and sadness permeating the dark parlor, Annette went back outside for another walk with her newest close companion. She and Maggie had formed a close attachment at once, and the two became inseparable, walking the property as often as they could manage it. A roar at the foot of the drive caught her attention and a mud-spattered, faded green pickup wheeled in, spun up the slick driveway, and slewed to a stop abreast of them. The driver's window disappeared into the door to reveal a ruddy, mustached face, which then leaned out with a wide smile and uncomfortable leering gaze.

"Well, well, if it ain't Goldilocks, all growed up and pretty as a picture. Now, don't tell me—you're Mary's niece from Beverley— ah—Nanette, right? Or maybe you're Little Red Ridin' Hood and that's the low-down, thievin' wolf next to you," indicating Maggie, who turned away with a low growl and slunk away.

"I'm John—that'll be Uncle John after tomorrow—and this here's my buddy, Lenny." Brighton jerked a thumb back at the shadowed figure in the passenger seat. "Gonna be my best man tomorrow at the weddin', he is. Lenny's father owns about half this town, ya know."

The tension inside the house for the next couple of hours was palpable, as Brighton bulled his way into the dreary gathering and explained the car trouble they'd had and the delay getting the money because the buyer's check had to clear. Claire excused herself at the first opportunity and Ginny tried her best to keep Mary from accepting all this without protest and anger.

The groom-to-be pulled a small white box from his vest pocket, removed the top, and handed it to Mary. Inside was a heart-shaped gold locket on a chain, and inside the locket, of all things, was a picture of Christ, with sad dreamy eyes and a glowing halo. An odd gift from a man like Brighton, especially since Mary wasn't big on organized religion herself. But on the back in tiny characters was the inscription: "To Mary, my beautiful bride, Love, John."

Pleased with himself, Brighton smiled at Mary. "Never did buy you a proper engagement ring, Mary, but maybe this'll hold you until I can slip this weddin' band on your finger tomorrow," he said and produced a blue velvet box from his shirt pocket. Apparently, the wedding was still on for the next day so Ginny and Annette excused themselves to prepare dinner in the kitchen.

"That Annette's sure a pretty girl," Brighton commented, nodding toward the kitchen door. "How come she's not hitched to some rich guy, a lawyer or something?"

"Annette's a student at Vassar College," Mary responded proudly. "Got herself a full scholarship, she did, and in a year or so she'll be graduating with a degree in archeology. Isn't that something?"

"Archeology? Seems like a royal waste of time and money to me. Young woman that good lookin' should latch onto a rich husband and start raisin' a family."

Annette came in from the kitchen with a steaming pot roast, which she set down hard before Brighton, silencing him instantly. Then, standing up straight and looking him in the eye, she said, "There are other interests for women in this world, Mr. Brighton, besides marrying the first dull man that comes along so he can keep her doing his laundry and tending babies the rest of her life, and I intend to explore those alternative possibilities."

With that she turned on her heel and pushed open the kitchen door, nearly toppling her mother, who was on her way to the dining room with the mashed potatoes.

"John," Mary asked quietly, after the dinner dishes were cleared and Ginny and Annette were in the kitchen preparing dessert, "Whose truck is that outside?"

"That's mine, Mary. Like I told you, the car just up and quit and fixin' it was out of the question. Besides, we'll need a pickup 'round this place if we're gonna farm it."

"I'm almost afraid to ask, but how much did it cost, John?"

"Well, a thousand dollars, Mary, but I told him we were puttin' in crops, so he let me take it with $550 down, and the rest in the fall."

"So you brought back $450?"

"Well, a week of livin' in the city, new shirt and pants for the weddin', locket and weddin' band for the bride, let's say I still got two hundred somethin'...."

"Two hundred dollars, John? That's...."

But Ginny was just coming in with the rhubarb pie and Mary's concerns had to wait.

Mary was married in the simple white dress Claire had given her. It had been worn only once, when Claire's sister graduated from high school. Claire had to take it in some here and there so it wouldn't hang too badly on Mary's thin frame. Mary was more challenged trying to keep the wedding ring from sliding off her finger onto the floor. It had a masculine heft to it and would probably have fitted the boxer, Joe Lewis. The pouring rain continued, and just getting into the cars at the justice's house and then running from the cars to the hotel restaurant were enough to soak everyone to the skin.

The wedding dinner was, at best, inauspicious. The hotel had lost the dinner reservations, and when the soaking party arrived late Saturday afternoon, there were no tables available. The manager apologized and ushered them into the bar to wait, which helped the groom and best man get off to a bad start. Dinner—which was chicken, since the steaks that had been pre-ordered had disappeared along with the reservations—was complemented by a champagne toast, but Brighton and his cohort supplemented this with a fresh bottle of whiskey.

The effects of the liquor became apparent as the pair's stories became increasingly lewd and hard to follow, and Brighton began leaning on and pawing at Annette, who held her seat next to the drunk only out of love and respect for her Aunt Mary. From the bride's point of view, the ordeal could not possibly end soon enough, and she would have happily foregone the cake if by some chance it had been misplaced along with the other arrangements. But it had not, and Mary had to endure the ludicrous sharing of the first piece with her new husband.

As the sorry dinner was concluding, the Reverend and Mrs. Daniel Phillips from the Methodist Church came by the table to pay their respects to the bridal couple. Attired in a well-pressed suit that looked as though it might have been presentable forty years before, the disturbingly thin clergyman first offered Mary their sincere best wishes, adding only that they were disappointed it had not been a church wedding.

Turning to the groom, the minister said, "You are indeed a fortunate man, Mr. Brighton. Today you have married a very fine woman."

"What I've married today, Reverend," Brighton retorted, slowly releasing each syllable so as not to slur, "is a very fine damn farm." And at that he and Lenny burst into a roaring fit of laughter.

Speechless at this response, the horrified Phillipses nodded to Mary and quickly withdrew.

When at last things reached a point so unpleasant and ridiculous that continuing was out of the question, Will Richardson excused himself and walked over to the cashier to settle up as previously arranged. As he turned to go back to the table and rescue Claire, he found Brighton right in his face.

"Listen, pal," Brighton hissed. "I know how you've been cuttin' our hay, keepin' it all and givin' Mary a few cents a bale for her half, which she never even counts...."

"Forty cents a bale, just like anyone else," Will interjected evenly.

"Well, that don't sound like much to me, mister." Brighton's sweaty red face and whiskey breath were too close for comfort. "This year it's gonna be different. This year I'm keepin' my share. I can sell it for twice that with no trouble, a'tall."

Will Richardson kept silent. He glared intensely into Brighton's eyes and the drunk gradually withdrew his face a few inches. Then Will said quietly, "Well, it appears like we'll have something to talk about another time, doesn't it? Right now I'm fetching Claire and driving her home. I suggest you do the same with your bride, Mr. Brighton."

In the longest night of her life, Mary McCorison—now Mary Brighton—learned exactly how loathsome and inconsiderate a brute can be when, half drunk, he insists on exercising his full rights as a husband. Before two weeks had passed she began to recognize the scope of her mistake, and how far in over her head she really was.

The last week of May, while Mary worked feverishly to get in an extra-large kitchen garden, "Buckshot" Wade from the Seed and Feed turned up with three thousand tomato seedlings, a hundred bags of fertilizer, and a sizable bill Mary could only sign. Brighton was in town, picking up parts for the worn-out farm equipment as well as avoiding the real work.

He had managed to plow about eight acres of rich but rough land, which was close to what he had planned. The problem was that much of it was not turned nearly enough and was rolling back in big clots into its former bed, and the disk harrow was not up to the task of finishing the job, no matter how many times it was dragged and bounced over the ridges. Brighton had gotten about half of it flat enough to consider plantable, but there was still a lot of grass sticking up like spiny islands on a rolling sea.

On half of the plantable area he started planting corn in rows less than straight. The old seed planter neither scratched the trenches deep enough nor covered the seeds sufficiently, and it was Mary's bone-jarring lot to ride the bucking relic behind the tractor. Her task, amid a blizzard of dust and choking gasoline fumes, was to feed buckets of the sticky purple crow-tarred kernels into the hopper. The better part of the corn seed still lay under a hole-ridden tarp at the field's edge, where it overheated, soaked up moisture, and moldered, while the ground that had been "prepared" for it grew slowly back to grass and weeds.

The acre and a half for the tomatoes was equally ill prepared and the tedious work of setting the seedlings by hand did not suit Brighton in the least. Right after breakfast he and Mary would set out together at the start of adjacent rows, and work steadily for the first hour, with Mary's seedlings going in more evenly spaced and more firmly set. An hour later Mary would be half a row ahead. By eleven, and at least a row and a half behind, Brighton would abruptly quit and head into town for "parts and supplies." Skipping lunch altogether, Mary would plant another three rows before checking on Bessie who was due to calve sometime soon. After starting bread rising, Mary would hand-carry water to the thirsty new seedlings in their fresh mounds of sweet earth.

Halfway through the planting a drizzle started in the afternoon, heralding eight full days of light showers punctuated by occasional heavy rain. Nearly half of the fifteen hundred seedlings already in the ground were drowned. In a desperate push as soon as the ground dried, Mary, working mostly alone, managed to replace about half of those lost before time ran out and other priorities and emergencies demanded her attention. For one thing, most of the expensive fertilizer, left uncovered in its heavy paper sacks, received a thorough soaking and dried hard as cement. Brighton spent a morning cursing, swatting black flies, and pulverizing the rocklike slabs with a sledgehammer. Some of the resulting pebble-strewn powder was scooped up by Mary and distributed to the tomatoes. But another hard rain a few days later drove much of the remaining pile of the chemical into the ground, where it burned a large bare circle in the surrounding grass.

Mary was aware that Claire only visited now when Brighton had gone to town, but she didn't feel much like talking anyway, and always dodged Claire's questions about her situation. The flower seedlings Claire brought over seldom got planted, and the books piled up next to Mary's end of the sofa unread. Even Maggie was mostly ignored these days, and spent most of her time either beneath an old maple near the stone wall or visiting Bull, the Richardsons' aging dog.

One bright day in late June the black flies that had so proliferated during the wet spell finally thinned out a little and a rare breeze was keeping the survivors more or less at bay. Mary, looking thinner and more tired and distracted each week, was actually making some progress against the weeds that had begun choking her peas, green beans, and summer squash plants. Brighton, last she'd seen him, was in typical desultory fashion slashing away at the witch grass that appeared to be swallowing the corn.

Mary eventually awakened from her thoughts when Bessie's constant bawling intruded. The Jersey had produced a fuzzy golden bull calf a few days before, and this uncharacteristic mooing was impossible to ignore once it had penetrated Mary's consciousness.

"Can't imagine Bess needs more fresh grass," she mused. "Gave her two pitchforks full just before startin' here. Well, maybe she's spilt her water bucket or the calf's somehow gotten under the blamed fence!"

Rising slowly from her knees, she walked toward the barn. The sight that greeted her as she rounded the corner stopped her in her tracks, and she had to grab onto a fencepost with both hands to keep from collapsing.

There, and in full view of the wildly agitated cow, Brighton had strung up the brown-eyed golden calf by its hind legs and had slit its throat. Now, as the crimson pool that had formed beneath the calf's pink snout began to shrink into the dirt, he was peeling the split hide from the tiny haunches.

"John," Mary whispered, hoarsely at first. Then louder, "John, whatever have you done? And why, John? And right in front of poor Bessie? How...."

"You got a problem with veal, Mary?" Brighton shot back more loudly than necessary. "Well, I don't—and we don't need no hungry bull calf suckin' up all the milk and eatin' grass that could be cut and sold."

"But John, we have all summer. He could've had a summer with Bessie, then in the fall he'd provide lots more meat."

"You tellin' me my business, Mary?" he said, glaring into her averted eyes. "'Cause this ain't your farm no more, remember. We're married now, and what's yours is now mine. That understood, Mary?"

She could think of no reply. In fact, she could barely think at all.

"Good. Then you dig up some of them beet greens you been hidin' in that precious garden of yours, and we'll have ourselves a right feast tonight." He turned back to the little carcass, and ignoring the obvious distress of both his wife and the Jersey cow, ran his pocket knife down the inside of the calf's other hind leg, and peeled back the pink vessel-mapped hide. Mary turned away in disgust and sorrow while Maggie sat watching from a safe distance. Whenever Brighton came anywhere near her the dog would disappear, but a while later would be studying the behavior of this crude man from a different vantage point, as though preparing to write a book.

That evening Brighton wolfed down his veal, making a big mess while all the time licking his fingers and remarking how good it tasted. Across from him, Mary sipped her tea, ate only a little bread, and said nothing. She couldn't look at her husband as he devoured his meal.

Brighton's appetite was monumental, and fresh roasted chicken was his favorite dinner. Hens had been disappearing from Mary's flock faster than they could be replaced—a serious matter for Mary, who loved her chickens and depended on the egg money for a little income. Nonetheless, she would pluck and dress the smelly carcasses and roast them for her thoughtless husband—who would laugh when she'd suggest he was taking more hens than the flock could bear to lose.

One day he marched in with his filthy boots spattering the fresh-scrubbed floor, blood dripping from the throat of an agate-eyed hen, running off the comb and mixing with the tracked-in mud.

"Oh, John," Mary sighed, tears welling in the corners of her eyes and sliding into the deepening wrinkles. "That hen's been settin' on a nice clutch of eggs, and she's the best brooder in the coop. Couldn't you just have left her alone?"

"This here's the only one I could catch. But don't worry, Mary," he smiled, "I didn't forget the eggs." He held up the worn graniteware bowl filled with sixteen brown eggs that before long would have hatched into a brood of new hope for Mary's decimated flock. "These'll make us a great breakfast tomorrow."

When Mary refused to dress the hen, Brighton made for her as though he was going to strike her, but Mary didn't flinch. Apparently thinking better of it, he grinned to himself, started whistling an indiscernible tune, and commenced ripping out handfuls of auburn feathers, dropping them at his feet.

Around the end of June, Claire and Mary were talking outside the Seed and Feed, while Will and Buckshot loaded hundred-pound sacks of protein mix into the back of Will's pickup truck. Mary was looking thinner and more distracted than ever, and Claire's concern was obvious. However, Mary still had little to say to her friend.

Will finished loading the grain, folded up and chained the tailgate shut, and walked over to the women.

"Afternoon, Mary," he nodded. "Good growin' weather, don't you think?"

"I guess it is, Will. It's growin' plenty of weeds, anyway."

"Them, too," he laughed. "Say, that Maggie of yours is some dog. She's got the mice thinned right down to almost nothing, and we never see a rat on the place anymore. And I tell you, those heifers are all so scared Maggie'll latch onto their ankles, they don't go near the fence."

"She's a good dog all right. I only wish...." Mary cut herself off and visibly tightened as though bracing for a blow. John Brighton, scowling and weaving slightly, a whiskey bottle poking from the bag under his arm, lurched into the conversation.

He ignored Will's greeting, but beamed a leering grin at Claire. "Afternoon, Missus Richardson." Then to Will, "See you're about ready to cut our hay next to the old orchard."

"That's right, I am, John. Just waiting for a clear forecast. Might mow on Thursday, actually."

"Well, don't forget what we talked about. You won't pay better'n forty cents a bale for my half, I'll take 'em myself and sell 'em to someone who'll pay fair."

"Forty cents is about average, John," Will stated calmly, not allowing himself to be drawn in to an argument by this scoundrel.

"Ain't much, seein' you're taking the lion's share, and it's hay cut on my farm to start with. There's some buyers from Vermont payin' a lot better than forty cents, I hear, and I aim to sell to them."

"Suit yourself," Will replied, trying hard to keep things civil.

"And don't go takin' no hay off the field 'fore I get a chance to count it, you hear?"

"Well, if the hay's down and baled, I'm not leaving it in the field begging to get rained on. Now, if you're thinking I'm going to cheat you out of your share, Brighton, then we got a little misunderstanding to sort out."

Will was clearly near the end of his patience. Both men were about the same height, but Brighton had him by about twenty pounds. And Brighton's reputation guaranteed he would fight plenty dirty, if it came to that.

Still, despite his narrow build, Will was hard as iron from practically endless farm and woods work, and Brighton would have to figure this adversary would have tremendous stamina. Where courage was concerned, everyone in the county knew that Will Richardson was a decorated fighter pilot. The story went that he got so involved protecting an advancing column from a squadron of harassing Messerschmitts that he failed to head back to base in time and was forced to bail out of his plane over the English Channel when he ran out of fuel. He was in the water for six hours before being picked up by a British corvette.

If a fight broke out between these two it would be a good one, and there was no predicting the outcome.

Brighton appeared to reconsider his odds and stepped back a little. "'Course I'm not accusin' you of cheatin', Richardson. Not what I meant at all. Just need to know how much hay I'll have to haul is all.... Well, get in the truck, Mary. We got work to do back at the place."

⸺

Once again the faded green pickup bucked and pitched ahead as Brighton tried to keep it from stalling on the grade approaching the farm. The jolt made the hay bales in the truck bed tip backward, quickly becoming an irresistible force despite Mary's efforts to hang onto them. For the third time that afternoon the bales, toppling tier by tier like dominoes, swept the struggling woman off the back of the truck, landing her on her back and nearly burying her.

"Jesus Christ, Mary!" Brighton swung open the windowless door and jumped out of the stalled truck. "You're supposed to hold the goddamn hay in place till the truck's movin'." He pulled off the bales that pinned his wife to the stubbly ground. Two of them broke, causing more swearing. Maggie watched from the nearby stone wall she had just cleared of a nest of field mice.

"Ask for a little help, so's we can get ahead for once, and what do I get?"

"Sorry, John, but the truck just jumped ahead. I tried holdin' the bales, but my shoes kept slippin' on the loose hay."

Brighton said nothing, just threw the unbroken bales back onto the truck. Mary, sore and out of breath, sweating from the exertion under the searing sun, climbed back on. It took all her strength to lift the bales three and four high, starting them with a boost of her thigh. The prickly hay scratched her skin through the threadbare overalls that had been her brother's and were miles too large.

Without another word, Brighton, his jaw set grimly, got back in the truck and again started up, and again the precarious load lurched. But this time Mary held the sweet-smelling wall more or less in place and avoided another avalanche. Brighton stopped the pickup a hundred feet farther along and began gathering the golden green bales of perfect clover hay within reach. One by one he tossed them onto the bed beside Mary, who was now standing precariously on the open tailgate as the loading neared its end.

Brighton, holding a bale by its strings in his left hand, strode a few feet and picked up another, then without warning he let out a hideous yowl. Dropping both bales, he fell backward full length upon the stubble. Mary's thought was "heart attack" and she leaped from the truck and ran toward her husband. But now he was back on his feet, nearly bowling her over in his desperate haste to get clear of something.

"John, what is it?" Then her eye caught movement on the side of one of the bales. The front half of a garter snake was writhing in a futile attempt to extract his crushed back half from between the compacted layers of hay. Apparently the unfortunate reptile had been picked up in a windrow of raked hay by Will Richardson's baler and had somehow survived the compression, only to be half crushed and trapped beyond hope. The gold-rimmed eyes on the bobbing head registered no pain or menace, and the forked tongue still flicked between the black scaly lips.

Brighton was bent over with his hands on his thighs, trying to catch his breath, his face and neck an alarming purplish red. He ordered Mary to drag the bale with its doomed prisoner fifty feet from the truck before he'd get in, then drove the load home minus the last six-bale tier. When they returned for the next load, he skipped the bale with the snake, and a half dozen around it, obviously keeping his distance.

Mary had first seen this phobia of snakes a couple of weeks earlier when she returned from town with Claire to find Brighton dismantling the neat stone wall that came off the back of the summer kitchen. The L-shaped dry wall of flat rocks had been built by Mary's grandfather and formed a little courtyard that Mary had spent years converting into a lovely flower garden. Having been startled by the harmless snakes that found the crannies between the rock inviting, Brighton had decided to eliminate this source of distress without consulting or warning Mary. In one thoughtless hour he had toppled and strewn the product of her grandfather's exacting work and negated the countless hours of planning, planting, and tending that had made the garden such an inviting and uplifting part of Mary's existence.

Now, figuring he'd sell the hay in a day or two anyway Brighton and Mary piled the bales outside the barn, saving the work of throwing it into the mows and stacking it there. The floor in the main bay of the barn sagged hopelessly between the decaying joists, and without a major reconstruction, would not support even a pickup with its load of thirty bales. After three terribly hard days of work, especially for Mary, a huge block of fourteen hundred bales stood dwarfing the former milk house. The straw-colored bales were tinted a subtle green, and even over by the house you could smell the sweet clover.

Exhausted, Mary sat on her porch rocker snapping green beans, worrying that it might rain and ruin all that beautiful hard-won hay before her husband found a dealer for it. Brighton was on the phone in the kitchen, trying to reach a buyer from upstate New York who was in the area buying quality hay for the fancy stables of thorough-breds near Lake George. He slammed the receiver down, flung open the squeaking screen door, which pulled itself closed with a sharp clap, clomped past his wife without a word, and strode toward the leaning outbuilding that had once served the McCorison men as a farm smithy.

The old forge still stood just inside the collapsed door, rusting from the rainwater that routinely poured in through the leaky roof. Brighton and Lenny had recently appropriated the building for their drinking bouts—which happened whenever the latter came wheeling up the drive after supper with a bottle on the seat beside him. No effort was made to hide from Mary or anyone else the growing mountain of empty whiskey bottle piling up outside the glass-less window.

Half an hour later, to Mary's great surprise, a trailer truck pulled up at the foot of the driveway. Two men stepped out and walked up the hill, stopping at the impressive block of hay, then peered inside the barn, no doubt wondering why anyone would risk leaving nice hay outside waiting to get rained on. The men pulled handfuls of the fragrant hay from a couple of the bales, tore it apart in their hands, smelled it, and nodded approval to one another as Mary approached them.

"Afternoon, ma'am," the older of the two offered. "Your husband around?"

"He is, all right," Brighton answered, rounding the corner of the stack a little unsteadily. He glared at Mary. "I'll handle this. You go back in the house and get my supper started. Hay is men's business."

Mary turned from the surprised dealers and walked away, but she stopped out of sight behind the honeysuckle where she could hear the conversation.

Dispensing with any pleasantries, Brighton got right to the point. "This here's damn fine hay, and I need eighty cents a bale if you're interested."

"Well, Mr. Brighton, this is mighty fine hay, all right. You must take good care of your fields. But we couldn't give you over sixty-five cents for it. Remember, we got to truck it all the way to New York and resell it."

"Now, that's not really my concern is it? I don't care if you have to truck the damn stuff all the way to China and back. My price is eighty cents and you can take it or leave it."

"If we don't take it this afternoon, like as not it'll get soaked tonight. Radio says there's a day or two of steady rain coming in. If this hay gets good and wet, nobody'll buy it at any price."

Mary turned around to face the east. Sure enough, the whole eastern sector of blue sky was filling up with mackerel clouds, white around the edges, but already darkening in the thicker areas. She bit her lower lip, and had there been a single drop of moisture in her apron it would have been wrung out, so relentlessly was she twisting it with her bony hands.

Brighton had swallowed a few belts of whiskey in the old smithy and was not in a bargaining mood. "Ain't no rain due around here, mister, or I'dve heard about it. I just talked on the phone to that feller from Vermont, been buying up hay down the valley. He'll be by day after tomorrow, and says he can guarantee me seventy-five cents. A little shower won't bother this hay anyways, way it's stacked so tight."

Before long the dealers from New York gave up and reluctantly started down the drive toward the truck. Mary wanted to yell after them to stop and of course they could have the hay for sixty-five cents. But she knew only too well what the consequences might be for such a rebellion.

Around 10:30 that night, Mary, lying awake next to her snoring, liquor-smelling husband, heard the first drops of rain on the tin porch roof. Ten minutes later it had grown into a deluge loud enough to rouse Brighton from his stupor. He swung his legs out of the iron bed, wove his way to the window, and peered into the darkness outside with his customary scowl. "Jesus Christ," he muttered, then wheeled round and thumped downstairs to the kitchen, where the whiskey bottle with two inches of golden liquid left in it sat on the kitchen table. Alone in the bed, Mary cried quietly and pictured the precious hay getting ruined in the downpour.

It rained hard all night and right through to mid afternoon the next day. Then even when the rain stopped the air was unbearably sticky, and when the sun broke out it set every sodden surface steaming. The following afternoon the dealer from Vermont wanted nothing to do with Brighton's steaming mound of once-premium hay. Enraged, Brighton vehemently insisted he examine the hay two and three layers down from the top. The buyer had his two boys dig out a few sample bales from these depths and made Brighton the only offer he was going to get. The top three layers, plus all the edge bales, were tossed aside, and the crew loaded the half that was left. They paid Brighton forty cents a bale for what they took.

———

Just as Brighton had predicted, theirs were the first tomatoes to ripen in the whole county. And since the new ground seemed to have plenty of nutrients without the wasted fertilizer, even the grass and tall prickly weeds couldn't suppress a good crop on the plants that survived. Grocers and vegetable-stand owners admired the firm red beauties Mary had carefully sorted, polished, and neatly packed into half-bushel wooden boxes. Throughout July they paid Brighton the handsome price of a half dollar a pound each morning when he brought them by, the boxes stacked in two layers in the bed of the pickup. The early sweet corn was meeting with similar approval.

In order to keep up with the crops Mary was up at four each morning cooking her husband's breakfast, and then helping him load the pickup with the tomatoes she'd polished and packed late into the previous evening. After the dishes were done she was out in the field picking tomatoes and sweet corn for the better part of the day. Maggie watched attentively when not hunting and wagged her tail whenever Mary reached the end of a row and stopped to empty the bucket of tomatoes onto the pile. "Nice dog, Maggie," Mary would say, "I just wish you had fingers so you could help me with all this pickin'." And as often as not, she'd stoop to scratch the dog's head on her way out to pick another pail-full.

Brighton would peddle all the produce by noon and invariably went to the hotel for lunch and a few beers. He'd return about mid afternoon and grudgingly finish what little picking was left while Mary made dinner.

After dishes, under the feeble light of a single bulb in the doorway of the connected shed, Mary cleaned and packed tomatoes into wooden boxes for the next morning's deliveries. Brighton normally read the paper and smoked a cigar, carelessly dropping the gray-white ashes on the floor next to his easy chair.

By the first of August other farmers began bringing ripe tomatoes and corn into town and the handsome prices immediately dropped. By mid-August tomatoes that had brought forty-five cents a pound just a month before were going for ten and even five cents. Sweet corn that had been worth ninety cents a dozen was down to fifteen or twenty cents and a farmer was lucky if he could sell all he brought. Rather than expend his energy for such insulting prices, Brighton stopped peddling altogether, content to let the produce—still worth several hundred dollars—rot in the field.

Near the end of August the seasonal cannery on the other side of town offered to buy a truckload—six hundred dozen ears of corn— from Brighton if he could have it picked, bagged, and ready to load in two days. The price was decent enough, considering the market, so he agreed. The temperature was already eighty degrees, with matching humidity, at 6:30 A.M. when Brighton and Mary entered the suffocating rows with their sacks across their shoulders. By 10:00 the temperature was up to 101 degrees and they had about half the corn picked and dumped in a big pile at the end of the field. They would have had more if they hadn't had to plow through the waist-high weeds clogging the lanes between the rows, and if Brighton had gotten around to spraying against the tip borers that had infested the crop, making about half the ears worthless.

Shortly after 10:00, Lenny drove up in a cloud of dust, and Mary knew well what that meant. Sure enough, Brighton opened the passenger door of Lenny's Packard and stepped in.

"Me and Lenny are goin' into town for a couple hours, Mary. You take a break from the heat. We'll be back 'round four and we'll finish up pickin' then." Mary said nothing, but she knew from hard experience the two would not be back till late at night, and Brighton would expect her to have the picking done by then.

At eight that evening Leo Miller from the cannery pulled up the drive in his truck with the big box body, his son, Buddy, following behind in the car. The plan was to leave the truck for Brighton and Mary to load when they got done bagging, but Mary was sitting exhausted and half buried in the sweet mound of corn when Leo walked over.

"Didn't think you was comin' till tomorrow morning, Leo. We haven't started baggin' the corn yet, but as you can see, it's all picked."

"We mean to get an early start tomorrow, Mary, so if it's okay with you, me and Buddy here will start baggin' right now, and we'll drive it on over to the factory tonight."

At that, Buddy climbed slowly out of the cab, unwinding his long frame like a spring, and started helping his father by holding open the bags. Leo nimbly started picking up and counting the ears as he tossed them in.

"Mary, you got any iced tea in the house, we could use some in about an hour," Leo said, insisting she get some rest while they tackled the daunting task that should have been Brighton's.

Although short-lived, the period of selling vegetables was a time of relative prosperity for the farm. But this didn't necessarily mean that the farm's creditors got paid. Each day, Brighton brought home bundles of expensive store-bought groceries, ignoring the bounty of fresh produce in Mary's garden. He was spending lots more time at the hotel bar and patronizing the liquor store. Occasionally he'd return from town with a new purchase for himself, perhaps a half dozen new white shirts.

Until now Mary had always spent enjoyable time at the Seed and Feed, visiting with Buckshot, the proprietor, and his amiable wife. She savored the molasses aroma of the milk-cow grain, and the smell of pungent leather tack. She could lose herself just moving slowly down the neat rows of farm and garden tools, galvanized washtubs, salt blocks, bins of seeds, and pots of flowers. But these days she slipped in like a thief, got her sack of laying mash for the hens with cash, and paid a few dollars on the huge bill Brighton had run up in the spring. Never casting her eyes higher than the countertop, she would quickly leave.

One afternoon Brighton returned from town with, of all things, a RCA console television set. The technology was still very new, and only a handful of homes around had the new-fangled sets to receive the two stations that intermittently cast their waves to hopeful believers. Mary had watched with fascination on occasion in the Richardsons' parlor before Brighton had come along and erased such pleasures from her life.

"I think you need some kind of antenna on the roof, John, if you want to pull in any stations 'round here," she suggested.

"That's how much you know about it," was the hostile response. "These rabbit ears the clerk at Nelson's sold me set right on top of the television and will work just as good as any antenna. You adjust it by moving these things," he said, moving the telescoping wands up and down and back and forth.

Still, the only reception was a whirling charge of white dots across the screen that resembled nothing so much as a blizzard of white locusts accompanied by the roar of deafening static. It seemed to make no difference which channel the dial was tuned to. "Bah, sonofabitch, it's just 'cause it's daylight. This thing's like the radio set. Come evenin' it'll come in clear as can be."

But the reception was no better that evening, and the roaring static was accompanied by a howling that was impossible to bear.

"Maybe it's the set, John," Mary offered softly, barely audible over the roar of the set. "You could bring it back tomorrow and...."

"Bring it back?" Brighton roared, knocking back an inch of whiskey that remained in the tumbler. "I'll bring it back all right, only I'll really give that sonofabitch somethin' to fix! I only put fifty dollars down, and the goddamn thing costs over three hundred." With that he stooped and seized the brick that normally served as a doorstop and shattered the picture tube with a dead-center shot.

A finer early October was difficult to imagine. Near-freezing nights were followed by bracing days with bright blue skies, warm sunshine, and fresh breezes from the northwest. Wild things were clearly on the move. Ragged chevrons of geese winging southward punctuated the sky. Their wingbeats and arresting calls reflected the ageless rhythms and patterns ingrained in all wild things, but conspicuously absent in most humans. Even the field mice were beset by the urgencies of the season, and this spike in activity did not escape Maggie's attention.

With the back ends and tails of two voles already hanging from her mouth, she focused her full attention on some rustling in the tall dried grass that could possibly yield the makings of a rare triple play. Her hunting instincts completely took over and she failed to notice two figures stepping into the break in the stone wall.

An impact like a kick from a horse and a searing pain in her right shoulder and foreleg pitched Maggie over like a dried leaf before the wind, and a concussion like thunder assaulted her ears as she rolled. Instinctively, she got up on her three good legs and vaulted into a thick copse of blackberries, ignoring the agony of her torn hide and muscle and shattered bone. A second load of number six birdshot blew a hole in the spiny stalks, leveling dozens of canes and scattering leaves, all but a few missing the dog. These stung like wasps at the base of her tail. Maggie churned through the tangles that clawed at her bloody hide until she was hidden deep inside the cover, where she lay flat to the ground and kept perfectly still.

"Damn bitch," Brighton laughed. "Too bad this thing wasn't loaded with buckshot or I'd have finished that ugly bitch once and for all."

"Think you might've anyway, partner," Lenny observed. "Judging from all this hair and blood, I don't believe she's goin' too far."

"And did you see how I tumbled her? I've been waitin' months to get even with that growlin' she-bitch."

"I don't think Mary's gonna like it much, John."

"Mary's not goin' to find out about it, is she?"

"Guess probably not. Let's head down to those apple trees and see if we can nail a pa'tridge half as good as we can a chocolate dog." And with that the two men commenced laughing.

When Maggie failed to appear over the next couple of days, Mary called Claire to find out if the dog had been staying over at their place.

"No, I haven't seen her, Mary. I don't think Maggie's been over here at all. Old Bull's been watching for her, and she hasn't taken any of the dry food I leave out, for at least a couple days."

"That's odd," Mary mused. "Don't seem like she'd up and leave just now. Though 'course we don't know where she came from."

"No, I don't think so either, I think she's settled at your place even if...well, never mind. I'll give you a call soon as she turns up over here, Mary."

The following afternoon in a cold drizzle, as Mary was on her way back to the house, she heard a rustle and a soft whimpering from behind some of the hay the dealer had left. There lay Maggie, her tongue extended, eyes dull, and dried blood, mud, and blackberry canes matting most of the hair on her right side. Still, when she recognized Mary her white-tipped tail started to beat weakly up and down on the bloody hay.

Brighton was off somewhere with Lenny, as usual, but Claire and Will roared up the driveway in their car just minutes after Mary called. "Looks pretty bad, Mary," Will spoke softly as he stroked the soft hair on Maggie's head. "Appears to be birdshot—from close range, the way the hide's torn back. Probably ought to put the poor girl out of her misery."

"Oh, Will!" Mary couldn't bear the thought. "She took a little water a minute ago. I've got a few dollars tucked away. Couldn't we take her to Doc Fuller's? Let him have a look at her?"

"Sure, Will," Claire piped in. "Harold's great with cats and dogs, same as he is with big animals."

"Got a rug or something, Mary? We're going to have to be real careful puttin' Maggie in the car."

A little later, Doc Fuller dried his hands and shook his jowly head. "That's some nasty wound on her shoulder. Picked out at least twenty pellets," he said, nodding toward a steel bowl filled with bloody tissue and the lead beads stained red. "But the infection's not as bad as it could be. This penicillin should help some, but she's seriously dehydrated. She's a damn tough dog if she pulls through this."

He poked at the limp, shattered foreleg. "Looks like this is beyond saving though. Just isn't enough bone left whole to think of setting it."

"She won't be the first dog ever had to get along on three legs, Harold," Claire interjected. "We want to give Maggie every possible chance of makin' it."

Mary nodded in agreement as a tear ran along her cheekbone onto her upper lip.

Luckily Brighton didn't stumble home until late that night and Mary never said a word about finding Maggie. Her suspicions were pretty firm regarding the source of the birdshot.

The next day Claire and Will picked Maggie up at the vet's and brought her to their place. Claire prepared a bed for Maggie in the summer kitchen where she was still doing some late-season canning—mostly pears, grape jelly, and applesauce. The first night Maggie's breathing was heavy and irregular and her eyes dull. But she was still alive the next morning and lapped up a little water from a bowl Claire held for her. That evening she took some beef broth and at one point tried to rise, but Claire settled her down.

Mary managed to sneak over every day to clean the wounds and change the dressing on Maggie's stump. She brought with her cooked eggs, chicken broth, and other treats as the dog's appetite improved. Before long Maggie was hobbling around the room and began going outside to do her business. By the eighth day she insisted on staying outside, and at dusk curled up next to Bull in his cozy corner of the hay barn.

The following day Brighton's truck came screeching to a stop when he noticed Maggie hobbling across the Richardsons' lawn.

"'S'matter, John? Never seen a crippled dog before?" Will inquired, stepping out from behind the baler he'd been lubricating before putting it up for the winter.

"Mary's been wonderin' what happened to that useless stray,"

Brighton lied, his voice even as ice. "Looks like she might've had an accident."

"Some worthless sonofabitch shot her with birdshot. But it looks like she's gonna be all right."

"Likely someone caught her chasin' deer or somethin' and she got just what she deserved." Brighton jammed the truck into gear and spun off, kicking up a shower of dust and gravel.

A week later Brighton and Lenny polished off a bottle in the sugarhouse that they'd taken over for their drinking now that a little warming fire was in order. Grabbing their shotguns, they headed out for the overgrown pasture that usually sheltered a few grouse. The partridges were there, but as usual the reactions and shooting of the impaired hunters were not up to the challenge. Defeated, but still feeling no pain from the whiskey, the men returned to the farmyard.

Brighton came to a halt just abreast of the hen yard. Only seven hens had survived his gluttonous campaign to keep a chicken in the pot at all times. These wary veterans kept an eye on the men even as they clucked in alarm and nervously scratched the dusty yard for feed. Slowly and deliberately Brighton eased his way to the door of the coop, and the hens strutted cautiously out of reach. He closed the door, to shut off their usual refuge, and their clucking increased dramatically. Brighton backed off a few steps and then, raising the rusty single-shot 16-gauge, waited until two hens were lined up in range before squeezing the trigger. The surviving hens squawked wildly, flapping around the yard in confusion. They skittered to the coop's door, but of course this time it did not welcome them, and a second blast took two more of the black biddies as they stood huddled on the ramp. Two additional reports from Lenny's double-barreled 12-gauge and one more from Brighton's, and the last of Mary's flock were finished.

Laughing so hard he could barely stand up, Brighton staggered around collecting the carcasses while Lenny held both guns.

"Now that's what I call huntin'," Brighton laughed. "If our teeth can stand all the shot, we've bagged ourselves about twenty-five pounds of eatin'."

On the floor in the kitchen Mary lay sprawled where she had fainted when she'd looked out the window.

———

Around the first of November Brighton was introduced to the Ace Finance Company, which offered interest rates that would make a Chicago loan shark blush. But the company was eager to loan money to anyone with collateral. Winston Brewster, the proprietor, knew the McCorison place, and, on the conservative side, he figured he could safely lend a few thousand dollars even to a major risk like John Brighton—but not all at once. Brighton succeeded in obtaining $1,800, and with that and the old Case tractor for a trade-in, he was able to get a good used Farmall "Super H" tractor with a bucket loader, a trailer mower, and a set of chains thrown in to sweeten the deal.

Mary was justifiably alarmed she saw the tall red tractor being unloaded from the dealer's trailer. By the next morning, Brighton still had presented no explanation and Mary dared not voice her concern.

"If you're gonna sulk in the corner and bury your foolish head in the sand about this tractor, that's your business, Mary. But I'd like to know how you think I'm gonna to get firewood to burn, and pulp to sell if I don't have a decent machine to twitch it outta the woods."

With that he was out the door, collecting his chainsaw—a rare capital contribution he'd made to the farm—from the shed as he went. He climbed aboard the gleaming red monster, which roared to life on the first pull of the starter switch, and machine and driver bounced off toward the woodlot.

Mary was as surprised as anyone at the quantity of four-foot wood Brighton was pulling out of the woods on the rebuilt hemlock scoot that had been her father's. Apparently cutting wood was something he did well and seemed to enjoy. Normally Mary would have saved enough sewing money from the previous winter to purchase ten cords of chunked-up firewood. This would feed the gargantuan rust-coated furnace in the cellar throughout the impending winter, and Will Richardson always brought over a couple of cords of fitted kitchen wood as "part of the hay deal." But Mary wasn't expecting that gesture of generosity this particular fall, and frankly hadn't known how she would heat the rambling house during the cold weather ahead.

Now there was a growing wall of hardwood lining one side of the dooryard and an even longer pile of spruce, scrub pine, and fir pulpwood neatly stacked along the other. Soon Scott Burrill began picking up the pulpwood in his big stake-body truck and delivering it to the mills in Berlin and Rumford.

To Mary's even greater surprise, Brighton spent a couple of hours each morning bucking the maple, ash, and beech bolts into stove lengths with the chainsaw and splitting the larger chunks with a maul. When a late-season wet spell kept him from working in the woods, he would climb into the pickup with no explanation and head off for town.

Mary was feeling a bit stronger after the near breakdown brought on by the chicken shoot. She still had lots of stamina for a small woman who had not led an easy life, and one afternoon she felt up to tossing some of the split wood into the cellarway and stacking it in the big bin alongside the furnace. In an ancient pair of leather work gloves, a kerchief, and her father's old barn jacket, she worked outside in the bracing air for a half hour, then rested a bit scratching Vincent's ear and watching small flocks of crows winging toward the southern horizon. Then she descended the bark-strewn granite steps into the musty cellar and by the light of a single bulb in a porcelain socket, she stacked the wood she had just tossed down.

She was just tossing her third batch into the depths when Brighton came roaring in with the pickup and skidded to a sudden stop alongside.

"Jesus Christ, Mary, what the hell you think you're doin'?" he yelled out the window, his face a bright red.

Taken aback by his fury, Mary mistook the reason behind his concern. "I don't mind stackin' the wood, John—you done all the cuttin' and haulin', the least I can do is toss it into the cellar...."

"Get away from it! Away! Hear me?" Brighton sprang from the truck and put his liquor-reeking maw so close to Mary's face that she had to turn away. "Wood's my business. That means I'll take care of movin' it around and if I need help I'll ask for it. Understand? Now git inside and fix me a decent supper for a change. And leave the wood movin' to me!"

Mary thought she had hardened beyond tears over the last few months, but as she stumbled toward the back door, her shoulders convulsed and tears stung her eyes and ran down her cheeks.

The next day the real reason for Brighton's rage was revealed when Burrill backed up to the hardwood pile and, with his boy, began throwing the chunks into the body of the truck, which was now fitted with solid sideboards instead of stakes.

At first Mary didn't comprehend—she hadn't slept much the night before and was thankful that Brighton was once again off someplace. She threw on a thin sweater, dried her red hands with a gray dishtowel, stepped off the porch, and approached Burrill.

"Mornin', Scott. Nippy one, ain't it?"

"Guess so, Mary, but not as nippy as it's gonna get accordin' to the almanac." He and Scott Jr. continued heaving firewood into the truck.

"Don't mean to tell you your business, Scott, but ain't you supposed to be takin' that pulpwood across the yard?"

"Not today, Mary. We got an order for this hardwood over to the Whipples we have to take care of first. We'll come get the pulp in a day or two when we're done with this."

Now Mary understood. Of course! Why did she ever believe anything different? Brighton had sold the hardwood for cash, leaving who-knew-what to heat the house all winter long. She stood silently through the entire loading process, an icy wind slicing through her threadbare sweater.

"Well, Mary, better get yourself inside 'fore you freeze," Burrill said as he hoisted himself up into the truck cab and closed the door.

When Burrill had finished hauling what he'd bought, all that was left against the approaching winter were about three cords of fir pulp too soft for acceptance at the mill, the cord or so Mary had thrown into the cellar before Brighton had stopped her, and the green wood of two apple trees—both good bearers that shouldn't have been cut. When the snow came and began piling up a few inches each day, there would be no more twitching wood with the Farmall until after the spring mud season dried up.

—

The first day of December was cold and still but around noon the sun had climbed just high enough to warm what surfaces it touched. Vincent the cat always sought out the best exposures and mid afternoon found him stretched out in the driveway on a patch of dark gravel that absorbed the warmth of the retreating sun. So luxurious did the sunlight feel on his straw-colored fur that he was slow getting to his feet as Brighton rounded the corner of the barn with the Farmall in high gear. For his part Brighton couldn't be bothered with slowing or veering for a one-eared cat, and for the first time Vincent's agility was not enough to get him out of harm's way.

This blatant display of cruelty and callousness was more than Mary could dismiss, and she let fly at Brighton saying exactly what she thought of his senseless, cruel behavior.

The next day, when Claire stopped in, Mary was unusually silent and withdrawn, and it was the first but not the last time Claire would notice bruises on her friend's delicate cheekbones and a puffiness on her brow.

Thankfully Brighton was around less and less these dark December days, spending more time in town and over at Lenny's. Will Richardson brought over the usual two cords of kitchen wood when he knew Brighton was on a bender in town.

"A little Christmas present, Mary. No, I don't want any money for it. You can bake us a couple of your apple pies if you get a chance some day."

—

On a bitterly cold night in early January. Mary was lying under a mountain of quilts in their unheated upstairs bedroom marveling at the silver moonlight illuminating the thick frost on the windowpanes,

Jerry Stelmok

and trying not to think about anything. Presently she heard Brighton's truck pull up at the foot of the driveway—not unusual in itself because the drive was now choked with drifts and totally impassable. But although she heard the truck door slam shut, the engine continued to run.

A mixture of terror, revulsion, and anxiety set Mary trembling under the covers. When she heard the dreaded footsteps on the stair treads, Mary closed her eyes and feigned sleep, although she knew it would do no good. Not that Brighton pestered her sexually anymore, but he always woke her just to rant and rave, disturb her sleep, and instill the element of fear. This time he didn't collapse fully clothed into bed as had become his habit, but instead switched on the light and began pulling clothing out of the drawers of the maple dresser that had been built by Colonel McCorison himself in the 1880s.

Besides the wool pants, vest, mackinaw, and boots he was wearing, the only clothes he owned that were not rags were a couple of graying union suits, some summer undershirts, a second pair of wool pants, and a dozen white dress shirts. All of these he stuffed into a large maroon carpetbag, leaving behind in the closet only the suit in which he had married Mary.

"Leaving, John?" Mary rolled over to face the door as Brighton was about to depart.

"Christ, Mary, don't startle me like that. Why ain't you sleepin', anyhow? Me, I'm headin' down to the coast. Ain't nothing I can do 'round here to make enough money to live on. I'll take my job back at the shipyard, return in the spring for plantin'. You take care of things here, understand? I'll give you a call when I'm settled in." Then he was out the door and down the stairs and Mary took her first relaxed breath in many months.

Next morning a patrol car pulled up to the mailbox alongside the road and Sheriff Fred Murdock walked up the drifted path to the porch. Murdock had served as sheriff of Franklin County for sixteen years, overseeing his outsized beat with two deputies and a calm, intelligent manner. There was little serious crime for the most part, and when something significant did occur Murdock never got overly excited. When there was a break-in or a theft he usually had a pretty good idea as to the identity of the perpetrator and where he might be found, often still in possession of the goods. Murdock didn't hesitate to call in help from the state police or the warden service when appropriate, and anyone convicted and doing time in his jail could count of being fed well and treated like a human being. Now sixty years old with short gray hair, steel gray eyes, deep lines like isobars on a weather map distinguishing his tanned face, and without a trace of excess weight, he still looked in control.

"Mornin', Mary, don't suppose your husband's around?"

"No, he's not, Sheriff. He's down at the coast lookin' for work."

"I'll bet he is, Mary, and he was smart to leave."

Mary's heart skipped a beat. "What'd he do, Fred?"

It turned out that in the bar the night before, Brighton, with too much liquor in his blood, had baited young Billy Calder, repeatedly using offensive language and thinly disguised insults directed toward Calder's girlfriend, a half-blooded Indian. Eventually Billy took the bait and swung an ill-directed right at his tormentor, setting himself up for a brutal attack. Brighton beat the boy with his fists, feet, and knees and kept hammering even after Billy was pretty much helpless. Now Calder was at his parents' house, too sore to stand or move much at all, and it was wait-and-see if there would be any permanent damage. Both of Billy's eyes were swollen nearly shut, one cheekbone was cracked, and his jaw dislocated, not to mention several broken teeth and any number of blue and yellowish bruises.

"Calder's a tough kid, Mary, and I believe he'll be all right in awhile, but John had no call to beat a kid or anyone else like that, and I just want to know where to find him if something goes wrong. Technically it was Billy threw the first punch, but that won't matter in court if he turns up crippled."

As Sheriff Murdock went to the door, he turned back toward Mary. "John Brighton's a lowdown mean animal, Mary. I think he's dangerous as hell, and I hope for your sake he never comes back."

Mary could hardly disagree, but only looked at the sheriff's feet and said nothing.

In the days that followed, despite a rattling cough and a general lack of energy, Mary made the most of what seemed like a vacation. She took in several good sewing jobs that helped her get by, and gathered fallen branches from the orchard, the sugar bush, and along the overgrown fence rows to supplement her meager wood supply. These she cut up with a rusty bucksaw, sawing two or three billets of a wrist-sized branch before having to stop and rest.

Claire started coming around again with baked goods, boxes of tea, and even a copy of the latest sensation from her book club. Maggie also began paying visits, both with Claire and sometimes on her own. She was getting around so well on three legs that you had to look hard to see if one was actually missing. She'd come into the kitchen some days to sit by the welcoming stove, wagging her tail anytime Mary so much as glanced her way.

One sunny day in late February, a determined Mary put a halter on old Bessie the cow and walked her all the way around by the road to the Richardsons' place. Will agreed to keep her when Mary explained that she feared for Bessie's safety should her troublesome, unpredictable husband return.

The first of March, Mary's niece, Annette, arrived for a visit. She was on her way to Europe to complete her degree in archeology and would be doing field work in both France and Italy. Annette was as excited about the year-long sojourn as any bright, adventuresome young woman would be, and Mary was as excited about it as she was. Once again Annette and Maggie were inseparable. Annette had been terribly upset when she'd heard that Maggie had been shot and had lost a leg. But now, watching her bounce around, and hunt as she always had, she felt a little more at ease. Her concerns about her beloved aunt were not as easily dispelled. Clearly, Mary had failed a great deal and Annette was deeply concerned with Mary's lack of strength and energy and her persistent hacking cough. With Claire's support, she tried persuading Mary to see the doctor, but even she was unable to make her aunt take this step for her own well being.

The morning she left, Annette held her arms around Mary for a long time. She underscored the importance of seeing a doctor, told her she loved her, that she would be writing from Europe, and finally that she was sorry for Mary's troubles with Brighton, adding that she hoped he'd never return.

Then she knelt down to hug Maggie goodbye before getting into the Richardsons' car for the ride to the bus station.

By the second week of March the unrelenting cold seemed to lose its grip. With the increasingly longer days the sunshine gathered enough strength to pull the mercury up above the freezing mark. Normally this would be time for shoveling out the doorway of the sugarhouse, tapping the metal spiles into the rough bark of the giant maples, and getting the evaporator into shape. But this spring there was no firewood worked up to fuel the fire, the sugarhouse was a wreck inside from Brighton and Lenny's drinking bouts, and Mary just plain didn't have energy enough to launch what usually ranked alongside garden work as a favorite activity.

With the resilience of youth, Billy Calder recovered from the worst of his injuries more quickly than expected. He had a few gaps where his teeth used to be, and something about his face looked just a bit crooked, with a persistent purple bruise along the left cheekbone. There were no charges filed against Brighton, and somehow, probably through Lenny, he got word down in Portsmouth that the coast was clear.

The twentieth of March marked the first truly warm sunny day of spring, and Mary moved a rocking chair from the shaded porch out into the yard to catch the warming sun. Soon Maggie appeared from her hay bed in the barn, glancing sideways at Mary with calm, "smiling" brown eyes, her tail beating back and forth like a metronome. She got to within five feet of Mary and stopped short. Her ears went up and her tail stopped wagging. She scanned the road below, but it was empty of traffic as usual. Still, sensing something that Mary could not detect, Maggie spun around and with her tail and head down trotted back toward the barn, went past it, and ascended the snowy hill toward the Richardsons'.

Five minutes later Mary heard the growl of her husband's pickup laboring down the road as if a piston or two were frozen up.

Brighton's greeting was short and unfriendly. "What're you doin' out here? Ain't there work enough to do in the house?"

Other than the kitchen, which was warmed by the cookstove, the rest of the house was freezing cold. Brighton stalked out to the woodshed, slammed the door, and thumped down the open stairs into the cellar.

When he came back up empty-handed, he started in. "Jesus Christ, Mary, there's no damn wood anywheres. How're we supposed to stay warm in this icebox?" He pulled a quart jar half full of bluish pickled eggs and a bottle of whiskey from his frayed bag and sat down at the head of the kitchen table. He helped himself to the half loaf of bread Mary had wrapped in well-used wax paper on the sideboard and began wolfing down what he termed a "damn poor dinner."

"Tomorrow I'll cut us some firewood and get in a few groceries so we can live like humans. This is damn pitiful."

When Brighton went upstairs to the bedroom, Mary, too weak and despondent to climb the stairs, stayed down on the daybed in the kitchen. Any gains she had made physically in the past few months seemed to seep away, and suddenly she could think of nothing but sleep.

She didn't hear Brighton go outside in the morning, but from time to time her sleep was interrupted by a strange droning that wove in and out of her dream world and consciousness. Eventually it struck her that it was Brighton's chainsaw she'd been hearing, and now she could hear him swinging open the creaky bulkhead doors, probably to throw down some firewood for the furnace, but again she drifted off into a deep sleep.

When she awoke it was dark. There was still a warmth in the kitchen from the fire Brighton must have built, but he apparently had gone into town or over to Lenny's. Claire soon appeared, stoking the fire with the green wood, and ladling out a mug of steaming soup from a pot she had brought with her wrapped snugly in a couple of heavy towels. The chicken soup tasted good and the warmth sliding down to her stomach began to have a positive effect. Still, Mary could manage very little before she launched into another coughing fit that seemed as though it would never stop.

"Mary, I'm going upstairs to get you some things and you're coming with me to our house, and we're getting Dr. Miles to have a look at you. You can't stay here now that *he's* back. You need some rest, dear, and some care and hot food, and you don't need anything from John Brighton."

"Thanks for the soup, Claire, and the kind offer," Mary's words came out slow and deliberate and no louder than a whisper. "But this is my home, and John's my husband, and this is the bed I made myself." There was a long pause while she caught her breath. "This soup will help a lot and that lemon tea you brought the other day helps, too. I'll rest up and be all right. Then I'll decide what to do."

Mary's condition worsened daily and each day Claire marched in despite Brighton's hostile presence. When he discovered that this wouldn't keep her from "meddling," he'd simply leave or be absent whenever the determined friend appeared.

A week of this forced care passed and Mary seemed to be gaining some strength. She was sitting in the kitchen rocker the next time Claire came by, and ate a small bowl of macaroni and melted cheddar along with a slice of Claire's sourdough bread with butter.

"I am feeling better, Claire, thanks to all your care and fine cooking." Setting down her teacup, she rose stiffly from the rocker. "That gardenin' book Annette brought me when she was here—I never even had a chance to look at it. It's out here in the parlor, and I want you to borrow it."

"No," Claire said, jumping up from the kitchen chair she always sat in while visiting. "Let me get it for you, it's awfully cold in there. Is it on the end table?"

"Listen, Claire, I'm fine. I haven't gone any farther than the bathroom for over a week. Time I got a bit of exercise."

"No, Mary!" but she was too late. Mary pushed open the dark paneled door and a rush of cold musty air swept past them into the warm kitchen. Mary walked carefully and a bit unsteadily to the stand beside her favorite chair with the red leather upholstery and dark clawed feet. She picked up a book with bright flowers and lush green tones on the jacket and her eyes drifted up to the window beyond the chair.

"Oh, my God, Claire!" Her face turned even paler. Trembling, she sank down onto the red ottoman, the air beneath the leather cover exiting with a short whoosh. "How could he?" she breathed.

From the window the view behind the house took in the beloved maple sugarbush. But instead of the stately grove of ancient trees with their impressive trunks and intertwined crowns, the south-facing hill-side was a clutter of huge fallen trunks whose branches had been amputated and cut up for firewood. The limbless trunks, represent-ing too much work for Brighton to cut up and split, lay forlornly scat-tered over the hillside like so many beached whales.

The shocking sight of the savaged sugar bush marked the point from which Mary's condition rapidly deteriorated. On a raw day a week into April, Claire met Brighton on the rickety porch just as he was coming out the door. Her hands were full with yet another steam-ing pot of soup and a couple of quart bottles of ginger ale, a liquid Mary seemed willing to swallow from time to time. Instead of allow-ing him to brush past as usual, Claire stepped directly into his path, forcing the man she loathed to stop.

"Listen, Mr. Brighton, Dr. Miles couldn't come with me this morning because he was needed at the hospital, but he's coming out this afternoon to see Mary."

"I don't recall orderin' no doctor."

Ignoring his dismissal, her eyes flashing, Claire continued. "Will's runnin' me down to Sumner for a few days so's I can stay and help out our niece there, just had a baby boy."

"So?"

"So, you make sure the doctor gets to see Mary, and if she needs hospitalizin', make sure she gets there. Don't worry about the bill...."

"I can pay for our own doctorin' don't you think I can't...."

"If Doc doesn't have her admitted here's some chicken soup, and muffins. You be sure to keep that kitchen fire burnin' and...."

Brighton had had enough. He shoved Claire aside to gain passage down the steps. "I'll take care of my own wife in my own home, Mrs.

Meddler, the way I see fit, don't you worry about that."

Tossing back his shoulders he strode off into the gray day. A cold wind struck up, twisting and spinning the snow flurries as they fell onto the frozen mud.

Four days later Will picked up Claire at his niece's and started back home in a blossoming spring snowstorm. By the time they reached the home stretch it was late afternoon, prematurely dusk, and six inches of new snow had fallen. A stiff northeast wind was drifting it dangerously wherever it had a fetch. Claire glanced up anxiously at the McCorison place as they drove slowly past the drive.

"Wait, Will. Stop!" There was no light in the house, no smoke from the chimney, and Brighton's truck was nowhere in sight. The couple struggled up the driveway, the wind battering them like the wings of a thousand swans and the driven snow stinging their faces. They were surprised and relieved to see Maggie on the porch, curled up on a discarded jacket, out of the wind behind the empty kindling box. She looked up and thumped her tail in greeting. Using a coal shovel with the D-handle broken off, Will had to clear drifted snow away from the door even on the protected porch before they could get in. Inside, it was dark and frigid as a tomb, and their momentary relief at seeing Maggie quickly faded. "Must've taken Mary to the hospital, dear," Will said. Groping, he located the dangling string that operated the lightbulb over the table. The soup pot was empty and unwashed, the handle of a big wooden spoon sticking out. The stove was stone-cold and the faucet that had been left dripping had secreted a little stalactite of ice reaching to the slate sink below. Suddenly there was a rustling and a moaning from the pile of ragged blankets on the daybed, and Mary's friends knew their worst fears were true. Mary was under those covers and she'd been without heat or any measure of care for some time.

—

"No, Claire, Brighton wouldn't even let me onto the porch." Dr. Miles's big voice boomed from the telephone receiver. "Said Mary was doing better and that Ginny, her sister, was on her way up to care for her...told me the same thing when I saw him in town later on. Other- wise I'd have gotten the sheriff involved. Hold on, I'll be right over."

Will had gotten a fire started in the stove and was heading over to his place to get the Willys truck with the plow so the ambulance could get up the driveway. Claire was perched on the edge of the daybed, stroking Mary's forehead and her wonderfully fine silver-gray hair, waiting for the water in the kettle to thaw so she could prepare a hot-water bottle.

Mary was shivering and the rattle in her chest sounded like a dull saw being drawn across concrete. She tried to speak, but did not seem to have the strength. Each breath was a desperate effort, and a signif- icant triumph, only to be followed by the next agonizing cycle.

Claire had filled the rubber bottle with hot water and placed under the covers next to Mary's skeleton-like form by the time Dr. Benjamin Miles burst through the door. His unbuttoned overcoat and scarf were coated with snow, but his reassuring leather bag was gripped tightly in his bare hand.

"Ambulance's off the road outside Strong. Will's started plowing down at the foot of the drive. Soon's we can, we'll drive my station wagon up here." He felt Mary's forehead and held her birdlike wrist in his big hands searching for the feeble throb of her pulse.

"Well, Mary, we're going to have to get you to the hospital, looks like, hook you up to some oxygen, and give you something for that congestion. Meantime, Claire, see if you can find a sheet or something, so we can set up a little vapor tent here." Turning to his bag he added, "I got something here that'll make it a bit easier for her to breathe."

Claire dragged a floor lamp to the side of the bed to drape the sheet over. Already Will was in the front yard slamming through the dense drifts with his plow truck, scraping up clods of half-frozen gravel and mud along with the snow.

"Great! Never mind this, Claire. I'll go fetch my wagon. The sooner Mary's in the hospital, the better." As Dr. Miles opened the door partway and slid out, Maggie pushed past his legs and hopped over to the daybed in her odd three-legged gait. Her ears were down and her liquid brown eyes looked sad. She nestled her chin on the covers near Mary's head, and Mary, wheezing unevenly, turned her face toward the dog. She seemed calmer all at once, not struggling so hard.

"Maggie," she whispered hoarsely, "oh, Maggie."

By the time Will and Dr. Miles had the station wagon backed up to the porch Mary was gone, a look of peace and contentment finally bestowed on her face.

Claire, Will, and Maggie sat with their departed friend that night in the snowbound house, keeping the kitchen fire crackling. Toward dawn Will let Maggie outside. It had stopped snowing and a quarter moon revealed itself as the clouds dissipated. Maggie made her way over to the snow-covered site of Mary's garden. Lifting her head, she howled again and again, then lay down in the new snow, watching something only she could see.

———

John Brighton pulled the seven-foot blade from the cutter bar of the mowing machine. The weather looked good and he had a pile of hay to mow the next two days. That was going to be his ticket out of this godforsaken valley. Things had not gone all that well for him since Mary's death. Although he was not actually charged with a crime for his blatant neglect, the folks and establishments in town were not nearly as tolerant of his misdeeds and excesses as they had been. His credit was at rock bottom, and he was fast running out of cash.

The evening after Brighton's disgraceful behavior at Mary's funeral service, Will Richardson had caught up with him just outside the Rusty Nail. A small clot of witnesses, and the widower himself, found out once and for all that no amount of experience in barroom mayhem tactics was enough to defeat a younger opponent with muscles of iron, especially when that opponent came armed with courage and determination. From his patrol car parked across the square, Sheriff Murdock watched the whole thing approvingly without lifting a finger to interfere. When Brighton could no longer rise from his hands and knees for more punishment, Murdock started the car and pulled slowly away. Two months later Brighton's ribcage was still inflamed from the pounding and he was finding his womanizing severely curtailed with a big hole in his smile where four front teeth had once been.

In May Brighton had returned to the Ace Finance Company and borrowed the entire amount his credit would bear using the farm for collateral, ostensibly for fixing up the sagging and leaking barn. Instead, he had used most of it to buy a nearly new Ford Fairlane 500, two-toned, sky blue and white. Two weeks later, driving drunk late at night, he left the road at Parson's Corner. By sheer dumb luck, he'd managed to fly the Fairlane between two big ash trees and stumbled away from the accident unhurt. But the damage to the car's axle, drive shaft, and crankcase was considerable, not to mention the crushed right front fender. Naturally Brighton carried no collision insurance and now the car sat at Duffy Henderson's garage with an $850 estimate for the work to be done, while he was left once again driving the less-than-dependable pickup.

He applied for work at the sawmill, but quickly discovered that Billy Calder's half-brothers worked there and didn't want to risk finding himself being shoved into the monstrous circular saw or having a lift of studs somehow dropped on his head. His credit at the hotel for rooms, meals, and drinks had been exhausted, and even Lenny's low-grade companionship was no longer available. Word was, Lenny had left town after knocking up Ebel Stockton's eldest daughter, whom many folks considered simple. Ebel was stalking the county with a shotgun in the back seat determined to either march the culprit to the altar or put him into an early grave.

The McCorison farm was now so far into hock that selling it would present its own set of hoops to jump through, and truth be told, it had become so run down that it was unlikely the purchase price would equal the debt against it. Even Will Richardson was no longer interested in a portion of it.

An undeserved chance came Brighton's way as he was walking along the Carson Road after another truck breakdown. Two hundred yards down the road he was picked up by an animated fellow in a new Chevy truck.

"Stew Freeman's the name, and I'm lining up hay for my crew to bale and haul to Maryland. Quality feed only, that is. Preferably clover mix." A lot of acreage around was no longer being farmed, but the better fields still grew hay and Stewart Freeman had the means to process it and a market to sell it to. "I'm payin' forty cents a bale, but if you save us the trouble of mowing I'll give you fifty cents if the hay's as good as you claim, Mr. Brighton."

Brighton had him pull over by one of the fields the Richardsons had nurtured over the past several years. The tall, clover-rich grasses tossed their heads in the gentle breeze and Freeman had to admit it was the finest crop he had seen so far this season.

"Tell you what, Mr. Brighton, the forecast's good for the next three or four days. You knock down that hay and get it drying. I'll be here with the baling crew on Wednesday. Looks like you've got at least three thousand bales here, and I'll be happy to buy it all." He paused, "'Course the deal's off if it gets rained on. That's your risk till it's baled."

Brighton didn't mention that half the crop was rightfully Richardson's. "Fifteen hundred bucks," he thought. "That'll get my car back on the road with enough cash left to get me well on my way out west. And it'll be a real nice surprise for that meddlin' Will Richardson!"

Brighton replaced a half dozen triangular knives on the long, flexing sawblade, flattened out the rivets expertly, and then began filing the bevels on the remaining teeth. He was getting dry and the incessant barking was getting on his nerves.

"What's that yapping, anyway? Haven't seen a dog 'round here all spring, and it sounds like it's coming from the barn." He'd taken to talking to himself when he was alone—which was most of the time, nowadays.

"I wonder if it's that three-legged bitch? Probably got a ground hog cornered 'round the side." He grinned. "Might just be an opportunity to get even with that nuisance once and for all."

He grabbed a pitchfork and stalked off toward the frenzied barking. Off the west side of the barn the crumbling remains of the old heifer tie-up stood at a right angle to the larger structure. In the days before electricity it had been the first milk house. Now the roof was mostly fallen in and the interior was an obstacle course of collapsed roofing boards and crisscrossed collar ties a man had to practically crawl through. A sliding door that once led into the barn itself had long ago been boarded over.

Sure enough, to Brighton's grim delight, the chocolate-colored dog with three legs apparently had a critter cornered in there and was paying attention to nothing else. Her head was down under an old stanchion, and her tail beat back and forth as she barked relentlessly at a victim just out of reach.

Clutching the pitchfork, Brighton eased into the outside doorway, effectively blocking any means of escape. He took a couple of careful steps toward the preoccupied dog, the pitchfork leveled for a fatal thrust. Sensing his presence, Maggie lifted her head, whirled around to face her enemy, and seemed to realize that she was trapped. The dog growled menacingly with teeth bared, and began backing up. She never took her eyes off her antagonist.

"This is gonna be too easy, you she-bitch," Brighton grinned, advancing by ducking under each sagging rafter in turn. Maggie was soon up against the immovable inside door with nowhere to go but past the gleaming tines of Brighton's fork. His grin broadened as he ducked under one final collar tie to put himself into optimum striking position.

But it was Maggie who had set the trap, and as Brighton straightened up to thrust the pitchfork, his head came up squarely into the ash-like whorls of a huge paper wasp's nest. The blow crushed open the bottom of the nest and a swarm of whining defenders were on him in a cloud before he'd realized what had happened. Instantly the malicious grin was replaced by a terror-stricken countenance and a scream, and as he dropped the fork Maggie was past his flailing legs in an instant.

Every inch of Brighton's exposed skin was crawling with angry wasps, and in his hasty retreat he slammed his head against every sagging collar tie in turn and banged his shins painfully on at least a dozen lower obstacles. The tenacious wasps pursued him around the barn and continued stinging until he dove into the shelter of his pickup. By the time he'd killed the tormentors who had followed him inside, his face, arms, and neck were swelling rapidly and only his right eye remained partially open. Squadrons of vengeful wasps kept circling the truck.

The pain was excruciating. He discovered a Mason jar half full of warm stale water on the seat beside him and with difficulty, manipulated the stubborn spring. His swollen hands were nearly useless and his vision was greatly reduced, but eventually he was able to remove the glass lid. He took a few swallows and poured the remainder over his swollen face and neck. Suddenly his sense of distance and space began playing tricks on him, and his chest felt oddly constricted. Brighton was fighting for each breath as he felt himself falling backwards into a dark tunnel—and everything turned black.

By the time he regained consciousness it was dusk. He could see very little and the dozens of stings felt like hot coals burrowing through his flesh. The swelling had stabilized but not yet begun to subside. Still, Brighton felt lucky that he hadn't succumbed to shock from the huge dose of venom. The water jar was empty, his shirt, overalls, and the seat of the truck still damp. If the damn truck would only start he could probably drive himself to the hospital in Farmington. With swollen fingers and blurred vision it was hard to coordinate the key and starter button. "Goddamn!" he swore when the response was only a series of annoying clicks.

Cautiously, Brighton opened the truck door and listened for the drone of wasps, but of course they were long gone. Stepping out he was nearly overcome by dizziness, but after leaning against the fender for a few minutes the spinning decreased to no more than that after a good drunk, and he could manage that. Naturally the phone in the house had been disconnected, but he could at least bathe the burning, swelling welts with cold water and baking soda or something. Then he figured he could manage the walk down the driveway to the road, where someone was bound to pick him up. Then a better idea hit him—what he really needed was a good drink. There was still a half bottle of whiskey over by the tractor just waiting for him. The ideal antidote!

Brighton wobbled over to the tractor. The bottle was sitting on the old chopping block where he'd split so much wood and beheaded so many chickens. In the gloom he failed to notice the dark form curled up beside the locust block, but just as he spotted the bottle's white label, Maggie stood up, grabbed the bottle in her mouth, and limped off with it.

"You she-bitch." Brighton growled through clenched teeth. "You drop that bottle, hear? I ain't chasin' you. I'll get the friggin' gun." But Maggie wasn't moving well. She covered about twenty-five feet, whimpering as she hobbled along, then stopped and put down the prize. Apparently she'd gotten her share of wasp stings, too.

Heartened, Brighton lurched ahead, grabbing a large crescent wrench from the tractor. But just as he was reaching for the bottle, Maggie snatched it back up and hobbled off another thirty feet before stopping and again dropping the bottle. Rage building as pain and frustration mounted, Brighton followed. Four more times Maggie picked up the bottle just as Brighton approached, moving it another thirty or forty feet before dropping it. Now they were along the eastern side of the barn where yet another collapsing outbuilding leaned precariously as the forces of nature drew it toward the ground. Here, a tangle of raspberry canes and chokecherries attested to the continued neglect of the once-groomed farmyard.

"Hell with this!" Brighton yelled. "I'm not chasin' you to hell and back. I'm fetchin' the shotgun, then we'll see who's in charge!"

But Maggie appeared completely spent. She dropped the bottle on a pile of rubble and this time moved off into the gathering darkness limping painfully.

Sensing triumph—and giddy with the anticipation of the smooth whiskey sliding down his throat—Brighton lunged ahead. Consumed by this vision, he abandoned normal caution and ignored the warning that was pulsed dimly in his addled memory. Unseeing, he pushed past the faded shingle Mary years before had nailed to a small pine post: "Danger—Abandoned Well—Keep Out"

Beneath Brighton's considerable weight, the dry-rotted planks and motley slabs that served as the shaft's cover caved in instantly, much of the wood crumbling almost into dust. Feeling himself falling, Brighton's survival instincts took over. His arms flew out, clutching desperately at one crumbling slab after another. Just before plunging into the abyss he managed to catch one sound locust plank with his left arm, jolting his descent to a stop. Though his right hand was still numb from the wasps, he closed it in a death grip on an angular rock that had kept its place along the rim while others had dislodged and tumbled along with the rotten boards to the bottom of the dry well thirty feet below.

For a long minute, in utter terror, John Brighton, legs dangling, hung in the shaft, his left armpit cocked painfully over the old locust plank and his right hand gripping the rock so tightly there might be impressions of his fingertips in it even today. Ironically, the bait—the half-empty bottle of whiskey—remained perched on the lip of the well, level with his swollen and grimacing face. But it might have been a thousand miles away for all the good it was doing him now. No matter how vigorously he kicked and flailed his legs, his feet could not locate a solid toehold in the crumbling shale sides of the well. His shouting and wailing went unnoticed, swallowed by the raspberries, the decrepit buildings, and the deepening darkness. The locust plank groaned under his weight and shifted slightly, and Brighton began to cry and then to bawl.

Then a sudden movement to his right caught his attention. Maggie, just barely discernible in the near darkness, drew up to the edge of the well just above him. The three-foot-long milk adder she held gently just behind the head writhed desperately. With a little toss of her head Maggie released the snake, sending it down toward the suspended man. With reptilian presence of mind, the floating snake extended its tail, reached Brighton's neck, and used this purchase to wrap itself again and again around the doomed man's head. With a final choking scream, John Brighton released his grip on the plank and rock and tore at the powerful serpent as he plunged downward.

━

In October a bird hunter parked his truck in the weed-choked barn-
yard and stalked carefully around the barn to check the old apple tree
that clung to life amid the brambles there. As he had anticipated, two
grouse were perched in the branches, feeding on the small scaly apples
They lit out in a burst of energy just as he brought the shotgun to his
shoulder, firing one blast, then a second. But the birds whistled away
untouched. Shaking his head the hunter snapped open the breech and
the ejected shells tumbled into the dark shaft he had failed to notice
and had just missed stepping into. A deputy was sent out to investi-
gate after the hunter reported the hazard. The roving beam of his
five-cell flashlight traveled down the dark cylinder, picking up little
outside an occasional spider web—until it reached the distant bottom
and came to rest on the gruesomely contorted remains of John
Brighton.

━

Two years later a late-model sedan pulled slowly up the rutted and
overgrown driveway of the old McCorison place. It stopped before
the nearly collapsed porch of the weathered farmhouse. The driver's
door opened and a somber-looking man stepped stiffly out into the
weeds that were taking over the yard. He wore a corduroy cap and a
vest of the same gray material over a white shirt. By contrast, the
woman on the passenger side practically bounced out of her door and
spun slowly around, taking in the forlorn desolation of what had once
been a thriving farm. Her fair hair was cut short and barely reached
the collar of her tweed coat. A blue silk kerchief was tied in a casual
knot on top of her head.

From the back seat the man lifted a toddler of perhaps a year and
a half, who was already blessed with the same golden curls as her
mother. The man, walking with an obvious limp, carried the little girl
as he and the woman took a sobering turn around the dilapidated
farmyard. Half the barn roof had caved in and the red cedar silo was

cocked like the Tower of Pisa, the top half pulling well away from the side of the barn where it had once been firmly attached. Sheds and outbuildings were collapsed entirely or leaned beyond hope of recovery. The porch on the house leaned outward, and the wood-shingled roof riddled with gaping holes. Scores of clapboards had come loose and either hung by one end or piled up around the granite foundation as they fell off entirely. Dozens of windowpanes were missing and as many more had been broken by stones thrown by mischievous boys. The front door, with top and middle hinges pulled free by the wind, hung at a ridiculous angle as though a circus clown might swing it open and step out. All the lawns and gardens were choked with milkweed, goldenrod, and burdocks.

"Oh, my, Claude," the young woman said, finally breaking the silence. "This is much worse than I ever imagined. I am so sorry for dragging you way out here. This was once a really nice farm. But now—but this—this is hopeless."

"Yes, Annette," the man replied calmly with a slightly foreign accent. "I'm sure this was a very fine farm at one time, and it could be again, I think." The gray hair at his temples suggested a man a bit older than his wife.

"But think of the work, Claude. Just to get the place in shape."

"Annette, dearest," he said softly, setting down the young child. "Don't forget, I come from a village that had been shelled by the Germans; occupied; bombed by the Allies; occupied by them, who were chased out once more by the Germans. Then finally, with much fighting house to house, it was liberated again. At our family farm just outside town, there was not one stone left sitting on top of another. We spent three full years rebuilding it for my brother and his family. This looks like not such an impossible job to me."

"Well, the asking price is certainly low enough," Annette said, and brightened.

"It is incredibly low, Annette. In France, in order to be...."

He was interrupted by his wife's squeals of joy, and then and then her sudden sobbing. A three-legged dog had come up to her and was now bouncing around like a puppy. The white-tipped tail was whipping back and forth excitedly as Annette knelt to greet her old friend and receive a dose of wet kisses.

"Claude, this is Maggie. Claire mentioned she was still around, but I still can't believe it!"

"Either that, my dear, or there are a lot of three-legged chocolate dogs in this country," Claude joked.

The baby, Kathleen, toddled up to Maggie and clutched her short hair with both hands to keep her balance, laughing with a series of bubbling squeals. Maggie stood patiently, her tail still wagging. Then she turned her head and gently licked the child's face.

Claude bent at the waist, trying to get his face down close to the dog's. In his youth he had been a daring and very successful courier for the Résistance until he had lost his right leg, and his artificial limb did not easily permit kneeling. He stroked Maggie's shoulders with his strong hand, as his wife said, "Oh, Claude, it's so good to see Maggie again. She's such a nice dog, and very intelligent."

Claude leaned closer, his green eyes peering directly into Maggie's soft brown ones. "Yes," he said, "I can see that Maggie is a very intelligent dog." Then he added, "And I think a very brave one, as well."

THE NORTH SHORE*

A s the hulking plow truck crawled along the lakeshore highway, the swirling snow swallowed the beams of its headlights before they penetrated fifty feet. The combined efforts of fog lamps, taillights, cab lights and flashers would have been futile in the face of the blizzard even had they not been heavily coated with damp clinging snow. Even the greenish-white pulsating beam of the strobe was invisible beyond a hundred feet.

Chewing a wad of wintergreen gum and nervously humming a berserk tune, driver Larry Schneider strained to see out the oily swatch cleared momentarily by the passing wiper blade, then just as quickly clogged with new snow. Beads of sweat broke out on his forehead despite the fact that he was driving in his shirtsleeves, so high did he have the fan and defroster set to melt the incoming blobs.

"A few degrees colder, and I could cut the damn defroster altogether and this foolish snow wouldn't melt, just bounce off and I could see something." Having spent so much time isolated in the glowing comfort of the plow truck's cab, talking to himself had become as natural as anything. He swallowed the tasteless gob of gum and drew two new sticks from a large pack. After nearly thirty years patrolling the remote stretch of highway that snaked along Lake Superior's North Shore, linking Duluth and the rest of the state with Canada, he had become accustomed to the wild, wet blizzards that swept in from the unfrozen lake—backlashes from storms that were supposed to be moving in the opposite direction.

Still, this was about as bad as Larry had ever seen, and he was

* The author and the editors realize that Lake Superior is not in Maine....

thankful he'd started out from Two Harbors at 2:00 A.M. rather than waiting until 5:30 A.M. as his crew leader had suggested. Had he made that mistake and the snowfall continued at its present rate, he'd have been lucky to get through. At Castle Danger he'd had to lift the plow's extended wing, concentrating all the power on pushing aside just the drifts directly ahead of the truck. Widening the lane would have to come later.

"Lucky thing I know this road like the back of my hand," he said to himself, "or I'd really be in trouble."

The pilot in him sensed the grade down to the bridge over the Split Rock River before it was apparent. "Holy Cow!" he yelped as an unburied length of bridge guardrail suddenly loomed out of a drift directly alongside. "Good thing the wing was up, or that would have been an expensive mistake."

Larry was a model public servant. He'd learned to enjoy his job and he respected the state's equipment as though it was his own. A dent or broken part on his truck that showed up later at the garage slapped him with a sense of failure and remorse, even though it was seldom his fault, and any other operator would have joked about it with the mechanics.

The CB radio came to life as the driver of another rig checked in with the dispatcher. The reception was lousy with static and garbled voices. It was a hell of a storm.

For a moment the intensity of the storm seem to wane a little. But Larry knew better than to expect things to end so soon. Approaching a turnout overlooking the lake, Larry glimpsed what could be the reflection of taillights off to the side. He slowed to a crawl and after a blinding gust spent itself, he spotted the back end of a red sedan. It was listing as though the passenger-side wheels were off the road into the ditch.

It wasn't unusual to come across abandoned vehicles in a heavy snowstorm, and Larry was glad that this one, at least, was not obstructing the highway. He always stopped to be sure no one was still inside, and would use his radio to summon a state cop and possibly a wrecker if assistance was needed. In lesser storms Larry usually offered to pull the vehicle back onto the road—clearly against regulations, but the one exception to his strict adherence to the rules.

He pulled to a stop and lowered his right-side window. A rush of snow-laden wind roared into the cab, lashing him with the force of a fire hose. He quickly ran the window back up, and now at least the top half was momentarily free of snow. Larry switched on the powerful searchlight and deftly directed the beam toward the stricken car. It took a few seconds for his vision to adjust to the charging snow rushing toward him, but presently the intense light made it possible to identify a bright red Mustang, probably thirty years old, over its rocker panels in drifted snow. And standing next to it, his forearm shielding his squinting eyes from the blinding beam was a smallish man wearing neither hat nor coat.

Caught by surprise, Larry held the beam directly on the car and the man as he stared in disbelief. Quickly coming to his senses, he diverted the beam just enough so it was not shining directly in the stranded man's calm white face. This fellow seemed unwilling or unable to walk over to the plow truck, so Larry pulled on his heavy, lined canvas coat and rabbit-fur bomber cap and climbed down the leeward side of the cab. The drifted snow was deeper than the tops of his felt-lined boots. The force of the wind struck him as he rounded the plow and he had to lean into it to hold his place and advance into the gale.

The man waited for him as if rooted beside the Mustang, appearing neither distressed nor relieved. He wore a white oxford shirt and gray light-wool trousers.

"Holy cow, mister!" Larry yelled into the wind when he was within a couple of yards of the man. "Don't you have a coat or nothing to put on?"

The man's mouth moved, but because of the roaring wind Larry couldn't understand what he said, so he repeated, "Don't you have a coat or something in there?"

Without a word the pale man, nearly bald on top, opened the driver's door, pulled out a suit coat of the same light material as his pants, and slowly pulled it on, as though he would never have thought of doing this had Larry not suggested it.

"Screwy," Larry thought to himself. "Either that or he's already hypothermic and disoriented." A lull in the blizzard allowed the pair to exchange a few sentences.

"What were you thinking, out on a night like this without so much as a warm coat and hat?"

"Oh, I never wear a hat," the man replied. "Besides," he continued as though Larry was a complete idiot, "I was inside the car."

"Well, 'course you were, but that car of yours must be thirty years old, and this is probably the worst storm we've seen up here since it was built."

There was no reply and Larry figured he had a bit of a nut case here and had better get on with business. The velocity of the wind-driven snow was again building. Larry looked around and it was easy to see the car would not be easily extracted from the growing drift.

"Don't think I can pull you out without hurting your car," Larry yelled.

"You're not just going to leave me here, are you?" the man said, barely loud enough to be heard.

"No...yes, but first I'll call the state police on the radio, and they'll send someone out to get you in a four-wheel-drive truck or something."

"Why can't I ride with you?"

"They don't allow that." Larry yelled, but the man appeared not to hear.

"They don't allow that," Larry repeated louder. "I could lose my job. I'll call this in. You get inside your car and start it up so you don't freeze to death." Larry instinctively glanced at the car to be sure its tailpipe wasn't buried in the snow.

"The car's dead," the man stated flatly.

"Dead? What do you mean?"

"The battery must be dead. There's no power whatsoever."

"Are you sure?"

The man stepped to the side. He hadn't bothered to button his thin coat or even turn up the collar against the raging storm. He extended his hand, palm out toward the driver-side door, inviting Larry to try it for himself.

"Want me to try 'er?" He opened the door to the funky sixties sports car, but the dome light failed to come on. Larry felt self-conscious piling into the little bucket seat in his huge coat and snow-covered boots. The man closed the door behind him. Once inside, Larry was transported into the past. He was back at Mesabi High, he had the hottest car in the parking lot, and the Beach Boys were working their magical harmonies on the radio.

The startling white face at the window brought him back to reality. The keys were in the ignition and the sliding T-grip shift lever on the console was in Park. Larry depressed the accelerator and turned the key.

Click. Nothing more, and the same on the second try. Larry climbed out of the Mustang less gracefully than he would have back in high school. "Battery's dead all right," he shouted. The pale stranger appeared satisfied.

Off to the side the state truck loomed gigantic, like a snorting Cyclops from a Greek myth, half covered in snow, all its lights bouncing off the swirling snow.

"Tell you what, sir. I'll call this in and we'll try jump-starting your car. If it starts, you can wait inside until help arrives."

"It won't work. I might as well ride along with you in the truck. At least you're going in the right direction."

"Sorry, they'd never allow it. Only in real emergencies." Inside the warm cab, Larry reached for the radio mike. Heat from the idling engine had melted the snow surrounding the wiper paths, and water was running down the windshield in sheets. Larry pushed the button to send.

"Unit 40 to Base, do you read me? Base, this is Larry, Unit 40, just past Split Rock Bridge, come in."

There was no response, not even a crackle or a sputter. He tried again, but with the same results. He unwrapped another stick of gum and added it to the wad in his mouth. He glanced at the new cellular phone—useless at best in this region of poor coverage, even under ideal conditions. As he climbed down he was startled once again: he hadn't expected the stranded driver to be standing just outside the cab in the shelter of the truck.

"Radio's not working for the moment, but that's not unusual. Let's start your car and I'll try again." He climbed back up to move the rig into position and to fetch jumper cables. Like most state property, the cables were the best money could buy, and unusually long.

The man remained standing alongside, looking up at Larry his arms now crossed, hands clasping opposite elbows. For the first time he actually looked cold.

Larry climbed down. "You can sit inside the truck while I set this up. Don't you even have gloves?"

Silently, and with surprising agility, the man climbed up into the cab and slid over to the passenger side. Larry noticed he was wearing low shoes of some expensive leather Larry couldn't identify, and they looked totally inappropriate for the season and the conditions. When Larry got back in to move the truck, the man turned to him and simply said "Thank you." His breath was almost hot—strong, but not exactly foul—faintly familiar yet still as mystifying as the rest of his presence.

The terrible visibility made it difficult for Larry to maneuver the plow truck alongside the Mustang, but once the hoods of both vehicles were lifted, the generous length of the cables made the connection. The traveler made no effort to help in any way, and when Larry suggested he switch back over to his car to try starting it, he said, "It's no use, the car's *dead*."

Larry shrugged, gave the truck a little gas, fought his way over to the car, and used his flashlight to confirm that everything was in position for starting. He pressed down the accelerator and turned the key.

"YEOW!" His hand leapt from the keys, his fingertips tingled from the electrical shock that traveled up his arm and through his body. There was a flash that briefly lit up the black vinyl interior and continued on outside. He rolled down the window and couldn't believe what he saw—the cables were on fire along their whole length to his truck.

Jerry Stelmok

"Holy cow!" he cried, and bolted from the Mustang. "What the hell?"

Small yellow flames flickered along the cables. He reached his rig, climbed up onto the plow frame, and disengaged the alligator clamps, again burning his fingers. Steaming, hissing, and now bare wires with the rubberized insulation completely burned off the cables fell onto the snow. But to Larry's amazement the battery was not blown and the truck continued running with its lights burning and no sign of damage from the considerable flash he'd witnessed.

Larry glanced up, his eyes still wide, but the pale man was gazing down from the cab impassively. Weird.

The snow and wind were once again picking up. Larry directed the flashlight beam onto the Mustang's battery. Its top had blown into about a hundred pieces which lay scattered all over the little V8 engine. The exposed cells of the battery were smoking or steaming, and the whole mess smelled of burnt sulfuric acid.

"Christ!" Larry swore, and swallowed the wad of gum. He closed the hood so it wouldn't fill up with snow and returned to the truck.

Larry thought the whole interior of the cab now smelled like the stranger's breath, but maybe it was just burnt insulation he was detecting. The tips of his fingers also smelled a little burned.

"Did you see that?" Larry blurted. "Holy damn! It was hooked up right, too. I've never seen anything like that in my life!"

"I told you it wouldn't work," was all his passenger had to say. In the glow of the lighted dials and gauges, the complexion of the pale man now took on an eerie greenish hue, which was accentuated with each flash of the strobe outside. Larry checked all the gauges and everything appeared normal. He tried the CB again but there was no response, and it didn't appear to be picking up any outside traffic, either.

"Well, this is something, isn't it?" Larry turned toward the man, who was sitting erect and looking straight ahead, completely unperturbed. "Guess I can't leave you here, can I? Guess this qualifies near enough to an emergency, wouldn't you say?"

"Precisely," was the response.

Larry folded two new sticks of wintergreen into his mouth and began to settle down once he got his truck back onto the buried highway. With his guidance the plow efficiently moved the considerable snow from the path ahead. Once or twice he gave the CB a try, but it was clearly dead. The odd passenger had little to say. He sat there so silently that Larry found it a bit unsettling.

"So, er...I don't think you've given me your name or where you're from," Larry began.

"No, I don't believe I have," the man said, and there was a finality to it. After a few more minutes Larry tried again.

"That Mustang of yours is a beauty. It looks to be in perfect shape. I had one just like it back in sixty-six."

"You don't say."

"Yeah, really. Same candy apple red, black interior, automatic, fake wire wheels with spinners—same exact car. I can picture it like it was yesterday."

"Hmmmm."

Larry glanced again at his perplexing passenger. There was something oddly familiar about him. Not so much as a personal acquaintance, perhaps, but more like a character he'd seen on TV or at the movies.

"Yeah, 1966. Boy, that was a long time ago. Things sure have changed a lot in thirty years."

"You don't say."

"Yep, back then I thought I'd be setting the world on fire—especially after I got that Mustang. I wouldn't've believed it for a second if someone'd told me I'd end up working thirty years for the state, driving a snowplow in winter and a gravel truck the rest of the year."

The passenger seemed to be perking up a little, possibly taking an interest in the one-sided conversation. "So that was some car for a senior in high school, wasn't it, Lawrence?"

Larry started at the use of his formal Christian name. He hadn't heard it spoken for years. Even more disquieting was that he couldn't remember telling this man his name at all—but guessed he might have.

Outside, the storm continued raging. Inside, the normally cozy cab felt unusually cold. The windshield directly before his passenger was actually beginning to accumulate frost on the inside surface. Larry bumped up the defroster another notch, and turned the blower up to full. He wished he hadn't removed his coat.

"The Mustang?" Larry said, getting back to the conversation. "You bet. For a short time it almost put me on top of the heap."

"How's that?"

"Well, you know. I wasn't no genius in high school or nothing. But that would have been okay if I'd had other things."

"Like what, Lawrence?" the passenger asked, again using his formal name.

"Please, just call me Larry." But now he was thankful for someone to talk to. "Oh, I guess mostly things girls notice, like good looks or money or being good at sports."

"Surely you must have been big enough?"

"Oh, yeah, I was plenty big, but I was slow and clumsy as hell. In gym class even Coach Sumner called me Lard Ass. You can imagine what the other guys called me."

"I probably can."

"I was a stupid dork, period. A laughingstock. Girls wouldn't have anything to do with me."

"How did you manage?"

"Oh, I coped, or rebelled sometimes, and made do with friends as hopeless as I was."

Ahead in the blinding snow, barely discernible, was a road sign to Beaver Cove. The going was not getting any easier, and Larry was glad he had the sometimes troublesome tire chains that now were allowing him to proceed.

"Got into the wrong crowd, did we, Lawrence?" the stranger probed.

"You could say that, but what choice did I have? At least these guys knew how to get dope—you know, pot, mostly, and acid once in awhile. And we were a comfort to each other. We kept telling ourselves we were really cooler than those popular jerks."

"Did you believe that?"

"Well, no, 'course not. I looked at these pathetic creeps, supposedly my friends, then I'd look at the popular guys with their girls like Betsy Graves, Linda Larrabee, and Bev Jennings—now *she* was really something—and it was easy to see it was us who were really the losers."

Suddenly, oncoming headlights greeted them as they rounded a bend.

"Now who the hell could that be?"

Larry rolled down his window as they passed abreast a four-wheel-drive Dodge Ram with a pair of wide-eyed loggers in the cab. The bumper of the pickup was plowing snow as it churned along.

"Hope those guys know what they're doing. Well, anyway, now they can use our side of the road—not likely they'll meet anyone else." Sure enough, in the rearview mirror Larry saw the Dodge pull over into the plowed path behind his truck and continue on south.

"You were saying, about Marilyn Meunch, Lawrence?"

"Did I mention Marilyn? Didn't think I did, but I guess I must've. Yeah, Marilyn, the one girl who had it all—good looks, nice tits, good grades, cheerleader, and sexy as hell. I was obsessed with Marilyn. She was in my homeroom, and she was pretty nice, even to me. Man, I wanted her something awful." Larry's gum-chewing grew faster and faster.

"Did you ask her for a date?"

"No, 'course not. Not for a long time, anyway. I wasn't stupid or crazy. She was going steady with Daryl Larsen, anyhow. Big blonde football player—drove a little two-seater T-Bird. What chance did I have? I didn't even have a car. Well, not really. Sometimes my old man let me take the station wagon. Some cool, huh?"

"Is that where the Mustang came in?"

"Well, sort of. How'd you guess?"

"Not difficult to figure, really. Or maybe I have some inside information."

"What do you mean by that?" Larry glanced over at his enigmatic passenger.

"Well, from what you're saying, I'd bet you were ready to do just about anything to get a crack at Marilyn Meunch."

"That's the truth. Practically anything."

There was a pause. "You don't remember me, do you Lawrence?"

Glancing at his passenger, Larry said, "You? Well no, I guess not. Should I?" The hair was beginning to stand up on the back of his neck.

"How about now, Lawrence?"

Larry looked again and let out a scream. He covered his eyes with both hands, letting go of the wheel. In the seat next to him the eerie passenger had somehow changed into a terrible creature with a beaked nose, waxy skin, and a mouthful of rotten tooth stumps. A thin black tongue flicked rapidly between the stubs. Worst of all were the bulging yellowish eyes with their tiny red irises. Larry shrieked again, his hands still covering his eyes, but the plow truck continued along the highway without straying or faltering.

"Now you remember me, don't you, Lawrence? We made a little deal awhile back involving a red Mustang and certain other favors."

Larry was now trembling like a gun-shy setter, and whimpering like a raccoon caught in a trap. "No!" he cried. "Go away! You're not real. You're not here."

"Oh, but Lawrence, I kept my side of the bargain. You got what you wanted, right?"

Larry's right hand slid down past his eye just a bit. He spread his fingers, dreading but wanting a second look at the creature. Instead, next to him sat the pale passenger in the suit. The truck continued along the road, and Larry reflexively grabbed the steering wheel to take back control. His breathing was irregular and his sobbing had not entirely subsided.

"You remember now, don't you?" The rider's mouth was twisted into a thin grin. "Sorry about the theatrics, Lawrence. I never really like resorting to that, but most people expect it. Otherwise they don't believe I can deliver my side of the deal. You were in a receptive mood for them that night, if I recall."

"But that's not fair. I was on pot and I'd dropped some acid, and you were just part of a weird dream—a nightmare, I'd call it."

"What does that change?"

"What does that change? Why, everything. I was drunk and I was stoned. I don't think I was even conscious. What kind of shape is that to make a deal in?"

"There's nothing in the rules against it," the passenger observed. "Besides, you'd have made the same deal if you'd been wide awake and sober as a judge, wouldn't you have, Lawrence, to get Marilyn?"

"Well...well, probably I would have, but that wasn't the case."

"A deal's a deal, Lawrence."

Larry swallowed the ball of gum he'd been violently chewing. "Sure, b-but this is crazy. I was stoned. You weren't real. And...and it wasn't you gave me the Mustang, anyways."

"Where did you get the car?" the man asked patiently.

"It was my grandfather's."

"Your grandfather's. Wasn't that a little bit strange, Lawrence?"

"Well, y-yes. But it was Gramps's car, sure enough. He bought it about a year after losing Gram. Everyone said he'd gone off his rocker or he was having his second childhood or something."

"And how did you happen to get it?"

"Gramps died, of course. Choked to death at home on a pork chop bone. Wait! Oh, no! You didn't, did you? Did you kill Gramps?" Larry's feet hit the clutch and brake.

"Let's not stop here, Lawrence." Suddenly Larry's feet felt like they were on fire. He jerked them from the pedals and the pain ceased. The plow truck continued along precisely on its route.

"Let's just say, Lawrence, that sometimes it takes a little intervention to move things along in their intended direction. You got the Mustang, and you were in heaven—pardon the expression—and you never gave your grandfather another thought. Correct?"

"Well, I...er...."

"Exactly. And did that get you Marilyn?"

"No. No, it didn't. She was still going with Daryl Larsen. There, see? It wasn't you at all. You may have used Gramps to get me the Mustang, but that didn't get me Marilyn."

"What did?"

"Well...me askin' her, mostly. After Daryl had the accident in his T-Bird Marilyn, was a little...."

"Daryl had an accident, did he?"

"I'll say, he totaled his car and it paralyzed him from the hips down. He didn't even want to live, but they pulled him through..... Wait! Oh, no! That was you, too, wasn't it? Oh, my God."

Suddenly Larry's fingers felt on fire.

"Let's not use that name, please. Not when there's a discussion between the two of us. Okay, Lawrence?" The pain subsided instantly. "Daryl was in the way, so he had to be removed from the picture if you were going to have any success. Did you say Marilyn was a little upset?"

"She was a wreck. She didn't know what to do. She loved Daryl, but only the way he'd been. You know, a tall, handsome athlete, not the broken, bitter kid jammed into a wheelchair. She felt guilty about it. Took up smoking joints. Doing crazy things."

"And there was your chance, right?"

"Right. I'm ashamed to say it, but you're right."

"Shame is something you need not confess to me."

"I couldn't help myself. She started riding to school with me in the Mustang. She lived just two streets over. Her family wasn't rich or anything. One day she said she'd go to the movies with me. I was on top of the world."

"Did you get what you wanted, Lawrence?"

"By and by. First it was just driving around, smoking and drinking on weekends. Then we were parking out around the lake, like everyone else. Then one night her folks were away and we were on the couch in her living room, and it happened."

"It happened. You got what you'd been after. You must have felt good about yourself."

"It was a rush all right. But it wasn't really what I'd anticipated. She didn't love me, and by then I don't think I loved her, either. It had been, like, one of those unattainable goals, but once we did it, it wasn't as magical as I thought it'd be."

"Was it just that once?"

"Oh, no; after that we did it pretty regular for about six months, I'd say. But her head was really getting weird. I think it always had been. Anyway, it wasn't what I thought it would be. She was still pretty, though, and I enjoyed the attention I got. I lost twenty pounds. Even my zits cleared up some. The dorks that used to be my pals couldn't believe it."

"So what happened?"

"Well, Marilyn Meunch was always a little unstable and not really so very nice. She took an interest in the older brother of one of her chums, a scary guy who'd quit school and joined the army. He was visiting home on leave and they just got together. She dropped me like a hot rock and ended up following this soldier to Tennessee. I heard they were married after he completed a hitch in 'Nam."

"But you still had the Mustang?"

"Well, yes, for a few more months, anyhow. I lent it to my kid brother for a big dance and he skidded off the road and totaled the damn car. He wasn't hurt much, but the car was gone. Because he was a minor and had had a few beers, the insurance company wouldn't pay. I didn't speak to him for two years."

The passenger grinned. "Easy come, easy go, eh, Lawrence?"

The two-way radio suddenly sprang to life.

"Base to Unit 40. Unit 40 come in. Where are you, Larry? Do you read me? This is Mike, the dispatcher. Why haven't you checked in? Do you read...."

Larry reached for the transmitter, but the pale man pointed his finger at the set. There was a spark and a snap, and the radio fell silent. The temperature in the cab was falling again. Larry shivered, and for fifteen or twenty minutes there was just the snow and the road and the silence. Larry stuck a couple of sticks of gum in his mouth.

"N-now what happens?" Larry broke the silence, his voice cracking.

"What do you think?"

"W-well I g-guess you take me off, or k-kill me or something."

Jerry Stelmok

He couldn't keep the sob out of his voice.

"Something like that, but not exactly."

"Well, what then?" He'd stopped watching the road, as the truck obviously didn't need his guidance to stay true to its course. There was no reply. "B-but I've led a good life since then, I ain't hurt no one."

"I should hope not."

"Doesn't that count for anything?"

"What?"

"Living a good life. Not hurting no one."

"It's something, but I don't recall any clause that would get you off the hook for that. Tell me about your good life, Lawrence."

"W-well, let's see. I ain't never been in jail. Never broke any important laws really...might've kept a few short fish."

"That doesn't mean anything. Most laws are idiotic. The rest are just ways of manipulating people by those in power, so they can stay in power."

"I was a good husband."

"You're divorced, correct?"

"Sure, have been for fifteen years. Tina run off with another fella. A bread salesman."

"Why was that?"

"Tina's always been a little wild. Married me to make another guy jealous, if that tells you anything! That didn't work so good, so she settled in. We had a half dozen or so pretty good years."

"Then what?"

"Then she got restless, I guess. Started jerking me around. I knew she was seein' other fellas. But for a while at least she kept it pretty quiet. But it got worse. After awhile everyone knew our marriage was a joke."

"Then the bread salesman?"

"Yep, then the bread salesman."

They'd reached the mouth of the Temperance River. The wind blew stronger through the little canyon that led to the shore. Larry was into his plowing again. Even this troubling conversation had relaxed him a bit, but his gum-chewing was just as intense. He raised the plow a foot and made an initial pass across the bridge and its approaches. Then he backed all the way back, lowered the blade to its normal position, and scraped it clean with a second pass. Otherwise, he'd never have made it through.

"This storm is really something. I can't remember a worse one."

The pale man watched, then asked, "So what have you done that's so commendable?"

"W-well, I c-coached the kids some. Baseball mostly. We had a few pretty good teams. I coached the first team around here that let a girl play on it. Cassie Knowlton. Damn, she could hit the ball farther and better than most of the boys."

"But you enjoyed that—the coaching?"

"Yeah, I enjoyed it all right. I like children."

"But you never had your own?"

"No. Tina didn't want any. Too demanding, she said. Besides, she didn't let me touch her the last five years or so."

"Anything else besides coaching kids' baseball?"

"Well, there was the Morrison kids. I took care of them after their folks died."

"How did the Morrisons die?"

"Fell through the ice and drowned."

"Both of them?"

"Yep. Damnedest thing, really," Larry said thoughtfully. "They had a farm just down the road from my place. One day in late November Mary spotted a duck frozen into their farm pond. Still alive. It was a freezing day, wind blowing like crazy, but the ice in the middle had just frozen the night before. Wasn't thick at all. Barry was out hunting deer, so Mary got half a sheet of plywood and dragged that across the field to the pond. She slid it out onto the ice ahead of her. When she got near the duck she lay down on it like a toboggan or something."

"Go on."

"Well, she broke through. Slid off the plywood into the water. For a while she held onto the plywood that was wedged across the hole in the ice. But she couldn't climb out. Her mother's an invalid, watched the whole thing from her wheelchair in the house. Called the fire department, but it was too late."

"Barry come home from hunting and saw her out struggling in the pond. He dropped his gun and run out, not thinking at all. He crashed right through, and they both drowned, or froze to death, one or the other. Terrible accident and needless, and you know what was the strangest thing?"

"What?"

"When Barry went barreling through the ice, it freed up the duck. The thing shook its feathers and flew off toward the river that still had open water."

"And they had children?"

"Two teenagers. Luke was thirteen and Elaine was fifteen when it happened."

"And you took care of them?"

"Yeah, but I didn't have legal custody or nothing. That was their Uncle Wilbur. He and his wife, Fat Kate. Mean, mean people. They was beating up on poor Luke pretty regular, and I'm sure that snake was bothering Elaine. I'd watched those kids grow up and they ended up over at my place. So I let 'em stay. I fed 'em, bought clothes for 'em, taught 'em to drive, just like they was mine."

"And Uncle Wilbur never came for them with the law?"

"Oh, no. He didn't want the law hearing about what he done to those kids. Besides, he kept collecting the money from Human Services, and he didn't have to spend a cent of it on them. I told 'em not to say nothing, and they was happy, so they didn't."

"What became of them?"

"Oh, they both graduated from Mesabi High eventually. Elaine married a fella from Boston. Luke went into the service. He's got a family of his own up in Alaska. They write me two or three times a year and they never forget to send something nice at Christmas. They're real good kids." A tear started in the corner of Larry's right eye and traveled down his cheek to his chin. "They're real good kids," he repeated.

"That's a pretty good story," the pale man observed.

"It's all true. You can check up on it if you want."

"Oh, I know it's true."

"Does that mean maybe I'm off the hook?"

"I didn't say that."

"W-well, what then? Don't things like that matter? Don't *He* keep track of things like that? Oww!" Again, a burning shock surged through Larry's fingers.

"Let's leave that name out of it. Once a contract is agreed upon, no one but me can change it for any reason."

"That don't seem fair to me." Larry was starting to shake again.

"It was fair enough for you when all you wanted was to get between Marilyn's legs."

Distracted by the conversation, Larry passed right by the junction of Route One. Normally he'd have turned up it as far as the highway department garage. There he would have fueled up, gotten a cup of coffee, loaded more sand, and begun clearing the south lane back to Two Harbors. Now they were almost to Silver Bay, its few houses still in darkness, shut in by the blizzard. Just outside town the storm let up considerably, and soon it was barely snowing. Above them the three-quarters moon was dimly visible behind the inky racing clouds.

Up ahead Larry spotted what looked like taillights alongside the highway. The usual crew had plowed a couple hours before, but six additional inches of new snow had piled up in the interim. Larry pulled up beside a red Mustang. Not surprisingly, it was a 1966 model. The headlights were on, wipers working, but no one was inside. Incredibly, no snow had accumulated on the vehicle.

Larry began trembling. His chin was on his chest and he was blubbering. "Now what? Oh, gosh, now what? Please just give me a chance. J-just one more chance. I'll be good, I promise. Please, please?"

"Oh, shut up, you fool. I'm getting out now. Thanks for the lift."

"Y-you're getting out? You're letting me go?"

"I didn't say that."

"W-well, what then? W-what are you gonna do?"

"I'm going to think things over. I haven't decided."

"You're letting me go?"

"Not necessarily. I have to weigh a few things. You might end up as part of a bigger bargain."

"You mean I'm free?" Larry's face was as hopeful as a child's on Christmas morning.

"For now, anyway. But nothing has changed—*yet*—and I know how to find you."

The man climbed down and stepped over to the car, turning back toward Larry. He made a sweeping motion with his arm, indicating Larry should drive off. It didn't register. Larry sat at the wheel, his mouth open, watching the pale man. Again the man motioned Larry to pull out. But this time he jabbed Larry's fingers with a shock through the steering wheel.

"Yeoww!" Larry shook his head, put the plow truck in gear, and slowly pulled away. He watched the rearview mirrors but didn't see the man get into the car. And the Mustang's headlights didn't advance, as Larry had feared they would, only receded into the distance.

As he rounded a long curve the snow began falling again—at first just flurries, but gradually building in strength. A few miles down the highway and Larry was plowing again, the heavy snow sweeping in from the great lake. Larry continued to monitor the view behind, but now he was starting to concentrate on plowing carefully. He knew he should be looking for an opportunity to turn around and get back on his own stretch, but he hadn't the courage to go back and perhaps meet the red Mustang with its hideous driver. He was still shaking, but the whole episode was beginning to seem unreal. But it *had* been real! How could he have made it up? And it wasn't a dream, because he hadn't been sleeping. He sniffed the air for the unsettling burnt aroma that had permeated the cab during the bizarre drive, but it was no longer detectable.

"Of course it isn't," he said to himself. "I've had the vent on for ten minutes trying to get rid of it."

Larry turned on the dome light. He felt sure there would be some evidence of the pale man's earlier presence. Just what it might be, he wasn't sure. but there was nothing. No trace.

"Why should there be. anyways?" He was small enough, so of course there'd be no impression in the seat. And he wasn't stupid enough to leave a shoe or anything behind.

But there was not even a hint of dampness on the seat or on the floor in front of it from the melted snow. That was eerie. But Larry had no doubt the frightening visit had been real enough.

The blizzard continued to rage as ferociously as ever. Visibility was minimal. Larry was plowing practically on instinct alone. All his thoughts were concentrated on the terrifying visit. The pilot light on the CB radio was once again glowing, indicating it was probably working. Suddenly he thought he should check in with the dispatcher, who must be wild with anxiety. Larry hadn't checked in for hours. Now he was miles beyond his assigned stretch.

"Unit 40 to Base, do you read me? Come in Base. This is Unit 40. Over."

"Unit 40, this is Base. Read you loud and clear. Getting thick out there is it, Larry? This is supposed to be a good one. Over."

"Base, this is 40. It's a good one all right. Don't you wanna know where I'm at? Over."

For a moment there was silence.

"Unit 40, this is Base. We figure you must be near Castle Danger by now. Is there some problem out there, Larry? Over."

"Castle Danger!" Larry exclaimed to himself incredulously. Then he got it: Headquarters must think he'd come back that far on the return trip already!

"Base, this is Unit 40 again. Well, actually I'm not anywheres near Castle Danger.... You want to guess where I am? Over."

"Unit 40, this is Base. Get back to you in a few minutes. Unit 16 is having a problem with a stuck trailer truck blocking the road. Talk to you later. Out."

The radio conversation made Larry feel much better. But now he had to find a place to turn the rig around. Damn, the snow was coming down hard. What was odd was how familiar this new stretch of highway felt to him. It was like he'd been plowing it all his life. He

Jerry Stelmok

had no idea what time it was. Daylight would break late in this slop. He glanced at the clock.

"Six sixty-six—SIX SIXTY-SIX? What in the hell kind of time is that? Christ! Must have fried the clock when I jumped the Mustang—if I really jumped a Mustang at all."

He pulled back his left sleeve and looked at his watch.

"TWO-THIRTY! The damn thing must have stopped. It's gotta be almost seven, anyways." He reached for more chewing gum, but the pack was empty. "Christ," he groaned. Then he remembered he had a brand new pack in the emergency monkey suit under the seat. Still driving, he leaned forward and felt around under the seat with his right hand.

"It's here somewhere. Oh, yeah, here it is right behind the jumper cables. He pulled the cables out to get at the coveralls, then jammed on the brakes and almost sent the truck off the road as his mind caught up to the obvious: Not only were the cables in their usual place under the seat instead of lying in the snow where he'd left them, but they were in perfect condition!

"Holy cow! Holy shit!" he said over and over to himself. "That really was a dream. Thank God. Oh thank you God!"

As if to confirm this conclusion, Larry noticed for the first time the road sign alongside the passenger window. The blowing snow made it difficult to read, but in the erratic light of the strobe the letters eventually became legible: "Castle Danger 2 miles" and in a smaller shield above it "61 North."

The signs made Larry feel even better, until he thought he caught a flash of light in his rearview mirrors.

"Holy cow! Who could that be out driving at this hour, in this mess?" But now he wasn't sure he'd really seen anything. The mirrors showed nothing but blackness beyond the end of the dump body.

A glance a minute later revealed another flash, then a glimpse of headlights. But these disappeared, as well. Despite himself Larry was getting edgy. As he ground his way down a long grade, the glow of headlights at the top was now unmistakable. Larry exercised all his discipline to remain calm, but on the next straightaway, when the two bright dots actually became visible, Larry lost it.

"It's *him!* I know it. He's been playing with my mind. Oh, God! Oh shit!" Larry pressed on the accelerator. He wanted to shift into a higher gear, but knew he'd only stall out. The big plow truck lumbered into the storm, Larry leaning into the windshield as though that would move the truck faster. Still, the following headlights were growing both in size and brightness.

"Holy shit! Oh, God, please help me!" Larry thought of raising the plow, but the snow was deep, and it was heavy with moisture from the lake. He wouldn't get far.

Now the pursuer was really gaining on him and Larry was sure the headlights belonged to a Mustang.

"Oh, God! Oh, please!" His heart was hammering so hard, he thought it might let go and fly out of his chest. The headlights continued to ease closer. There was a garbled call on his radio, something to do with the state police. But that would have to wait.

Just before the bridge over the Split Rock River the road curved and dropped at a respectable grade. Larry was pushing the rig much too fast for the conditions, but he felt he was still in control.

As he reached the bridge itself, a strong gust laden with snow from the lake rushed through the chasm and visibility suddenly ended altogether for a few seconds. When it let up, Larry knew he'd corrected a little too much to the right. He jerked the wheel and touched the brake, but the surging juggernaut slid straight ahead, unmindful of Larry's command. Snow flew and the truck rammed the steel guardrail like a train, sending a twenty-foot section flying into snowy space while the truck sailed through and over the side. It fell thirty feet before striking the huge rock that gave the river its name. On impact, the plow broke free and the cab exploded into a yellow ball of flame. The dump body somersaulted over the burning cab, continuing the truck's violent descent into the chasm. It crashed through the ice in the pool below and settled standing on its tailgate, only the burning cab projecting above the surface shrouded in swirling snow.

The patrol car that had been closing on the rig pulled to a stop just beyond the ragged hole left in the guardrail. The blue strobes came on and two troopers bounded out, pulling on their parkas and fur hats. Shielding their eyes against the blinding snow, they peered down incredulously at the burning cab on top of the ice.

"Holy Christ, Bill!" one of them exclaimed. "Ever see anything like that before?"

"That's Larry Schneider's rig, isn't it?" asked Bill. "Poor bastard. I wonder why he didn't answer our call. Why the hell was he driving so fast, anyway? Hell, you'd think the Devil himself was on his tail."

The Three Requests

The rude intrusion of the telephone's relentless hammering slowly drew Willie Canton from the depths of an utterly sweet slumber. Having been the object of a serious and perfectly unrequited crush throughout high school, the delectable Marcia Staples had suddenly appeared in his dream all these years later. Remarkably, Marcia didn't look a day older than she had twenty years earlier. Having moved back into town, she had looked Willie up to invite him to dinner at her apartment. This diaphanous dream held within its folds a happiness unimaginable in the stark bleakness of his present existence. But no matter how hard he fought to hold onto this delightful delusion, it was being wrenched from him by the repeated blats of an intruder he couldn't ignore.

Swinging a sleep-numbed arm around and knocking a glass of water from the wooden crate that passed for a nightstand, he got his hand on the receiver and lifted it to his ear. There he held it without speaking as he tried in vain to recall exactly the vision of Marcia that had just slipped away.

"Hello," the phone said. It was a woman's voice, someone he would've recognized had he fully taken command of his awakened consciousness.

"Hello, is anyone there? Is that you, Will?"

"Um..., hello, yeah, it's me." He was sitting up now on the ratty sofa that doubled as his bed. The window behind him was half open and a cold wind swept through the sad apartment above the studio that everyone referred to as his shop.

"Hello, Will, it's me, Harriet. Did I wake you?"

"Um...." He glanced at the noisy plastic bedside clock—10:30! "Oh, no, 'course not, Harriet. I was just coming upstairs to get something. So, how's Mom?"

"That's just it, Will. I'm afraid she passed away...late last night."

"Oh."

"I'm so sorry, Will. It was about one-thirty. She'd woken up a few minutes earlier. Mandy, Doris's sister—you know, the nurse—woke me and I was there beside her, too. We couldn't reach Reverend Hamill, but he'd been by yesterday afternoon. Your mother didn't say anything, but she looked wide-awake and alert. I asked her if we could get her anything, but she just stared ahead for a minute or two, and then closed her eyes. And that was it, bless her soul.... You still there, Will?"

"Um...yeah, I'm still here."

"Anyway, Mandy checked her pulse and listened with the stethoscope for a heartbeat, but she was gone, just like that." Harriet sounded as though she was about to cry, but instead she continued.

"I thought about calling you, but there wasn't much sense, really. I mean, what could you possibly do under the circumstances? I figured I'd let you sleep, and I'd call this morning to find out your plans."

"Plans?"

"Well, the coroner was just here to make out the certificate, and the fellows from Leighton's Funeral Home should be here shortly. You remember she wanted to be cremated right off...Will?"

"Yeah, I remember."

"Well, Bud Leighton said we can have the ashes sometime tomorrow, so you have to decide what you want to do, and then there's the cat, of course. But look, the hearse is just pulling into the drive. I'm going to be here all day, and so is Doris, so we can talk later, okay? And, Will, I am so sorry. Are you all right?"

"Yeah, I'm all right."

"Well bless you, Will. I've got to let Bud in. We'll talk later. Bye."

"Bye, and oh yeah, thanks, Harriet."

Willie was cold—numbed by the news of his mother's death and shivering from the wind that still blew across his bed. The first thing was to close the window. There were only two, one at each gable end of the unfinished loft. Foil-backed insulation stuffed between the rafters and stapled years before was beginning to lose its grip, the upper corners peeled down to reveal the dirty yellow batting stained by leaks and embedded with mouse droppings. He walked stiffly to the sectioned-off corner behind the stairwell where there was a toilet, a sink, and a rust-streaked claw-footed tub with raw half-circles pocking the rim where the enamel had chipped off. From another wooden crate, this one nailed to the wall, he took a plastic bottle of ibuprofen and downed three of them with a handful of water from the tap.

His first attempt at starting a fire in the little cast-iron stove resulted in a fog of stinging smoke and he was forced to open the window again. On the second try he remembered to open the damper and soon there was an ambitious little blaze roaring inside, and tongues of flame were licking at the edge of the door that had been left ajar.

He poured some Cheerios into a metal bowl then realized the milk had gone sour and he'd poured it down the sink the day before, where it continued to release traces of sour unpleasantness from the trap. Rummaging around in the old fridge he located a can of Pepsi and sat back in a padded chrome chair with his feet up on the cluttered table to enjoy his breakfast. He ate the dry cereal like popcorn, washing down each mealy mouthful with a slug of soda. Before long his thoughts were drawn back to the morning's phone call, and from there it was an easy step to revisiting his recent trip home to visit his dying mother.

⁓

A nearly horizontal rain was ricocheting off the paved driveway as the boxy Dodge Colt limped in. Willie strained to see through the foggy, rain-streaked windshield that was being poorly served by the indifferent defroster and the flayed wiper blades. The familiar Shingle Style house sat among towering oaks and maples on top of a rise fifty yards off the road. The lawns, still as green as in summer, fell away in back to the shore, the perfect stone wall hugging the contoured slope like a giant angular snake. The pelting rain and stiff breeze off McKay's Cove were tearing the last stubborn leaves from the oaks. Only a solitary beech appeared able to hold some of its copper leaves in the face of this double assault. The beech had been Willie's favorite climbing tree growing up, the gray, wrinkled skin of its sweeping branches like the trunks of elephants.

Once Willie eased up on the accelerator, the Colt lurched and sputtered to an abrupt halt alongside a burgundy BMW. Willie climbed out, and oblivious to the rain, walked up the glistening slate walk between the cedar hedges. Though it was only two in the afternoon it was dark enough to fool some of the lampposts into prematurely starting their night's work.

He climbed the wide brick steps, passed beneath the shingled archway onto the front porch, and made for the outsized French doors. Just as he reached for the latch, one door swung open from within and Willie was surprised to see a pleasant looking gentleman standing there in a charcoal trench coat, holding a briefcase and black fedora in his left hand. The man's pleasant demeanor noticeably faded when he, in turn, registered the sight of Willie, who was now holding the door open for him. This change of mood was so dramatic Willie cast a glance at his own reflection in the glass, curious as to what had turned the fellow's expression so suddenly sour. But the reflection revealed nothing out of the ordinary—only a slightly overweight man in his thirties with a mop of wind- and rain-whipped orange hair, a self-conscious grin on his wide mouth, and smallish pale eyes squeezed between heavy orange eyebrows and full, freckled cheeks. His zippered sweatshirt ranged in hue from dirty gray to sooty black and was notable mostly for the dozens of holes apparently burned into it, as well as for its blown-out elbows and ragged cuffs. This was complimented by Carhartt overalls, once a burnt sienna, but now mostly just burnt, as though the wearer had just run through a grass fire. The frayed, high-cut Chuck Taylors in which his bare, wet feet squished did little to discredit this possibility. The overall image was sorry enough that even Willie regretted he hadn't taken the time to clean up and change clothes before driving down from his place outside Thorndike. But his mother's condition had sounded so grave that he hadn't given that idea much thought.

The gentleman with the briefcase had not budged nor taken his eyes off Willie, and now Harriet stepped around him and made the introductions.

"Mr. Bradbury, this is Will," she said. "Catherine's younger son."

"Oh, yes, indeed. The welder," Bradbury said, without acknowledging Willie's extended hand.

"Will," she continued, "this is Ransom Bradbury, your mother's attorney."

Now it was Willie who looked puzzled and she hastened to add, "Ever since Don Hinckley, whom you remember, retired last March."

"Pleased to meet you," Willie offered, reaching out and snatching the lawyer's reticent right hand, then pumping it enthusiastically.

"Yes, indeed," Bradbury responded, wrenching free as quickly as possible and tucking his hand into the pocket of his coat. "Mr. Hinckley and I were partners at Brougham and Hinckley."

"Really," Willie pondered. "Then how come your name isn't Mr. Brougham?"

"Er...well, naturally there have been more than just the original founding partners in the firm over the past thirty-five years. But I really must be on my way, and I know you must be anxious to see your mother. Good day." And nodding back to Harriet in the doorway, Bradbury said goodbye.

Harriet had been Willie's mother's personal secretary for as long as he could remember. She and Catherine had been friends since childhood, but when Catherine had gone off to Oberlin, Harriet had to be content with a local two-year business program. Bright, friendly, and gracious, Harriet was one of the few people beneath her own situation, that Catherine really respected, and probably her only friend. Harriet had always been able to calm the rough waters that typified Catherine's relations with her neighbors, local tradesmen, staff, and even members of her social circle. It didn't hurt that Harriet's husband was a partner in a successful financial firm in Portland. It put Catherine's mind at ease to know that Harriet wasn't staying around simply because she needed the money.

Once they were inside, Harriet gave Willie a warm hug.

"Your mom's a little better now, but early this morning when I called you things looked very grave. We've had a hospital bed moved into the parlor and there's a nurse here all the time, and usually also Doris or me.

"Your mother really loves you, Will; I don't think I need to tell you that. She can be hard on you, I know, but she really wants to see you."

There was a crashing sound and a scream from the direction of the parlor, loud enough to bring Doris running from the kitchen. The French door leading into the parlor was thrown open and a dark-haired nurse in white blouse and slacks hurried out, her right hand spread across her upper chest and throat.

"Good heavens, Mandy, what's happened?" Doris ran up to her and steadied her with a reassuring hand on the small of her back. "Is Mrs. Canton all right?"

The nurse took a couple of deep breaths and tried to settle down.

"My! Oh goodness!" she gasped. "Yes, Mrs. Canton's fine. It's that cat of hers. I was just starting to sponge her neck and face when the creature jumped up on the bed from nowhere. She landed practically in the washbasin, and then she arched her back and hissed at me. It was hideous. I guess it just startled me."

"Harriet! Doris! Where is everyone?" A deep, throaty voice issued from the room. "This so-called nurse has upset Fidget and almost drowned me with this bath water. Someone bring in more towels and fresh sheets. Must I do it myself?"

While the three women were in with his mother straightening things out, Willie walked over to the dining room windows with a view of the cove. The drenching rain cast a somber veil across the lovely backyard and the pebbly beach with the long dock resting on its granite piers. Sheets of rain and fog swept across McKay's Cove revealing sections of the little bay for a moment or two before again

Jerry Stelmok

closing in and shrouding them with a pearly gray curtain. The floats were pulled up onto the shore and secured to pilings against any unusually high tides. The dinghy, wherry, and sailboards were apparently stored for the winter in the boathouse, and the mooring for *Sweet Promise* had been pulled for the season. The Friendship sloop was no doubt hauled out at a yard on Georgetown. This former family yacht was now the responsibility of Willie's older brother, Philip, and that was fine with Willie. Just like his father, Willie had never cared for, nor gotten the hang of sailing. This was beyond the comprehension of the imperious Catherine, whose family tree had maritime roots that were easily traced back to the War of 1812.

When the room was ready, Willie was admitted into the grand parlor. His mother was sitting up in a reclining chair by the bed, a light blanket across her lap and draped over her legs. She was wearing an embroidered silk jacket over her flannel nightgown, and her silver hair was unbound but brushed back. Her naturally sharp features were now exaggerated by the weight she had lost, and the lines and wrinkles were poorly disguised by the fresh makeup, no doubt applied by Harriet. Beside her crouched her beloved cat, Fidget, a rumpy Manx tabby glowering at the intruders.

The contrast between the institutional hospital bed and the rich leather-upholstered furnishings, dark paneling, and finely bound books was jarring. Willie shifted his eyes to the birch fire crackling in the raised-hearth fireplace.

"Nothing like an open fire to cheer one up, is there Willard?" Catherine asked in a raspy lifelong smoker's voice, breaking the silence between them. "Come over here so I can get a good look at you.

"Jesus, Willard, what happened to you? Did that wreck of yours finally blow up?"

As Willie approached he extended his hand to stroke Fidget, who swatted at it, spat, wheeled around, and in one clean motion leaped onto an empty bookshelf a yard above the back of the recliner. Willie bent down to peck his mother's forehead and was forced to notice her waxy skin and her thin, brittle hair. There was also a slightly sweetish smell he couldn't place.

"I don't know as I should let you get so near, I might catch something from you," she added. "And you terrified poor Fidget."

"Don't start in on me, Mother. I came as soon as I got off the phone with Harriet. You seem to be doing better."

"Better than what? Better than a salted codfish, maybe, or a stranded whale, perhaps. Better than dead, anyhow. Maybe."

Willie had learned over the years never to rise to such bait, and was making no exceptions even as she sat before him, dying.

"You gave Harriet and the nurse quite a scare this morning. Is the pain any better?"

"If the pain were better, Willard, it would be even stronger. Am I in as *much* pain? Well, not so much now. They've got me pretty much doped up. Mr. Morphine can be a good friend at this stage of things. We Pickett women have withstood much worse than this, you know. I'm sure I've told you about your great-great-grandmother, Eliza?"

"Yes, Mother, you have."

"Eliza's husband, Harold Pickett, your great-great-grandfather, was master of a four-masted coastal schooner, Bath built, named.... You know what, Philip? I can't think of the schooner's name. Can you believe that?"

"I'm Will, Mother. Philips's in China, remember?" And indeed he was startled that his mother had forgotten the name of one of her ancestor's vessels. He couldn't remember that ever happening.

"Anyway, they were running from Charleston to Portland in January or February of 1919 when they got caught far out at sea in a winter storm. Most of the crew were helpless in their berths with a terrible flu. Turned out to be the Spanish Influenza. Two of them died of it later, if I'm not mistaken. Philip, dear, would you please hand me that glass of water?

"Thank you. Well, Eliza was with child, eight months' worth. Here, put the glass back on the end table, there. But during the worst of the storm, with the snow swirling around so thick she couldn't see the forward doghouse from the ship's wheel, and with the ship plunging down into the great troughs, shaking with each new gust, and dark water washing over the decks, your great-great-grandmother stood there at the helm. Captain Pickett and one able deck hand took down frozen sail, dislodged ice, and manned the pumps to keep them afloat. Well, Eliza fought that wheel, holding courses her husband yelled to her, and she brought the *Heaven Sent*—that was the schooner's name, appropriate wouldn't you say?—right into Boston Harbor. That's what the women in this family can do."

But her voice had grown weaker, no more than a hoarse whisper, and Willie had to lean in close to catch the end of the familiar story. He sat quietly, watching her breathe, and soon her eyes closed.

Philip, of course, was Willie's older bother, and clearly his mother's favorite. Schoolwork and nearly everything else that had proven difficult for Willie had come easily to his brother. Teachers loved him, and their great expectations for Willie when he walked into their classrooms two years after his brother were inevitably met with disappointment. Catherine's friends, ministers, self-important bores at the yacht club in their silly hats, all loved Philip, and Willie came to accept this as natural.

Still, these guileless people didn't see a side of his brother that Willie knew all too well. Philip was the kind of big brother who turned loose Willie's beloved hamster outdoors, and would run his little brother's bicycle with its awkward training wheels into the ditch and then say it was an accident. Or he would pull Willie's kite into the treetops while pretending to "help." With his friends, Philip would run and hide from Willie, who couldn't keep up and wanted so much to belong. And it was Philip who tagged him with the despised nickname "Carrot Head" that—much to Willie's distress—caught on at school and around the neighborhood.

His thoughts were interrupted when Doris, the housekeeper, appeared to check on Catherine and bring Willie a cup of hot chocolate with real whipped cream floating on top. As usual, she had spiked the creamy rich drink with a jigger of Bailey's. Doris had been Catherine's housekeeper and cook for seven or eight years, coming in each morning except Sundays and, in her efficient manner, keeping the house immaculate. Before leaving she would make dinner. They were lucky to have her, really. She liked the work, but had difficulty understanding Catherine's selfish moods and probably would have left long before if it weren't for Harriet's calming influence.

Catherine's eyes opened as Doris was leaving the room, and for a moment she looked a little startled. After a minute she reached for a glass of juice the housekeeper had brought, and Willie steadied her trembling hand while she took a few sips. Her wrists were little bigger around than a broomstick and her skin as dry as parchment. When she was finished, Willie gently wiped her mouth with a clean face towel.

"So, tell me, Willard, how is the market in rusted sunflowers these days?"

She was referring to the outsized flowers that Willie cut out of scrap steel, welded together, and sold at fairs, garden shows, at a seasonal tourist trap in a barn on Route One, along with other lawn ornaments and an occasional weathervane. Like any artist, he would have preferred more creative and challenging constructions, but most years it was the big flowers, frogs, grasshoppers, and, this past summer, metal goldfish that allowed him to nearly pay the bills. But he said nothing as he waited for his mother's next unkind attack; he was used to it.

"I don't suppose you've any exhibitions opening at the Museum of Modern Art or anything?"

"Not at the MoMA, I'm afraid, but I think I did send you those photos of the logging sculpture, didn't I? I finished that piece and it went to the Farnum Museum for installation in September."

"Surely you're kidding, Willard. Did you say the Farnsworth? That heap of rusted junk that looked like what's left after a barn burns down? I can't believe no one told me anything about it. Why, every year I...."

"No, Mother, not the Farnsworth. The Farnum Logging Museum. Outside Millinocket."

"Oh, of course. What could I have been thinking? The Farnum *Logging Museum,* and were you paid for it?"

"Of course I was. It was a big hit." This was a small exaggeration.

A benefactor of the museum had pledged $1,500 for a logging-related piece of art to be hung in the new visitor's center of this small but very fine institution dedicated to the history of the timber industry in northern Maine. For his inspired construction that conjoined dozens of old peaveys, pike poles, boom chains, whiffletrees and double trees, bendy crosscut saws and circular mill blades and such in a complex and ingenious spiral—which had taken him several months to construct—Willie was paid half of the bequest. The remainder was spent on better fixtures to illuminate it. The piece did receive a lot of attention, including some from individuals who knew and appreciated art. Willie had already been approached by an agent from down state whose client was interested in a similar piece for the lobby of a new bank, but utilizing the gear and hardware of the fishing industry.

"Well, whoever said education didn't pay off?" Catherine's sarcasm was little diminished by her depleted condition, but her delivery was considerably softer.

A misfit throughout high school, though intelligent and creative, Willie had not been interested in applying for college until a friend of his mother sent over a catalog for Bennington. The admissions office looked past his dismal academic record to his creative energy and he was enrolled. But Willie proved a square peg even among this eclectic student body, whose sophisticated social excesses and dependencies went way beyond his naïve comprehension. Lacking the discipline and the proper tools to design his own program, he floundered through a confusing semester finding solace only in the barn-like sculpture studios under the guidance of a brilliant, if schizophrenic, visiting artist from Chile. In fact, he was totally captivated by the process of cutting metal components and assembling them into creative designs.

A year later Willie enrolled in a museum art school in Boston with similar results. Since there was no program in metal sculpture, he slogged away at painting and sculpting in clay with indifferent effort. He did enjoy Boston, however, particularly the park along the Charles and the Public Gardens. He even enjoyed a brief fling with a sculpture intern from Ireland that produced many firsts in his life, including his first seriously broken heart when Alice returned home at the end of the term to her waiting boyfriend.

Following a period of brooding, Willie got a job lumping fish on the piers of the Portland Fish Market, a position that suited his temperament and self-esteem at the time and gave him a legitimate outlet for his pent-up, directionless energy. One day, as he was reading the help-wanted ads with no actual expectations, he noticed an ad for a welding program at a vocational college. He read the description of the comprehensive course several times and was charged with real excitement for the first time in a long while.

Philip, on the other hand, had continued his charmed, focused, success, graduating from MIT in aeronautical engineering, then following that up with a masters in business from Stanford. He worked for a San Diego-based aircraft manufacturer for a short time before being lured to a better offer in Washington State. Now he was heading up a four-year plant conversion in China for his company.

While at Stanford he had met his future wife, Elaine, a former Miss Nebraska who was clerking for a federal judge. They were married at an opulent wedding in Lincoln six months before leaving for Beijing, where Elaine landed a job at the U.S. Embassy. Catherine often credited her vivacious daughter-in-law with "actually having the talent and the brains to match her spectacular boobs."

Now, Catherine seemed to find another charge of energy. "I've picked a damned inconvenient time to die, Willard," she said.

"You're not going to die, Mom." And he gently picked up her bony hand, only to have her pull it back sharply.

"Oh, cut the crap, Willard. Face reality for just once in your life. Of course I'm dying, and it's probably about time.

"Unfortunately, Philip's off setting up those damned Chinese in the serious aircraft business—a very poor policy, if you ask me, but a good opportunity for him nonetheless. Did I mention that Elaine's now a solicitor working at the U.S. Embassy?"

"Yes, Mother, I know."

"Well, anyway, when they were here last month you really should have come down to see them, you know. Anyway, we pretty well got things in order. Ransom Bradbury and I had updated my will before-hand. As you know, Philip is getting this house, since he's in a posi-tion to best appreciate and maintain it. The house is being appraised to get a current value and the sum will be transferred to your half of the estate. Five or six years ago, Lincoln Boyce, the realtor from Bath, said it was worth half a million. Can you believe that? When Papa bought the house for your father and me when we were married, he was outraged that he had to pay thirty-five thousand for it. Of course, the house is really only a small part of the estate.

"So, Willard, thanks to your shrewd—some called them ruth-less—forebears, you'll be in a position to buy quite a pile of scrap metal, won't you?"

Willie had nothing to say to that, but grinned meekly.

"Don't get your hopes up! Believe me, I've learned my lessons about giving you too much money to play with."

Willie knew exactly what she meant, and shifted his eyes to gaze at the oriental carpet at his feet.

"So the firm of Brougham and Hinckley will administer a trust fund for you, and with their guidance and your brother as executor, you should be quite comfortable, and...."

"Mother, thanks, but I don't think that's really necessary. I've...."

"Oh, it's necessary all right, and it's been done. Now Philip and Elaine will be coming for a few weeks in May. We've arranged for a memorial service during that visit, here at the house. The grounds are lovely then and the grass will be nice and green...." But the old woman trailed off, and for the first time, tears welled from her sunken eyes.

"Mother?" Willie said.

"It's all right, Willard. Just give me a second here." She refused his help drying her eyes with a tissue. "Anyway, at that time you and your brother can get any details settled between you that aren't explicitly covered in the will.

"Now, I'm getting very weary. Tomorrow morning we'll go over just a few matters that you must attend to. Oh, I do wish Philip was here. If you'd tell Harriet to please come in—I don't think she's left yet."

Just then there was a knock and the door opened as Harriet and the night nurse came in, affording Willie an opportunity to withdraw.

He wandered around the house that, while familiar, was hard to think of as his childhood home. Each year it was feeling more like a museum and less like someone's actual residence. On the paneled walls of the hall leading to the library, formerly his father's den, hung portraits, both paintings and photographs of Pickett family patriarchs, but none of the Canton family ancestors. Most were stern-looking men in vested suits with watch chains or in nautical attire—merchant sea captain or naval officer uniforms. Catherine had always stressed the seafaring roots of the family to her sons or anyone else whom she could corner. But despite this rich tradition, the real wealth of the family could be attributed to her grandfather, in the photograph a frail-looking man with a thin mustache and John Lennon spectacles. Philip Worden Pickett had been sickly throughout his youth, and therefore unable to follow a life at sea. Instead he went to work in a bank, and at forty-three leveraged the modest family fortune to found a small independent savings bank in Brunswick that competed successfully, as Catherine often boasted, with the much larger financial institutions in Bath and Portland.

In the kitchen, Willie found a delicious homemade minestrone soup to warm up along with some sourdough bread Doris had prepared before she left. He ate two bowls of soup and half the loaf, and considered his mother's references to his past performance squandering money when it was made available.

After the welding program, Willie had begun a search for a place to live as well as set up his studio. As always, his father, Robert Canton, was excited about his new prospects and after what must have been endless and painful, if not actually humiliating, negotiations with Catherine he managed to persuade her to finance their son's efforts. But even he was a little disappointed when Willie settled on an unfinished gambrel-roofed shell on six acres of cut-over woodlot in the hilly countryside of Waldo County.

Even though this was the late seventies, the low-priced fallow farms there were still a magnet for dreamers of all persuasions, all of them labeled "hippies" by the skeptical locals. In fact, a number of these hippie settlers had befriended Willie and convinced him that for the $50,000 limit his mother had set, he could buy land and studio, with an apartment upstairs his friends would help him finish. And according to them, he'd have plenty left to purchase all the torches, chain falls, band saws, and other equipment he would need to get started.

Within a couple of weeks of moving up and while living in a tent, Willie and the crew had hooked up the existing well, installed a kitchen sink and bathroom upstairs, and a trailer furnace and deep sink in the shop. They had also insulated both levels and were nailing up plywood as a practical choice for the interior studio walls.

After an inspection, Willie's father was so thrilled by the progress, as well as by his son's exuberance, that he handed over the check for the remaining half on the spot, and took the crew into Belfast for a celebratory night out.

That visit pretty well marked the end of any appreciable progress on the place, although it was now hard to tell because of clutter that had accumulated over the past twenty years and the scars of hard use. Once his opportunistic neighbors became aware of the extent of this new source of wealth in their midst, the amount of work accomplished per case of beer or bag of pot began diminishing exponentially. This steady drain became a deluge when the group persuaded Willie to "invest" in their scheme to convert a huge three-story, aluminum-sided chicken barn into an incubator for gourmet mushrooms that the restaurants of Portland and Boston were supposedly screaming for. Two of the clan's young women suddenly took an intense romantic interest in the artist, and were plenty skilled in administering their wholesome charms, both singly and together, and Willie readily agreed to help finance the project.

The last remaining few thousand bought a trip to Iceland for four of the group, the girls included, for the purpose of researching which breeds of Icelandic sheep might best be suited for the Waldo County environment. Willie, who was originally supposed to be part of the mission, found himself grounded, watching from the departure gate at the Bangor airport as his friends gaily disappeared into the boarding area. Apparently there had been a mysterious "mix-up" when the tickets had been reserved a few weeks before. Nor surprisingly, neither the mushrooms nor the sheep succeeded, the hippie group split up, and Willie was left poorer and only slightly wiser.

Then, just two years ago, Willie had gotten an opportunity to redeem himself when his brother took over ownership of the sloop *Sweet Promise*. To be fair, Catherine compensated her younger son with a check in the amount of the marine surveyor's appraised value of the boat—not all that much, considering the amount of yard work that would be necessary to put her back into top shape. Willie managed to use up the entire windfall on a trip to the highlands of Mexico, where the former Chilean mentor from his Bennington days was conducting a series of workshops. Besides airfare, tuition, and living expenses, all quite reasonable, other costs included a used Escort for his teacher's wife, who'd was injured in an accident that had totaled their ancient Toyota. He also sprang for the tuition of a cute black-eyed Venezuelan girl who was unable to come up with her own funding, and he picked up the check for countless evenings of cheap beer and great food involving fellow students, teachers, American snowbirds, and aimless travelers.

As Willie finished off his introspective supper with some of Doris's delicious pear cobbler, the night nurse came into the kitchen to brew coffee. Surprisingly, she seemed interested in his art and asked some thoughtful questions. She also asked him how prepared he was for his mother's impending death. Later, Willie sat reflectively at Catherine's bedside while the nurse read a mystery and the ever-vigilant Fidget glared at him from the foot of the bed. Then he climbed the stairway to his old room to retire. The downpour had abated, so he opened wide a window to breathe in the damp ocean air and listen to the gong on the channel marker rolling with the swells at the mouth of the harbor.

The following morning, after showering and changing into some

Jerry Stelmok

decent jeans and a clean shirt from his closet, Willie ate a breakfast of bacon, eggs, toast, coffee, and the rest of the pear cobbler. He waited until the nurse had finished the morning routine, then went in to see his mother.

Catherine looked rested and much stronger. She was sitting up in bed stroking Fidget, who still regarded Willie with suspicion. She cut the preliminaries short, and got right to the point.

"It's such a pity Philip can't be here. But that's how it stands, so I'm afraid there are a few details you'll have to take care of. Do you think you can do that for me, Willard?"

"Of course I can, Mom. Anything."

"Well, I hope you can manage them. You haven't always been that dependable.

"First of all there's the matter of sweet Fidget here. She's such a sweet baby." The cat craned her neck, gazing lovingly up at Catherine, then again fixed her glare on Willie.

"She's a purebred Manx you know, a breed developed on the Isle of Man. Most Manx are born without a tail, or only a little bitty one. There was a myth that they were a cross between a shipwrecked cat and a rabbit. Hence the short tail and the unusually long hind legs. But of course that's ridiculous. Anyway, Fidget loves me and doesn't really care for anyone else."

"I've noticed that."

"Philip is not only allergic to cats, but he's living in China. He wanted me to put the poor baby into a kennel while he and Elaine were visiting last month. But we couldn't have that, could we, Fidgie? So Philip's out and your living situation, up over that dump, is preposterous. And Harriet isn't a cat person, so I've made arrangements with the Clausens, who live in Thomaston.

"If you remember, they were the breeders who sold me Fidget. They've agreed to take her back into their home and keep her as one of their own pets. It's far from ideal, but they do know Fidget, and she'll be in a familiar environment."

"Do you want me to take her there now?"

"No. Don't be stupid. Of course not yet. For one thing Rob and

Nita are in South Carolina until sometime next week. And I want my baby with me until the end. Don't I, little baby?" and she scratched the cat's fat jowls.

"Harriet has all the information and the travel cage and knows about Fidget's special toys. Now, if I go before the Clausens return, you are to take Fidget to her veterinarian, Dr. Crosby—Harriet has all that—until they return home. Then you can deliver the poor little darling."

Fidget watched and listened as though understanding every word.

"Second, Willard, there is the matter of my ashes. Now I have no idea why your father was so devoted to that ramshackle camp on that fog-ridden, godforsaken cove in—where was it—Cutler?"

"Trescott, Bailey's Neck, actually."

"Trescott then. For my part I detested the place, and after seeing it once I refused to go near it. But Robert spent more and more time there every summer right up until his death, which I can't understand when we have all this." She swept her open hand in an arc across the bed, indicating the whole McKay's Cove complex.

"But naturally we honored his request and spread his ashes on that jumble of boulders he called a beach, and that puts me in an uncomfortable situation."

"How's that, Mom?"

"How's that? Well I'll tell you how's that! Your father was, of course, my husband, and it's normally expected that the ashes of a married couple will be either interred or scattered at the same location. At least that's the way it's always been in our family. But Robert was being very unfair, you see. He knew just what I thought about Bailey's Neck, or whatever it's called. Hell's Door is more like it. And still he went and requested that without really consulting me or getting my approval."

"For a change," Willie thought to himself. "Good for him." Then, aloud:

"So, Mom, where would you like your ashes scattered? Here on the cove?"

"No. I would prefer a dignified family gathering after the memorial service at King's Pine Park with my ashes inside an urn, then buried and a proper headstone installed."

"Well, then, Mother, that's what we'll do."

"You haven't been paying attention, Willard. First you must honor your father by flinging *half* of my ashes across that windswept, barren shore. Because like it or not, that is my duty as his wife."

"Are you sure that's what you want, Mom?"

"Clearly it's *not* what I want, Willard, but it's what must be done, and you're the one who's going to have to do it."

"Why don't we all go next summer, when...."

"No, Willard. I won't have everyone dragged down there to that wasteland to witness this humiliation. And besides, you remember I sold that dump as soon as I could after Robert's death, and now some other sucker owns the place. And whoever it is, is likely to be there in the summer. But I can't imagine anyone in his right mind being there in November. They'd die of depression for sure.

"Now, you were there, Willard, and you helped scatter your father's ashes. I want you to spread mine on the same rocks on the shore, and I want it done before there's snow on the ground. I don't think even dead, and reduced to ash, I could bear being consigned to that bleak shore when it's covered with snow.

"So, Willard, when you get that call, Harriet will have half my ashes, and I want you to drive down there at your first opportunity before the snow starts falling, and you are to cast my remains to join those of your father."

Tears were welling in Willie's eyes with his mother's less than respectful references to his beloved father.

"You know, Willard, I had it all before your father came along."

"What do you mean, Mom?"

"Well, there I was—young, poised, quite a stunner if I do say so myself. From a good family with money, and there were those who thought I could have made a mark as a concert pianist. Others thought that after school I'd land one of the millionaires' sons who used to come courting each summer.

"But then along came your father. Poor Robert, broke, a little goofy, teaching sociology part-time at a crummy little college. And still working summers at the Sand Dollar restaurant on Orr's Island, where he'd worked during college. But Lord, he was handsome! And he was funny and could we ever dance together! I loved him so, and I couldn't be without him, no matter what anyone said—and they said plenty. And I can't say that it was ever perfect, or that I was easy to live with. But even with all the prospects I turned my back upon, I could never bring myself to regret marrying your father."

She was silent for a couple of minutes, her eyes closed. When she opened them she dried her eyes with a tissue.

"I'll take care of that, Mother. You can count on me."

"And the last thing, Willard, there's the matter of your great-great-great-grandfather's weatherglass."

"My great-great-great-grandfather's what?"

"Weatherglass. An antique barometer. I'm sure I've told you about it. You're named for him—Willard Leonard Pickett. Although of course your name's not Pickett. He was a privateer during the Civil War. He sailed a shallow-draft schooner and he caused the Confederacy a lot of trouble. Plus he got his hands on vital supplies no one else could easily get. For his services, years later he was presented this historic instrument by the vice president of the United States, Schuyler Colfax."

"Oh, yeah, I remember now. Where is it, anyway?"

"I'm not finished yet, Willard. He had his ship blown out from under him in a fog off Cape Hatteras and escaped into the night with most of his crew in the ship's boat. The following night they stole a Confederate cutter off its mooring and sailed it home, not knowing until they were underway that its hold was filled with military rifles that had been stolen by the Rebels from a Yankee garrison."

"Yes, Mom, I do remember you telling me that."

"Well, that weatherglass, with its inscribed brass tag, is going to be on permanent display at the maritime museum. It was already an antique when it was presented to Captain Pickett. It's from a British vessel captured during the War of 1812. It's in the long, narrow wooden box on the writing table in the den."

"So you want me to take it to the museum?"

"No, Willard. You're to take it to Mr. Daryl Stedderman in Searsport. He's a museum conservationist who specializes in marine antiques. The wood parts need reconditioning, the fluids need to be changed or recharged, and the gimbals need repair."

"Then do I take it to the museum?"

"No. Mr. Stedderman will deliver it when he's completed the work. All you have to do is bring it to his studio. Harriet has all the information and will make the appointment.

"Now, I know what condition your vehicle is in, and how undependable it is, so I want you to take the Volvo. Harriet's having it serviced later this week, then you can keep it."

"Thanks, Mom. But I really don't...."

"Yes, Willard. It's all set. Philip and Elaine have no interest in a five-year-old station wagon. Now, Willard, I'm feeling very tired. I do appreciate your driving down to see me."

"Really, Mom, I wanted to, and I was planning to come even before Harriet called."

""Now I want you to go back home, if that's what you call it."

"But, Mom, I think I should stay here to be near you."

"No, Willard. I still have some loose ends to tie up, and Harriet will help me. I'll need all my strength for that. Harriet will call you when the time comes. Then you must come at once and take care of these three matters. Is that understood?"

"Mom!" he tried to protest, but she shook her head and closed her eyes. "All right, Mom, I understand."

"Goodbye, Willard."

"I love you, Mom." He leaned over and kissed her on the forehead but there was no response, only her shallow breathing.

At the doorway he turned and watched her resting peacefully, still sitting up.

"Goodbye, Mom."

"Willard, I do so worry about you."

That had been just the previous week, and as Willie had expected it was be the last time he would see his mother. Now there were things expected of him and he pledged to himself that for once he would not disappoint her, wherever she might be. He would call Harriet back and as soon as his mother's ashes were available, he would drive down and discharge his obligations. But before he'd deposited his cereal bowl onto the mound of crusty dishes in the sink, his phone rang again.

"Hello."

"Hiya, Carrot Head. It's your rich and famous big brother in China."

"Hi, Philip."

"Well, the old dame's finally up and done it, hasn't she? And here everyone was betting she was just too stubborn to die."

"What?" Willie couldn't believe his brother was being so callous.

"Oh, nothing, serious one. How's the weather in bleak old Maine? It's beautiful here today. I'm in Shanghai lining up some subcontractors. This is a fascinating place."

"I'm sure it is. It's getting pretty cold around here. I think we'll be getting some snow before long."

"Well, Laney and I will be returning stateside for a couple weeks in May, and we'll get the memorial service or whatever out of the way and settle up on odds and ends. I think everything's pretty well set. You'll be hearing from Ransom Bradbury and getting a copy of the will, I suspect. Everything's pretty black and white, except for dividing up the contents of the house. I'm willing to have it all appraised and buy you out, then we won't have to deal with going over it all piece by piece."

"We don't have to talk about all that right now, do we?"

"Carrot Head, life is busy and it just keeps getting busier. You know if the old girl had hung on much longer, we wouldn't have anything left to split."

"What do you mean?"

"Well, Old Tightwad suddenly got very generous once she knew the end was in sight. You know what the old girl did? She wrote in Harriet for fifty Gs."

"Harriet's been a great...."

"That's fifty grand, Carrot Head, and the same thing for the church. The way that weasel Reverend Hamill has been skulking around, I'm sure he had his hopes set a lot higher than that."

"Well, Mom was pretty involved in the church, Philip."

Philip ran on, ignoring Willie's comment. "Then there's a year's pay for the maid, and for the gardener—you know, old Michelson, who sat on his ass while his wife planted the flowers. Can you believe it?"

"Well, sure."

"Oh, give me a break, Carrot Head. And you know what else? Twenty-five grand to the friggin' Nature Conservancy. The Nature Conservancy! To protect ducks! Since when did our mother give a fuck about ducks?"

"The Nature Conservancy's a good organization, they do lots of good things."

"Right, Willie-boy, like stealing twenty-five grand from old women who no longer know what they're doing," Philip scoffed. "And then there's fifteen grand for the care of that vicious cat of hers that ought to be thrown over the Bath bridge in a sack!"

"Philip, that's not funny. Mother loves...er...loved that cat."

"And twenty grand to the maritime museum. And you know what that's for don't you? That's a bribe so they'll display that old barometer that's in the library and not lose it in some storage space. I'd love to have that thing hanging in my own office. I tell you it's a good thing she signed off when she did or half the estate would have disappeared. Anyway, Carrot Head, I've got an appointment and I have to run. Now listen, don't touch a thing. Okay?"

"What?"

"I said, don't touch anything. I know she gave you the Volvo, that's part of the will. But don't touch anything else until I get there.

Got to go, Willie-boy. Take care." And the line went dead.

—

Harriet came to the door and greeted Willie with a warm hug. She said most things were ready, but there'd been a couple of small glitches. The first was the Volvo wagon. They'd called from the dealership and had found an unusual problem with the automatic transmission and were going to replace it free of charge. However, they wouldn't be able to install it until early the next week.

"They offered to give you a loaner, if you wanted, Will. What do you think?"

"Oh, my Colt's all right. Let's not bother with that."

Harriet appeared skeptical. "Are you sure, Will? You know you could wait until next week."

"I don't want to wait Harriet. It's almost Thanksgiving and it could start snowing any day now. And you know how Mother felt about being scattered over the snow."

The second problem had to do with the cat breeders. They were not due back from their vacation until the next day, and Willie couldn't possibly bring Fidget to them until the day after that.

"But if you wanted to stay here until then, that wouldn't be a problem," Harriet suggested.

"I think I'd rather get started, Harriet. I'll take Fidget and the barometer home with me. Then on Wednesday I can deliver her to Thomaston and from there take the barometer to Searsport. Thursday I'll drive to Trescott and spread the ashes. And for once I won't have disappointed Mother." Willie was decisive, and Harriet looked stunned for a moment.

"That's a very good plan, Will. I'm sure Catherine would be very pleased. But we have one more little obstacle, I'm afraid."

She led Willie down to the laundry room in the basement. Outside the closed door sat Fidget's fashionable traveling cage. "She won't let anyone near her, Will, let alone catch her and put her in this cage.

"Careful," she cautioned when Willie cracked the door for a peek inside. The light was on but the cat was nowhere to be seen. Only a low menacing growl reached his ears from its origin behind the dryer.

"You better put these on," Harriet suggested, handing him a pair of heavy leather work gloves.

Willie shook his head, but hearing the ominous growl a second time he took her advice and pulled the stiff things on. Then, swiftly opening the door, he slid inside, closing it just as quickly. Wild crashing and howling ensued, but in just a few minutes the door opened and Willie emerged. His hair was disheveled, both sleeves of his flannel shirt were shredded, and two sets of crimson streaks crossed his forehead and left cheek. But the cat was in the madly swinging carrier in his left hand, though still emitting blood-curdling yowls.

"That wasn't so bad," Willie offered, feigning a grin, but his eyes, showing twice the normal amount of white, attested to the intensity of the recent battle.

Upstairs, with Fidget simmering down in the cage by the front door, Harriet led Willie into the library and opened a narrow walnut case that protected the fragile antique barometer. To Willie it looked like a turned post from a railing, or perhaps a king's scepter. But Harriet pointed out the small glass door at the top, and behind it the pair of thin glass tubes that disappeared into the long shaft. There were numbers on a scale behind the tubes, and above the door a brass plate was inscribed in old-fashioned script too small for him to read without his glasses. The case had a swelling a bit below the door to accommodate the gimbals, which had been used to mount the instrument to a bulkhead and keep it riding level in a rolling sea.

"It's awfully fragile, Willie, I needn't tell you. But it fits snugly in its case and we can wrap it in a blanket. But I'd be careful what I put near it—no heavy tools or anything."

"Don't worry, Harriet. I took all the junk out of the car before I left, just in case."

This also seemed to amaze Harriet, and Willie couldn't help wondering just how hopeless everyone considered him.

Eventually they got the barometer in its case, bundled in a blanket, along with Fidget's carrier, the litter box, a case of special cat food, favorite dishes and toys aboard the squat Colt wagon. Only then did

Harriet bring out a faux-leather cube-shaped box about five inches across each side. Inside was a lovely lidded urn decorated with hand-painted irises. Willie hadn't expected anything less from his mother, who insisted on managing every detail of her funeral in the same distinctive style with which she had managed her life and the lives of the people around her.

"Your instructions are to dash this urn on the rocks after you've scattered her ashes," Harriet informed him. "The other half of the ashes will stay in the library until the memorial service."

She then handed him a leather bank pouch with a zipper. Inside it was two thousand dollars in new currency. "And this is to tide you over until the allowance from your trust fund starts in about a month. Mr. Bradbury will be contacting you about that. And the Volvo should be ready by the time you get back." She gave Willie another warm hug and a kiss and wished him good luck.

"Your mother would be very proud of how you're handling this, Will," she said as he sank into the broken-down driver's seat.

Five miles outside Brunswick, Willie pulled over because of Fidget's dreadful yowling from the carrier in the back seat. He moved the box containing the urn to the back and put Fidget's cage on the front passenger seat, which seemed to settle her down. With the urn in the front seat, he felt as though Catherine was sitting beside him, no doubt criticizing his driving and the unpromising performance of the rattletrap car. The pouch of cash he slid under his seat.

As he crossed the new bridge spanning the Kennebec River, he glanced down at the old Carleton lift bridge and the gray frigates moored at the Ironworks. Until a few years before the old bridge had provided passage for all vehicles as well as trains traveling between Bath and Woolwich on busy Route One. The now-humbled bridge was dwarfed by its new suspended counterpart, but it had been an impressive example of modern technology to Willie and his brother when they were youngsters.

Suddenly Willie recalled the one common interest they had shared as kids: a giant erector set their father had bought them. They both fell upon it instantly. Two additional sets later, Philip had constructed a scale model of the Carleton Bridge, including the lower railway level over which he ran his electric trains. The center section actually lowered and lifted with the help of a battery-powered winch. For his part, Willie assembled as realistic a representation of the Japanese movie monster, Godzilla, as could be accomplished using short lengths of perforated steel and assorted gears. It also articulated but was not battery-powered like his brother's bridge.

The erector sets provided nearly a month of shared enthusiasm and unparalleled cooperation between the brothers. But, much to Willie's regret, this eventually came to an end as Philip tired of it and began drifting toward new distractions. Before it entirely ended, Philip had taken up the annoying practice of cannibalizing sections from his younger brother's projects to integrate into his own.

———

That evening Willie found himself sitting alone in Smitty's, a favorite little tavern in Belfast, devouring his second deluxe cheeseburger along with this third beer. The place was dark, smoky, and rough, the way most establishments in town had been before the blue-collar poultry and mill workers were displaced by clever young telemarketers and money shufflers from the huge financial firm that now dominated the region. Mangled butts in the tin ashtray on the dark oak table attested to the fact that Willie was smoking once again—a habit he embraced whenever he was under pressure.

When he'd gotten home that afternoon, he'd made the decision to let the unhappy and urine-soaked Fidget out of her carrier for the night, so she could eat and perhaps calm down. Carefully he set out a dish of her fancy wet cat food, another of water, and even remembered to bring up her litter box before taking a deep breath and sliding open her door. To his amazement and great relief the cat stepped calmly and confidently out of her little prison, took a turn around the cluttered apartment, ate a few bites of food, and began cleaning herself.

On the way out Willie was careful to pull the door at the head of the stairs to, and made doubly sure to close the outside shop door after himself as well—just in case. Still, he was becoming overwhelmed by the several things he would have to coordinate and manage over the next day or two.

Smitty's door swung open and in walked a tall figure in a pea coat and watch cap, flared jeans and motorcycle boots. Alongside him on a length of fraying hemp rope plodded a huge black dog, probably mostly Newfoundland.

"You know damn well I don't allow dogs in here, Farrin," Casey, the bar tender, short order chef, and owner threatened in his gravely voice.

"Sure I do, Casey, but this here's my reincarnated grandmother," the man replied with a grin, easily swinging one leg over a barstool. "Now draw me my usual and put two burgers on the grill—one for me and one for old Bear, here."

Casey laughed and worked the tap, and Bear collapsed behind the stool, resting his big head on his paws and closing his eyes. Hod Farrin cast his glance around the dingy establishment and spotted Willie next to the greasy window that looked out on the darkening harbor.

"Well, it's my lucky day after all. If it ain't the famous artist himself havin' supper and beer with all his friends." He snatched up his draft, strode over to Willie's table, and pulled up a chair.

"How's it going, Hod?"

"I tell you, Will, it's goin' a lot better now that Bear and I have found a ride home."

Hod Farrin was a capable jack-of-all-trades living about two miles past Willie's place on the Unity Road. No one was able to pinpoint exactly where it was he was from, but he'd been in the area at least a few years longer than Willie. Usually he stayed pretty much to himself at his primitive but cozy log cabin. Socially, he shunned most of the new flush transplants into the county, just as he had the often inept and arrogant back-to-the-landers years before. But he seemed to like Willie well enough, probably because Willie never presumed too much.

Hod supported himself modestly doing carpentry and a little plumbing, gathering wild honey, and processing maple syrup, along with plenty of hunting, not all of it according to the game laws. In late summer he might be off down east raking blueberries with the Indians and migrant laborers, and if he'd had a really thin winter, he'd been known to spend a whole summer up north planting seedlings for the paper companies. Earlier this fall he'd helped Willie assemble and weld together all the implements in the logging sculpture, contributing his own torch when Willie's gave out.

"I read about your mother in the Sunday paper. Sorry to hear it, buddy. That must be why you're smoking."

"Thanks, Hod. It's all right, I guess. She seemed ready to go. What's wrong with your truck, anyway?"

Hod fixed Willie with dark eyes set deep under his heavy brows. A scar running the length of his right jawbone was barely discernible beneath a couple of days' of black stubble.

"Damned transmission. The one I found outside Bucksport wasn't any good. Truck is over to Luke's. He'll have a rebuilt one stuck in it in a day or two. Then all's I'll need is the five hundred it's gonna to cost me."

"That's pretty cheap for a rebuilt."

"Only because I installed new windows in his hunting camp last week. Otherwise it'd be twelve."

By nine o'clock the pair had polished off a dozen beers between them, and along with Bear, had downed a half dozen or so burgers. When two suits in their twenties came in and began talking loudly about the infantile incentives they were employing to get more production out of their workers, they decided it was time to leave. Willie deposited a fifty on the bar on the way out.

"We appreciate the lift," Hod remarked, helping old Bear, who was getting a little stiff, into the very back of the wagon. "Say, I don't suppose we could stop by your place and get those cylinders I left, could we? Friday I'm helping Gus fix his saw rig and we're junking up his firewood and getting it covered before it snows."

At Willie's the pair went into the shop to get the gas bottles and torch while Bear sniffed around outside, hoping against the odds to find something edible.

"By the way, if I could borrow those Stones CDs of yours, I could burn a set while I'm at Gus's." Willie knew Hod didn't have power at his cabin, but guessed he'd listen to the music while driving his pickup.

"Listen, Hod, you've helped me out lots of times, especially this fall, and I never paid you a thing for all that work." They were back at Willie's wagon, and had slid the empty three-foot-long gas bottles into the back. Willie pulled out the bank pouch from under his seat, unzipped it, and counted six hundred dollars into his friend's palm.

"Oh c'mon, Will. You can't afford to do that," Hod protested.

"Oh, yes I can, and that's just what I want to do. Now get Bear into the back and I'll run up and get the CDs."

"Okay, buddy. Thanks a million."

Not yet past the effects of the beer, Willie stumbled on the first step and had to concentrate on what he was doing as he ascended the dark passageway. "First thing I'm doing tomorrow is changing this friggin' lightbulb," he reminded himself as he kicked the bottom of the stubborn door to get it open. As soon as he succeeded, a dark streak shot past his legs, tore down the stairs, and unerringly continued the length of the unfamiliar studio, and out through the open door.

"Fidget!" Willie yelled once his addled brain grasped what had just happened. "Fuck!"

Outside, under the unnatural bleaching radiance of the mercury light, Hod had just managed to coax Bear off some unspeakable reeking offal and had hoisted him once again into back of the wagon. There, he spread out a blanket he found and cinched the rough rope around one of the gas bottles to keep Bear from jumping back out. Just as he was about to close the lid, Fidget shot by, yowling in surprise when Hod almost stepped on her.

In an instant the big dog launched himself from the car in hot pursuit, the rope still tied to the cylinder and, unfortunately, hitched through the strap of the barometer case.

The panicked cat veered around Willie's uncovered firewood and miscellaneous junk, and streaked into the brushy ravine that separated the yard from the woods. Bear plunged after her, the gas bottles and antique barometer still caught on the rope and bouncing behind like ponderous flails. They ricocheted off the woodpile and old utility trailer before being keel-hauled through the alder-choked ditch until finally fetching up against a clump of willows, bringing the bellowing dog up short.

———

Two days later, Willie got an early start on his way down east to Bailey's Neck, outside Cutler. The morning was bright with the low-angled November sun, but a front coming up the coast promised snow over the entire state by the next day.

Willie puffed nervously on a cigarette as he relived the bizarre events that had turned the past few days into a nightmare. He and Hod had spent an hour with flashlights trying to recover Fidget from the silent, brooding woods. Since Bear wouldn't stop barking from the back of the car, Willie finally drove them home and returned to resume the hunt alone. Several times he was certain he heard Fidget meowing beyond the reach of the flashlight beam. But the spooked feline evaded him each time Willie closed in. Around 1:00 A.M. he gave up in frustration and exhaustion. Before collapsing into bed, he set out a dish of Fidget's food on the driveway side of the ditch. In the morning, still drunk from inadequate rest, he was disappointed to discover the offering had been left untouched. He spent another hour calling and searching the neighboring woods to no effect. He alerted the few neighbors he was comfortable approaching and tacked a notice up at the variety store down at the four corners. He was not reassured by all the stories he heard about cats in the area that had allegedly been dragged off by fishers and coyotes. Then he gathered up what fragments he could find from the shattered barometer and its case.

Somehow Willie located the number Harriet had given him for the Clausens in Thomaston. They were back from their vacation and anticipating his call. Rob was quite surprised when he learned Willie wouldn't be bringing Fidget down for a couple days, but was too gracious to probe for an explanation.

Later that afternoon in Searsport, Mr. Stedderman had been shocked into silence when Willie had shown him the remnants of the antique barometer. The carrying case had been splintered in its berserk dash across the cluttered yard behind the powerful dog. The glass door to the barometer was lost, as was the graduated scale. The glass tubes had been sheared off inside the compartment, and by the sounds, shattered their full length within the wooden shaft, which itself was broken nearly in two where it had fetched onto the willows. Naturally, the fluids had all drained out. The only surviving component still intact was the commemorative brass tag swinging freely from the crown of the instrument by the one surviving escutcheon pin.

"Th-th-this is utterly hopeless!" Stedderman stammered once he gathered his wits enough to speak. "I have n-n-never in my life seen its like. There is nothing to be done with this wr-wr-wreckage. It is disappointing beyond words."

Willie was getting the message there would be no magic resurrection of the barometer. "So, um, I guess you won't be restoring it after all."

"Restoring it! All the king's horses and all the king's friggin' men couldn't put this thing back together. It's a travesty! Have you any idea how rare a piece this was? A dog, you said? I'd have the dog drawn and quartered if it were mine."

As Willie turned to leave, the peculiar little man stopped him in his tracks.

"And what about my fee? Shall I send the bill to Harriet Monroe or to Brougham and Hinckley?"

"Fee? You just said you couldn't do anything."

"My fee for this consultation. I am a professional conservationist, and my time is worth money."

Willie was not quite ready to break any of this bad news either to Harriet or Mr. Bradbury.

"Um, I guess I'll pay it. How much is it?"

"Four hundred dollars. I'll write a receipt," and he turned toward his desk.

Willie gulped and was about to ask if he'd heard correctly, but he knew he probably had. He went out to his car and counted the money out of the pouch.

On the road again, he told himself, "Best put this all out of my head, for now and concentrate on getting Mom's ashes to Bailey's Neck. I'll have plenty of time to suffer the consequences of these screw-ups later."

At Milbridge Willie drove right past what had been his father's favorite restaurant, a place the two of them had enjoyed together the pitifully few times Willie had joined him. The forecasters continued to threaten snow, and after the events of the past couple of days he was determined not to repeat his pattern of failures.

The countryside kept assaulting Willie with images and subtle associations with his father, whom he hadn't thought a lot about lately. It was from his father, Robert, that Willie had inherited his red hair, only it had stood out less in his father's case because it was kept short and neatly groomed, including a tidy little mustache. He had also been a good deal taller than Willie, much thinner, and although quiet, certainly less self-conscious.

Robert Canton had been patient in all things, and was perhaps the only figure in Willie's youth who seemed to prefer Willie's company to that of his brother, although outwardly he was fair and even-handed with them both. His existence seemed at times to be filled with an unexpressed sadness and a quiet resignation to a life dominated at every turn by Catherine, whose family was the source of their wealth and social standing, about which Robert cared little. For her part, Catherine, always ready to impress, outshine, or one-up everyone in their circle, felt betrayed by her husband's casual indifference.

He had been quite content teaching sociology at Gorham Normal School when their hot romance flared up largely because they were both such fine ballroom dancers. In those days the pay at the state college was ridiculously low, and although the couple lived well because of Catherine's independent means, Robert felt pressured into giving up teaching and accepting a position in her father's bank. For more than twenty years he dutifully put on a dark suit each morning and discharged the sometimes distasteful duties of his office with minimal competence and little interest or enthusiasm.

He was rewarded with a salary beyond what his work warranted, but although technically family, he always felt like an outsider alongside the more dedicated personnel. Much to Catherine's distress, he willingly stepped aside to allow more deserving colleagues to ascend the ladder of success ahead of him. When the bank was bought out by a large regional institution, about the time Willie was beginning high school, it was one of the happiest days in his father's adult life. As a bank officer, he received a nice severance package, and wouldn't have signed on with the new firm under any circumstances.

This boost allowed him to take a job with the newly reorganized Department of Human Services, which really suited him. The euphoria was short-lived however, as a scandal within the department, having nothing to do with him, set off another politically motivated shake-up, and after only a year and a half Robert found himself without a position.

Catherine practically went through the roof when he accepted a teaching position at a nearby high school, but by then he didn't care. He spent at least half of the summer break as well as April vacation at the neat little cottage he'd bought at Bailey's Neck. There he could drink coffee all morning long in his pajamas, if he cared to, gazing out at the wheeling gulls and the sea wrack being tossed about by the treacherous currents that stretched all the way to Grand Manan Island in New Brunswick. Willie soon came to realize that perhaps his father's greatest attraction to the place was the fact that Catherine refused to accompany him.

Ten years had now passed since his father had slumped over the steering wheel while starting his car in the high school parking lot. He had just celebrated his sixty-third birthday, and Willie's intentions of spending more time with his dad never materialized.

—

The side road leading to Bailey's Neck was easy enough to find from the shore road connecting Cutler and Lubec. But Willie's dad never took that route, preferring instead to poke along several little gravel roads after leaving East Machias, which brought him to his cabin after a series of critical yet unmarked turns. Willie had never learned the nuances of this "shortcut" and found himself creeping along a narrow path he didn't recognize.

As in much of the region, once the spectacular coastline was left behind, one was surrounded by quite unremarkable country—relatively flat and distinguished mainly by cut-over woodlots, sour-looking bogs with stunted black spruce and tamarack trees, or thin-soiled rocky barrens good for growing blueberries and little else. For a brief spell around the beginning of October, these barrens were transformed as the low blueberry bushes were stained a stunning cardinal red by the first frosts. By late November, however, the country was as bleak as it was at any time during the year.

To Willie this particular road appeared endless and virtually uninhabited. The two rusted house trailers he passed sat askew on their cinder-block supports, much of the window glass broken away and the yards littered with cannibalized vehicles, worn tires, sheet plastic, and other trash. Finally rounding a bend he came upon a small cottage with a thin column of smoke spiraling out of its crooked, gap-toothed chimney. The few shingles that still clung to the walls were a black-streaked silver-blue, curled and split and riddled with holes that had once been occupied by knots. A box-like windowless addition, sheathed in wafer board on one side, was sagging away from the original structure.

As he was about to step from the Colt to knock at the door, Willie spotted two figures farther along the road that appeared to be hailing him. Pulling ahead, he rolled down his window to a pair of desperate-looking women. The older one was enormous, had a green kerchief wrapped around her head, and wore a threadbare red-and-black-checked hunting coat much too large for her, despite her corpulence. Coral polyester pants covered with thread pills sprouted from the jacket's hem, and frayed two-dollar tennis shoes protected her feet. In one meaty hand she clutched a plastic grocery bag stuffed with clothing, and with her other she supported her companion by holding her elbow. This second female, now mostly hidden by the first, was as skinny as the other was huge and wore a thin yellow cotton dress under a maroon windbreaker that seemed to be harboring a basketball. On her feet were imitation leather sandals.

"Holy Jesus, mistah," the big one bellowed through nearly toothless gums and colorless lips. "Ain't we glad to see you drivin' up. This heah's my girl, Emmy," indicating the startling pale wraith beside her. "Her water's broke, and we got to get her to Machias."

With that she wrenched open the rear door, threw in the plastic sack, and shoved her daughter in behind it. Then she filled the door opening with her own bulk, cramming herself onto the narrow seat while propelling Emmy across to the passenger side at the same time.

"Have you called an ambulance or anything?" was all Willie could think to ask.

"Jesus, mistah, do you think we'd be beggin' you to ride in this shit-box if a real ambulance was on the way? Phone company disconnected the phone six weeks ago. Lovah-girl, here, been talkin' to her husband to the tune of eight hundred dollars. That's the reason. Now get goin'!"

At the mention of her husband, the young woman let out an ear-splitting wail, then hyperventilated for an endless half minute before screaming at the top of her lungs, "Oh, Mama, I'm going to die!"

"Not that way, for Chrissakes," the woman bellowed at Willie, who had commenced driving in the direction they had appeared to be headed.

"I said Machias! You deaf or somethin'?"

Not knowing how to proceed, Willie simply stopped and turned his head for instructions.

"See that side road up theyah? Turn around and head back the way you come from. You ain't from around heah, are ya?"

"Mama, Mama, help me!!"

"Oh, calm down, girl. You ain't the first woman evah had a baby."

Willie turned around and drove cautiously along the road in the direction indicated.

Jerry Stelmok

"Mama! It hurts so! What's *wrong,* Mama?"

"You'll be all right once we git to Machias, deah."

"Yeah," Willie added, hoping to comfort the wretched girl. "They'll take care of everything once we get you to the hospital."

"You evah been to that hospital, mistah?"

"Well, no, but...."

"Well, if you ain't been theyah, don't go tellin' her how great it is," she said, gruffly cutting Willie off. "It ain't no Taj Mahal."

"Sorry," Willie said, and focused on his driving.

"OWWWWWW! Mama, I'm scared. It hurts so. Why does it hurt? AHHHHH!"

"Prob'ly if you'd a' quit smokin' that weed of yours and ate somethin' decent the past few months, you'd feel a whole lot bettah than you do."

Attempting to change the subject, Willie glanced at the pathetic girl with the dark gray pockets around her dull eyes and greasy hair plastered to her forehead.

"So where's your husband now, Emmy?"

"AHHHHHH!" the girl howled in grief and despair.

"Jesus, mistah," Big Mama interjected. "Just stick to your damn drivin'. Look what you done. Her old man's in jail. In Kentucky or Tennessee."

"Tennessee." Emmy whispered, "but he's gettin' out next month. What's he gonna say, Mama?"

Having not yet learned his lesson, Willie offered, "Well, just think what a great homecoming gift you'll have for him."

At that Emmy let out the most heartrending wail yet, followed by another of excruciating pain.

"You numbskull," Big Mama hissed. "Can't you keep your friggin' trap shut? He's comin' home next month, all right. And he's been in jail the past fourteen months."

"Oh Mama! What's he gonna do?"

Finally the implications registered, and Willie indeed shut his trap and concentrated on navigating the narrow crowned road laced with stretches of glassy ice.

While Emmy sobbed, Big Mama spotted the bank pouch under Willie's seat. Carefully keeping her hands lower than the back of the driver's seat, she slid the pouch out and opened the zipper.

"Jesus!" she couldn't help exclaiming, but not too loudly. She quickly extracted the money, and watching Willie's eyes in the mirror, chose a safe moment to pull forward the elastic waist of her slacks and stuff the wad of bills into her feed sack-sized drawers. Then she replaced the pouch.

During this profitable distraction she had neglected to point out a left-hand turn they needed to take to reach their destination, and Willie had kept driving straight ahead.

Emmy was still thrashing around, crying and wailing in pain and fear.

"Jesus, mistah," Mama yelled in Willie's ear. "You missed the friggin' turn, for Chrissake! Don't you know anything?"

"I—er...."

"Nevah mind. Just find someplace to turn around—and fast."

That was easier said than done. The narrow road would not have allowed even two small vehicles to pass one another, and for the last couple of miles it was bordered by a low bog on either side, sprouting dense clumps of alder and willow with no prospects of a turnoff. To make matters worse, the patches of ice were now more numerous, causing the Colt to swerve and fishtail dangerously, especially when Big Mama shifted her weight in the back seat, and Emmy screamed and thrashed around.

Eventually Willie spotted a narrow turnoff on the left—probably a single load of gravel dumped into an opening in the brush barely wider than the car. Gingerly he eased the Colt forward down into the little turnout and his heart sank when he felt the deceptively steep angle of the incline into which his front tires had descended.

Nervously he shifted into reverse and eased up on the clutch, and for an instant thought he might actually back up and out of the trap. But halfway out the bald front tires started to spin on the ice coating that covered the gravel. They spun moderately at first, then faster as he gave it more gas, and finally they burst into an honest free-wheeling spin. Instinctively, Willie eased the car forward and tried rocking it back. But the sorry tires only spun on the polished icy sheet beneath them. Emmy was moaning pitifully, but for once Big Mama was speechless.

Willie got out and stared despairingly at the half inch of solid ice that coated the full extent of the incline. He couldn't help thinking about his mother's Volvo with its new studded Perellis, but realized that wasn't really helpful. He lit up a Camel, and then extinguished it, as though it mattered at this point to the struggling infant inside Emmy's bloated belly. He opened Mama's door. "You better drive, and I'll push," he informed her with surprising authority.

"Jesus. I don't drive. Haven't for twenty yeahs and never drove a standard. What are you thinkin', anyways?"

He realized how ridiculous it would be with this cow crammed behind the wheel trying to gently release the clutch while backing up a grade—having never driven a standard. With the engine off he put the stick into neutral then ran around to the front and tried pushing with all his strength, but he couldn't budge the rig an inch up the glassy slope. In fact he had to jump in quickly and jam it into gear as the car had actually started pushing him deeper into the swamp.

Next he tried to free up some gravel from the rutted road, but the earlier rain followed by intense cold had frozen the fine, coffee-colored gravel into a matrix the consistency of concrete. He couldn't dislodge a teaspoonful with his heel, and he broke the blade of his pocketknife when he gave that a try. Normally there'd be a shovel, probably a sledgehammer, and maybe even a come-along with other useful tools stashed in the rear. But he had carefully emptied the car to accommodate the fragile barometer and Fidget, the now-missing cat.

"Jesus," he heard himself say. "Fuck."

"Jesus, mistah, don't you even carry no sand? Where are you from, anyways?"

Emmy, who'd been sobbing quietly, let out another scream. "Mama! It's comin'! I can feel it!"

The thought came to him like a bolt of lightning. The ashes! He quickly put any thoughts of his mother out of his mind, jumped into the front passenger seat, and turned around. Emmy was slumped down as far as possible in the seat behind, her spread knees pressed against the back of the front seat, her cotton dress hiked immodestly up around her hips.

"'Scuse me!" Willie offered, and averting his eyes he plunged his arm down between her legs, his hand groping along the floor beneath her for the cube-shaped box.

"What kind of preevert are you, anyways?" Big Mama bellowed, a flush of crimson overtaking her face. "Don't you know that girl's about to have a baby?"

"I just have to get hold of this box down here," he explained, "It's got...."

But a jarring smack on his right cheek jolted his head back.

"You sick preevert. You get your friggin' hands away from her," and this time she made a proper fist and drew back her arm.

"This one could kill me," Willie thought, but just then his fingers closed around the container. "It's just I need this," he said, showing his surprised assailant the box.

"What the...."

But Willie was already back outside. He tossed the box, opened the lid of the little urn, and gazed at the granular contents.

"Mostly ground-up bone," he thought. "Mother would die all over again if she could see what I'm about to do." And the vision was enough to make him stop and reconsider. He picked up the box with the gold sticker—Catherine Pickett Canton 1920–1992. "Maybe someone will come along and pull us out," he thought.

Then Emmy let out another scream.

Willie got down on his hands and knees and very carefully spread an even band of the gritty ashes on top of the ice from the right front tire all the way up the ramp to the road. Then he rounded the car, and using the rest of the contents, laid down a similar track on the driver's side. Finally, he got into the wagon, started it up, put the shift lever into reverse, and ever so slowly eased up on the clutch.

ACKNOWLEDGMENTS

I am deeply indebted to my publisher, Jennifer Bunting, for having the courage (and let us hope foresight and wisdom) to take on publishing this collection of stories in the first place. Thank you, Jennifer. And thanks also to her talented team of editors and designers at Tilbury who crafted the material into its pleasing form.

And a heartfelt thanks goes to Andrea Myers for her patient and considerable work lifting my handwritten words from the pages of all the lined yellow pads, and scrunching them into those little plastic disks that the rest of the world demands in order to deal with them—and for doing it all with style and without apparent exasperation.

For the dialect of Jean Batiste in the title story I relied upon the model set forth by the nineteenth-century poet of the St. Lawrence Valley, Henry Drummond. I offer Jean Batiste's dialogue with the same admiration and respect conferred by Drummond upon his beloved "Habitant" neighbors. I wish to thank retired educator, poet, and friend Roger Davies for scrutinizing these passages, along with friend Linda Viollette, and for offering suggestions to better square them with Drummond's style. If you ever have the opportunity to hear Roger recite from Drummond's work, do not miss it.

In *Ulysses*, Alfred Lord Tennyson wrote, "I am a part of all that I have known," and I believe that simple line best describes the source writers like myself draw upon in creating any fiction with at least a hint of truth to it. So although none of the characters in these stories portrays an actual person, nor the settings actual places except in the broadest sense, each has risen to the surface, and emerged from that bubbling cauldron of chowder that represents my life experiences. I am grateful for that flavorful blend, rich in inspiration and detail, into which I can dip the ladle and with luck come up with something interesting.

Jerry Stelmok
Atkinson, Maine